THE
GRACE
YEAR

Kim Liggett, originally from the rural Midwest in the US, moved to New York City to pursue a career in the arts. She's the author of *Blood and Salt*, *Heart of Ash*, *The Last Harvest* (Bram Stoker Award Winner), *The Unfortunates*, and *The Grace Year*.

Kim spends her free time studying tarot and scouring Manhattan for rare vials of perfume and the perfect egg white cocktail.

THE GRACE YEAR

KIM LIGGETT

DEL REY

DEL REY

First published by Del Rey in 2019

1 3 5 7 9 10 8 6 4 2

Del Rey, an imprint of Ebury Publishing
20 Vauxhall Bridge Road,
London SW1V 2SA

Del Rey is part of the Penguin Random House group of companies
whose addresses can be found at global.penguinrandomhouse.com

Penguin
Random House
UK

www.penguin.co.uk

A CIP catalogue record for this book is available from the British
Library

Hardback ISBN 9781529100587
Trade Paperback ISBN 9781529100594

Printed and bound in Great Britain by Clays Ltd, Elcograf S.p.A.

Penguin Random House is committed to a sustainable future for our
business, our readers and our planet. This book is made from Forest
Stewardship Council® certified paper.

MIX
Paper from
responsible sources
FSC
www.fsc.org FSC® C018179

For all the daughters,
and those who revere them

A rat in a maze is free to go anywhere,
as long as it stays inside the maze.

—MARGARET ATWOOD,
THE HANDMAID'S TALE

Maybe there is a beast . . . maybe
it's only us.

—WILLIAM GOLDING,
LORD OF THE FLIES

No one speaks of the grace year.

It's forbidden.

We're told we have the power to lure grown men from their beds, make boys lose their minds, and drive the wives mad with jealousy. They believe our very skin emits a powerful aphrodisiac, the potent essence of youth, of a girl on the edge of womanhood. That's why we're banished for our sixteenth year, to release our magic into the wild before we're allowed to return to civilization.

But I don't feel powerful.

I don't feel magical.

Speaking of the grace year is forbidden, but it hasn't stopped me from searching for clues.

A slip of the tongue between lovers in the meadow, a frightening bedtime story that doesn't feel like a story at all, knowing glances nestled in the frosty hollows between pleasantries of the women at the market. But they give away nothing.

The truth about the grace year, what happens during that shadow year, is hidden away in the tiny slivers of filament hovering around them when they think no one's watching. But I'm always watching.

The slip of a shawl, scarred shoulders bared under a harvest moon.

Haunted fingertips skimming the pond, watching the ripples fade to black.

Their eyes a million miles away. In wonderment. In horror.

I used to think that was my magic—having the power to see things others couldn't—things they didn't even want to admit to themselves. But all you have to do is open your eyes.

My eyes are wide open.

I follow her through the woods, a well-worn path I've seen a thousand times. Ferns, lady-slipper, and thistle, the mysterious red flowers dotting the path. Five petals, perfectly formed, like they were made just for us. One petal for the grace year girls, one petal for the wives, one for the laborers, one for the women of the outskirts, and one for her.

The girl looks back at me over her shoulder, giving me that confident grin. She reminds me of someone, but I can't place the name or the face. Maybe something from a long-forgotten memory, a past life, perhaps a younger sister I never knew. Heart-shaped face, a small red strawberry mark under her right eye. Delicate features, like mine, but there's nothing delicate about this girl. There's a fierceness in her steel-gray eyes. Her dark hair is shorn close to her scalp. A punishment or a rebellion, I cannot say. I don't know her, but strangely enough, I know that I love her. It's not a love like my father has for my mother, it's protective and pure, the same way I felt about those robins I cared for last winter.

We reach the clearing, where women from all walks of life have gathered—the tiny red flower pinned above their hearts. There's no bickering or murderous glares; everyone has come together in peace. In unity. We are sisters, daughters, mothers, grandmothers, standing together for a common need, greater than ourselves.

"We are the weaker sex, weaker no more," the girl says.

The women answer with a primal roar.

But I'm not afraid. I only feel a sense of pride. The girl is the one. She's the one who will change everything, and somehow, I'm a part of all this.

"This path has been paved with blood, the blood of our own, but it was not in vain. Tonight, the grace year comes to an end."

As I expel the air from my lungs, I find myself not in the woods, not with the girl, but here, in this stifling room, in my bed, my sisters glaring down at me.

"What did she say?" my older sister Ivy asks, her cheeks ablaze.

"Nothing," June replies, squeezing Ivy's wrist. "We heard nothing."

As my mother enters the room, my little sisters, Clara and Penny, poke me out of bed. I look to June to thank her for quelling the situation, but she won't meet my gaze. She won't or she can't. I'm not sure what's worse.

We're not allowed to dream. The men believe it's a way we can hide our magic. Having the dreams would be enough to get me punished, but if anyone ever found out what the dreams were about, it would mean the gallows.

My sisters lead me to the sewing room, fluttering around me like a knot of bickering sparrows. Pushing. Pulling.

"Ease up," I gasp as Clara and Penny yank on the corset strings with a little too much glee. They think this is all fun and games. They don't realize that in a few short years, it will be their turn. I swat at them. "Don't you have anyone else to torture?"

"Stop your fussing," my mother says, taking out her frustration on my scalp as she finishes my braid. "Your father has let you get away with murder all these years, with your mud-stained frocks, dirt under your nails. For once, you're going to know what it feels like to be a lady."

"Why bother?" Ivy flaunts her growing belly in the looking glass for all of us to see. "No one in their right mind would give a veil to Tierney."

"So be it," my mother says as she grabs the corset strings and pulls even tighter. "But she owes me this."

I was a willful child, too curious for my own good, head in the clouds, lacking propriety . . . among other things. And I will be the first girl in our family to go into her grace year without receiving a veil.

My mother doesn't need to say it. Every time she looks at me I feel her resentment. Her quiet rage.

"Here it is." My oldest sister, June, slips back into the room, carrying a deep-blue raw-silk dress with river-clam pearls adorning the shawl neckline. It's the same dress she wore on her veiling day four years ago. It smells of lilac and fear. White lilac was the flower her suitor chose for her—the symbol of early love, innocence. It's kind of her to let me borrow it, but that's June. Not even the grace year could take that away from her.

All the other girls in my year will be wearing new dresses today with frills and embroidery, the latest style, but my parents knew better than to waste their resources on me. I have no prospects. I made damn sure of that.

There are twelve eligible boys in Garner County this year—boys born into families that have standing and position. And there are thirty-three girls.

Today, we're expected to parade around town, giving the boys one last viewing before they join the men in the main barn to trade and barter our fates like cattle, which isn't that far off considering we're branded at birth on the bottom of our foot with our father's sigil. When all the claims have been made, our fathers will deliver the veils to the awaiting girls at the church, silently placing the gauzy monstrosities on the chosen ones' heads. And to-morrow morning, when we're all lined up in the square to leave for our grace year, each boy will lift the veil of the girl of his choosing, as a promise of marriage, while the rest of us will be completely dispensable.

"I knew you had a figure under there." My mother purses her lips, causing the fine lines around her mouth to settle into deep grooves. She'd stop doing it if she knew how old it made her look. The only thing worse than being old in Garner County is being barren. "For the life of me I'll never understand why you squandered your beauty, squan-dered your chance to run your own house," she says as she eases the dress over my head.

My arm gets stuck and I start pulling.

"Stop fighting or it's going to—"

The sound of ripping fabric causes a visible heat to creep up my mother's neck, settling into her jaw. "Needle and thread," she barks at my sisters, and they hop to.

I try to hold it in, but the harder I try, the worse it gets, until I burst out laughing. I can't even put on a dress right.

"Go ahead, laugh all you want, but you won't think it's so funny when no one gives you a veil and you come back from the grace year only to be sent straight to one of the labor houses, working your fingers to the bone."

"Better than being someone's wife," I mutter.

"Never say that." She grabs my face in her hands, and my sisters scatter. "Do you want them to think you're a usurper? To be cast out? The poachers would love to get their hands on you." She lowers her voice. "You cannot bring shame on this family."

"What's this about?" My father tucks his pipe into his breast pocket as he makes a rare appearance in the sewing room. Mother quickly composes herself and mends the tear.

"No shame in hard work," he says as he ducks under the eave, kissing my mother on the cheek, reeking of iodine and sweet tobacco. "She can work in the dairy or the mill when she returns. That's entirely respectable. You know our Tierney's always been a free spirit," he says with a conspiratorial wink.

I look away, pretending to be fascinated by the dots of hazy light seeping in through the eyelet curtains. My father and I used to be thick as winter wool. People said he had a certain twinkle in his eye when he spoke of me.

With five daughters, I guess I was the closest thing to a coveted son he'd ever get. On the sly, he taught me how to fish, how to handle a knife, how to take care of myself, but everything's different now. I can't look at him the same way after the night I caught him at the apothecary, doing the unspeakable. Clearly, he's still trying for a prized son, but I always thought he was better than that. As it turns out, he's just like the rest of them.

"Look at you . . . ," my father says in an attempt to draw my attention. "Maybe you'll get a veil after all."

I keep my mouth clamped shut, but inside, I want to scream. Being married off isn't a privilege to me. There's no freedom in comfort. They're padded shackles, to be sure, but shackles nonetheless. At least in the labor house my life will still belong to me. My *body* will belong to me. But those kinds of thoughts get me in trouble, even when I don't say them out loud. When I was small, every thought showed on my face. I've learned to hide behind a pleasant smile, but sometimes when I catch my reflection in the glass, I see the intensity burning in my eyes. The closer I get to my grace year, the hotter the fire burns. Sometimes I feel like my eyes are going to sear right out of my skull.

As my mother reaches for the red silk to tie off my braid, I feel a twinge of panic. This is it. The moment I'll be marked with the color of warning . . . of sin.

All the women in Garner County have to wear their hair the same way, pulled back from the face, plaited down the back. In doing so, the men believe, the women won't be able to hide anything from them—a snide expression, a wandering eye, or a flash of magic. White ribbons for the young girls, red for the grace year girls, and black for the wives.

Innocence. Blood. Death.

"Perfect," my mother says as she puts the final touches on the bow.

Even though I can't see the red strand, I feel the weight of it, and everything it implies, like an anchor holding me to this world.

"Can I go now?" I ask as I pull away from her fidgeting hands.

"Without an escort?"

"I don't need an escort," I say as I cram my sturdy feet into the fine black leather slippers. "I can handle myself."

"And what of the fur trappers from the territory, can you handle them as well?"

"That was one girl and it was ages ago." I let out a sigh.

"I remember it like it was yesterday. Anna Berglund," my mother says, her eyes glazing over. "It was our veiling day. She was walking through town and he just snatched her up, flung her over his horse, and took off into the wilderness, never to be heard from again."

It's odd, what I remember most about that story is that even though she was seen screaming and crying all through town, the men declared she didn't fight hard enough and punished her younger sister in her stead by casting her to the outskirts, for a life of prostitution. That's the part of the story no one ever speaks of.

"Let her go. It's her last day," my father pleads, pretending to give my mother the final say. "She's accustomed to being on her own. Besides, I'd like to spend the day with my beautiful wife. Just the two of us."

For all intents and purposes, they appear to be in love. The past few years, my father has spent more and more time in the outskirts, but it's given me a fair amount of freedom, and for that, I should be grateful.

My mother smiles up at him. "I suppose it'll be all right . . . as long as Tierney's not planning on skulking off into the woods to meet Michael Welk."

I try to play it off, but my throat goes bone dry. I had no idea she knew about that.

She tugs down on the bodice of my dress, trying to get it to sit right. "Tomorrow, when he lifts Kiersten Jenkins's veil, you're going to realize how foolish you've been."

"That's not wha . . . that's not why . . . we're just friends," I sputter.

A hint of a smile slips into the corner of her mouth. "Well, since you're so eager to be out and about, you can fetch some berries for the gathering tonight."

She knows I hate going to the market, especially on veiling day when all of Garner County will be out on full display, but I think that's the whole point. She's going to make the most out of this.

As she takes off her thimble to fetch a coin from her deerskin pouch, I catch a glimpse of the missing tip of her thumb. She's never said as much, but I know it's a memento from her grace year. She catches my gaze and shoves the thimble back on.

"Forgive me," I say as I look down at the worn wood grain beneath my feet. "I'll get the berries." I'd agree to anything to get out of this room.

As if sensing my desperation, Father gives a slight nod toward the door, and I take off like a shot.

"Don't stray from town," my mother calls after me.

Dodging stacks of books, stockings drying on the banister, my father's medicine bag, and a basket full of unfinished knitting, I rush down the three flights of stairs, past the disapproving clucks of the maids, bursting out of our row house into the open air, but the sharp autumn breeze feels alien against my bare skin—my neck, my collarbone, my chest, my calves, the bottom half of my knees. It's just a little skin, I tell myself. Nothing they haven't seen before. But I feel exposed . . . vulnerable.

A girl from my year, Gertrude Fenton, passes with her mother. I can't help but look at her hands; they're covered in dainty white lace gloves. It almost makes me forget about what happened to her. *Almost.* Despite her misfortune, even Gertie seems to still be hoping for a veil, to run a house of her own, to be blessed with sons.

I wish I wanted those things. I wish it were that simple.

"Happy Veiling Day." Mrs. Barton regards me as she clings to her husband's arm a little tighter.

"Who's that?" Mr. Barton asks.

"The James girl," she replies through gritted teeth. "The middle one."

His gaze rakes over my skin. "I see her magic has finally come in."

"Or she's been hiding it." Her eyes narrow on me with the focus of a vulture pecking away at a carcass.

All I want to do is cover up, but I'm not going back inside that house.

I have to remind myself: the dresses, the red ribbons, the veils, the ceremonies—they're all just distractions to keep our minds off the real issue at hand. The grace year.

My chin begins to quiver when I think of the year ahead, the unknown, but I plaster on a vacant smile, as if I'm happy to play my part, so I might return and marry and breed and die.

But not all of us will make it home . . . not in one piece.

Trying to get hold of my nerves, I walk the square where all the girls of my year will be lined up tomorrow. It doesn't take magic or even a keen eye to see that during the grace year, something profound happens. We'd see them when they left for the encampment each year. Though some were veiled, their hands told me everything I needed to know—cuticles picked raw with worry, nervous impulses flickering through cold fingertips—but they were full of promise . . . alive. And when they returned, the ones who returned, they were emaciated, weary . . . broken.

The younger children made a game out of it, taking bets on who would make it back, but the closer I got to my own grace year, the less amusing it became.

"Happy Veiling Day." Mr. Fallow tips his hat in a gentlemanly fashion, but his eyes linger on my skin, on the red ribbon trailing down my backside, a little too long for comfort. Geezer Fallow is what they call him behind his back, because no one knows exactly how old he is, but he's clearly not too old to give me the once-over.

They call us the weaker sex. It's pounded into us every Sunday in church, how everything's Eve's fault for not expelling her magic when she had the chance, but I still can't understand why the girls don't get a say. Sure, there are secret arrangements, whispers in the dark, but why must the boys get to decide everything? As far as I can tell, we all have hearts. We all have brains. There are only a few differences I can see, and most men seem to think with that part anyway.

It's funny to me that they think claiming us, lifting our veils, will give us something to live for during our grace year. If I knew I had to come home and lie with someone like Tommy Pearson, I might walk straight into the poacher's blade with open arms.

A blackbird lands on the branch of the punishment tree in the center of the square. The scratching of its claws against the dull metal limb sends a sliver of ice through my blood. Apparently, it used to be a real tree, but when they burned Eve alive for heresy, the tree went with her, so they built this one out of steel. An everlasting emblem of our sin.

A group of men pass by, shrouded in whispers.

There have been rumors circulating for months . . . whispers of a usurper. Apparently, the guards have found evidence of secret gatherings in the woods. Men's clothes hanging from branches, like an effigy. At first, they thought it might be a trapper trying to stir up trouble, or a jilted woman from the outskirts trying to get even, but then the suspicion spread to the county. It's hard to imagine that it could be one of our own, but Garner County is full of secrets. Some that are as clear as fresh-cut glass, but they *choose* to ignore. I'll never understand that. I'd rather have the truth, no matter how painful the outcome.

"For the love of God, stand up straight, Tierney," a woman scolds as she passes. Aunt Linny. "And without an escort. My poor brother," she whispers to her daughters, loud enough for me to hear every syllable. "Like mother, like daughter." She holds a sprig of holly to her upturned nose. In the old language it was the flower of protection. Her sleeve slips from her wrist, exposing a swath of pink puckered skin on her forearm. My sister Ivy said she saw it once when she went on a call with Father to treat her cough—a scar runing all the way from her wrist to her shoulder blade.

Aunt Linny yanks down her sleeve to block my stare. "She runs wild in the woods. Best place for her really."

How would she know what I've been up to unless she's been spying on me? Ever since my first bleed, I've gotten all kinds of unwanted advice. Most of it asinine, at best, but this is just plain mean.

Aunt Linny glares at me before dropping the sprig and continuing on her way. "As I was saying, there's so much to consider when giving a veil. Is she pleasant? Compliant? Will she bear sons? Is she hardy enough to survive the grace year? I don't envy the men. It's a heavy day, indeed."

If she only knew. I stamp the holly into the ground.

The women believe the men's veiling gathering in the barn to be a reverent affair, but there's nothing reverent about it. I know this because I've witnessed the last six years in a row by hiding in the loft behind the sacks of grain. All they do is drink ale, sling out vulgarities, and occasionally get into a brawl over one of the girls, but curiously, there's no talk of our "dangerous magic."

In fact, the only time magic comes up is when it's convenient for them. Like when Mrs. Pinter's husband died, Mr. Coffey suddenly accused his wife of twenty-five years of secretly harboring her magic and levitating in her sleep. Mrs. Coffey was as meek and mild as they come—hardly the levitating sort—but she was cast out. No questions asked. And surprise, Mr. Coffey married Mrs. Pinter the following day.

But if I ever made such an accusation, or if I came back from my grace year unbroken, I would be sent to the outskirts to live among the prostitutes.

"My, my, Tierney," Kiersten says as she approaches with a few of her followers trailing behind. Her veiling dress might be the prettiest one I've ever seen—cream silk with strands of gold woven in, glinting in the sun, just like her hair. Kiersten reaches out, skimming her fingertips over the pearls near my collarbone with a familiarity we don't share. "That dress suits you better than it did June," she says, looking up at me through her sugary lashes. "But don't tell her I said that." The girls behind her stifle wicked giggles.

My mother would probably be mortified to know they recognized it was a hand-me-down, but the girls of Garner County are always on the lookout for an opportunity to dole out a thinly shrouded insult.

I try to laugh it off, but my undergarments are laced

so tight, I can't find the air. It doesn't matter anyway. The only reason Kiersten even acknowledges me is because of Michael. Michael Welk has been my closest friend since childhood. We used to spend all our time spying on people, trying to uncover clues about the grace year, but eventually Michael grew tired of that game. Only it wasn't a game to me.

Most girls drift away from the boys around their tenth birthday, when the girls' schooling is over, but somehow, Michael and I managed to remain friends. Maybe it's because I wanted nothing from him and he wanted nothing from me. It was simple. Of course, we couldn't run around town like we used to, but we found a way. Kiersten probably thinks I have his ear, but I don't get involved in Michael's love life. Most nights we just lay in the clearing, looking up at the stars, lost in our own worlds. And that seemed to be enough for both of us.

Kiersten shushes the girls behind her. "I'll keep my fingers crossed you get a veil tonight, Tierney," she says with a smile that registers on the back of my neck.

I know that smile. It's the same one she gave Father Edmonds last Sunday when she noticed his hands were trembling as he placed the holy wafer on her awaiting pink tongue. Her magic came in early, and she knew it. Behind the carefully arranged face, the cleverly tailored clothes meant to accentuate her shape, she could be cruel. Once, I saw her drown a butterfly, all the while playing with its wings. Despite her mean streak, she's a fitting wife for the future leader of the council. She'll devote herself to Michael, dote on their sons and breed cruel but beautiful daughters.

I watch the girls as they flit down the lane in perfect formation, like a swarm of yellow jackets. I can't help wondering what they'll be like away from the county. What will happen to their fake smiles and coquetry? Will they run wild and roll in the mud and howl at the moon? I wonder if you can see the magic leave your body, if it's taken from you like a bolt of heat lightning or seeps out of you like slow-leaking poison. But there's another thought creeping into my consciousness. What if nothing happens at all?

Digging my newly buffed nails into the fleshy part of my palms, I whisper, "The girl . . . the gathering . . . it's only a dream." I can't be tempted into that kind of thinking again. I can't afford to give in to childhood fancies, because even if the magic is a lie, the poachers are very real. Bastards born to the women of the outskirts—the reviled. It's common knowledge they're out there waiting for a chance to grab one of the girls during their grace year, when their magic is believed to be most potent, so they can sell their essence on the black market as an aphrodisiac and youth serum.

I stare up at the massive wood gate, separating us from the outskirts, and wonder if they're already out there . . . waiting for us.

The breeze rushes over my bare skin as if in response, and I move a little quicker.

Folks from the county are gathered around the greenhouse, trying to guess which flower the suitors have chosen for which grace year girl. I'm happy to hear my name isn't on anyone's lips.

When our families immigrated there were so many different languages being spoken that flowers were the only common language. A way to tell someone I'm sorry, good luck, I trust you, I'm fond of you, or even I wish you ill. There's a flower for nearly every sentiment, but now that we all speak English, you'd think the demand would have faded, but here we are, clinging fast to the old ways. It makes me doubt anything will ever change . . . no matter what.

"Which one are you hoping for, miss?" a worker asks, swiping the back of her callused hand over her brow.

"No . . . not for me," I say in an embarrassed hush. "Just seeing what's in bloom." I spot a small basket tucked under a bench, red petals peeking through the seams. "What are those?" I ask.

"Just weeds," she says. "They used to be everywhere. Couldn't take a step out your house without comin upon one. They got rid of em round here, but that's the funny thing bout weeds. You can pull em up by the root, burn the soil where they stood, might lie dormant for years, but they'll always find a way."

I'm leaning in for a closer look when she says, "Don't worry bout it none if you don't get a veil, Tierney."

"H-how do you know my name?" I stammer.

She gives me a winsome smile. "Someday, you'll get a flower. It might be a little withered round the edges, but it'll mean just the same. Love's not just for the marrieds, you know, it's for everyone," she says as she slips a bloom into my hand.

Flustered, I turn on my heel and make a beeline for the market.

Uncurling my fingers, I find a deep purple iris, the petals and falls perfectly formed. "Hope," I whisper, my eyes welling up. I don't hope for a flower from a boy, but I hope for a better life. A truthful life. I'm not usually sentimental, but there's something about it that feels like a sign. Like its own kind of magic.

I'm tucking the bloom into my dress, over my heart for safekeeping, when I pass a line of guards, desperately trying to avert their eyes.

Fur trappers, fresh from the territory, click their tongues as I pass. They're vulgar and unkempt, but somehow it seems more honest that way. I want to look in their eyes, see if I can sense their adventures, the vast northern wilderness in their weathered faces, but I needn't dare.

All I have to do is buy the berries. And the sooner I get this over with, the sooner I can meet Michael.

When I enter the covered market, an uncomfortable din permeates the air. Normally, I pass through the stalls unnoticed, slipping in and out of the strands of garlic and rashers of bacon like a phantom breeze, but today, the wives glare as I walk by, and the men smile in a way that makes me want to hide.

"It's the James girl," a woman whispers.

"The tomboy?"

"I'd give her a veil and then some." A man elbows his young son.

Heat rushes to my cheeks. I feel ashamed and I don't even know why.

I'm the same girl I was yesterday, but now that I'm freshly scrubbed and squeezed into this ridiculous dress, marked by a red ribbon, I've become entirely visible to the men and women of Garner County, like some exotic animal on display.

Their eyes, their whispers feel like the sharp edge of a blade grazing my skin.

But there's one set of eyes in particular that makes me move a little faster. Tommy Pearson. He seems to be following me. I don't need to see him to know he's there. I can hear the beating wings of his latest pet perched on his arm. He has a fondness for birds of prey. It sounds impressive, but there's no skill involved. He's not gaining their trust, their respect. He's just breaking them.

Prying the coin from my sweaty palm, I drop it in the jar and grab the closest basket of berries I can find.

I keep my head down as I maneuver through the crowd, their whispers buzzing in my ears, and just as I've nearly cleared the awning, I run smack into Father Edmonds, mulberries spilling all around me. He starts sputtering out something cross, but stops when he looks at me. "My dear, Miss James, you're in a hurry."

"Is that really her?" Tommy Pearson calls out from behind me. "Tierney the Terrible?"

"I can still kick just as hard," I say as I continue to gather the berries.

"I'm counting on it," he replies, his pale eyes locking on mine. "I like them feisty."

Looking up to thank Father Edmonds, I see his gaze is fixed on my bosom. "If you need anything . . . anything at all, my child." As I reach for the basket, he strokes the side of my hand. "Your skin is so soft," he whispers.

Abandoning the berries, I take off running. I hear laughter behind me, Father Edmonds's heavy breathing, the eagle furiously beating its wings against its tether.

Slipping behind an oak to catch my breath, I pull the iris from my dress only to find it's been crushed by the corset. I clench the ruined bloom in my fist.

That familiar heat rushes through me. Instead of dampening the urge, I breathe it in, coaxing it forward. Because in this moment, oh how I long to be full of dangerous magic.

A part of me wants to run straight to Michael, to our secret spot, but I need to cool off first. I can't let him know they got to me. Plucking a hay needle, I drag it along the fence posts as I pass the orchard, slowing my breath to my measured steps. I used to be able to tell Michael anything, but we're more careful with each other now.

Last summer, still reeling after I caught my dad at the apothecary, I let some snide comment slip out about his father, who runs the apothecary, runs the council, and all hell broke loose. He told me I needed to watch my tongue, that someone could think I was a usurper, that I could be burned alive if they ever found out about my dreams.

I don't think he meant it as a threat, but it certainly felt like one.

Our friendship could've ended right then and there, but we met the next day, like nothing happened. In truth, we probably outgrew each other a long time ago, but I think we both wanted to hang on to a bit of our youth, our innocence, for as long as possible. And today will be the last time we'll be able to meet like this.

When I come back from the grace year, *if* I make it back, he'll be married, and I'll be assigned to one of the labor houses. My days will be spoken for, and he'll have his hands full with Kiersten and the council during the evenings. He might come by for a visit, under the guise of some type of business, but after a while, he'll stop coming, until we both just nod to each other at church on Christmas.

Leaning on the rickety fence, I stare out over the labor houses. My plan is to lie low, get through the year, and come back to take my place in the fields. Most of the girls who don't get a veil want to work as a maid in a respectable house or at least at the dairy, or the mill, but there's something appealing about putting my hands in the dirt, feeling connected to something real. My oldest sister, June, loved to grow things. She used to tell us bedtime stories about her adventures. She's not allowed to garden anymore, now that she's a wife, but every once in a while, I catch her reaching down to touch the soil, digging a secret cocklebur from her hem. I figure if it's good enough for June, it's good enough for me. Fieldwork is the only job where men and women work side by side, but I can handle myself better than most. I may be slight, but I'm strong.

Strong enough to climb trees and give Michael a run for his money.

As I make my way to the secluded woods behind the mill, I hear guards approaching. I wonder why they're all the way out here. Not wanting any trouble, I dive between the bushes.

I'm crawling my way through the bramble when Michael grins down at me from the other side. "You look—"

"Don't start," I say as I attempt to untangle myself, but a pearl gets caught on a twig and pops off, rolling into the clearing.

"Such poise." He laughs, dragging his hand through his wheat-colored hair. "If you're not careful, you might get snapped up tonight."

"Very funny," I say as I continue to crawl around. "Won't matter anyway, because my mother is going to smother me in my sleep if I don't find that pearl."

Michael gets down on the forest floor to help me look. "But what if it's someone agreeable . . . someone who could give you a real home? A life."

"Like Tommy Pearson?" I loop an imaginary rope around my neck to hang myself.

Michael chuckles. "He's not as bad as he seems."

"Not as bad as he seems? The boy who tortures majestic birds for fun?"

"He's really very good with them."

"We've talked about this," I say as I comb through the fallen scarlet maple leaves. "That's no life for me."

He sits back on his heels and I swear I can hear him thinking. He thinks too much.

"Is this because of the little girl? The girl from your dreams?"

My body tenses.

"Have you had any more?"

"No." I force my shoulders to relax. "I told you, I'm done with all that."

As we continue to search, I watch him out of the corner of my eye. I should've never confided in him about her. I should've never had the dreams at all. I just have to last one more day and then I can rid myself of this magic for good.

"I saw guards on the lane," I say, trying not to be too obvious about my prodding. "I wonder what they're doing way out here."

He leans in, his arm grazing mine. "They almost caught the usurper," he whispers.

"How?" I ask a little too excitedly, and then quickly rein it in. "You don't have to tell me if—"

"They set up a bear trap, out in the woods, near the border of the county and the outskirts last night. It went off, but all they caught was a light blue stretch of wool . . . and a lot of blood."

"How do you know?" I ask, being careful not to seem too eager.

"The guards called on my father this morning, asked if anyone had come into the apothecary looking for medicine. I guess they called on your father, as well, to see if he treated any injuries last night, but he was . . . indisposed."

I knew what he meant. It was a polite way of saying my father was in the outskirts again.

"They're searching the county now. Whoever it is, they won't last long without proper care. Those traps are nasty business." His gaze eases down my legs, lingering on my ankles. Instinctively, I tuck them under my dress. I wonder if he thinks it could be me . . . if that's why he was asking about my dreams.

"Found it," he says, plucking the pearl from a bit of moss.

I brush the dirt from my palms. "I'm not knocking it . . . the whole marriage thing," I say, desperate for a change of subject. "I'm sure Kiersten will worship you and bring you many sons," I tease as I reach for the jewel, but he pulls his hand back.

"Why would you say that?"

"Please. Everyone knows. Besides, I've seen the two of you in the meadow."

A deep blush creeps over his collar as he pretends to clean off the pearl with the edge of his shirt. He's nervous. I've never seen him nervous before. "Our fathers have planned out every detail. How many children we'll have . . . even their names."

I look up at him and can't help but crack a smile. I thought it would be strange picturing him like that, but it feels right. How it's meant to be. I think he went along with me all those years mostly on a lark, something to pass the time, away from the pressures of his family and the grace year ahead, but for me, it was always something more than that. I don't blame him for becoming who he was supposed to be. He's lucky in a way. To be at odds with your nature, what everyone expects from you, is a life of constant struggle.

"I'm happy for you," I say as I peel a red leaf from my knee. "I mean it."

He picks up the leaf, tracing his thumb along the veins. "Do you ever think there's something more out there . . . more than all of this?"

I look up at him, trying to gauge his meaning, but I can't get caught up in this again. It's too dangerous. "Well, you can always visit the outskirts." I punch him on the shoulder.

"You know what I mean." He takes a deep breath. "You must know."

I snatch the pearl from him, slipping it into the hem of the sleeve. "Don't go soft on me now, Michael," I say as I stand. "Soon, you'll have the most coveted position in the county, running the apothecary, taking your place as head of the council. People will listen to you. You'll have *real* influence." I attempt a simpering smile. "Which brings me to a tiny favor I've been meaning to ask."

"Anything," he says as he gets to his feet.

"If I make it back alive . . ."

"Of course you'll make it back, you're smart and tough and—"

"*If* I make it back," I interrupt, dusting off my dress the best I can. "I've decided I want to work in the fields, and I was hoping you could use your position on the council to pull some strings."

"Why would you want that?" His brow knots up. "That's the lowest work available."

"It's good, honest work. And I'll be able to stare up at the sky anytime I want. When you're eating your supper, you can look down at your plate and say, my, that's a fine-looking carrot, and you'll think of me."

"I don't want to think of you when I look at a damn carrot."

"What's gotten into you?"

"No one will be there to protect you." He starts pacing. "You'll be open to the elements. I've heard stories. The fields are full of men . . . of bastards one step away from being poachers, and they can take you anytime they want."

"Oh, I'd like to see them try." I laugh as I pick up a stick, lashing it through the air.

"I'm serious." He grabs my hand, midswipe, forcing me to drop the stick, but he doesn't let go of my hand. "I worry for you," he says softly.

"Don't." I jerk my hand away, thinking how strange it feels to have him touch me that way. Over the years, we've beat each other senseless, rolled around in the dirt, dunked each other in the river, but somehow this is different. He feels sorry for me.

"You're not thinking straight," he says as he looks down at the stick, the dividing line between us, and shakes his head. "You're not listening to what I'm trying to tell you. I want to help you—"

"Why?" I kick the stick out of the way. "Because I'm stupid . . . because I'm a girl . . . because I couldn't possibly know what I want . . . because of this red ribbon in my hair . . . my dangerous magic?"

"No," he whispers. "Because the Tierney I know would never think that of me . . . wouldn't ask this of me . . . not now . . . not while I'm . . ." He pulls his hair back from his face in frustration. "I only want what's best for you," he says as he backs away from me and goes crashing into the woods.

I think about going after him, apologizing for whatever I've done to offend him, take back the favor, so we can part as friends, but maybe it's better this way. How do you say good-bye to your childhood?

Feeling irritated and confused, I walk back through town, doing my best to ignore the stares and whispers. I stop to watch the horses in the paddock being groomed by the guards for the journey to the encampment, their manes and tails braided with red ribbons. Just like us. And it occurs to me, that's how they think of us . . . we're nothing more than in-season mares for breeding.

Hans brings one of the horses closer so I can admire its mane, the intricate plaiting, but we don't speak. I'm not allowed to call him by his name in public, just "guard," but I've known him since I was seven years old. I'll never forget going to the healing house that afternoon to find Father and instead finding Hans lying there all alone with a bag of bloody ice between his legs. At the time, I didn't understand. I thought it was some kind of accident. But he was sixteen, born to a woman of the labor house. He'd been given a choice. Become a guard or work in the fields for the rest of his life. Being a guard is a respected position in the county—they get to live in town, in a house with maids, they're even allowed to buy cologne made from herbs and exotic citrus at the apothecary, a privilege Hans takes full advantage of. Their duties are light in comparison to the fields—maintaining the gallows, controlling a rowdy guest or two from the north, escorting the grace year girls to and from the encampment, and yet, most choose the fields.

Father says it's a simple procedure, a small cut and snip to free them of their urges, and maybe that's true, but I think the pain lies elsewhere, in having to live among us—being reminded day in and day out of everything that's been taken away from them.

I don't know why I wasn't afraid to approach him, but that day in the healing house, when I sat down next to him and held his hand, he began to weep. I'd never seen a man cry before.

I asked him what was wrong, and he told me it was a secret.

I said I was good at keeping secrets.

And I am.

"I'm in love with a girl, Olga Vetrone, but we can never be together," he said.

"Why?" I asked. "If you love someone you should be with them."

He explained that she was a grace year girl, that yesterday she'd received a veil from a boy and would have no choice but to marry him.

He told me that he'd always planned on working in the fields, but he couldn't stand the idea of being away from her. At least if he joined the guard, he'd be able to be close to her. Protect her. Watch her children grow up, even pretend they were his own.

I remember thinking it was the most romantic thing in the world.

When Hans left for the encampment, I thought maybe when they saw each other, they'd run away, forsake their vows, but when the convoy returned, Hans looked as if he'd seen a ghost. His beloved didn't make it home. Her body was unaccounted for. They didn't even find her ribbon. Her little sister was banished to the outskirts that day. She was only a year older than me at the time. It made me worry that much more for my sisters, but also, about what would happen to me if they didn't make it back.

Come winter, when I saw Hans alone in the stable, practicing his braiding, his cold fingers deftly weaving in and out of the chestnut tail with the ribbon, I asked him about Olga. What happened to her. A shadow passed over his face. As he walked toward me, he stroked his hand over his heart, again and again, as if he could somehow put it back together again, a tic he carries to this day. Some of the girls make fun of him for it, the constant rubbing sound it makes, but I always felt sorry for him.

"It wasn't meant to be," he whispered.

"Will you be okay?" I asked.

"I have you to look after now," he said, a hint of a smile in his voice.

And he did.

He stood in front of me in the square to block my view of the most brutal punishments; he helped me sneak into the meeting house to spy on the men; he even told me when the guards had their rounds, so I could steer clear of them when sneaking out. Other than Michael, and the girl from my dreams, he was my only friend.

"Are you scared?" he whispers.

I'm surprised to hear his voice. He usually isn't brazen enough to speak to me in public. But I'll be leaving soon.

"Should I be?" I whisper back.

He's opening his mouth to say something when I feel someone tugging on my dress. I whip around, ready to clobber Tommy Pearson or whoever touched me, but I see my two little sisters, Clara and Penny, covered in goose feathers.

"Do I even want to know?" I ask, trying to stifle a laugh.

"You gotta help us." Penny licks a sticky substance off her fingers. I can smell it from here: sugar maple sap. "We were supposed to fetch Father's parcel at the apothecary, but . . . but—"

"We got waylaid." Clara rescues her, giving me that confident grin. "Can you fetch it so we can get cleaned up before Mother comes home?"

"Please, pretty please," Penny chimes in. "You're our favorite sister. Do us this one favor before you leave us for a whole year."

When I look up, Hans is already at the stables. I wanted to say good-bye, but I imagine good-byes are harder for him than most.

"Fine." I agree just to get them to stop whining. "But you better hurry. Mother's in a mood today."

They take off running, laughing and pushing each other,

and I want to tell them to enjoy it while it lasts, but they won't understand. And why taint the last bit of freedom they have.

Taking a deep breath, I head to the apothecary. I haven't been since that hot July night, but there's a part of me that wants to face the ugly truth—to be reminded of where I could end up if I'm not careful. The bell jingles as I open the door, the tinny metallic sound setting my teeth on edge.

"Tierney, what a pleasant surprise." Michael's father takes in an eyeful. When I don't blush, stammer, or avert my eyes, Mr. Welk clears his throat. "Picking up your father's parcel?" he asks as he fumbles with the packages lined up on the back shelf.

Fixing my gaze on the cabinet, I feel the memory rising in the back of my throat like thick bile.

I'd snuck out, like I did most every night to meet Michael, and on the way home, I noticed the soft flicker of candlelight coming from inside the apothecary. Creeping closer, I found Michael's dad opening a hidden compartment behind the cabinet of hair tonics and shaving tools. My heart started pounding against my ribs when I saw my father step from the shadows to inspect the tidy rows of secreted glass bottles. Some were filled with what looked like dried bits of jerky, others a deep red liquid, but there was one in particular that caught his eye. Pressing my forehead against the warm glass to get a better view, I saw an ear, covered in small white pustules, suspended in murky liquid. I went to put my hand over my mouth, but I accidentally bashed my knuckle against the glass, drawing their attention.

Though I denied seeing anything, Mr. Welk insisted that I be punished on the spot. "A loss of respect is a slippery slope," he said. The heat of the switch coming down on my backside only seemed to cement the image in my mind.

I never spoke of it. Not even to Michael, but I knew those were the remains of the girls who were poached during their grace year, their bits and pieces being sold on the black market as an aphrodisiac and youth serum.

Father was a man of medicine, working on cures for disease. I always got the sense that he thought of the black market as superstition, nothing more than going back to the dark ages—that's why I never expected him to be so vain, so low, so desperate, as to be a customer. And for what? So he could have the stamina to father a precious son?

That earlobe belonged to someone's daughter. Someone my father might've treated when she was ill, or patted on the head at church. I wondered what he'd do if I was the one in those little glass bottles. Would he still want to eat my skin, drink my blood, suck the very marrow from my bones?

"Oh, I almost forgot," Mr. Welk says as he thrusts the rough brown-paper-wrapped package into my hands. "Happy Veiling Day."

Tearing my eyes away from the cabinet, from their dirty little secret, I give him my best smile.

Because soon, I'll be coming into my magic, and he should pray that I burn through every last bit of it before I come home.

As the church bell tolls, men, women, and children rush toward the square.

"It's too early for the gathering," someone whispers.

"I heard there's a punishment," a man says to his wife.

"But it's not a full moon," she replies.

"Did they find a usurper?" A young boy tugs on his mother's bustle.

I crane my head around the crowd, into the square, and sure enough, the guards are rolling out the staircase for the gallows. The squeaky wheels send a jagged chill through my blood.

As we gather around the punishment tree, I'm searching for a hint of what's about to happen, but everyone stares straight ahead, as if transfixed by the dying light glinting off the cold steel branches.

I wonder if this is what Hans was trying to tell me. If it was some kind of warning.

Father Edmonds steps forward to address the crowd, his white robes clinging to his bulbous shape. "On our most sacred eve, a grave matter has been brought to the attention of the council."

I don't know if I'm just being paranoid, but my mother's eyes seem to dart in my direction.

The dreams. I swallow so hard I'm sure everyone can hear it.

Searching the crowd for Michael, I find him near the front. Could he have ratted me out? Was he so angry at me that he could've told the council about the girl from my dreams?

"Clint Welk will speak on behalf of the council," Father Edmonds says.

As Michael's father steps forward, it feels like my heart is going to burst through my rib cage. My palms are sweaty; my mouth is chalk dry. Penny and Clara must sense my distress, because they nuzzle in a little closer on either side of me.

Standing before us, in perfect alignment with the punishment tree, Mr. Welk lowers his head as if in prayer, but I swear I catch the rise of his cheekbones—the hint of a smile.

I feel sick. Every sin I've ever committed runs through my mind, but there are too many to count. I got too comfortable, careless. I should've never spoken of the dreams . . . I should've never had them at all. Maybe I secretly wanted this to happen. Maybe I wanted to be caught. Just as I'm getting ready to speak up, promise to repent, vow to rid myself of this magic and be good from now on, Mr. Welk's lips part. I'm watching his tongue—waiting for it to move to the roof of his mouth to form a *T*, but instead, he presses his lips together to form an *M*. "Mare Fallow, come forth."

I let out a gasp of pent-up air, but no one seems to notice. Maybe every girl in the square did the same. Despite our differences, that's the one thing we all share in. The fear of being named.

As Mrs. Fallow walks to the front, the women push forward to spit and jeer, my mother always the first among them. I don't know why she feels the need to rub salt in the wound. Mrs. Fallow was kind to me once. In my fourth year, I'd gotten lost in the woods. She found me, took me by the hand, and led me home. She didn't scold my mother, she didn't tattle on her that I was out where I shouldn't be, and this is how my mother thanks her? It makes me feel ashamed to be her daughter.

Focusing in on the gate, I try to escape in my mind, but Mrs. Fallow's measured steps, the swish of her underskirts, burrow their way into my senses, like the softest of death knells.

I don't want to look at her. It's not out of disgust or shame—I feel like it could just as easily be me. Michael knows it. Hans knows it. My mother, too. Maybe they all do. But I owe her my full attention. She needs to know that I remember . . . that I won't forget her.

She looks like a ghost as she passes. Pale papery skin, salt-and-pepper braid lying limp against her curved spine, her husband shadowing her like a bad omen. I wonder if she knew her time was up. If she could feel it coming.

"Mare Fallow. You stand accused of harboring your magic. Shouting obscenities in your sleep, speaking in the devil's tongue."

I can't imagine Mrs. Fallow raising her voice above a whisper, let alone shouting obscenities, but her season has changed. She bore no sons. Her girls have all been assigned to the labor houses. Her womb is a cold, barren wasteland. She has no use.

"Well . . . what do you have to say for yourself?" Mr. Welk prods.

Other than the thin stream of liquid trailing over the tip of her worn leather boot, she gives away nothing. I want to shake her; I want her to tell them she's sorry, beg for mercy so she can be sent to the outskirts, but she just stands there in silence.

"Very well," Mr. Welk announces. "On behalf of God and the chosen men, I hereby sentence you to the gallows."

By law, the women—wives, laborers, and children—are required to watch a punishment. And choosing to do this on veiling day is no accident. They want to send us away with a message.

Before climbing the rickety steps, Mrs. Fallow looks to her husband, perhaps waiting for a last-minute reprieve, but it never comes. And in that moment, I know if she had any magic left in her, she would use it. She would choke the life out of him, the entire council . . . maybe all of us. And I can't say I'd blame her.

When she finally reaches the top of the platform, and they place the rope around her neck, she opens her hand, revealing a small red bloom. It's so tiny, I wonder if anyone else even notices it.

Right before she steps off the ledge, it hits me like a cast-iron kettle.

Scarlet red, five delicate petals. It's the same flower from my dreams.

I start pushing to the front. I need to stop this. I need to ask her where she got it, what it means. My mother grabs me, squeezing my hand. It's not a nurturing squeeze. It's rough and tight. *Stand down, child. Do not bring shame on this family,* it says.

And so I stand there with the others, watching the red petals dance with every spasm, every final impulse, until her hand finally goes limp.

There's a moment of silence that follows every hanging. Sometimes it feels like it stretches on forever, like they want us to dwell in it for as long as possible—dwell is the right word, to be domiciled, take up residence, to abide—but this time, it feels too short, like they don't want us to really think about what just happened . . . how *wrong* it is.

Mr. Welk steps to the front, seemingly oblivious to the macabre sight of her corpse swaying gently behind him, or maybe in spite of it.

"And now there are *thirteen* eligible men," he announces as he motions toward Mr. Fallow.

Mr. Fallow stands with his hands clasped piously in front of him. Geezer Fallow. I can't stop thinking about seeing him this morning in the square. He seemed happy as a lark. Not a man who was about to condemn his wife to death, but a man who was on the hunt for a new one.

As the crowd slowly begins to disperse, instead of backing away with the others, I push forward. I don't want to see Mrs. Fallow up close, but I need to find that flower. I need to know that it's real, but Michael stands in front of me like a brick wall. "We need to talk—"

"I forgive you," I say as I peer around him, scanning the ground for the bloom.

"*You* forgive *me*?"

"I just . . . this isn't a good time . . . ," I say as I drop to my knees to look. Where could it be? Maybe it slipped through the cracks. Maybe it's wedged between the cobblestones.

"There you are." Kiersten bounces on her tiptoes in front of him. "Is everything all set?" she whispers.

Michael clears his throat. He only does that when he's at a complete loss for words.

"Oh, I didn't see you down there," Kiersten says through her tight smile. "We're going to be the best of friends. Isn't that right, Michael?"

"Okay, lovebirds." Michael's father clamps his hand over his shoulder to pull him away. "You'll have plenty of time for that later. Right now, we have a choosing ceremony to attend."

Kiersten squeals in delight and flutters off.

At last, I think I'm free, when I'm yanked to my feet from behind.

The guards are herding the women back toward the church.

"Wait . . . there was a flower—" I start to yell, but one of the women elbows me hard in the ribs.

I lose my breath; I lose my bearings. I get swept up in the crowd, and the further I get from Mrs. Fallow's swaying body, the less I'm certain the bloom was ever there to begin with.

Maybe this is how it starts—how I lose myself to the magic lurking inside of me.

But even if it was real, what would it matter anyway?

After all, it's just a flower.

And I'm only one girl.

Before all the women are locked inside the chapel to await the veils, we're counted. Normally, this would be my cue to make a round, do something annoying to get myself noticed, which would be followed by a swift admonishment from my mother to keep quiet and behave. I'd then sneak into the confessional booth and disappear through Father Edmonds's quarters. That was always the creepiest part—the smell of laudanum and loneliness seeping from his bedchamber.

But there will be none of that tonight. Even though I'm not getting a veil, the girls who receive one will want to rub it in, soaking up the envy and disappointment in the room like emaciated ticks.

Standing with my back against the curtain of the confessional booth, I grip the oxblood velvet with hungry fingers. It's killing me that I won't be able to witness my own year. But if I close my eyes, I can feel the hay itching my nose, smell the ale and musk wafting up to the loft, hear the names of the girls escape their feverish lips.

I already know the prettiest girls with superior breeding and gentle graces will get a veil, but there's always at least one wild card. I scan the room wondering which one it will be. Meg Fisher looks the part, but she has a strange savage streak. You can see it in her shoulders, the way they roll forward when she feels threatened, like a wolf trying to decide whether to attack or retreat. Or Ami Dumont. Delicate, sweet. She would make for a docile wife, but her hips are too narrow, beddable to be sure, but not sturdy enough to withstand childbirth. Of course, some men like breakable things.

They like to break them.

"Bless us, Father," Mrs. Miller says as she attempts to lead the women in prayer. "Please guide the men. Let them use your holy voice to do your bidding."

It takes everything I have not to roll my eyes. By now, the men will have cracked open a second barrel, telling tall tales of the women in the outskirts, the wicked things they'll do for coin, bragging about all their bastards roaming the woods, hunting for a girl to poach.

"Amen," the women say, one after the other. God forbid they do anything in unison.

This is the one night a year the women are allowed to congregate without the men. You'd think it would be our opportunity to talk, share, let it all out. Instead, we stand isolated and petty, sizing each other up, jealous for what the other one has, consumed by hollow desires. And who benefits from all this one-uppery? The men. We outnumber them two to one, and yet here we are, locked in a chapel, waiting for them to decide our fate.

Sometimes I wonder if that's the real magic trick.

I wonder what would happen if we all said what we really felt . . . just for one night. They couldn't banish us all. If we stood together, they'd have to listen. But with rumors swirling about a usurper among us, no one is willing to take that risk. Not even me.

"Do you have your sights set on a particular labor house?" Mrs. Daniels asks, eyeing my red ribbon. As she leans in, I get a whiff of pure iron, but I also smell the decay. No doubt she's been using grace year blood to try to hang on to her youth. "I mean, if you don't get a veil . . . of course," she adds.

I think about giving her a polite rehearsed answer, but her husband's on the council, and now that Michael and I are on the outs, maybe she can be of use. "The fields," I reply, bracing myself for the cluck of disapproval, but she's already moved on to her next victim. She didn't really want an answer; she just wanted to infect me with fear and doubt.

"Tierney! Tierney James." Mrs. Pearson, Tommy's mother, beckons me over with a single wizened claw. She came back from her grace year missing the other four fingers on her right hand. Frostbite, I presume. "Let me look at you, girl," she says as she juts out her bottom lip to survey me. "Good teeth. Decent hips. You seem healthy enough," she says as she gives my braid a hard tug.

"Pardon," June says, coming to my rescue. "I need to borrow my sister for a moment."

As we're walking away, Mrs. Pearson says, "I know you. You're the oldest James girl. The one who can't get pregnant . . . the one with no bairn."

"I don't care if she only has six fingers," I say as I clench my fists and start to head back, but June pulls me away.

"Breathe, Tierney," she whispers as she leads me to the other side of the room. "You're going to have to learn to control that temper of yours. You don't want to make enemies going into your grace year. It's going to be hard enough for you as it is, but everything can change with a seed of kindness," she says as she pats my arm before let- — ting go to join Ivy. I follow her with my eyes, wondering what she meant by that.

Ivy's stroking her prized belly, bragging about how she can tell it's a boy. I swear, she got all of my mother's vanity, but none of the tact. June stands by her side, smiling, but I can see the strain in the corners of her mouth. Even June must have a breaking point.

"Look at Mrs. Hanes," someone says behind me, which sets off a string of agitated whispers.

"I wonder if she let another man see her with her hair down?"

"I bet he caught her out in the meadow again, looking at the stars."

"Did anyone see her ankles? Maybe she's the usurper they've been searching for."

"Don't be daft, if that were the case, she'd be dead by now," another woman snaps.

As Mrs. Hanes walks down the center aisle, toward the altar, the women stand back, giving her a wide berth, their eyes affixed to the blunt end of her lopped-off braid, splayed out in anger . . . in violence. We're forbidden from cutting our own hair, but if a husband sees fit, he can punish his wife by cutting off her braid.

A few of the women pull their plaits over their shoulders for comfort, but most avert their eyes, as if her shame might rub off on them. It's not until she's safely tucked away in the front pew that they resume their vapid conversations.

The whiff of rose oil perfumes the air as Kiersten slips

by with Jessica and Jenna trailing behind her. You'd think they might be triplets, the way they move in perfect synchronicity, but Kiersten seems to have that effect on whomever she chooses to shine her light upon. With or without magic, it's a powerful gift. They quickly zero in on Gertrude Fenton, who's standing in the corner, doing her best to blend into the cherry-paneled wall, but her fine dress won't let her.

"Don't you look fetching in that blush-colored lace," Kiersten says, toying with the edging on Gertrude's sleeve. "The gloves are a nice touch."

Jenna snickers. "She thinks if she covers her knuckles, she'll get a veil."

Jessica whispers something in Gertrude's ear; her cheeks turn crimson.

I don't need to hear it to know what she said. What she called her.

Up until last year, Kiersten and Gertrude were inseparable, but all of that changed when Gertrude was charged with depravity. Since she still possessed a white ribbon, the details of her offense were kept hidden, but I think that made it all the worse. Our imaginations ran wild with what it could be. And when they dragged her into the square, whipping her knuckles clear to the bone, that's when I first heard the name, whispered from girl to girl.

Dirty Gertie.

From that moment on, any chance of receiving a veil was obliterated.

And still, they pick at her. It reminds me of my mother and the other hyenas, always ready to cast the first stone.

A part of me wants to throw myself on the pyre, give Gertrude a chance to escape, but that goes against my plan. I promised myself I was going to get through my grace year with as little fuss as possible and that means steering clear of Kiersten and the like. As much as I hate watching them dismantle such an easy target, maybe it's time Gertrude learns to toughen up a bit. The year ahead will be full of terrors much worse than Kiersten.

I've heard as long as we stay within the encampment, no harm will come to us. It's considered hallowed ground. Not even the poachers would dare cross the barrier for fear of being cursed. So what made the girls leave the safety of the encampment in the first place? Did their magic consume them . . . make them do foolish things? No matter the cause, some of us will only be returning to Garner County in pretty little bottles, but at least that's an honorable death. The worst fate, by far, is not returning at all. Some say vengeful ghosts are to blame, some say it's the wilderness, madness that makes them take their own lives, but if our bodies go unaccounted for, if we disappear, vanish into thin air, our sisters will bear the brunt of our shame and be banished to the outskirts. I look at Penny and Clara, playing behind the altar, and I know, no matter what, dead or alive, I need to make it back to the county, for their sakes.

As the hours tick by, and the refreshments disappear, the tension in the room is palpable. I want to believe we can be different, but when I look around the church, at the women comparing the length of their braids, reveling in another woman's punishment, scheming and clawing for every inch of position, I can't help thinking the men might be right. Maybe we're incapable of more. Maybe without the confines placed upon us, we'd rip each other to shreds, like a pack of outskirt dogs.

"The veils are coming, the veils are coming," Mrs. Wilkerson finally calls down from the bell tower as she pulls the rope—the manic dull clang, the pinching of cheeks, the stomping of heels, kicking up the stench of desperation.

The doors open and a hush falls over the chapel, as if God himself is holding his breath.

Kiersten's father is the first to step inside, his face a perfect portrait of maudlin hope. As he places the veil on her head, Kiersten looks at every single one of us, making sure we're all choking on her good fortune. She's not only been veiled—she's the first. An honor.

Jenna's and Jessica's veils aren't far behind. No surprise there. They've been setting the bait since their ninth year with diminutive gazes and clear-skinned smiles. God help the boys who fell into that trap.

Mr. Fenton walks in, his face ruddy from drink or emotion, maybe both, but when I see him tenderly place the veil on Gertrude's head, I can't help but feel a twinge of happiness for her. Somehow, against all odds, she showed them all.

One after another the fathers file in, the pretty maids are veiled, and with each one down, I feel the chains begin to loosen around my chest. I'm one step closer to building a life on my own terms.

But when my father enters the chapel, the veil held out in front of him like a stillborn calf, it feels as if I'm being gutted with the dull end of an axe.

"This can't be . . ." I stagger back against the sea of women, but they only push me forward, rejecting me like a heavy tide.

Through bleary eyes, I look to my mother. She seems

just as surprised as I am, wavering on her feet, but she manages to raise her chin, giving me a stern signal to behave.

I feel the heat take over my face, but it's not embarrassment. I'm furious. And as I look at the other girls, stationed around the room, who would've killed for a veil, I feel a pang of guilt.

How is this even possible? I've done nothing to encourage a suitor. In fact, I've done just the opposite. I openly ridiculed every boy who showed even a glimmer of interest.

I look to my father. But his eyes won't leave the veil.

Scraping my memory, I search for a hint of who it might be, when it hits me—Tommy Pearson. My stomach roils when I think of him hollering at me when I dropped the mulberries, the way he looked at me when he said he liked them feisty. I search the room for Mrs. Pearson, to find her looking on with great interest.

Kiersten gives me a ghost of a smile from beneath the lacy gauze, and I wonder if she knew . . . if Michael's behind this? Just today, he was defending Tommy, said he wasn't that bad. Did he talk Tommy into claiming me to save me from the fields? He said he only wanted what's best for me. Is this what he thinks I deserve?

As my father places the veil on my head, he still can't meet my eyes. He knows this is nothing but a slow death for me.

I've practiced every possible expression from despair to indifference, but I never imagined I'd have to fake happiness.

With trembling fingers, he lowers the veil over my raging eyes.

Through the dainty netting, my eyes dart around the room, the jealousy, the whispers, the knowing glances.

I was the wild card.

Tonight, I became a wife.

All because a boy claimed it so.

While my parents escort me home, my sisters twitter around us, spouting off the names of every eligible boy, trying to gauge Father's expression, but he stays stone-faced. As per tradition, I won't know the name of my future husband until he lifts my veil tomorrow morning at the farewell ceremony. But I know. I can still feel Tommy Pearson's eyes on my skin like a festering rash. And soon his eyes on me will be the least of my worries.

Husband.

The word makes my knees buckle, but my parents only tighten their grip on my elbows, dragging me along until I regain my footing.

I want to spit and scream like a trapped animal, but I can't risk being cast out, bringing shame on my younger sisters. I need to hold it together until we're safely behind closed doors. Even then, I must watch my tongue. I have a few skills, but if I were to get thrown out of the county now, the poachers would hunt me down within a fortnight. That much I'm sure of.

As my older sisters pair off to their own homes, and my mother chases my younger siblings off to bed, I'm left alone with my father for the first time in months—the incident at the apothecary still fresh in my mind.

I grip the banister, imagining the wood bruising beneath the weight of my fingertips.

"How could you let this happen?" I whisper.

I hear him swallow. "I know this isn't what you planned, but—"

"Why did you teach me those things? Show me what it meant to be free, and for what? I'm just like the rest of them now."

"I wish that were true."

His words are cutting, but I turn to face him. "Did you even try to stand up for me? You could've told him I haven't bled or I smell bad . . . anything!"

"Believe me. There were plenty of protests all around. But your suitor's mind was set."

"Did Michael at least try to dissuade him, or was he the one behind all this? Tell me that much."

"Sweet daughter," he says as he eases the back of his hand over my cheek—the scratchy veil irritating my skin, his placating touch irritating *me*. "We only want what's best for you. There are worse fates."

"Like the girls in those little jars?" I advance on him with a viciousness that not even I recognize. "Was it worth it? All for the chance at a precious son?"

"Is that what you think?" He staggers back a step as if he's afraid of me.

And I wonder if this is the magic taking over. Is this how it starts—the slip of the tongue? A loss of respect? Is this how I become a monster the men whisper of?

I turn and run up the stairs before I do something I regret.

Slamming the door behind me, I rip off the veil. I'm tearing at the dress, contorting my hands behind my back trying to get at the corset strings, but it's no use. They're tucked away beyond my reach, which only seems fitting.

After a lifetime of planning, wishing, hoping, all it took was a whisper, "Tierney James," and as soon as the words left his traitorous lips, the life I knew was over. No longer would I be able to pass unnoticed in the lanes. There would be no more dirt allowed beneath my nails, no more scuffed boots and sun-tangled hair. No more days lost in the woods, lost in the curiosities of my own mind. My life, my body, now belonged to another.

But why would Tommy Pearson choose me? I'd made no secret of hating his guts. He was cruel and stupid and arrogant.

"Of course," I whisper, thinking of his pet birds. His birds of prey. The thrill was in the taming, and once they were tamed, he lost interest, letting them starve to death before his very eyes. This was all a game to him.

I slump to the ground, the raw blue silk billowing around me in a perfect circle. It reminds me of one of the fishing holes my dad and I used to carve out at the deepest point of the lake. How I wish I could slip under the ice—disappear into the cold abyss.

My mother enters the room, and I quickly throw the

veil back on. It's tradition for her to remove it while she tells me of my wifely duties.

As she stands before me, the veil still fluttering in agitation, I'm expecting her to yank me to my feet, tell me to buck up, tell me how lucky I am, but instead, she sings an old tune, a song of mercy and grace. Tenderly, she removes the veil, setting it on the dressing table behind her. Slipping off the red ribbon, she runs her fingers through my braid, letting my hair fall in soft waves over my shoulders. She takes my hands, pulling me to my feet, helping me out of the dress, and when she unlaces the corset, I take in a deep gasping breath. It's almost painful being able to fill my lungs again. It only reminds me of freedom. Freedom I no longer possess.

As she hangs up the dress, I try to gain control of my breath, but the harder I try, the worse it gets. "This . . . this wasn't supposed to happen," I sputter. "And not Tommy Pearson—"

"Shhh," she whispers as she dips a cloth in the bowl of water and washes my face, my neck, my arms, cooling me off. "Water is the elixir of life," she says. "This has been collected from high on the spring, where it's freshest. Can you tell?" she asks as she holds the cloth to my nose.

All I can do is nod. I don't know why she's talking about this.

"You've always been a clever girl," she continues, "a resourceful girl. You watch. You listen. That will serve you well."

"In the grace year?" I ask, watching her berry-stained lips.

"In being a wife." She leads me to sit on the edge of the bed. "I know you're disappointed, but you'll feel differently when you return."

"*If* I return."

She sits next to me, taking off the silver thimble, giving me a full view of her missing fingertip, the angry puckered skin. This rare show of intimacy brings fresh tears to my eyes. "You know the stories June used to tell about the rabbits that lived in the vegetable garden?"

I nod, wiping away my tears.

"There was one that was always getting into trouble, venturing out where she shouldn't go, but she learned valuable things, about the farmer, the land, things the other rabbits never would have known. But knowledge comes at a great cost."

My skin prickles up in goosebumps. "The poachers . . . did they do this to you?" I whisper as I touch her hand. Her skin is hot. "Did they try to lure you out of the encampment? Is that what happens to the girls?"

She pulls her hand away, putting the thimble back on. "You've always had a vivid imagination. I'm merely talking about the rabbits. We don't speak of the grace year, you know that. But I suppose I do need to tell you of your wifely duties—"

"Please . . . don't." I shake my head. "I remember my lessons," I say as I wring my hands in my lap. "Legs spread, arms flat, eyes to God."

I learned all that ages ago, long before our lessons. I've seen countless lovers in the meadow. One time, Michael and I were trapped up an oak while Franklin did it to Jocelyn. Michael and I sat there, trying not to laugh, but it doesn't seem at all funny now—the idea of having to lie with Tommy Pearson, his red face grunting over me.

As I'm staring down at the floor, I see a drop of blood run down the inside of my mother's leg, staining her cream-colored stocking. Catching my gaze, she tucks her leg back to hide it.

"I'm sorry," I whisper. And I mean it. Another month without a son. I wonder if her season is coming to an end, which puts her at risk. I can't imagine my father replacing her, like Mr. Fallow did, but I can't imagine a lot of things lately.

"Your father and I were lucky, but respect . . . common goals can grow into something more." She tucks a loose strand of hair behind my ear. "You've always been your father's favorite. His wild girl. You know, he would never give you to someone he thought . . . immature."

Immature? I don't understand. That's Tommy by definition.

"Your father only wants the best for you," my mother adds.

I know I should keep my mouth shut, but I don't care anymore. Let them cast me out, let them whip me until I can't stand. Anything will be better than silence. "You don't know Father the way I do . . . what he's capable of," I say. "I've *seen* things. I *know* things. Like last night, the guards came to see him and he—"

"As I said . . ." She stands to leave. "Your imagination will be the death of you."

"What about my dreams?"

My mother stops. Her spine seems to stiffen. "Remember what happened to Eve."

"But I don't dream of murdering the council. . . . I dream of a girl. . . . She wears a red flower above her heart."

"Don't," she whispers. "Don't do this to—"

"She speaks to me. Tells me things . . . about how it could be. She has gray eyes, like mine, like Father's. What if she's one of his . . . a daughter from the outskirts? I've seen him leave the gates more times than I can count—"

"Watch yourself, Tierney," she snaps with an intensity that makes me flinch. "Your eyes are wide open, but you see nothing."

As I sink back on the bed, my eyes fill with tears.

My mother lets out a deep sigh as she sits next to me. Her skin is clammy, a sheen of cold sweat dotting her brow. "Your dreams . . . ," she says as she gently takes my face in her hands, "it's the one place that belongs only to you. A place where no one can touch you. Hang on to that as long as you can. Because soon, your dreams will turn to nightmares." She leans in to kiss me on the cheek. "Trust no one," she whispers. "Not even yourself."

I catch a strong whiff of iron, the metallic smell gripping my senses. As she pulls away, I notice a chalky red substance clinging to the corners of her mouth. A sliver of ice moves through me. Her lips aren't berry stained.

They're blood stained.

The bottles from the apothecary. Pieces of poached girls adrift in a sea of blood and moonshine. I always thought my father was buying it for himself, but what if he was buying it for her—all for a taste of youth? Was she so desperate to stay young that she felt the need to consume her own kind? Is that what the grace year does to us? Turns us into cannibals?

As she slips out the door, I rush for the window, opening it, gulping down the fresh air. Anything to drown out the scent of blood.

Aside from the faint crowing of drunken boys, and the muffled weeping of girls who didn't receive a veil, it's eerily quiet.

Staring out at the dim lanterns shining from the woods, the outskirts, I wonder if the poachers are watching me now . . . if they see an easy kill.

Taking a deep breath, I close my eyes and hold out my arms like an eagle, letting the bitter wind unfurl around me. I sway to the rhythm of the night until it feels as if I'm soaring high above Garner County. Michael and I used to do this when we were little, when the world felt as if it might swallow us whole. A part of me wants to step off the ledge, see if my magic will kick in, letting me fly away from here, but that would be too easy.

And none of this is going to be easy.

When I wake, I'm alone, nestled beneath soft cotton and goose down. My eyes narrow on the thin strip of hazy yellow light nipping at the edges of the heavy curtains. It could be early morning or late afternoon. For a moment, I think maybe they forgot to wake me, or I dreamt the entire thing, but when I look around the room, at the veil innocently draped over the edge of the dressing table like slow-oozing poison, I know it's only a matter of time before they come for me. I can hide under the covers, luxuriate in my childhood bed, my childish notions, or I can face this head-on. My father always told me that a person is made up of all the little choices they make in life. The choices no one ever sees. I may not be in control of much, like who I marry, the children I'll bear, but I have control over this moment. And I'm not going to waste it.

My body shivers in revolt as I rip off the covers. The cold wood floor groans under my weight, as if it senses how heavy my heart is today.

Just as I'm about to peek out the curtains, my sisters come barging into the room.

"Are you mad?" Ivy says as Penny and Clara crash into me, pushing me back. "Someone could see you."

We're not allowed to be seen by the opposite sex without our veils on until the ceremony. We're no longer children . . . not yet wives. But we've been marked as property.

As soon as I'm safely out of view, Ivy flings open the curtains; I shield my eyes.

"Consider yourself lucky," she says as she pulls down the lace valance. "My year we were drenched rats before we even reached the county line."

"Knock, knock," June says as she comes in with my traveling cloak. It's the only personal item we're allowed to have. The rest of our supplies are county issued, probably already packed in gunnysacks and loaded on the wagons by now.

"I lined it four times, one for each season," she says,

draping it over my chair. "Cream wool with gray fur trim. To match your eyes."

"Cream wool? That's dumb." Ivy runs her greedy fingers over the cloak. "Come spring, it will be filthy."

"It's lovely." I nod at June. "Thank you."

She looks down, an embarrassed flush blooming in her cheeks. Most of the girls, including Ivy, came back from their grace year even more spiteful than when they left, but not her. June returned with the same placid smile as when she left. It made me wonder if that was her magic—having no magic at all. They say my mother came back much the same, but it's hard to imagine her ever being at ease or pleasant about anything.

"Make way," my mother says as she comes in with a tray full of enough food to feed an army, but when my little sisters reach for a biscuit, she slaps their hands away. "Don't you dare. This is for Tierney."

Without a veil, I'd be downstairs, eating porridge alongside my father in flinty silence, but my mother seems more than pleased to wait on me hand and foot, now that I'll be coming home to a husband.

Mrs. Tommy Pearson. The thought makes my stomach churn.

I sneak one of the biscuits into my napkin and slide it over to the edge; my little sisters seize it like urchins, crawling under my bed to eat it. I can hear them giggling and making fun of Mother, but she turns a deaf ear. She was so strict with June and Ivy, but I think I wore her down.

"Eat," my mother urges.

I'm not even hungry, but I cram as much sausage, eggs, stewed apples, milk, and biscuits into my belly as I can.

Not out of duty or to please my mother. I do it because I'm not an idiot. The guards who escort the girls to the encampment are gone for four days. So I figure it's a two-day journey each way. The wagons are for the supplies, which means we'll be on foot. And I'm not about to faint out there with the poachers watching our every move, looking for an easy mark. I'll need my strength.

Penny crawls out from under the bed and grabs the veil off the table, putting it on, checking herself out in the mirror. "Look at me . . . I'm the first wife chosen." She bats her eyelashes and fans herself.

I know she's just teasing, but seeing her like that sets something off inside of me. "Don't!" I yell as I snatch the veil off her head. She looks up at me in shock, as if I'd just given her a fresh slap. She probably thinks I'm being selfish, that I don't want her touching my precious veil, but it's the exact opposite. She can be so much more than this. I want to tell her as much, but I bite my tongue. I can't give her the same false hope my father gave to me. It makes it so much harder in the end.

But in that same breath, if anything close to the girl in my dreams is real . . . maybe there's hope for her yet. For all of us.

I lean down to tell her I'm sorry, but she kicks me in the shin. It brings a smile to my face. There's still fight in her. And maybe there's still fight in me.

My mother braids my hair with the red ribbon and then helps me dress. A high-neck cotton chemise with a linen traveling smock, followed by my cloak. It's heavier than I imagined, but that's because it's well made. June would make for a wonderful mother. I catch her eyeing Ivy's swollen belly, and it pains me. Life can be cruel. No one is immune to that, no matter how good you are.

Before my thick wool stockings go on, my brown leather boots laced up tight, I need to be printed. It's tradition. Clara and Penny are laughing, fighting over which one gets to do what, but my older sisters, my mother, stand stock-still. They know the gravity of this moment. What it means. Clara rolls the gloppy red ink on the sole of my right foot; Penny holds the stiff sheet of parchment in place. I stand, putting my full weight into it. As they peel it off, a shiver runs through me, but not from the cold ink alone. This is my mark, the brand of my father's sigil that I received at birth, a stretched rectangle with three slashes inside, signifying three swords. Should I be taken by a poacher, only to come home in tiny bottles, this is how they'll identify my body.

The bell echoes over the square, snaking its way through the narrow streets and narrow minds, until it reaches my house, reaching straight into my chest, squeezing tight.

Hurriedly, my sisters help me finish dressing.

As my mother places the veil on my head, I glimpse my ghostly reflection in the looking glass and take in a shallow breath. "Can I have a moment?"

She nods in silent understanding.

"Girls, out you go," my mother says as she herds them out of the room, gently closing the door behind her.

Raising the veil, I practice a demure, flaccid smile, over and over and over again until I've mastered something that can pass for pleasant. But no matter how hard I try I can't dim the fire burning in my eyes. Again, I wonder if it's my magic kicking in. With any luck, flames will start shooting out of my eyes, burning them all to a crisp on the spot. I think about keeping my eyes downcast, but maybe it's not such a bad thing, the discord between my mouth and my eyes. Tommy will lift my veil expecting an eagle, and I will give him a dove.

But I won't be a broken bird.

Not for anyone.

I never thought I'd be grateful for a veil, but the delicate netting makes the walk to the square almost dreamlike. Leers turn to glances. Sharp words are muffled. The falling aspen leaves look more like a celebration than the death of summer.

Snips of obscenities needle their way into my senses as I pass—

"How did she . . ."

"Who did she . . ."

"She must have . . ."

Normally, I'd focus in on every word, searching for clues, but the words have never been about me before.

Burying my trembling hands in the pocket of my cloak, I find a river clam pearl inside. The odd shape, the bluish pink luster. It's the same one I slipped into the hem of June's dress for safekeeping. She must've placed it here for me as a memento. I roll it between my fingertips, feeling a certain kinship. Like this pearl, I'm the tiny bit of irritant that worked its way into the soft tissue of the county. If I can survive the year, burn through my magic, maybe I'll come back just as resilient.

The buffalo horn bellows from the outskirts, signaling the approach of the returning girls and the start of a new hunting season.

"Vaer sa snill, tilgi meg," my father whispers in the language of his ancestors, *please forgive me,* as he hands me the flower my suitor chose for me. A gardenia. The sign of purity, secret love. It's an old-fashioned flower, one that's long gone out of favor. The only thing I can think is that Tommy's mother must've picked this out for him, because it's much too romantic for his brutish nature. Or perhaps he's twisted enough to find delight in the pure, knowing he's the one who ultimately gets to take it away.

While my family gathers around to say their good-byes, a final prayer, I have to clench my jaw to keep from crying. They say the poachers can smell our magic a mile away. That you can hear the girls screaming for days as they skin them alive. The more pain, the more potent the flesh.

As we take our place in line, with the onlookers crowded behind us, I notice Kiersten standing next to me. She's dying for me to notice her—the camellia precariously balanced between her delicate fingertips. A red camellia, the symbol of untethered passion, a flame within your heart. A bold choice for Michael, but again, I didn't know this side of him. I'd be happy for him if I still didn't want to strangle him.

As the boys start their march from the chapel to the square, the drums begin to beat. Everything wells up inside of me at once—shame, fear, anger. I close my eyes, trying to match my heartbeat to the drum, their heavy footsteps, but my body won't allow it. Even in this simple act, there's a part of me that refuses to give in. Surrender.

Boom.

Boom.

Boom.

I steal a glance and immediately wish I hadn't. Mr. Fallow is first in line, wetting his paper-thin lips in anticipation. I can't stop picturing his wife's body, gently swaying behind him as they announced he would be taking on a new wife.

A new wife.

And just like that, it feels like I've been hit square in the chest with an anvil. My breath grows short, my knees weak, my thoughts are racing—the way he looked at me yesterday morning in the square, the way he tipped his hat and wished me a happy veiling day, the way he stared at my red ribbon trailing down my backside. The old-fashioned flower. The saccharine sentiment. I wouldn't be surprised if he gave the same bloom to his last three wives. And my mother telling me that Father would never give me to someone he thought . . . *immature*. That's what she was trying to tell me. Geezer Fallow is my husband-to-be. The thought is so repulsive I have to choke back the bile nipping at the back of my throat. I want to pretend it's my imagination, dread getting the best of me, but when I look over again, he's staring right at me. The truth feels all at once shocking and like something I've always known. Maybe this is God's way of punishing me for wanting something more. The dreams . . . the things my father taught me, they were all for nothing. Because here I am . . . getting what's best for me.

Boom.

Boom.

Boom.

As he comes toward me, I'm trying to keep it together, not give myself away, but my veil is trembling under a dead calm sky. Lowering my eyes, I wait for it, wait for the moment he claims me, but his footsteps pass me by, settling in front of a girl to my left who's holding a pink nasturtium. The flower of sacrifice. I watch him lift her veil, and my heart sinks a little when Gertrude Fenton's face is revealed. He leans forward to whisper in her ear; she doesn't smile or blush or even cringe. She doesn't do anything at all but run her thumb over her scarred knuckles.

I should be relieved it's not me. The thought of his old wrinkly skin pressing up against mine makes me sick to my stomach, but no one deserves Geezer Fallow. Not even Gertrude Fenton.

Boom.

Boom.

Boom.

I steal another glance to see Tommy and Michael smiling at one another, until all I can see is red. Clenching my eyes shut, I try to simmer down, but I can't stop picturing Tommy's ruddy face grunting over me. I thought I'd prepared myself for this moment, rehearsed my part to perfection, but the closer he gets, the hotter the fire burns. I want to run . . . set myself on fire . . . disintegrate into a pile of ash.

Boom.

Boom.

Boom.

Kiersten's veil flutters next to me. A gasp as her red camellia falls to the ground. No doubt so she can embrace Michael dramatically. She always knew how to put on a show.

Boom.

Boom.

Boom.

A pair of freshly shined boots settle before me. The heavy breath of anticipation. The susurration of the crowd behind me. This is it. His fingers graze the edge of my veil, lingering in a hesitant, unexpected way. Slowly, he lifts the netting, every movement weighted with intention.

"Tierney James," he whispers, but his voice is all wrong.

I raise my eyes to meet him, and I feel like a bluegill that's been tossed on the riverbank, mouthing for air.

"Michael?" I manage to get out. "What are you doing?"

In confusion, I glance over at Kiersten to find Tommy Pearson pawing all over her, the heel of his boot crushing her red bloom into the soil.

"This . . . this is a mistake," I sputter.

"No mistake."

"Why?" Feeling light-headed, I rock back on my heels. "Why would you do this?"

"You didn't think I'd let you be assigned to the field house."

"But that's what I wanted," I blurt, then quickly lower my voice. "How could you sacrifice your happiness for me?"

"I did no such thing." He looks up to the sky for a moment, an anguished smile playing across his lips. "Tierney, you must know." He takes my hands. "I've been trying to tell you for so long. I love y—"

"Stop," I say a little too loud, attracting unwanted attention. "Stop," I whisper.

I feel hundreds of eyes on me, their judgment prickling the back of my neck.

"I tried to tell you yesterday," he says as he takes a step closer.

"But I saw you . . . with Kiersten . . . in the meadow."

"And I'm sure you saw her with many others, but you were too kind to tell me."

"I'm not kind." I look down at the ground, the tips of our boots almost touching. "I will never be the wife you need."

He places his warm fingers beneath my chin. "I want more than that," he says as he closes the gap between us. "You don't have to change for me."

Tears burn my eyelids. Not out of happiness, or relief. This feels like the ultimate betrayal. I thought he understood.

"It's time," Mr. Welk calls out, staring daggers into me. He must've been one of the other protestors my father spoke of at the choosing ceremony. I'm far from the daughter-in-law he imagined.

Michael leans in to kiss my cheek. "You can keep your dreams," he whispers. "But I dream only of you."

I don't have a chance to react, to even take in a breath,

before the gates open, signaling the arrival of the returning grace year girls. Instantly, the atmosphere shifts. This is no longer about veils . . . and promises . . . and hurt feelings . . . and dreams—this is about life and death.

As the bell begins to toll, we all stop to count. Twenty-six. Which means nine of the girls have met the poachers' blade. That's two more than last year.

There are no elaborate good-byes. No public displays of affection. Everything has been said. Nothing has been said.

As we're led out of the square, I notice a long line of men waiting their turn at the guard station, men I don't recognize from the county, but I quickly lose interest as we pass the returning girls, bone weary, emaciated, reeking of wood smoke, rot, and disease.

The girl in front of me slows to stare at one of the returning girls. "Lisbeth?" she whispers. "Sister, is that you?"

The girl raises her head, exposing a blood-crusted scab where her ear used to be. She blinks hard, as if trying to wake herself from a never-ending nightmare.

"Move it." The girl behind her pushes her along, the tattered remains of her soiled red ribbon hanging limply from her severed braid.

And to think—these are the lucky ones.

Frantically, I search their faces for a hint of what happened to them out there . . . what's in store for us. Beneath the dirt and grime, their gaunt expressions, there's a glimmer of seething hatred in their eyes. I can't shake the feeling that their ill will isn't for the men who did this to them but for us, the pure, unbroken girls who now possess the magic they've lost.

"You're dead," Kiersten says as she passes, jabbing me hard in the ribs. I'm doubled over, trying to catch my breath, when the other girls from my year walk by hissing insults.

"Slut."

"Traitor."

"Whore."

Michael may think he saved me from a life in the fields, but all he's done is put a target on my back.

I think of my mother, blood clinging to the corners of her mouth, telling me to trust no one.

As I look back on the closing gate, at the sisters, daughters, mothers, and grandmothers gathered around to watch the broken birds, it hits me. Maybe the reason no one speaks of the grace year is because of us. How could the men live among us, lie with us, let us care for their children, knowing the horrors we inflict upon one another . . . alone . . . in the wilderness . . . in the dark?

There's no specific marker in the road, no proclamation of our arrival, but I can tell we're nearing the outskirts.

It goes beyond the guards tightening their formation around us, beyond the glimpses of thatched stone cottages dotting the woods, and flashes of red darting through the dwindling foliage—it's the smell that gives it away: a thick gamey scent of fertile soil, freshly tanned hides, green ash soot, flowering herbs . . . and blood.

I can't decide if it's pleasant or repugnant, maybe somewhere in between, but it's absolutely dripping with life.

Though the women of the outskirts are unprotected by the gates, the church, the council, they seem to survive. I've heard the wives who are banished here never last long. If no one wanted them in the county, they certainly wouldn't want them here, but if they're young, lucky enough to be taken in, they can be of use serving the men of the county in exchange for coin. Their bastard sons are raised to be poachers, and their daughters age into the family trade. I used to wonder why they didn't just leave—there's nothing stopping them . . . no gates, no rules. It's easy to tell myself I can't leave because my younger sisters would be punished in my stead, but deep down I know it's more than that. I've never heard of a soul who's lived to tell the tale of what lies beyond our world. The men say Garner County is a utopia. Heaven on earth. Even if it's a lie, there's no denying our tradition, our way of life, has kept us alive for generations now. And if it's the truth, I shudder to think what lies beyond the woods, beyond the mountains and plains. Maybe it's the fear of the unknown that binds us here. Maybe we have that much in common.

As the women from the outskirts emerge from the woods, gathering alongside the trail, Kiersten raises her chin, higher than I even thought possible. The other girls follow suit, but I can see their fear—veins protruding from rigid necks, like winter geese stretching out on the chopping block, instinctively striving for a clean death.

Not me.

I've been waiting to see this my whole life.

I know I said I'd leave the dreams behind, but I know my father has been sneaking off to the outskirts for years. What if the girl is here . . . waiting for me? A long-lost half sister I never knew. Maybe she's been dreaming of me, too. I feel dizzy with the prospect. All I need is a fleeting moment of recognition . . . just to know she's real.

As I search the crowd, I notice the young girls are all wearing natural linen frocks, while the women wear clothes of beet-dyed linen. It reminds me of our red ribbons. Maybe it's a symbol that they've bled . . . that they're open for business.

With hair loose and wild, threaded with withered flower petals, the women press in as we pass—so close I can feel the warmth from their unbound bosoms. A low hissing sound swells through the crowd, making my skin prickle. No, it's not mere curiosity that brings them here. There's an undercurrent of seething jealousy. I can almost taste the bitterness on the tip of my tongue.

With their heads held low, they glare up at us through heavy strands, zeroing in on the girls with veils. For a moment, I forget that I'm one of them. I try to tuck away the gauzy netting in my cloak, but it's too late.

To them, we must represent everything they'll never have, everything they think they want.

Legitimacy. Stability. Love. Protection.

If they only knew.

As uncomfortable as it is, I meet each and every face, Young. Old. Everything in between. There are certain features that remind me of her—a dark widow's peak, the slight cleft chin—but no one bears the small strawberry mark under the right eye.

I'm feeling stupid for giving in to this, for even entertaining the idea to begin with, when I spot a tiny red petal threaded into a strand of hair of one of the women lining the path. It's not the girl, but I'd know that flower anywhere. It has to mean something. I'm gravitating toward her when I'm shoved from behind.

Falling to my knees, I feel a burst of red warmth bloom through my wool stocking, seeping through my chemise and traveling smock. And by the time I get to my feet, the woman is gone. Or maybe she was never there to begin with.

"You should watch your step." Kiersten smiles back at me.

Something inside me snaps. Maybe it's the magic rising in me, or maybe I've just had it, but as I start to go after her, I feel someone grip my elbow. I turn, ready to lay into one of the guards for touching me, but it's Gertrude Fenton.

"It'll only make things worse," she says.

"Let go." I try to pull away but she clamps on even tighter.

"You need to lay low."

"Is that right?" I'm finally able to jerk my arm away, but she's stronger than she looks. "And how has that helped *you*?"

A deep flush creeps up her neck, and I immediately feel bad.

"Look," I try to explain. "If I don't stand up for myself, she'll treat me—"

"Like me," she cuts me off. "You think I'm weak."

"No," I whisper, but we both know it's a lie.

"You've always thought you were better than us. You think you're so good at hiding, at pretending, but you're not. Everything shows on your face—always has," she says as she continues walking.

I want to let it go, sink back into my solitude, but I feel bad for never coming to her aid before. I wanted to, plenty of times, but I didn't want to draw attention to myself, and here she is, going out on a limb for me. That's far from weak.

Catching up with her, I match my footsteps to her own. "You and Kiersten used to be best friends. I remember seeing you together all of the time."

"Things change," she says, staring straight ahead.

"After your . . ." I can't help staring down at her knuckles.

"Yes," she replies, tugging down on her sleeves.

"I'm sorry about that . . . about what happened to you."

"Not as sorry as I am," she says, fixing her gaze on the back of Kiersten's skull. "If you're smart, you'll stand down. You don't know what she's capable of."

"But you do," I reply, fishing for answers.

"It wasn't even my lithograph," Gertrude says under her breath.

"It was a lithograph?" I ask. Everyone knows Kiersten's father has a collection of lithographs from long ago.

Gertrude clenches her jaw before lowering the veil over her eyes, signaling the end of our conversation.

And all I can think about is that phrase my father used to say. Still waters run deep.

One thing is certain.

Gertrude Fenton has something to hide.

Maybe we're not so different after all.

The guards march us east, well past sundown, to a sparse campsite. There's a strip of dirty linen marked with fresh blood draped over a rotting log. This must be the same spot the returning girls camped last night.

"Two coins on the Spencer girl," one of the guards says as he spits between the spokes of the wagon.

"You can kiss that money good-bye," the one with the dark mustache says as he lays down his bedroll. "It's the Dillon girl." He glances back at the girls huddled around the campfire.

"The big one?"

"Bingo." He gives a lopsided grin, but there's a bittersweet quality to his voice. "Doubt she'll last a fortnight."

As they're sizing us up, I'm sizing them up, too.

These guards are different from Hans. Escorting the girls is the lowest work available, so they're either too old, too young, too dumb, or too lazy to do anything in the county. They act like they're disinterested in their virgin cargo, but I can see that's not entirely true. The way they look at the girls, such longing, such despair, but at the same time they despise us for taking away their manhood. I wonder if they still think it was worth the trade.

I'm leaning against a knotty pine, situated halfway between the guards and the girls. For me, it's the best observation point. I can listen in on both sets of conversations and still have a good vantage point of the woods surrounding us, but I can see how this must look to the others. And maybe Gertrude's right, maybe I did think I was better than them. I thought I had it all figured out, that I could slip beneath the surface, unnoticed, unscathed, but that's certainly over now. Michael betrayed me by giving me a veil, the girl wasn't in the outskirts, and now I have a target on my back. But all is not lost. There's Gertrude Fenton—possibly a friend, one that I never thought I needed.

I watch her from the shadows, sitting with the other outcasts, fiddling with the end of her red ribbon. But even her fellow outcasts know to keep their distance. I wonder what really happened to her. If it was Kiersten's lithograph, and she let Gertie take the blame, that would mean Kiersten is capable of absolutely anything.

As much as I feel the urge to protect her, I keep coming back to my mother's words. *Trust no one. Not even yourself.*

A breeze rustles through the camp, and I pull my cloak tighter around me. I'm dying to warm my aching limbs by the fire, but I'm not ready to join the other girls.

Slipping off my boots, I try to rub some feeling back into my toes. I was smart enough to wear the boots around the house as soon as they arrived to try to break them in, but I can tell some of the others weren't as fortunate.

Without our grandfather clock or the bells of the county, I have no idea what time it is. I guess it doesn't really matter anymore. The only time that matters will happen thirteen moons from now. Thirteen long moons. But I can't get ahead of myself. My father always told me that you only have to solve one problem at a time, and right now, my biggest problem is Kiersten. I need to stay out of her way until we reach the encampment. Maybe we'll all have cozy little cabins to ourselves, and I'll scarcely have to deal with her.

For now, I'll do what I do best.

I'll watch.

I'll listen.

The wind forces its way through the forest, making the pines creak and yaw.

"Do you think the poachers are watching us right now?" Becca asks as she peers into the dense woods.

"I heard they follow us the entire way to the encampment," Patrice whispers.

"Let's find out." Kiersten stands up. "Is this what you want?" she yells, raising her skirts, flashing her legs to the darkness surrounding us.

"Stop that." They pull her back down, giggling, like this is some kind of game.

"My oldest sister said they wear shrouds over their whole bodies," Jessica says.

"Like ghosts?" Helen asks.

"Ghosts don't wear shrouds, stupid." Jenna laughs. "That's only in the Christmas pageant."

"I heard it's because they're deformed," Tamara says, a dark tone to her voice. "They have giant mouths full of razor-sharp teeth."

"I bet they're not even out there," Martha says. "We haven't seen them or heard them this entire time. They probably just tell us that to scare us."

"But why?" Ravenna asks, clinging to her veil, the scratchy sound of the netting grating between her fingertips.

I inch closer. Maybe I'm not the only one with doubts.

"So we don't escape," Kiersten says. "They can't have us running wild with all that magic . . . all that power." She leans forward, lowering her voice. "I feel it happening already. There's a tingling deep inside of me, right *here*," she says as she opens her cloak, stretching out her fingers below her navel.

A flutter of excitement rushes through the group, the same as when the blades are being sharpened in the square before a punishment.

"I can't wait to find out what my magic will be," Jessica says, sitting up a little taller.

"I heard speaking to animals runs in our family." Dena looks to Kiersten for approval.

"Maybe I'll be able to command the wind," another girl says, spreading her arms out wide.

"Or be impervious to fire." Meg runs her finger through a lick of flame.

"There now," Kiersten shushes them as she looks over at the guards. "We mustn't get carried away. Not just yet."

"What are you hoping for?" Jenna nudges Kiersten gently with her knee. "Please tell us."

"Do tell . . . ," the other girls join in.

"I want . . ." She pauses dramatically to make sure they're hanging on every word. "I want to be able to control people with my thoughts. Lead them to their rightful path . . . deliver them from sin, so we can burn through our magic and return purified women."

Gertrude lets out a huff of air. I'm not sure if it's a sigh, a yawn, or a chortle, but Kiersten glares at her from across the fire. "Maybe even *you* can be pure again, Gertie."

The muscles in Gertrude's jaw flex, but that appears to be the only reaction Kiersten will get out of her.

"And what about you, Betsy?" Kiersten turns her attention to the girl sitting next to Gertrude. The next-closest target.

"Me?" She looks around the campfire as if searching for a witness.

"Is there another Betsy Dillon?" Kiersten asks. "What magic are you hoping for?"

"Not to be so big and ugly?" One of the girls snickers. Kiersten smacks her in the leg.

Even in the dim light, I can see the heat taking over Betsy's cheeks; she's either embarrassed or flattered that Kiersten is paying attention to her. "I . . . I want to fly, like a bird," she says as she looks up into the treetops.

"Fat chance," someone murmurs; Kiersten shushes her.

"And why's that?" Kiersten asks sweetly. Too sweetly.

"So I can fly far far away," Betsy says, a dreamy look coming over her.

"Trust me." Kiersten narrows in on her. "We *all* want you to fly far far away."

The other girls let out a burst of pent-up laughter.

With tears streaming down Betsy's face, Kiersten turns her back on her and continues talking to the others.

Gertrude reaches over to try to console her, but Betsy jerks her hand away and gets up, bolting into the woods.

"What'd I tell you," the guard with the dark mustache says as he watches her run off. "The Dillon girl."

"Every year . . . ," the other guard says as he digs two coins out of his pocket and hands them over. "I don't know how you do it."

I'm about to go after her, tell her to ignore them, when I hear it—a high-pitched yelp. Followed by another. And then another, all coming from different points in the wood. A classic call and response. At first, I think it must be a pack of wolves, but then I hear it again, closer this time, followed by coarse laughter. I don't need anyone to tell me that's the call of the poachers. And they're herding her.

I look to the guards to do something, but they're just going about their business of settling in for the night.

"You have to go after her," I say.

The taller one shrugs me off. "If you run, we're not responsib—"

"But she's not running away . . . she just wanted to cry . . . in private."

"Don't stray from the path. Those are the rules—"

"But no one told us . . . no one said—"

"Shouldn't you just *know*?" he says, looking me over, shaking his head.

I start to go after her, but then I hear screams. Blood-curdling screams, echoing through the woods. It feels like the sound is penetrating straight through my skin, sinking deep into my bones, freezing them in place.

"Did you see what I made her do?" Kiersten whispers to Jenna. Jenna then whispers it to Jessica. And just like that, news of Kiersten's magic spreads like wildfire.

As I glance back at the girls, their faces lit by the flames, inky shadows nestling into the hollows of their skulls, they look to Kiersten, a mix of fear and reverence taking over.

A hint of a smile pulls at the corners of Kiersten's perfect rosebud lips.

I know that smile.

Huddled up on the damp ground, I can't sleep. I don't know how anyone could. Not with all that screaming. I've heard the rumors, how the poachers keep us alive as long as possible as they skin us, how pain brings the most potent magic to the surface, but even the guards seem a little unnerved by this one. It's as if the poachers want us to hear every cry, every cut; they want us to know what's in store for us.

But as the sun rises, heavy, bloated, on the eastern ridge, the color of a late-summer yolk, the screaming dies down to the occasional whimper, until it finally stops all together. I've never been more horrified and relieved at the same time. Her suffering is finally over.

Silently, we pack up for the rest of the journey to the encampment. They take Betsy's bundle out of the wagon and leave it behind, like it's nothing. Like *she* was nothing.

The heavy fluttering of wings pulls me from my reeling thoughts. I look up at the sparse bony branches to find a wren staring down at me. Plain and plump, wanting to be seen.

"Fly far far away," I whisper.

After we're lined up and counted, we walk the path. I'm conscious of the woods around me in a way I never thought of before. Last night was proof that we're being studied. Stalked. And I've hunted enough with my father to know they're probably looking for a weak link.

Taking a cue from Gertrude, I lower my veil. I know it dehumanizes me, the same way we put a sack over a hog's eyes before slitting its throat, but I don't want to let them in. I don't want them to memorize my face. Dream of me. I won't give them the thrill of seeing my fear.

A girl stops abruptly in front of me to pick up a heavy stone from the side of the path, tucking it inside the pocket of her cloak. It's Laura Clayton, a quiet, spindly girl who will probably be sent to work in the mill upon her return. "Sorry," she murmurs as she presses on, but she won't meet my eyes. I wonder if she's looking for a weapon. The way she's walking, I can tell this isn't the first heavy object she's picked up along the way. I'm looking for my own heavy rock when Gertrude slows her pace so she can walk next to me.

"See?" she says as she stares straight ahead up the path.

I look up to find Kiersten whispering to a set of girls. She glances back at me before moving on to the next cluster of eager ears.

"What about it?"

"She's setting the stage as we speak."

"I'm not afraid of her."

"You should be. You saw what she can do . . . her magic—"

"I didn't see anything other than a hurt girl running off to cry."

Gertrude looks at me sharply, but I can see it in her eyes: I'm not the only one with doubts.

"Magic or not . . . there are other ways she can hurt you."

I remember watching Kiersten do the same thing to Gertrude last year. Spreading that vile name like a plague. But that was done in the confines of the county, with the men watching over us, making sure we stayed in line. This is something new.

A part of me wonders if I had this coming. The way I turned a blind eye watching Kiersten bully whomever she saw fit. I could've stopped her then, but now . . . anything goes.

"I have to ask . . . ," I say, stealing a nervous glance in her direction. "Did you take the blame for her . . . for the lithograph? Is that what happened to you?"

Gertrude looks at me, her eyes glassy . . . haunted.

"Are you talking about Betsy?" A girl sidles beside me, startling us both. It's Helen Barrow.

Feeling flustered by the intrusion, Gertrude ducks her chin and rushes ahead.

"Gertrude, wait," I call after her, but she's gone.

"I know I don't have a veil," Helen says. "But you've always seemed like a nice girl . . . nice family. Your father did my mother a great kindness once—"

"Yes. He's a great man," I murmur without inflection, wondering where she's going with this.

"There's talk," she says, glancing up in Kiersten's direction. "You should steer clear of Gertie. You don't want people to think you're dirty, too."

"I really don't care what they think," I say with a deep sigh. "And neither should you."

She looks at me, her cheeks flushed with embarrassment. "I didn't mean any offense."

"Just because you didn't get a veil doesn't mean you're anything less. We're all the same here."

Her eyes well up; her bottom lip puckers out.

"What is it? What's wrong?"

"I'm afraid. Afraid of what's going to happen when we—" Helen stumbles over her own feet, careening off the path.

Grabbing the edge of her cloak, I yank her back just as a slender blade whizzes past her cheek, embedding into a nearby pine.

"Did you see that?" she gasps, fresh tears making her eyes look even bigger.

Slowly, we turn to look behind us, but there's nothing there. Only the woods. But I swear I can feel them out there . . . their eyes on my skin.

"Is Kiersten looking at me?" Helen whispers in horror, keeping her eyes trained on the ground in front of her. "Did she make me trip?"

I don't want to give it any credence, but when my eyes veer up the path, I swear I catch the swish of Kiersten's braid. The hint of a smile.

My skin explodes in goosebumps.

"Don't be silly." I pull her along. "You tripped over a root, that's all." But even as I'm saying it, I'm not entirely sure.

It feels like Kiersten is flowering right before my eyes, a belladonna, ripe with poison.

By day's end, the forest has become so dense that only an occasional burst of dying light filters through. Every time it's taken away it feels like an insult, until it doesn't come back at all.

With every step, the air grows thicker, the terrain more uncertain; the scent of decaying oak and wintergreen gives way to hemlock, fiddlehead ferns, moss, clay, and algae.

The path narrows to the point that it feels like the woods might snuff us out.

Some of the girls have to take off their boots, their feet bloody and blistered beyond recognition. Because of our slow pace, the guards decide not to camp. Maybe it's for the best; that way we don't have the time to sit and ponder our fate. It seems baffling to me, but in the short span of two nightfalls, we've somehow become resigned to it all.

I have to stop to relieve myself. I'm not even sure where it's coming from since they haven't given us a drop to eat or drink. Maybe it's just a phantom urge. Something my body used to do. Spotting a cluster of ferns, I stumble forward, pull up my skirts, push my underclothes aside, and crouch.

I'm waiting for it, even a drop to satisfy, when the last

guard passes by without a word. As I watch the torchlight disappear down the path, I realize he didn't see me. They don't know I'm gone, and probably won't know until we're counted at the encampment. A spark of adrenaline races through me. I could run right now. Not back the way I came, but somewhere new. The poachers will be following the pack of girls, and by the time anyone figures out I'm gone, I will have found a stream of water to lose my scent in. I will be untraceable. I know how to hide. I've been doing it for years, in plain sight. Michael was right about one thing . . . I'm strong and I'm smart, and I may never get an opportunity like this again.

I'm starting to gather my skirts when I hear the unmistakable sound of footfalls. Glancing over my shoulder, I see their silhouettes. An endless parade of dark figures emerging from the woods. *Poachers.*

The realization quickly sinks in that I somehow strayed from the path. I wasn't thinking. I just saw the ferns and went for it. I'm only a few feet away, ten at the most, but I can't tell how close the poachers are, how fast they're coming . . . because when I look at them, all I see is black clouds floating through the forest like wraiths.

I want to run for the path, cry out for help, but I'm so petrified that all I can do is sink deeper into the foliage and close my eyes.

It's childish to think that if I can't see them, they can't see me, but in this moment, that's exactly what I feel like—a child. They can dress me up, marry me off, tell me I'm a woman now, but in no way do I feel ready for this. For any of it.

I should bargain with God, promise to never stray from the path again, but I can't even do that. We're not allowed to pray in silence, for fear that we'll use it to hide our magic, but where is my magic now when I need it the most?

As the poachers begin to pass my hiding spot, I can't believe how quiet they are. They walk at exactly the same pace, so it's impossible to tell how many of them there are, but I can hear the steel of their blades hum when a breeze catches the sharp edge. No words are spoken; there's only breath, deep and measured with precision.

After the last of their footsteps dissipate, I open my eyes. I'm thinking maybe my magic did kick in, maybe I'm invisible, when I feel something warm pulsing against the side of my neck. Slowly, I turn to find a curved blade poised at my artery, a set of eyes staring back at me like wet gleaming marbles, but the rest of the poacher remains shrouded in darkness.

"Please . . . don't," I whisper, but all he does is stand there. Those eyes . . . it's like staring straight into a sinkhole.

Easing away from him, I crawl toward the path.

I'm waiting for the sickening caw, waiting for him to grab me by my ankles and pull me into the forest to skin me alive, but when my fingertips reach the cleared strip of earth, I scramble to my feet to find he's gone. Nothing but the void pressing in all around me.

Running ahead, I deftly slip back into the weary herd. I'm trying to act normal, but my body won't stop trembling. I want to tell the others about the poacher, how close I came to death, but as I look behind me, into the dark, I'm not even sure what really happened. There's no way a poacher would've just let me go. And the truth is, I didn't even see a body—just a blade . . . and those eyes.

My chin begins to quiver. It could be exhaustion or the magic slipping in, but no matter what did or didn't happen, I need to pull myself together, stay alert, because one false step in any direction could very well be my last.

As the sun rises once again, we pass a run-down cabin. I'm wondering if this is where we'll be spending our grace year, but they spur us forward, all the way to the end of the earth, only a vast wasteland of water stretched out before us. But if you squint just the right way, you can see a tiny speck of land sprouting up in the distance.

And I know this is it.

The beginning of the end for some of us.

We're assigned to canoes, but given no oars.

Only the guards get the privilege of steering us to our prison. Maybe they don't want us going feral and knocking them out. Maybe Laura Clayton has been gathering stones for that exact purpose. I keep my eye on her, ready for the slightest hint of a revolt. I don't know where we'd go, what we'd do, but I think I'm willing to find out.

No one says a word as they begin to row us over the glasslike water. Each stroke of the wood carving through the deep blue feels like someone's gutting me. Piece by piece. Stroke by stroke, stripping me of everything I've ever known, everything I thought I believed in.

Midway across the great lake, I see Kiersten reach her hand over the side, skimming her fingertips along the surface, creating long sensuous trails—it does something to me. Does something to all of us. The only person not looking her way is Laura Clayton. She's staring straight ahead, clutching the heaviest stone in her lap. Her lips are moving, but I can't make out what she's saying.

As I lean closer, she gives me the queerest look.

"Tell my sister I'm sorry," she says, right before she slowly keels over the side of the canoe.

"Laura—" I call out her name, but it's too late.

As her black wool cloak envelops her body, she quickly sinks to the depths.

And I realize the only rebellion she had in mind was her own.

No one moves. No one even flinches. If this is what we've already become, it makes me shudder to think what we'll be like a year from now.

Kiersten pulls her hand back into the boat, and the girls give her knowing glances. They think she made Laura do it.

And maybe she did.

A wave of panic rushes through me.

Two down, thirty-one to go.

Sunburned and weary, our bodies still swaying from the lull of the water, the emptiness of Laura's escape, we watch the awaiting guards pull the canoes onto the muddy bank. The scraping of the hulls against the rocky beach is like a razor to my frazzled nerves.

"The perimeter is clear," I hear one of the guards say. "No breaches to report."

I know that voice. Looking up, I see that it's Hans. I start to stand, but Martha, who's sitting behind me, yanks down on my skirts. "Don't draw attention to yourself. You saw what happened to Laura."

Hans steals a glance at me. A look of warning. Martha's right. No one can know that we're friends. I could get him in serious trouble.

"I can't believe you volunteered for this," the older guard says, shaking his head, looking back over the great lake. "An entire year in that crappy little cabin. Just you and Mortimer."

I wonder if that's the shack we saw on the other shore. I heard there were two guards that live nearby to maintain the barrier of the encampment, but it always sounded like more of a punishment than a privilege. Is this what Hans was trying to tell me the other day at the paddock?

Without another word, the guards load the supplies onto rickety wagons, pushing them up a wide dirt path.

We follow. What else can we do?

But it's more than that. We've been building to this moment our entire lives. The grace year is no longer a story, a myth, something that will happen someday.

That someday is now.

I take in every last detail of the terrain—just beyond the rocky shoreline, there appears to be a series of tall wooden structures in each direction. At first, I think maybe that's where we'll be living, but the guards continue to march us inland.

The sparse landscape slowly gives way to spindly white pines and ash. As I look ahead, the trees seem to grow thicker, in varying degrees of height, the tallest ones in the center of the island. I remember hearing stories from the trappers in my father's care about the islands to the north. Pinnacles of land cut off from the rest of the world. Where man and animal alike go mad.

Hans looks back at me. I think he's trying to tell me something, but I have no idea what it could be. I'm too tired for subtleties right now.

Through the foliage, I spot a tight curved line of enormous cedars that seem to wrap their way around the entire island, but they're too close together to be natural. It must be a fence—like the one we have in the county—but instead of the fence keeping us safe from the outside world, this is a fence to protect the rest of the world from *us*.

I have no idea what we're capable of, how the magic will consume us, but we haven't even reached our final destination and two of us have already fallen.

As my damp boots sink into the soft dirt, I think of my mother walking this path before me, June and Ivy, and Penny and Clara, who will be forced to follow in my footsteps.

There are deer tracks, and porcupine, fox, and fowl, but there's another set of tracks that makes my blood run cold. Large flat-soled imprints, alongside two long rivets, as if someone had been dragged.

Searching the woods, I look for the poachers, but I don't even know what I'm looking for. Eyes and blades, that's all I have to go on. Have they camouflaged themselves? Are they perched in the treetops or below our feet in trenches waiting for us to make a false step?

I know the poachers would never cross the barrier for fear of being cursed, so what would draw the girls out? Do they try to run? Do the poachers sweet-talk them? Or maybe they're forced out by their own kind?

As if Kiersten can hear my thoughts, she peers back at me over her shoulder, ice-blue eyes singeing a trail from my ankles to the top of my head.

I duck down, pretending to refasten my bootlace, anything to escape her gaze. I can't stop thinking about Betsy running off into the woods, Laura keeling over the side of the canoe—that look on Kiersten's face. Whether it's true or not, she believes she killed them with her magic.

And she's proud.

I try to shake it off, erase it from my memory, because no matter what happens, how things may appear, I need to keep a level head, my feet firmly rooted in the soil. No more superstition. No more fear.

As I gather my skirts to stand, I notice a tiny red bloom fighting against all odds to make its way to the surface. Reaching out, I touch the five petals, perfectly formed, just to make sure it's real. Tears prickle the backs of my eyes. It's the flower from my dream, the same one I saw in Mrs. Fallow's hand as she stepped from the gallows, the same bloom that was threaded into the outskirts-woman's hair. It's beyond me how it got here, how it managed to survive on this well-worn path, but it seems like a truer bit of magic than anything I've seen thus far.

"On your feet," Hans says as he wraps his arm around me, pulling me up.

"What are you doing here?" I whisper.

"I told you I would look after you," he says. I don't dare look at him, but I can hear the smile in his voice. "If there's a breach in the fence, they'll send for me. Do you understand? I will come for you."

I nod. But I have no idea what he's talking about.

As we approach the end of the path, we're faced with a towering wood gate, hundreds of lifeless ribbons nailed to the rough-hewn wood. Some are tattered, long since faded to the softest blush, but others are still crisp, the sharpest of crimson. I want to pretend the girls put them here themselves, one last rebellious act before returning to the county, but I'm done pretending.

These are the ribbons of the girls who've been killed.

It's more than a warning.

It's a message.

Welcome to your new home.

"Are we just going to stand here?" Kiersten asks, tapping her boot impatiently in the dirt.

"One of you will have to open the gate," the short, stocky guard says as he shifts his weight.

I can't stop my eyes from veering between his legs. It makes me wonder if he feels the cut more deeply here at the encampment.

Without the slightest hint of reverence for the moment in front of us, Kiersten yanks open the gate.

As the creaky wood swings open, a high whinny of lament, we're hit with an overwhelming burst of green wood smoke, burned hair, and the sickeningly sweet scent of decay. I can't help breathing it in. I'm woozy with it. It's so heavy, so deep, I swear I can feel it clinging to the tiny spaces between my ribs, almost as if it's afraid to be named.

"You'll need to take the supplies inside," one of the guards says, a slight quiver in his voice, like we've just opened the gates to hell.

As the girls hop to, dragging the carts inside, the men

edge away, never once turning their backs on us, as if just stepping over the threshold will unleash our magic, making us swallow them whole.

We wait for parting words . . . instructions . . . anything . . . but they just stand there in silence.

"Close it," Kiersten says, eyeing the heavy rope mechanism connected to the gate.

Meryl and Agnes jump at the chance to be noticed and pull it shut.

At the last second, Hans reaches in to unsnag the end of my ribbon from the wood post, his fingers lingering.

Another guard yanks him back. "Are you crazy? The curse," he reminds him. And I know this is his way of saying good-bye.

As the gate closes on the guards' troubled faces, it's clear they truly believe we're loathsome creatures that need to be hidden away for safekeeping, for our own good, to exorcise the demons lurking inside of us, but even in this cursed place, anger, fear, and resentment boiling inside of me, I still don't feel magical.

I still don't feel powerful.

I feel forsaken.

This is the first time we've been alone. Unsupervised.

There's a beat—a few weighted seconds—before it fully sinks in.

The energy swirling around us feels like a living, breathing thing.

As some of the girls rush off to explore, trills of excitement nipping through the air, others cling to the gate, weeping for the world that's been taken away from them, but most of us, out of obligation or curiosity, inch forward, one foot in front of the other, edging our way into a vast but barren half-moon clearing that's been carved out of the dense woods before us.

"It's a lodging house," Ravenna says as she peeks inside the long primitive log-cabin structure on the north end of the clearing. There are two small shacks positioned on either side, and beyond that, nothing but forest.

"This can't be it," Vivian says as she spins in a slow circle, dragging her veil in the dirt.

I gravitate toward the center of the clearing, to an old stone well and a lone tree, but that's not what has my eye. Placed at the foot of the tree, there's a pile of smoldering remains, a string of sumac leaves encircling it like a lewd gesture.

"I heard they did this," Hannah whispers. "But I didn't believe it."

"Did what?" Kiersten says as she kicks one of the leaves out of formation, breaking the chain, which makes most of the girls flinch.

"I shouldn't say." Hannah shakes her head, staring down at the ground. "It's forbidden to speak of the grace year."

Kiersten's nostrils flare like she's getting ready to lose it, but as she exhales, her face softens. "What's said here . . . what happens here . . ." She smooths her hand over Hannah's ruddy cheek. ". . . remains here forever. That's our most sacred vow."

Hannah purses her lips so tight they turn the shade of newly sprung blueberries before blurting, "It's the remaining supplies, everything they've built . . . everything they used to get through the year."

"But why would they burn it?" Jenna asks.

"Because it was done to them," Hannah says, studying the notches in the lone tree—forty-six. "Year after year. Why should we have a leg up when it was never given to them?" she says, running her fingers over the deepest, freshest cut.

I don't know why it surprises me, but I feel the betrayal deep within my bones. Not only did they want us to fail, they wanted us to squirm in doing so.

A scream comes from one of the smaller structures. Ruth Brinley is backing out, holding her cloak over her nose and mouth as a flood of black flies comes pouring out of the shack.

Martha cringes as she peeks inside. "I think we found the privy."

"Ashes," I say without thinking. "If we put the ashes in the privy it will cut down the smell, help break it down."

"How do you know that?" Gertie asks.

"My father. I used to go on calls with him to the field house. They have an outhouse similar to this one."

They all look to Kiersten.

"Well, what are you waiting for?" Kiersten barks out an order at me.

Grabbing a sleeve of fallen birch bark, I scoop up the ashes and carry them into the shack. The smell is unbearable; there's feces and who knows what else spread over the walls. I dump in the ashes, and when I come back for a second round, I notice the stone hidden beneath the debris. It appears to be etched with something. "Look," I say to the others. "Maybe it's a message."

I try to brush away the soot but only manage to kick up a thick cloud of ash.

"Are you trying to kill us?" Kiersten says, fanning the air in front of her. "Get some water to wash it away." She nods toward the well.

There's a part of me that wants to refuse on principle. After all, I don't want to set a precedent, but at least I'm doing something. Not just standing around like a bunch of sheep.

Gertrude joins me at the well. "See? This is smart," she says as she helps me pull up the heavy bucket. "If you make yourself useful, maybe you can get back in their good graces."

Green algae clings to the sides of the well, the rope, the bucket. Maybe I'm delirious from the journey, but there's something about it that looks unnatural. The bright green glow against the drab stone.

"Hurry up." Kiersten's brusque voice pulls me back.

I carry over the bucket, trying not to slosh too much over the sides. Kiersten grabs it from me, slinging water over the stone. The etched words come into focus.

Eyes to God.

My skin erupts in goosebumps. This is identical to the plaque we have in the town square. They position the gallows directly over it so when our necks snap, it's the last thing we'll see, which always struck me as especially cruel. If your neck is broken, how can you look up? Even in death we're a disappointment.

As the girls press in to get a closer look, a red drop appears, followed by another.

I crouch to see if it's rust seeping up through the stone, when a drop appears on the top of my hand.

As I look up, a cloud passes by, the late-afternoon sun filtering through the branches, illuminating hundreds of trinkets tied to the tree like yule ornaments.

Helen's pointing at the gnarled limbs of the tree, but she can't seem to find any words.

It takes me a moment to put it together, like a vile jigsaw. It's not rust. It's blood. And they're not yule ornaments, they're fingers, toes, ears, braids of all shades and textures affixed to the tree.

But while everyone is backing away, Kiersten steps closer.

"It's a punishment tree," she says, reaching out to touch

the rough bark. "Just like the one we have in the square, only this one is *real*."

Becca starts pacing. "I always thought the reason they came back with missing fingers was because they traded them with the poachers for food, not as some kind of punishment."

"Why would they trade for food, dummy?" Tamara says as she glances back at the wagons. "We have plenty."

"And yet they come back starving." Lucy wraps her arms around herself.

"Don't be so dramatic." Martha rolls her eyes. "We can always forage if we get scant."

"Not in *those* woods." Ellie shakes her head a little too rapidly as she stares past the log cabin into the surrounding forest. "I heard the animals are mad in there."

"Animals?" Jenna laughs. "What about the ghosts? We've all heard the stories. If you go in there, you don't come out."

There's a deep pause. A strange electricity among us. Suspicious glances quickly turn to panic as the girls take off running back toward the gate, clawing at the wagons for anything they can claim.

"I heard this is how it starts," Gertrude says.

"How what starts?" I ask.

"How we turn against each other."

I meet her gaze and I know she feels it, too.

I'm waiting for Kiersten to stop this, do something, but she just stands there, a hazy smile perched over her lips. Almost as if she wants this to happen.

Swallowing my nerves, I force my way into the fray. "We just need to stay calm," I say, but they're paying me no mind. Two girls fighting over a bag of food bash into me; the burlap rips, sending a cascade of chestnuts spilling to the ground. Girls are piling on top of each other to get to them. Leaping out of the way, onto the empty wagon bed, I yell, "Look at you . . . behaving like a pack of outskirt dogs."

They glare up at me, hate burning in their eyes, but at least I have their attention.

"All we have to do is take inventory. Ration. We're going to have to trust in each other if we want to get through this."

"Trust *you*?" Tamara lets out a strangled laugh. "That's rich coming from the girl who filched Kiersten's husband."

I'm opening my mouth to try to explain myself when Kiersten steps forward. "She didn't steal him from me." The girls ease back in anticipation of what's about to happen. "I wanted Tommy all along, a real man who can give me sons." But even as she's saying it, I feel a surge of repulsion rush through her. "No . . ." She looks me up and down before facing the crowd. "This is about betrayal. Tierney never wanted anything to do with us. And now she thinks she can come in and tell us what to do? How to live our grace year?"

"That's not what I'm trying to do." I yank off my veil and get down from the wagon. "I'm not trying to take over."

"Good," Kiersten says, but I can tell she's slightly disappointed. She was ready for a fight. "Everyone, put the supplies back. The only thing that belongs to you right now is your pack. Gather that."

The girls do as they're told, but they're still staring at each other skeptically.

As I'm searching for my bundle, out of the corner of my eye, I see something sail over the fence.

I turn to look, but all I find is Kiersten standing there, a priggish look on her face as a gaggle of girls hover around her trying, and failing, to stifle their laughter.

"All set?" Kiersten asks.

Looking around, I see everyone has their supplies, everyone except me. "I don't have mine."

"Oh, that's a shame," Kiersten replies. "Yours must've rolled off somewhere along the way. You're welcome to go back and find it." She nods toward the barrier.

I want to go after her, drag her to the gate, make her go out and fetch it, but then I think of Gertie's warning. As hard as it is, I need to show Kiersten that I'm not going to be a threat to her. And if that means being a little less comfortable than the others, so be it.

"I'm sure it will turn up," I say, lowering my eyes.

"That's the spirit," Kiersten says, smug satisfaction dripping from every syllable. "But hear me," she says as she walks through the group. "If someone took Tierney's supplies, stealing will not be tolerated. There will be punishment."

"But who's going to do the punishing?" Hannah asks. "At home, the punishers are men, chosen by God."

"Look around," Kiersten says as she stares me dead in the eyes. "We are the only Gods here."

As we pry open the door to the small structure on the left, we discover a narrow space with shelves lining each side.

"This must be the larder," Ravenna says.

"Or a place to stack the bodies," Jenna whispers to Kiersten.

"Oh no, pretty dovey," Helen cries, barging past everyone, coming out with a scrawny ringnecked dove cradled in her hands. "I think her wing is broken."

Kiersten picks up the rusty axe propped up in the corner. "I'll do it."

"No . . . you can't," Helen says, pressing the bird against her ample bosom.

"What did you say?" Kiersten snaps back.

"I mean . . . I'll take care of her." Helen quickly softens her tone. "You won't even know she's here."

"I've always wanted a pet," Molly chimes in, stroking the bird's smooth, drab head. "I'll help."

"Me, too," Lucy says.

Soon Helen is surrounded by girls offering to pitch in.

"Fine," Kiersten says, setting down the axe. "Anything to get you to shut up, but I hate birds."

"You better get used to them," someone mutters from the crowd.

Kiersten whips around. "Who said that?"

We all stand there, desperately trying not to laugh. It's common knowledge that her husband-to-be has an affinity for torturing majestic birds. I think Martha may have said it, but I can't be sure. Maybe we're just exhausted, but in this moment, it's the funniest thing I've ever heard. But the levity quickly dies when we realize how little they gave us in the way of supplies.

Taking inventory and setting up the larder is a tense undertaking. We end up having to count everything aloud, in unison, just like we did in our first year of arithmetic at the schoolhouse, only this time we're not counting beads, we're counting the things that will keep us alive over the next year. It's going to be tight, but as Kiersten seems more than happy to point out, not all of us will make it to the end. You'd think that would somehow bring us closer together, bind us in a common cause, but it feels tenuous at best, like there's only a single silk thread connecting us—one false move, one false accusation, and everything will unravel.

After gathering stray limbs from the perimeter, any kindling that seems dry enough to catch, I try to teach them how to build a proper fire, the same way my father taught me, but there's little interest. A few pay attention—mostly girls who will be assigned this type of work upon their return, Helen, Martha, Lucy—but Kiersten and the rest of her followers seem annoyed that I'm even bothering them with something so mundane.

It's only when Gertrude offers to take the first meal shift that they suddenly take an interest.

"She can't make our food . . . it'll be dirty," Tamara says.

Heated whispers erupt on the subject of Gertie, but she just goes about her business of filling the kettle with water, pretending not to notice. Maybe she's so used to it now that it doesn't even bother her. But it bothers me.

"Gertrude and I will take the first shift. If you don't like it, you can make your own," I say, which seems to quiet them down.

No matter what she did, there's no reason for her punishment to continue here. Veiled or not, depraved or saints, we're all equals in death.

As the conversation shifts to what they think their magic will be, Gertie and I work on putting supper together. It's meager, just some beans with a few rashers of thick-cut bacon thrown in for flavor, but all we can really taste is the well water—it has a pungent, earthy aftertaste that seems to cling to the roof of your mouth. Looking around at this landlocked parcel, I guess we should be grateful we have drinking water at all.

As we eat supper, the nervous chatter fades away to make room for the new world around us. Beyond the crackling fire, the sound of spoons scraping against the bottom of tin bowls, we find ourselves listening to the forest pressing in on us—the breeze rustling the last of the autumn leaves, the strange skittering sounds of unknown creatures, the lake water lapping against the pebbled shore. But it's not the water or the wind or the woods that has us on edge—it's the absence of the call of the poachers. Are they even out there? Or maybe that's exactly what they want us to think . . . how they'll lure us out. Not by cunning sweetness or threatening words . . . but by silence.

I can't stop thinking about the poacher I came face-to-face with on the trail. The look in his eyes—I try rubbing the chill from my arms, but it's no use. He could've killed me right then and there. I was fair game. I'm not sure what stopped him. But then again, I'm not even sure if he was real. Out here, the veil between our world and the unknown feels so thin that you could punch a hole right through it.

The wind moves through the camp, making the firelight dance.

"I wonder if it's them?" Nanette says, staring into the woods.

"Who?" Dena asks.

"The ghosts," Jenna replies.

Katie pulls her cloak tighter. "I heard it's the souls of all the grace year girls who died here."

"Katie should know," Helen whispers to me, the bird cooing in her lap. "All three of her sisters were poached."

"But they're not all benevolent spirits," Jenna adds.

"What do you mean?" Meg asks.

"The unclaimed girls, the ones who vanished, they still cling to their magic, even in death."

Though we're forbidden from speaking of the grace year back home, it seems we've all heard bits and pieces. Maybe truth, maybe lies, probably something in between. I can't help thinking that if we put all the pieces together we could somehow solve this elaborate puzzle, but it feels too slippery. Elusive. Like trying to catch smoke.

"There was a veiled girl in my sister's year who went into the woods," Nanette says. "It was near the end of her grace year. There was something haunting her every move. She would wake up to find her braid was different, the end of her ribbon hog-tied to her ankle. There were whispers in the dark. And when she finally went into the forest to confront her tormentor, she never came back. Her body was unaccounted for."

"Olga Vetrone?" Jessica whispers.

Nanette nods.

A chill breaks out over my flesh. That was the girl Hans joined the guard for. I'll never forget his face when he came into the square that day, and then watching her little sister being banished to the outskirts.

A deep thud comes from the gate. A few girls scream, gasp for breath, but every single one of us stands at attention. There's something in here with us.

With trembling hands, Jenna holds up a lantern, illuminating the outline of a large lump on the ground in front of the gate.

"What is it?" someone whispers. "A body?"

"Maybe it's a poacher . . ."

Taking cautious steps, we move in one huddled mass to investigate.

When Jenna gets close enough, she nudges the mysterious mound with her boot. It rolls over. "It's just a county-issued pack." She laughs.

"Hey, isn't that Tierney's family sigil?" Molly points toward the three swords embroidered in the burlap.

Helen noses her way in. "Did you do that, Tierney? Did you use your magic to make your bundle come back to you?"

"No." I shake my head. "I swear, it wasn't me."

"How can that be?" Meg asks. "We all saw what happened to it . . . when Kiers—"

"I'm not without mercy," Kiersten says with a smile.

Before the last ember dies out, we light a few more lamps and file inside the long, dismal log-hewn structure. No one says it out loud, but I don't think any of us likes the idea of being trapped inside with one another. We're not locked in and counted, like we are at the church, but something about it feels even more dangerous. We're so vulnerable during sleep. Anything can happen here, and no one will tell the tale.

There are only twenty iron beds set up with mattresses; the rest are piled up in a corner of the room like old bones. Half of those are missing their mattresses. I don't even want to think about what happened to them. It's a heavy reminder of how many of us won't make it home alive.

Kiersten lies down on one of the good beds to test it out, stretching out her long legs.

Jenna sits on the next bed over. "I can't believe we have to sleep here." She crinkles up her nose as she stares down at the dingy mattress. "I think this one belonged to a bed wetter."

"We're here to rid ourselves of our magic. That's all." Kiersten sighs. "Besides, as soon as the first girl with a mattress dies, you can have hers. Double up."

I look over at her sharply. I can't believe how casually that just rolled off her tongue. As if dying is a given—not a question of how, but when.

Glancing around the room, I'm wondering if we can somehow change this. Maybe Gertrude's right—if I can be of use, maybe they'll start to trust me . . . listen to me.

"I saw a lavender bush on the edge of the clearing," I say as I pretend to inspect the stacked-up bed frames. "If we mix lavender with baking soda, that will spruce them right up. In the morning, I can set up a washing station. We can also build rain barrels to collect drinking water and—"

"We don't need any of that." Kiersten cuts me off.

Jenna looks at her pleadingly. "But the well water tastes funny."

"We'll drink from the well, like every other grace year girl before us," Kiersten says.

"Is that her magic?" one of the girls whispers. "Knowing things . . . knowing about plants and how to fix things?"

"It's not magic," Kiersten snaps. "It's just because her father treated her as a son," she says as she gets to her feet, prowling toward me. "Do you have a willy under there? Maybe you're not a girl at all." Kiersten cups her hand between my legs. It takes everything I have to force myself to stand still and take it. "Or maybe you like girls? Is that your secret?" She's whispering in my ear. "Why you've always been so afraid to be around us?"

"Please stop," Gertrude says.

"What's it to you?" Kiersten's eyes flash toward her.

I shudder to think what the punishment for that would be. Back in the county it meant the gallows. Certainly, under Kiersten's rule, it would be something much worse.

"I wonder what your magic will be?" Kiersten says, picking at Gertrude. "Something depraved." She stares down at her scarred knuckles. "A power only a sinner could possess."

I know I told Gertrude I'd stand down, take the punishment, but I didn't say anything about standing by watching her punish someone else.

"Leave her alone," I say.

"There she is." Kiersten gives me a sly look. "I wondered how long it would take you to come out, Tierney the Terrible."

"That's right. You're good with nicknames, aren't you?"

"Don't." Martha tugs at my sleeve. "You saw what happened to Laura . . . what she can do."

"Laura had been collecting stones the entire way, slipping them into the hems of her skirts. She *chose* to die."

Kiersten stiffens as if a metal rod has been inserted in her spine. "Are you calling me a liar? After I took mercy on you and got your supplies back for you? Are you saying my magic isn't real?"

"No." I swallow hard. "I'm not saying that. I just think we should slow down. Examine everything . . . question everything . . . no matter how things may appear."

"You sound like a usurper," Kiersten says. "Back in the county, they'd tie you to the iron tree and burn you alive."

"But we're not in the county anymore," I say, forcing myself to meet her gaze. "If we stick together, if we're careful, maybe no one else has to die."

Kiersten laughs, but when no one joins in, she steps so close that I can feel her breath on my skin. "Deny it all you want, but deep down you feel it. You know what needs to happen here. You know what I can do to you."

The room goes completely still, the same hush that precedes a hanging.

Kiersten's eyes narrow on me. I'm trying to stay calm, act like I'm not afraid, but my heart is pounding so hard I'm sure she can hear it.

"That's what I thought." Pulling the red ribbon from her hair, she shakes her braid free, sending long tendrils of honeyed waves spilling over her shoulders. The girls seem to take in a collective breath, enamored and fearful of this wanton act. Other than our sisters, we've never seen a girl with her hair down before.

Ravenna starts to pull out her own ribbon, but Kiersten grabs her wrist, squeezing it so tight that I see her fingers blanch. "Only girls who've claimed their magic can remove their braid."

As she slowly walks back to the other side of the room, the girls watch her with envious eyes. Even I find myself wondering what it would feel like to be free of it.

"Veiled girls on this side," Kiersten says as she claims the bed against the far wall, center stage, so she can survey her new kingdom.

As the veiled girls scramble for the best mattresses,

jockeying for position near Kiersten, Gertrude and I stand back with the others. Kiersten is drawing a line in the sand. And this is clearly a test. She wants to see what we'll do. If we try to join them, she'll probably just laugh, cast us off with the others. But if we *don't* try, she'll take it as a sign of aggression.

I'm trying to figure out the right move when Gertrude laces her pinkie through mine. The strange warmth, the firm grip, catches me off guard.

"Come on, Tierney," she says as she pulls me back. I'm shocked that she's taking this stand, but I'm glad.

It's wrong of Kiersten and the others to flaunt their veils in this way. It must feel like salt in the wound to some. But on top of being cruel, it's foolish. The fact remains that there are more unveiled girls than there are of them.

Untangling the iron frames, the rest of us drag them into position on the other side of the room. The metal scraping against the well-worn oak floors sets my teeth on edge. I can't help thinking of the girls who slept here before us. Were they just as scared as we are? What happened to them?

After a few minutes, Jenna whispers something to Kiersten.

"Fine," Kiersten says with a heavy sigh. "Except for Tierney and Gertie, whoever wants to come over to our side can, but not too close."

Martha and the rest of the unveiled girls look at each other, then at me. I'm expecting them to jump at the chance and start dragging their beds to the other side of the room, but instead, they simply lay their bedding where they stand.

The familiar heat moves through my limbs, prickling the back of my eyes, but it's not anger this time. There's something in this simple act of rebellion that gets to me— gives me a bit of hope.

As I unpack my belongings, laying the bedding on bare springs, I find a braided leather tassel hidden inside, the same kind they use to adorn the riding crops in the stable. "Hans," I whisper, running my fingers over the elaborate braid. I know this is his handiwork. It's possible he slipped this into my pack as a memento when they brought the supplies to the gate, but what if he put it in there right before he threw the pack over the gate so I would know it was him? What if Kiersten's magic had nothing to do with it?

The girl leads me through the woods, but something's different.

The trees are taller, the birdsong has changed, even the sound of distant water has shifted; instead of the steady rhythmic trickling of the river, there's a slow swell, followed by something that sounds like lard hitting a hot pan. I remember that sound from when we arrived—it's the sound of waves hitting a pebbled shore.

"Where are we?" I ask, tripping over a slippery cluster of rocks. "Is there a gathering?"

She doesn't reply; she only presses forward, finally coming to a stop in front of a cluster of trees—only they're not trees—it's a fence made up of massive cedar logs.

Reaching out, she presses her palms against the wood; it begins to crumble.

I can't see anything on the other side, but I hear it—heavy breath moving in and out.

"Don't!" I pull her back. "There's poachers out there. They're waiting for us."

Peering over her shoulder, her gray eyes pierce right through me.

"I know," she whispers.

I wake with a gasping breath. It takes me a good minute to remember where I am.

Turning on my side, I find Gertrude staring straight at me. I can't even begin to decipher the expression on her face. It's strange that I never really noticed her before. I took her as plain, a scared rabbit among a den of wolves, but she's so much more than that.

"You were dreaming," she whispers.

"No, I wasn't." I wrap my cloak tighter around me. "I was just talking to myself."

"It's okay."

"But . . ." I look around to see who else has heard.

"Whatever happens during our grace year will never leave the encampment, you know that."

The way she says it, the dark tone in her voice—it makes me wonder if the rule was created by us. A way to avoid prosecution.

"Do you ever . . . *dream*?" I ask, having a hard time even getting the word out.

"I think I did once," Helen says, from the bed on the other side of me.

I turn to see her with her knees pulled to her chest, like my younger sister Penny does during a storm.

"But my mother put a stop to that," Helen adds, skimming her fingers over the ruler-sized scars on the top of her feet.

It makes me think of my own mother. She knew I had the dreams, but she never punished me for them. I never really thought about that before now.

"What do you dream of?" Gertrude asks.

I think about telling them that I dream of ponies and a dashing husband, but I can't bring myself to do it. I don't think I realized until this moment how I've been aching to share my secret . . . to feel connected to someone of my own sex . . . *friends*. Maybe they'll believe me. Maybe they won't. But I have to take that chance. "I dream of a girl." I glance up at them, trying to gauge their expressions.

"Oh," Helen says, a flush creeping into her cheeks.

"No. Not like that." And suddenly, I'm the one embarrassed by the suggestion.

"Go on," Gertrude whispers.

"She has eyes like mine, but her hair is dark and shorn close to her scalp. She has a small strawberry mark under her right eye. At first, I thought she must be a half sister from the outskirts—"

"That's why you stopped to look at them like that," Gertrude says.

"Yes," I whisper, surprised by how observant she was. "But she wasn't there."

"What does she do in your dreams?" Helen asks, nuzzling the dove under her chin.

"Usually, she leads me through the woods to a gathering."

"What kind of gathering?" Martha props herself up on her elbow.

I want to shut it down, stop talking, but as I look at her eager face, I think, *What do I have to lose at this point?*

"It's all the women—wives, maids, laborers, even the women from the outskirts, they've all come together, a red flower pinned above their hearts—"

"What kind of flower?" Molly whispers from two beds away.

I look over to find eyes on me from every direction. They appear to be hanging on every word, but I don't stop.

"It's a flower with no name. Five tiny petals with a deep red center. There's something about it that's so familiar, and yet I can't tell you where I've seen it before. But I think Mrs. Fallow was holding one between her fingers when she stepped off the gallows. And I think I saw a petal threaded into the hair of a woman in the outskirts. There was one on the path from the shore to the gate. Did anyone else see it?" I ask, my heart fluttering at the possibility.

They look around at each other and shake their heads.

As if sensing my disappointment, Gertrude adds, "But we weren't looking for it."

I stare at the door. "Tonight, the dream was different,

though. I wasn't home, in the county . . . I think I was here . . . in the woods."

"Was it scary?" Lucy asks, hugging her blanket.

I nod. I don't know why, but my eyes are wet.

"I wonder if that's your magic," Nanette says, her brow buried in deep thought. "The dreams . . . the girl . . . the flower. Maybe you can see the future."

There was a time when I wanted that to be true, more than anything, but in this last dream, there were no encouraging words, no comfort of the crowd. It was just the two of us in the dark woods. I'm trying not to let my imagination get the best of me, but I can't help wondering if she was trying to tell me something. If she was trying to show me how I'll die.

Pressing my palm against my stomach, I stretch out my fingers the same way I saw Kiersten do on that first night. "It doesn't feel like magic. Do you *feel* anything?"

"Not yet," Helen says. "But Kiersten—"

"Remember when Shea Larkin got those red itchy welts a few summers back and they got infected and she nearly died, and then all the other girls in her year fell down with the same?" I ask.

They look at each other and nod.

"They said it was a curse, that one of the girls came into her magic early, hid it and infected the others. My father treated them all, said the other girls itched themselves raw, but there were no welts to be found."

"Are you saying they were faking it?" Martha asks.

"No. I think they truly believed it," I say as I glance in Kiersten's direction. "And that's the scariest thing of all."

The sun seeping through the rough-hewn logs fills the air with glittering dots of moted light. If I didn't know they were flecks of pollen from long-forgotten weeds, or dead skin from grace year girls long past, I might call it beautiful.

There's something about it that makes me hold my breath, as if breathing it in might infect me with whatever they had, lead me to the same bitter end—just another stacked-up, mattress-less frame—a flaccid red ribbon nailed to the gate.

Easing out of bed, I slip on my boots and tiptoe through the maze of cots. My body aches from the journey, the spent adrenaline lingering in my muscles, or it could just be from the unforgiving springs crushing my spine, but all I want to do is find a soft bed of pine needles and sleep the day away.

As I slip out the door, I take in a deep breath of fresh air, but there's nothing fresh about it.

Every comfort, everything we've grown accustomed to in the county has been taken away from us. They even stripped us of our common language. There are no greenhouses here, no curated flowers, just weeds. Without it, I wonder how we'll communicate. I want to believe it's with words, but looking at the punishment tree, I can see it's with violence.

After all, it's what we know, how we've been raised, but I can't help thinking that maybe we can be different.

Walking around the clearing, I take note of everything we'll need to get through the year. At the very least, we'll need a covered area for cooking and eating, a washing station . . . enough firewood to get through the winter.

Stepping to the edge of the forest, I study the ragged, hacked-off stumps marking the perimeter. It doesn't appear the girls have ever ventured further than this. I wonder how deep it is, where it goes, how many creatures call this place home, but whatever lurks beyond the clearing, mad animals or vengeful ghosts, we're trapped in here together by a fence taller than giants. The wind filtering through the branches makes the last of the fall leaves shiver. There's something about it that makes me shiver, too.

I may not know much about the encampment, what happens to us here, but I do know land. This island doesn't care that we're grace year girls—that we've been put here by God and the chosen men to rid ourselves of our power—winter will descend upon us just the same. And I can tell by the chill in the air that there will be no mercy.

The sound of a stake being driven into the earth grabs my attention. Behind the punishment tree, toward the eastern fence, Kiersten appears to be erecting a series of tall sticks. I thought I was the first one up, but from the looks of it, she must've been up for hours collecting fallen branches, sharpening the ends. I'm thinking she must be building something for the camp—maybe it's the start of a washing shed or even maypoles for dancing—but when she drives the last stake into the dirt and stands back to survey her work, I understand what this is. A calendar. One post to signify each full moon. This year, there are thirteen. A bad omen. I want to believe it's simply a way to keep track of our time out here, but the placement is no coincidence. Back home, full moons are punishment days. Totems to our sin.

As if Kiersten can sense my presence, she turns and stares over her shoulder. My skin prickles beneath her gaze. There are twenty-six days until the next full moon. Twenty-six days to figure out how to turn this around. Because if I don't, I'm certain I'll be on the top of her list.

"Get back, veiled girls first," I hear someone holler.

Peeking around the larder, I find Jenna and Jessica pushing their way to the front of the well, grabbing the bucket from Becca.

I want to sink back, disappear into the grainy wood, but those days are over. And I certainly didn't help matters by getting in Kiersten's way last night. I thought I'd be a lone wolf out here, but even after this short amount of time I feel a certain responsibility for Gertie and the others. *The others.* That sounds terrible, but that's how we're raised to think of it—the unveiled, the unwanted, the undesirable—what I *should've* been. But if I start thinking about that right now, about Michael, I'll get so mad I won't be able to see straight.

Taking in a deep breath, I walk toward the well. "Is there a problem?"

The girls at the front lower their veils and glare at me before traipsing off to join Kiersten.

We're all standing there, staring at one another, wondering if anyone has changed in their sleep, but we all seem to be the same. Just as scared . . . just as confused. Last night, emotions were running high, lines had been drawn, but after a good night's rest, all of that could change. I wouldn't blame them. Kiersten clearly has it in for me. And Gertrude . . . well, Gertrude is a whole other story. I know they're still a little wary being around her, but I don't think she did anything wrong. I wonder how long it will take for Gertie to confide in us about what really happened.

"Do we have to drink this?" Molly asks, sniffing the water in the bucket.

"Didn't Tierney say something about a rain barrel?" Martha asks.

Gertie nudges me forward.

I clear my throat. "I thought we could use the well water for bathing and washing, and then rain water for drinking and cooking."

"You heard what Kiersten said." Tamara barges forward, fumbling to get her arm out from under her veil so she can scoop her pewter cup into the bucket. "We drink from the well."

As soon as she's out of earshot, Martha says, "How long do you think it would take to make one?"

"Couple of days," I reply. "*If* we had the right tools."

"Well, there goes that idea," Martha says, dipping her cup into the bucket, drinking it down. She gags a little. "Only the best for the grace year girls."

I don't know if she trips or just loses her footing, but Martha seems to wobble on her feet, accidentally pushing the bucket over the edge. She grabs the rope, nearly going down with it. "I'm fine," she calls out. With her skirts raised high in the air, we have to hold on to her legs to pull her back, and it hits me—literally hits me in the head.

"The hoops. We can use the boning from our skirts to bind the wood for the barrels."

"But you heard what they said." Becca chews on her cuticles.

Martha, now upright, her eyes bright with mischief, says, "They can have their water. We'll have ours."

The girls look at each other nervously before nodding in agreement.

Back in the county, cutting up our clothes, removing our underskirts would be enough for a whipping, but everything's different now. The realization gives us a surge of energy.

After a humble breakfast of cornmeal cakes, we gather the axe, and any nails we can dig from the ashes, and head off to the west, in the opposite direction of Kiersten and the others, who seem to be doing nothing more than kneeling in the dirt and praying.

Maybe our magic will consume us, making us little more than animals, but until that time comes, until the poachers lure us out of the gate to be cut up and placed in pretty little bottles, there's work to be done.

Toward the western edge of the clearing, we settle near a grove of ash and oak. I set my sights on a widowmaker near the perimeter. It's dead, so it's already seasoned, which will give us decent wood to burn until the other timber dries out.

I'm waiting for everyone to pitch in, give their opinions on the best angle for the first cut, but they look completely bewildered. Clearly, I'm the only one who knows how to do this, so I'm going to have to start with the basics.

"The key is a good split. Once you get it in there, it will eventually give. Like this," I say as I slam the axe into the wood. Prying it out, I hand it over to Molly. She takes it from me as gingerly as if she's accepting a flower from a suitor, but as soon as she gets her first bite of wood, she grins, gripping the axe a little tighter. When her arms have turned to soft custard, she passes it on to Lucy.

Lucy hauls it back for the first strike.

"Wait, wait, wait," I call out, grabbing the hilt. "You have to at least keep your eyes open."

Some of the other girls laugh.

"No, it's okay. You've never done this before," I assure her. "But this is serious. You wouldn't believe the timber injuries I've seen in the healing house."

At the mention of this, the girls pipe down.

"Here . . ." I position the axe in her arms. "Feet wide, strong grip, take in a deep breath through your nose," I say as I back away, "and when you exhale through your mouth, lock eyes on your target and swing."

Lucy takes her time, and when the blade makes contact with the wood, there's a satisfying crack. As the tree begins to lurch, I'm looking up trying to see which way it's going to fall, and when it starts to go down we all run to the other side, laughing, hooting, and hollering.

Cutting the tree into chunks and splitting the wood

into quarters is grueling work, but it seems to be exactly what we need. The girls take turns going back to the well for water, sneaking dried apples from the larder, and as the day goes on, we're talking and laughing, like we've been doing this for years. Maybe it's being away from the county, being able to use our bodies to do something useful, but I think opening up to them last night about the dreams, about the girl, seemed to have given them permission to do the same. To be themselves.

Looking around, it's hard to fathom that in a year's time we might turn on one another, sacrifice bits and pieces of our flesh, and burn this place to the ground, but if it's anything close to what Kiersten is claiming to be true? God help us.

As the girls pile up the boning from their skirts, I get to work on the rain barrels, cutting large discs from a mighty oak. I've only seen the men in the fields make these a few times, but I'm not about to tell them that. Confidence is key, that's what my father always said. When he went on calls, even if he wasn't certain how to treat someone, he never let on. He was afraid that if he showed even the slightest waver, they'd go right back to the dark ages— drinking animal blood, relying on prayer to heal them, or worse, the black market. He needed their trust. He needed them to believe he could help them even if he couldn't.

As I get to work, cutting the planks for the sides, Ellie asks, "Why did your father teach you all this?"

An unexpected wave of emotion comes over me. "I guess I was the closest thing to a son he was ever going to get." But even as I'm saying it, I'm wondering if it goes deeper than that. I want to believe he did this so I would be able to take care of myself out here, but if that's the case, that means he knows exactly what this place really is, and he sent me here anyway. The night before I left he said teaching me was a mistake . . . like *I* was a mistake.

"Tierney? Are you okay?" Ellie asks.

I look down to find my hands trembling. I don't know how long I've been standing here like this, staring off into nothing, but long enough that all the girls are watching me with concern. That's never happened to me before.

"Here, why don't you give it a try?" I say, putting the axe in Ellie's hands, anything to get the attention off me.

As she pulls it back to swing, she loses her balance and goes spinning round and round, until she finally collapses to the ground, narrowly missing cutting off her own foot in the process.

As we gather around, Martha says, "Give her some air."

Nanette brings a cup of water to her lips.

"I don't know what happened," she whispers, her cheeks flushed, her eyes struggling to focus. "It was as if my head got so light that it felt like it was going to drift away."

"Maybe it's your magic," Helen says. "Maybe you'll be able to hover above the ground . . . float among the stars."

"Or maybe we're just overworked," I say as I pick up the axe, burying it into the stump. "It was a long journey."

They look at each other; I can tell they're not entirely convinced.

"Tierney's right," Martha says, flopping down in the grass. "Until something happens . . . until we're certain . . . it's best to keep our heads."

One by one, we find ourselves lying in a patch of dried-up grass, staring up at the clouds, our bodies spent, our minds splayed open wide enough to speak without any more pretense.

"I don't know what I was expecting . . . ," Lucy says, squinting toward the fence. "But it wasn't this." A tiny moth flutters around her, landing on the back of her hand. "I thought we'd be fighting off poachers."

"Or battling ghosts and wild animals," Patrice says.

"I thought when we stepped through the gate, our magic would rip through us," Martha says, plucking a willow from the grass, blowing on the seeds. "But nothing happened."

"I'm glad we're away from the county," Nanette says. "If I had to look at my parents' disappointed faces for one more second, I was going to explode."

"We knew I wouldn't get a veil," Becca says, staring up at the cornflower-blue sky. "I didn't even have my first blood until May, and no one wants a late bloomer."

"Better than not having one at all," Molly says. "I never even had a chance at a veil, let alone a spot in the mill or the dairy. It'll be the fields for me."

"I didn't mind not getting a veil," Martha says.

They all look at her in shock.

"What?" she says with a casual shrug. "At least I don't have to worry about dying in childbirth."

They look appalled, but no one argues with her. What can they possibly say? It's the truth.

"I thought I was getting one," Lucy admits.

"From who?" Patrice props up on her elbow, excited for a juicy tidbit.

"Russel Peterson," she whispers, as if just saying his name is like pressing down on a fresh bruise.

"Why would you think he'd give you a veil?" Helen asks, feeding a bit of apple to Dovey. "Everyone knows he's been sweet on Jenna for years."

"Because he told me so," she murmurs.

"Sure." Patrice rolls her eyes.

"She's telling the truth," I say. "I've seen them together in the meadow."

Lucy looks over at me, her eyes welling up with giant tears.

I'm trying not to picture her—eyes turned to God as Russel grunts over her, whispering empty promises.

"And what were *you* doing in the meadow?" Patrice asks, clearly trying to dig up dirt.

"Michael," I reply. "We used to meet there all the time."

"Just like Kiersten said," one of the girls whispers.

"No . . . never." I lift my head to see who said that, but I can't tell. "Not like that. We're friends, that's all. I was as surprised as anyone when I received a veil. And even then, I was sure it was Tommy or Mr. Fallow."

"I wouldn't mind Tommy, at least he has all his teeth, but Geezer Fallow . . ." Ellie crinkles up her nose.

Nanette elbows her, nodding toward Gertrude, but Gertie pretends not to hear. It's sad to think how good she is at pretending.

There's an awkward pause. I'm trying to think of something to say, anything to divert their attention, when Gertrude says, "My parents called it a miracle. I mean, it's not every day a girl accused of depravity gets a veil." Her candor seems to disarm everyone. We all find ourselves staring at the thick scars on her knuckles. I want to tell her it wasn't a miracle, that she's worthy of a veil, but she's right.

A veil has never been given to a girl accused of a crime before, in all of grace year history, especially nothing as grave as depravity.

"It's funny," Gertie says, without the slightest hint of a smile on her face. "The same thing that prevented me from getting a veil from one of the boys in my year is the exact reason I received one from Geezer Fallow."

"What do you mean?" Helen asks.

She takes in a steeling breath. "When he lifted my veil and leaned in to kiss my cheek . . . he pinched me hard between my legs and whispered, 'Depravity suits me just fine.'"

I feel a strange heat move to my neck and cheeks.

Maybe we all do, because it's so quiet I swear I can hear one of the willow seeds settling between the blades of grass.

Whatever was in that lithograph . . . I know Gertrude Fenton didn't deserve this . . . and I'm fairly certain that Kiersten's to blame.

Returning to the camp with enough firewood to last the month, we start stacking it up in neat rows under the awning of the larder when screams echo from the eastern side of the clearing. Dropping everything, we run over to help, but what I find is all at once puzzling and chilling.

The girls are lined up behind Ravenna, holding hands, as if creating some kind of barrier. Ravenna's hands are raised to the sky. Muscles strained, veins bulging, sweat trailing down her neck, she appears to be grasping an invisible ball, trembling under the weight of it.

"Keep going," Kiersten says, urging her on. "Just a little lower."

"What's she doing . . . what's going on?" Martha whispers.

"Shut up, dummy," one of the girls hisses from behind her veil. "She's making the sun go down."

Patrice passes it on, as if everyone isn't hanging on every syllable. "She thinks she's making the sun set."

"Maybe she is," Helen whispers, staring in awe.

"It does feel earlier than yesterday," Lucy adds.

As they're watching her grunt and sweat and strain, I can see it in their eyes. This is what they've been waiting for. This is what they thought their grace year would be.

I want to tell them that the sun will set a little earlier every day until the solstice, but even I'm starting to wonder.

When the sun finally reaches its resting place, Ravenna collapses to the earth in a heap of sweat-drenched flesh. The girls rush in around her, picking her up, patting her on the back, congratulating her.

"I knew you could do it." Kiersten reaches for the end of Ravenna's braid, pulling the red silk ribbon free. The release I feel is undeniable. It's not just the idea of feeling dusk move through my hair, although that must feel like heaven—it's the sense of unwavering purpose they share.

As Ravenna kneels down to pray, they join her.

"Deliver me from evil. Let this magic burn through me so I can return a purified woman, worthy of your love and mercy."

"Amen," the girls whisper from beneath their veils.

Kneeling in the dirt, barefoot, eyes to God, bathed in golden light, they look like something not of this earth. No longer girls, but women on the verge of coming into their power. Their magic.

I promised myself I would keep my feet firmly rooted in the soil, that I wouldn't give in to superstition and flights of fancy, so why am I trembling?

Dinner around the bonfire is quiet, tense. Each group clinging to their secrets. I want to air our grievances, get everything out in the open so we can work together, but that's clearly never going to happen, not as long as Kiersten's in charge.

"What are you staring at?" Kiersten asks.

I quickly avert my gaze.

Kiersten whispers something to Jenna, Jenna to Jessica, Jessica to Tamara, and I know they're talking about me. I don't know what kind of lies she's spreading, what kind of clever new nickname she's given me, but she's obviously up to something.

A high-pitched shriek rings out from the forest, making everyone stop midbreath and stare into the dark woods.

"It's one of the ghosts," Jenna whispers. "I heard that if you get too close, they can take over your body. Make you do things you don't want to do."

"Isn't that what happened to Melania Rushik?" Hannah asks. "I heard they got into her head, whispered things, beckoned her into the woods with the promise of a veil, and when she finally succumbed, they spit her body out of the barrier in twelve different pieces."

The noise rings out again, which sets off a flurry of gasps and nervous whisperings of who the ghosts will go after first.

"It's an elk," I say.

"How would *you* know?" Tamara snaps.

"Because I used to go into the northern forests with my father this time of year to check on the trappers who didn't make it in for trading. It's looking for a mate."

"Whatever it is . . . it's creepy," Helen says, nuzzling Dovey under her cloak.

"You think you know everything, but you don't," Jessica says, glaring at me.

"I know that we chopped enough wood to last the month, made the meals, cleaned up, built rain barrels . . . what did *you* do?"

"You're wasting your time with all that," Kiersten says with a placid smile. "Every day that goes by that you don't embrace your magic is a day lost."

"We should get to bed," I say, standing up, faking a

yawn. "We have a big day ahead of us tomorrow . . . you know, building a washing station, a tub . . . things that will actually help us survive."

"You may think you're helping them, but you're not," Kiersten says. "You're only holding them back."

I pretend not to hear her, but I'm bad at pretending.

"I hope that tub's for Dirty Gertie," one of the veiled girls calls after us. "She's going to need it."

Laughter erupts around the campfire. I want to go back and clobber them, but Gertie shakes her head. Short. Precise. She fixes me with the same look my mother gave me when my father delivered my veil to the church.

"Don't," she whispers.

As the other girls file past us into the lodging house, I hold Gertie back. "I know it was Kiersten's lithograph. You should tell the others."

"That's my business," she says firmly. "Promise you won't interfere."

"Promise," I reply, feeling bad for pushing her. "But can you at least tell me why you took the blame?"

"I thought it would be easier," Gertie says, staring straight ahead, but I can hear the emotion in her voice. "I thought if I took the blame she would—"

"Coming?" Martha says, holding the door open.

Gertrude hurries along, more than happy to end the conversation.

With the lanterns low, we settle into our beds, peering up at the spiderwebs clinging to the beamed ceiling, trying not to imagine what's happening around the fire.

"What if it's true?" Becca says, breaking the silence. "What if we're wasting our time? You know what they'll do to us if we come back without getting rid of all of our magic."

"We just got here," I say, trying to position my body around the springs. "There's plenty of time for all that. They're just trying to scare us."

"It's working," Lucy says, pulling her blanket up to her nose.

"I for one am in no hurry to lose my mind," Martha says.

"But I was a late bloomer," Becca says, sheer panic in her hushed voice. "What if it's the same with my magic? What if it comes too late and I can't get rid of it in time?"

"It's not the same thing," Patrice says.

"How do *you* know?"

A low groan echoes through the woods, making us all hold our breath.

"It's just another elk, right?" Nanette asks.

I nod, though I'm not entirely sure.

"Did you see the way Kiersten was looking at me to-night?" Lucy says from beneath her covers. "She's always hated me. I have three younger sisters . . . if she makes me do something with her magic . . . if I walk into the woods and my body is unaccounted for—"

"We're getting carried away," I say. "This is what she wants. All we have to do is stick together. Be sensible."

"But you saw what Ravenna can do," Ellie says.

"All we saw was a girl holding an invisible ball," I say.

"But I felt it." Molly presses her palms against her lower abdomen. "There was a moment when I saw the sun in her hands. They were one."

"I thought it was about to crack open between her fingers like a soft yolk," Ellie whispers.

I want to say something, find a reasonable explanation, but the truth is, I felt it, too.

"Hey, where's Helen?" I ask, noticing her empty bed, the absence of cooing.

"She stayed by the fire," Nanette says, staring toward the door.

Maybe I'm reading too much into it, but I swear I hear a hint of sadness in her voice, longing.

Maybe they all wish they'd stayed behind.

As much as I want to deny it, bury the thought, there's a part of me that can't help wondering if Kiersten was right . . . if I'm the one holding them back.

Maybe there's nothing wrong with the grace year. Maybe there's something wrong with *me*.

In the weeks that followed, while we were busy clearing away the scorched debris, building a covered area for cooking, making rain barrels, chopping wood, divvying up chores, Kiersten was busy "helping" the veiled girls embrace their magic.

It started off with silly things, doling out little dares to try to jar their magic loose, singing hymns of Eve as they knotted flower crowns in the morning dew, sitting in a circle around the punishment tree telling cautionary tales, but what at first seemed like harmless tasks turned into something infinitely more dangerous. But isn't that how every horrible thing begins? Slow. Insipid. A twisting of the screw.

Night after night, Kiersten returned from the bonfire with another convert, glassy eyed, hair cascading down her back, making some wild claim or another.

Tamara said she could hear the wind whispering to her, and Hannah said she made a juniper berry wither just by looking at it. I could chalk it all up to their imaginations, social conditioning, superstition gone awry, but they weren't the only ones experiencing strange goings-on. Something was happening to the rest of us. Something I couldn't explain.

Along with dizzy spells, loss of appetite, double vision, it seemed like our irises were disappearing, soft black eroding away any color, any light. I kept thinking it was just exhaustion, or maybe some kind of illness passing through the camp, but the more I tried to make sense of it, the worse things seemed to get.

And as the full moon drew near, we bled. All of us at the same time, even Molly, just like a pack of wolves.

I tried to tell the girls that just because you can't explain something, that doesn't make it magic, but one by one they inched their beds closer to the other side of the room, drawn to wild tales of magic and mysticism.

Honestly, I couldn't blame them. I'd lived with these doubts about the grace year my entire life, and even I was starting to question things.

Question my sanity.

A few nights ago, as we were huddled around the fire, Meg swiped her hand through the flames. "I can't feel it," she exclaimed. As she looked to Kiersten, I felt something pass between them, a surge of invisible energy. Maybe it was all in my head, maybe it was Kiersten's magic, a language I couldn't understand, but in the next moment, Meg held her hand in the flames until her skin bubbled up like a hundred singing bullfrogs.

"What are you doing?" I yelled as I grabbed on to her, pulling her back from the heat.

Meg looked up at me, with those huge black eyes.

She didn't scream. She didn't cry. She laughed.

They all did.

Soon, wild rumors of ghostly activities swept through the camp. Things were disappearing, being smashed to bits in the night. Interestingly enough, the ghosts were only going after the things I'd built, but I didn't let it deter me.

As crazy as it got in the camp, I tried my best to stick to routine, keep up with the chores, but it was getting harder and harder to rally even myself, let alone the other girls. I suppose sitting around the fire talking about ghosts and magic is a lot more appealing than hard labor, but I promised myself that I would keep my head. If the magic takes me, so be it, but I won't give in without reason, without a fight.

In the early-morning hours, with whoever's willing, we head out to the western side of the clearing, to start on some futile project or another, but soon find ourselves lost in the clouds . . . the wind . . . the trees.

It makes me think of the women in the county—draping their fingers over the water, tilting their faces toward the late-autumn wind, is this what they're remembering? Is this what they're trying to get back to?

I feel like I'm missing something . . . a key piece of the puzzle. But when I look at the fence, the endless sea of stripped cedars stretching out for miles, it occurs to me—even though we're sent here against our will, to live or die like animals, this is the most freedom we've ever had. That we'll probably *ever* get.

I don't know why it makes me laugh. It's not funny at all. But I find Gertie, Martha, and Nanette laughing along with me, until we're crying.

Walking back to the camp, there's a sense of dread. Maybe it's just the weather turning, but it feels like something more. Every day the tension seems to be mounting. What it's mounting to, I cannot say, but it's palpable, something you can feel in the air.

As we approach the campfire, we find the girls already assembled, feeding on their own whispers, their dark eyes tracking us like slivers of wet shale.

Grabbing a pitcher of water from the rain barrel, a handful of dried fruit and nuts from the larder, we escape their heavy gaze, retreating into the lodging house, only to find four more beds have been moved to the other side of the room—Lucy, Ellie, Becca, and Patrice have all succumbed. No one says a word, but I know we're all wondering which one of us will be next. It doesn't even feel like an if anymore, but a when.

A mournful cry echoes through the forest, making me flinch. I'm not sure if it's a nightmare or reality, but they feel like one and the same as of late.

Listening closer, I only hear the heady lull of slumber all around me, the soft coo of Dovey sleeping in Helen's arms. "Everything's okay," I whisper to myself.

"Is it?" Gertrude asks.

I turn on my side to face her. I want to tell her yes, but I'm not sure anymore. I'm not sure about anything. I can't stop staring at her knuckles, the thick ropelike scars glinting pink and silver in the lamplight.

"Go ahead and ask," she whispers. "I know you want to."

"What do you mean?" I try to play it off, but as Gertie pointed out, I'm bad at pretending.

I'm trying to find the words, how I can phrase this without causing her any more embarrassment, any more pain, but then she does it for me.

"You want to know what was in that lithograph."

"If you don't want to say, I underst—"

"It was a woman," she whispers. "She had long hair that was loose around her shoulders, ringlets barely skimming her breasts. A red silk ribbon coiled around her hand like a serpent. Her cheeks were flushed; her head was tilted up."

"Eyes to God," I say, thinking of our lessons.

"No," she says in a dreamy tone. "Her eyes were half closed, but it felt like she was staring right at me."

"In pain?" I ask, remembering hearing about some pictures that were confiscated from the trappers a few years back. Women bound, contorted in ungodly shapes.

"The opposite." Gertrude looks up at me, eyes shining. "She looked happy. *Rapturous*."

My imagination is running wild. That goes against everything we've been taught. We've all heard the rumors about the women in the outskirts, that some of them might even enjoy it, but this woman had a red ribbon. She was clearly one of us. I swallow hard at the thought. "What were they doing to her?"

"That's the thing," Gertrude whispers. "She was alone. She was touching *herself*."

The notion is so shocking that my breath catches in my throat.

"Dirty Gertie," someone hisses from the dark, and the entire room erupts in giggles. Jeers.

I want to tell them it was Kiersten's lithograph, that Gertie took the blame, but I made a promise. It's not my story to tell.

As I watch her sink back into her covers, my heart aches for her.

To clear my head, get my mind off the deteriorating state of the camp, I set out to chop wood along the western perimeter.

I don't expect the rest of the girls to help out anymore, but Gertie's absence is a little more worrisome. Ever since the other night in the lodging house, when the girls overheard her talking about the lithograph, she's kept scarce . . . distant.

Some of the girls have been whispering, saying that she must be coming into her magic, but I think it's shame. It must feel like she's being punished in the square all over again. I want to help her, pull her out of whatever mood she's in, but I'm struggling myself.

Just this morning, I had the feeling that there were a million fire ants crawling on my skin, only to find nothing there. I don't have a name for what's happening . . . I don't know what to call it . . . but that still doesn't mean it's magic.

As I near the western edge of the clearing, I feel a heat move through me, like I'm burning from the inside out. Taking off my cloak, I lay it down over a stump and take in a deep breath of cool air. "Whatever this is, it will pass," I whisper.

Grabbing the axe, I set my sights on an old pine. As I place my hand against it to steady myself, my fingers begin to tingle. The deep ridges in the rough bark seem to be pulsing with energy. Or maybe the energy is coming from me, but I feel like it's trying to tell me something.

Pressing my ear to the bark, I swear I hear it whispering. I think this must be it, my magic taking over, when I realize the sound is coming from behind me.

Peering over my shoulder, I see Kiersten sitting on the stump, stroking my cloak, her nails scraping against the grain of the wool. I don't know how long she's been there watching me, but I don't like it. I'm searching behind her, wondering where the rest of her followers are, but I think she's alone.

"Put that down. It's mine," I say, gripping the axe in my hands.

"I don't want your cloak," she says, pushing it aside. "It's heavy. No wonder you're so muscular now."

Peering down at my arms, I know she doesn't mean it as a compliment.

"It feels good, to do something useful," I say as I snatch the cloak from her, putting it back on. "You should try it."

"Because isn't that the biggest sin of all for a woman?" she says, twirling a sunlit curl around her finger. "Not to be of use."

Her tone catches me off guard, but I need to stay cautious. "Why are you here, Kiersten?"

"I need you," she says with a deep sigh. "The *girls* need you. You can help them."

"If this is about the magic . . . I can't embrace something I don't have—"

"You're right. I don't think you have any magic, either."

"What?" I perk up.

"I think you've been hiding it for years, that you burned through it right under our noses." She gets up, stalking toward me. "That's how you got your father's attention, got him to teach you those things, and that's how you stole Michael from me. You squandered your magic, and now you want them to bury theirs. Is there no decency in you?"

"Decency?" I jut my head back. "You're one to talk. What about Gertie?"

"What about Gertie?" Her eyes narrow.

"You can cut the innocent routine. I know everything."

"Do you, now?" She flashes an uneasy smile. "It would be a shame if Gertie was the first girl in the camp to fall."

"Don't threaten me." I tighten my grip on the axe. "There's no reason we have to die here."

"We all die, Tierney." The corner of her mouth twists up. "In the county, everything they take away from us is a tiny death. But not here . . ." She spreads her arms out, taking in a deep breath. "The grace year is ours. This is the one place we can be free. There's no more tempering our feelings, no more swallowing our pride. Here we can be whatever we want. And if we let it all out," she says, her eyes welling up, her features softening, "we won't have to feel those things anymore. We won't have to feel at all."

Staggering back, I rest against the pine, feeling the wood beneath my fingertips . . . something real, something to anchor me to reality. But this is happening. Kiersten's human, after all. I think I finally understand her. She's *afraid*.

There's a part of me that wants to give in . . . wants to

believe . . . wants to be a part of this, so I can unleash my anger and be rid of it, but I can't do it. Maybe it's the memory of the girl from my dreams or maybe it's just me, but I know we can be more than this.

"I can't help you," I whisper.

"Then I can't help you," she replies, her face hardening back into its usual mask. "I think you've done enough," she says, taking the axe from me. "I'll take it from here."

After pacing the perimeter, trying to figure out what just happened, what to do, I'm heading back to camp to tell the others when I hear voices. I close my eyes, trying to block it out, but it's not in my head this time.

"It's the right thing . . . for both of you . . . for the good of the camp."

Peeking around the larder, I find Gertie standing there with Kiersten. "Hey," I call out.

Gertie looks up at me. Her face is red and damp with tears.

"The choice is yours," Kiersten says before returning to the camp.

"What choice . . . What's for the good of the camp?" I ask.

She wipes her face with the back of her filthy hand, clearly trying to pull herself together. "Kiersten's called a gathering tonight . . . for the full moon."

Thinking about what this means at home, I clench my hand into a fist, wondering which of my fingertips will be the first to go. "We can stay scarce."

"Everyone has agreed," she says as she glances toward the clearing. "Everyone but *you*."

"Oh," I say with a deep exhalation of breath, trying not to look as disappointed as I feel.

"The girls are talking . . . having doubts."

"Are you?" I ask.

She stares down at the shriveled sprig of elderflower cupped in the palm of her hand. It's an old flower, seldom used anymore, but it's the symbol of absolution.

"Did she give that to you?"

Gertie closes her fingers around it, like she's holding the most fragile egg.

"You know you can't trust her. She's not God. She can't absolve you from something she did herself. She's the reason you were punished. Remember what she did to you." I reach out for her hands to turn them over, to show her the scars, but she pulls away from me, staggering back a few steps in the process.

"She apologized," Gertie says as she slowly regains her balance. "We're friends again."

"Friends?" I laugh.

"You have no idea what it's like . . . being an outcast . . . being reviled."

"Look around . . . I don't see anyone trying to help me."

"But that's your *choice*." She shakes her head. "You never wanted to be one of us." A pained look comes over her. "All you have to do is accept your magic and—"

"I can't accept something I don't feel. Maybe it's an illness, but whatever's happening to us—"

"She's calling you a heretic," she says, her chin trembling. "A usurper."

I don't know why it makes me laugh. Back in the county, if you were accused of heresy, they didn't even bother with the gallows. They just burned you alive. I pull my cloak tighter around me. "Kiersten just wants chaos because she wants control."

"You're wrong." Gertie's brow knots up in a tight line. "She truly believes that by embracing her magic, turning herself over to the darkness inside of her, that she will get to go home a purified woman. Rid herself of her sins, start anew."

"What sins? The sin of being born a girl?"

"We all have sin," she whispers.

A caw rings out over the woods, making Gertie flinch.

"It's just a crow," I say, but I'm not sure this time. I'm not entirely sure I heard it at all. Looking up, I see the clouds race by so fast that it makes me dizzy. "Kiersten," I say, lowering my eyes, trying to regain my focus. "She came to see me today. She's just using you to get to me."

"Not everything is about you, Tierney."

"Then what's it about? Tell me. What's really bothering you?"

She looks up at me, her eyes large and glassy. "I don't want to be Dirty Gertie anymore. I just want it to stop."

"If this is about the other girls . . . I can talk to them . . . I can get them to—"

"I don't need your help anymore."

"I don't understand," I say. "Did she threaten you? Did she promise you something?" I'm searching her face, looking for any kind of clue, but Gertie's good at pretending. "What are you hiding?" I ask.

Gertie looks toward the punishment tree. I can't see the expression on her face, but I notice the tension in her jaw. It's almost as if she's clamping her mouth shut so nothing will slip out against her will. "I think it's best if we don't speak anymore," she says before joining the others.

I spend the rest of the day tapping maples, collecting tinder from the perimeter, anything to keep my mind occupied, keep away from the camp, but I feel myself drifting, like a piece of deadwood caught in a violent current.

My palms are blistered up beyond recognition by the time I decide to head back to camp. I take my time, in part because I don't want Kiersten to think I'm taking this gathering seriously, but also because there's a part of me that's scared. I overheard some of the girls saying they came into their magic just by staring into the flames. I keep thinking there has to be another explanation for all this. There's no denying we're in a weakened state right now, vulnerable, but I can't stop them if they want to succumb. People see what they want to see. Including me.

As I approach the fire, the wood isn't the only thing crackling. The very air surrounding the assembled girls feels charged. There's lightning in the distance, and a low grumble, like the echo of an avalanche from clear across the world.

On instinct, I find Gertie in the crowd, but she doesn't motion for me to join her. She doesn't acknowledge me at all. I want to fix this, apologize for whatever I did to offend her, but maybe she needs space right now. What I wouldn't give for a little more space. My eyes scan the fence keeping us from the outside world. So far, the poachers have made no attempt to lure us out. If I hadn't seen one of them with my own eyes, I might even question their existence. I wonder if they're watching us right now. Taking bets on which one of us will be the next to fall.

A roar of thunder releases. Closer this time.

"Listen. She's trying to communicate," Kiersten says.

"It's only thunder," Martha murmurs.

"Only thunder?" Kiersten says in a stern singsong voice. "Might I remind you of the story of Eve. Mother Nature herself. She was once a grace year girl. I think she's trying to reach out to one of us."

"What does she want?" Tamara asks, sinking deeper into her cloak.

"She's trying to warn us." Kiersten lowers her chin, the fire casting ghoulish shadows across the planes of her face. "What happened to Eve could happen to us. If we do not listen . . . if we do not heed her warning," Kiersten says staring directly at me. "Like some of you, Eve didn't believe. She laughed in the face of God. She held on to her magic, and when she returned home, she pretended she was purified, but every day that passed, the magic grew inside of her until it could no longer be contained. Under a full moon, on a night just like tonight, she killed her entire family."

A wave of repulsion swells through the crowd.

"If the men of the council hadn't stopped her, she would've killed them all."

I always thought it was just an old wives' tale, a fable, but looking around the campfire, I can see they're eating it up.

Kiersten raises her chin, looking up at the churning night sky. "When they burned her in the square, the sky opened up, taking her in, and there she remains as a reminder to us all."

A clap of thunder makes everyone jump.

"Listen," Kiersten whispers. "She will not be ignored. If she's communicating with someone in this group, speak up, claim your power. It's the only way to save yourself."

A girl from the back meekly raises her hand. "I hear her."

Kiersten motions for her to step forward.

Vivian Larson, a mouse of a girl, who received a veil from her cousin, someone that Kiersten has never paid any attention to a day in her life. I doubt she even knows her name, but now Vivi finds herself in the center of the sun, basking in Kiersten's approval.

"Tell us. What is she saying to you?"

"E-everything you said." Vivian clasps her hands in front of her. "She's warning us of what could happen."

"Did she say there's a heretic among us . . . a usurper?"

Another bolt of thunder groans above, and Vivian shoots me an uneasy look. The same look she gave me when I stumbled upon her in the meadow with a boy from one of the labor houses last year. "I'm not sure."

I pretend not to notice, but I can feel eyes on me from every direction.

"All in good time. Keep listening, friend," Kiersten says as she pulls Vivi's red ribbon free, running her hands through her unkempt, oily hair. Vivi smiles up at the moon, like she's just been released from the devil. From *me*.

"I only hope it's not too late for the rest of you." Kiersten paces around the fire. "All of these things you've been building, laboring over . . . ," she says, pushing over a cooking stand. "They're meaningless."

"They're not meaningless," I can't help blurting out. "You've certainly benefited from all of our hard work."

Kiersten turns on me with a focus that makes my skin prickle. "Being comfortable and well fed is not going to lead us to our magic. We're put here to suffer, to rid ourselves of the poison inside of us." Her eyes look wild in the firelight, menacing. "We're here because Eve tempted Adam with her magic. Poisoning him with ripened fruit. If we don't use our magic, if we don't rid ourselves of our demons, you know what will happen. You've seen what happens to the returning girls who try to hang on to their magic—they're sent to the gallows . . . or worse."

A shiver of fear ripples through the crowd . . . through me.

"But what if Tierney's right?" a small voice calls from the back. It's Nanette. She sleeps on the bed next to me. "What if it's just our imagination or some kind of illness?"

Instead of exploding in anger, Kiersten gets calm. Scary calm. "Is this because of Tierney's wicked dreams?"

I look around the campfire, wondering which one of them told, but I've got bigger problems right now.

"Don't you see what she's doing? Filling your heads with devious thoughts. Trying to distract you from the task at hand," Kiersten says. "She's not special. Look at her. She can't even keep the one true ally she has." Kiersten looks pointedly at Gertrude, and my worst fears are confirmed. She's just using her to get to me. And Gertrude knows it.

"Tierney wants you to hold on to your magic, and when you return to Garner County you'll be sent to the gallows. This is her way of getting rid of us."

"Why would I want to do that? We're all in this together."

"Together?" She laughs. "Did she ever reach out to any one of you back home? Has she ever shown the slightest interest in our ways? *This* is her magic. Turning us against each other . . . who we are . . . what we're meant to do."

"You're lying," I say, but no one seems to be listening to me anymore.

"You," Kiersten says, pointing to a girl in the middle of the group. It's Dena Hurson. Tentatively she steps forward. "Didn't you say communicating with animals runs in your family magic?"

"Yes . . . but . . ."

"Take off your clothes."

"What?" she asks, knitting her arms over her chest.

"You heard me. Take them off." Kiersten runs her hand down Dena's braid and whispers in her ear. "I'm going to help you. I'm going to set you free."

Dena looks around the campfire, but no one dares to intervene. Not even me. Letting out a shaky breath, she removes her cape, her chemise, her underpinnings.

As she stands there, shivering, trying to cover herself the best she can in the moonlight, Kiersten steps in behind her, pressing her palms against the girl's lower abdomen. "You should feel it right *here*," she says, fanning out her fingers, making the girl take in a shuddering breath. "Do you feel the warmth? Do you feel the tingling? Like your blood is reaching for the surface, wanting to scream?"

"Yes," she whispers.

"That's your magic. Latch on to it, welcome it, keep pulling it forward."

After a few heaving breaths, Dena clenches her eyes tight. "I think I feel something."

"Now get on all fours," Kiersten commands.

"Why?"

"Do as I say."

Dena obeys, getting down on the ground.

I want to step in, save her from this humiliation, but she's under Kiersten's spell. They all are. Maybe I am, too, because I can't seem to tear my eyes away.

As Kiersten removes Dena's red ribbon, pulling her long auburn hair free, Dena digs her fingernails into the soil.

The girls watch with rapt attention as Kiersten walks around her, coiling the red ribbon in her hand. "Reach out to the animals of the forest. Feel their presence."

"I don't know how," Dena says.

Kiersten whips the red ribbon through the air across her backside. I'm sure it doesn't hurt, but it surprises her . . . surprises all of us.

"Close your eyes," Kiersten commands. "Feel every heart beating in the woods. Find one. Focus in on that rhythm," she says as she paces around her.

"I hear something," Dena says as she lifts her head, eyes straining toward the forest. "I feel heat. Blood. The stench of damp fur."

A howl comes from the woods, making everyone hold their breath.

Kiersten yanks back Dena's hair. "Answer," she says.

As Dena howls back, stretching out her neck as far as she can, I see every tendon straining for magic. Yearning for greatness. Longing to be filled with something bigger than herself.

When Kiersten's finally satisfied, she releases her. Dena stands to face us—flushed cheeks, hair loose and wild, tears streaming down her face, her eyes glassy with madness. "The magic is real," she says before howling once more and then collapsing in Kiersten's arms.

I wake to the sound of muffled laughter, blood on my hands, blood between my legs.

Snapping up in bed, I find myself alone on my side of the lodging house, dark red seeping through my underclothes, girls pointing and giggling behind cupped hands.

"I made that happen." Kiersten laughs, a long feather in her hand, the tip coated in blood.

I look to Gertie, but she refuses to meet my gaze.

Grabbing my boots, I escape the stifling cabin and head to the rain barrel, to wash myself off, only to find it's been smashed to pieces. That was my last one. I spent weeks bending the wood just right, and with the weather turning, it will be nearly impossible to make another before spring. Kiersten will blame it on the ghosts, but I know this is her doing. Searing anger rises in my cheeks. I'm furious, but I need to keep it together. They're probably watching me right now, and the worst thing I can do is let them know they got to me.

Making a beeline for the well, I try to shove the bucket over the side, but it's frozen solid to the stone. I'm trying to pry it free when I hear the most eerie sound.

Singing. At least it sounds like singing.

Abandoning the well, I make my way toward the gate. There's a tiny figure hunched on the ground. The high voice, her small stature . . . for a moment I think it's the little girl from my dreams. I want to run to her, but I force myself to take measured steps. *Trust no one. Not even your-self.* My mother's words echo in my head.

I crouch in front of her, but I can't see her face. With trembling hands, I lift her filthy veil. It's Ami Dumont. She's stayed so quiet, so small, that I almost forgot she was here.

Leaning in close, I listen to her song.

Eve with the golden hair, sits on high in her rocking chair,

The wind doth blow, the night unfurls, weeping for all the men she's cursed.

It's an old nursery rhyme; I never gave it a second thought as a child, but now . . . here . . . in this moment, the words have taken on an entirely different meaning.

Girls beware, if you don't behave, you'll be sent to an early grave.

Never a bairn to call your own, never a care to—

Abruptly, she stops singing, with her eyes fixed on the gate; her breath grows shallow in her chest, but it's not in rhythm with the panting I hear. Following her gaze, I look behind me. At first, all I see is the gate, deep scratch marks embedded in the heavy timber, but beyond that, in the narrow cracks in the logs, I see eyes . . . dark eyes staring in at us.

"They can smell your blood." She smiles up at me.

I'm backing away, trying to get away from whatever's happening here, when my vision starts to blur. I'm staggering around the clearing trying to find anything to latch on to. The well. If I can just get some water. As I reach out for the stone ledge, my legs go out from under me. Smacking my head against the hard surface, I go down like a sack of bones.

As my eyes slowly come back into focus, I hear someone say, "All you have to do is run to the cove and back."

Tilting my head back, I see the girls huddled in front of the gate.

"As soon as you embrace your magic, I'll take out your braid," Kiersten says, as if she's talking to a child. "You can be one of us."

Getting to my feet is harder than I thought it would be. My head is pounding. The dizziness makes the fence blur in and out like the dial on Father's microscope.

"Can you hold Dovey for me?" Helen offers the bird to Kiersten. Kiersten cringes, shoving Jessica forward to take it. "She likes it best when you nuzzle her under your chin," Helen adds.

"Wait," I say as I make my way over. "She can't leave the barrier. There's poachers out there."

Jenna shoots me an exasperated look. "We thought you were dead."

"Yeah . . . no such luck." I brush past her. "Helen, you can't do this."

"But I'm invisible," she says with a grin.

"Since when?" I ask.

"Go away," Tamara says, pushing me aside. "Not that she needs any help, but we've got Ami distracting the poachers by the eastern fence with that awful singing."

I squint toward the east. I think I see Ami's tiny frame crouched by the barrier, but I can't be sure.

Frantically, I'm stumbling around the crowd, searching for anyone who can talk some sense into Helen, when my eyes settle on Gertie. "You have to do something," I whisper.

Although she's looking away, pretending not to hear, I see real fear in her eyes.

"All you have to do is concentrate. Feel your magic," Kiersten says, pressing the palm of her hand against Helen's belly. "Remember, if something goes wrong I can always use my magic to make the poachers do what I want."

Helen looks up at her and nods, but I can tell she's not right . . . she's not completely there. She looks like one of those dolls Mrs. Weaver makes with the huge blinking eyes.

"I'll even let you wear my veil. For protection," Kiersten says, placing the netting on top of her head. "That's how much I believe in you."

"Hey, that's *my* veil," Hannah says from the crowd, but she's quickly shushed.

As Kiersten lowers the netting, they open the gate. I know I should turn around, walk away, Helen's made her choice, but I can't stop thinking about those scars on her feet, the ones her mother gave her for dreaming. "A seed of kindness," I whisper.

I'm terrified of even going near the gate, let alone through it, but I can't let this happen.

Pushing past the girls, I dart out after her. Some are screaming at me to turn back, but Kiersten says, "Let her go."

The second I leave the safety of the encampment, the sheer force of the wind coming off the great lake hits me, taking the air right out of my lungs. I stagger back a few steps. The openness, the nothingness . . . maybe I've been cooped up in there too long, but I don't feel free here, I only feel . . . exposed.

A caw in the distance slips under my skin. I'm not sure if it's real or imagined, but it's what I need to regain my focus.

Searching the vast landscape, the muted palette of autumn giving way to winter—blue to gray, green to beige— I spot a blur of movement. Helen's veil clinging to her like a cloud of low river gnats.

When the second caw arrives, I know it's real because Helen freezes in place. I'm running toward her, motioning for her to come back, but her eyes are fixed to the north, on an advancing poacher. Just the sight of him makes me woozy. He's covered from head to toe in a gauzy charcoal fabric, a gleaming blade in his hand. Everything inside me wants to turn away, but I can't let her die like this. For nothing.

Picking up my pace, I call out her name.

She looks at me, sheer panic washing over her face. "You can see me?"

"Run." I shove her back toward the encampment and then take off in the opposite direction. "Run!" I scream. I'm looking over my shoulder, making sure the poacher took the bait, when I trip on a tree root, skidding to the cold earth. Instead of closing my eyes, bracing myself for what's to come, I flip over to face my executioner. He raises his blade to deliver the blow—and then stops.

"Kick me." A soft whisper emanates from the thin dark cloth covering his nose and mouth.

I have no idea if he said it or if it's just the sickness settling in, but I'm not about to stick around and find out.

Pulling my knees in, I kick him as hard as I can. He reels back before doubling over on the ground.

I think about taking his knife, slitting his throat right then and there, but there's something about the way he looked at me—something in his eyes. I wonder if it's the same poacher I met on the trail . . . the one who let me go before. Leaning over his body, I'm sure it's him. I feel it in my gut. I'm reaching out to remove the cloth obscuring his face when I hear caws coming from each direction. Backing away from him, I run toward the gate.

As Helen makes it through, the gate starts to close. I'm thinking it must be a mistake, they just don't see me yet, but when the latch locks into place, I know this is Kiersten's doing.

Between the poachers' fevered calls and the girls' screeching, I can't think, I can't breathe. I'm pumping my legs as hard as I can when a dizzy spell crashes over me, tilting the very ground I'm running on, but I can't afford to give in to this. If I don't make it back over the fence, the only way I'll be going home is in a row of pretty glass bottles. Leaping onto the gate, I grab the dead girls' ribbons, pulling my way up, and when I run out of ribbon, I dig my fingernails into the splintery wood and claw my way to the top edge. I'm kicking my legs up, trying to get a foothold, but my thighs feel like they're made of lead. As one of the poachers gets within cutting distance, I exert everything I have, managing to pull myself over, but as soon as I hit the ground on the other side, Kiersten is on top of me.

Nostrils flaring, eyes raging, she pins me to the ground, the axe pressed against my throat.

"Why did you do that?" she demands. "Why did you interfere? You almost got her killed."

"I *saved* her . . ." I strain against the force of the blade to get the words out. "If I hadn't interfered she would've been—"

"Perfectly fine!" Kiersten screams, veins bulging in her temples. "And who do you think it was that saved *you*?" She thrusts the steel in a little deeper. "*I* did," she says. "*I'm* the one who made the poacher stop. They all witnessed it." She glances back at the crowd of girls. "Do you still deny our magic?"

I'm trying to speak, but I'm afraid. Afraid of the blade going in any deeper, but more afraid of my answer. "I . . .

I don't know what made him stop," I whisper, my eyes tearing up. "But it happened before . . . on the trail."

Kiersten shakes her head in disgust. "If you want to deny your magic, risk facing the gallows upon your return, be my guest. But don't drag the rest of them down with you." She pulls the blade back and I take a deep gasp of air, clutching my throat.

Kiersten stands to face the crowd. "We've tried to help her, but she's lost to us now. Anyone caught consorting with this heretic will be punished."

As I lie on the ground, watching them walk back toward the camp, I can see it in their eyes. This is the final bit of proof they needed, when all I could offer them was a secondhand dream.

But I know what I saw. I know what I felt.

They can call it magic.

I can call it madness.

But one thing is certain.

There is no grace here.

Just before dawn, a sickening wave of caws echo through the woods, and when the sun rises, slow and thick over the eastern fence, Ami isn't sitting by the gate anymore. I hear the girls whispering, saying Kiersten made her do it so she would stop singing that song, but I saw it in Ami's eyes long before our grace year. She was always far too delicate for this world. And now she's gone.

No one speaks to me anymore. No one even looks at me.

With all of the rain barrels destroyed, I have no choice but to drink from the well, but every time I get near it they chase me off.

Crawling along the perimeter, I lick the morning dew from the leaves, but it only makes me crave water all the more. My tongue feels thick, like it's taking up all the room in my mouth, and there are times when I think I can feel it swelling, like it might choke the life out of me.

Walking the fence, in a half-moon shape, from the very edge of the clearing on the west all the way to the edge of the clearing on the east, I listen to the lake rush in and out with the tide, but that's not all I hear. There's breathing. Heavy. Constant. Like a living shadow. Sometimes, I convince myself that it's Michael walking beside me, but Michael always talked my ear off. Or maybe it's Hans, but it doesn't feel like a protective presence. It's the silence that's killing me. Silence, knowing in my gut that it's the poacher.

"I know you're there," I whisper.

I come to an abrupt halt and listen, but there's no response.

I feel like a crazy person, and maybe I am. I think I crossed that line the moment I arrived in this cursed place, but I want to know why he didn't kill me on the trail, why he let me go when I went after Helen. I know it wasn't Kiersten's magic, because she was nowhere near me the first time. So, what stopped him?

In the early evening, lured to the fire by the smell of burning stew, I take my place in the back of the line. I know I'm taking a risk, but I'm too famished to care. Without food or water, I won't last long.

As I reach the front, I hold out my bowl. Katie scrapes the bottom of the kettle for the last scoop and pours it onto the ground. My stomach lets out an angry growl, but I can't afford to be picky right now.

I'm leaning down to scoop it into my bowl when Katie presses her boot into it, the gravy gurgling around the edges of her muddy sole.

I look around at the other girls, waiting for someone to speak up for me, but no one does. It hurts. Especially after everything I've done to try to help them . . . to help the camp.

Taking in a steeling breath, I walk past their glaring eyes into the lodging house to find dead space where my cot used to be, my belongings gone. I could get another dead girl's frame from the corner, drag it over, have them cackling at me behind my back, but I'm too tired. Tired of fighting, tired of caring, tired of everything. Curling up on the floor, I'm trying not to cry, but the harder I try, the worse it gets.

When the lodging house door creaks open, I hold my breath, hold myself still. A single set of boots comes toward me. I feel like that possum Michael and I found on the road leading to the meadow a few summers back. We thought it was dead, but it was just pretending. It seemed like such a useless survival skill at the time, but what else can you do when you feel completely defense-less. Outnumbered. Beaten.

The footsteps stop just short of my lower back. I'm bracing myself for impact when there's a soft tap on the floor, followed by a quick retreat. Picking up the lamp, I manage to catch a glimpse of the hem of a moss-green cloak leaving the lodging house. Gertie.

And where she stood, there's a small potato.

Snatching it up, I sink my teeth into it. The skin is scalding hot. It burns my throat to the point that I can't even taste it, but I don't care, anything for a moment of warmth. It takes everything I have not to devour it in one fell swoop, but I have to be smart about this. After all, I'm not sure how long my punishment will last. Tucking the remaining half into my pocket, I feel the smallest shred of hope.

"You," Kiersten says, loud enough to wake the entire island. "You stole from the larder. How dare you."

"What?" I struggle to prop myself on my elbows. "I did no such thing."

"Empty your pockets," Kiersten yells at me.

The potato.

"Hold her down," Kiersten says.

The other girls grab me while Kiersten rifles through the pockets of my cloak.

A satisfied grin spreads across her lips like wildfire as she pulls the cold, half-eaten potato from my pocket.

"She's the one that told us we need to ration, trust in each other," Jenna says.

"She only did that so she could steal from us," a voice hisses against the back of my neck.

"I didn't steal it. I swear—"

"Then who gave it to you?" Kiersten asks.

I shoot Gertie a nervous look. "I . . . I just found it."

"Liar," she seethes.

The girls tighten their grip.

"And what happens to girls who spread lies?" Kiersten asks.

"They lose their tongues," the girls answer in unison.

Kiersten smiles down at me. I know that smile. "Get the calipers."

As the mob drags me out of the lodging house toward the punishment tree, I scream for her to stop, but I know it's no use. Kiersten is the only God here, and she wants everyone to know it.

Ellie skips over to us with a rusty iron clamp.

Kiersten then grabs my face, squeezing so hard that I can feel my teeth cutting into the inside of my cheeks. "Stick out your tongue," she commands.

I'm shaking my head, tears are burning the back of my eyes, clouding my vision, but I hear Gertie yelling, "Stop . . . I did it." She pushes through the crowd to get to us. "I gave her the potato," she says, pulling Kiersten away from me.

"How could you?" Kiersten seethes. "After I gave you a second chance? After I forgave you?"

"Forgave her?" I blurt. "You're the one who should be begging Gertie for forgiveness. I know what you did. That was *your* lithograph. You took it from your father's study and blamed it on Gertie. You ruined her life."

Kiersten raises a brow. "Is that what she told you?"

"Come on, Tierney, let's go," Gertie says, locking her arm through mine.

"Yes, it was my father's lithograph," Kiersten says. "But that's not why she was charged with depravity."

"Please . . . don't." Gertie shakes her head, a haunted look on her face.

"Do you know what she did?" Kiersten asks, her eyes welling up.

"Don't listen to her . . . ," Gertie urges, but I hold my ground.

"She tried to kiss me. And I knew then and there what she was . . . what she wanted," she says, her chin trembling with rage. "She wanted me to do the dirty things that were in that picture. Sin against God."

I feel the weight of Gertie's body and I realize her knees must've gone soft. Clenching my arm tighter around hers, we take our first step back toward the lodging house, when Gertie's head jerks back.

The sickening sound of a blade scraping against the back of her skull makes my blood turn cold.

I turn to find her crouched on the ground next to me, Kiersten standing over her with Gertie's ribboned braid coiled around her fist. At the end, a bloody patch of scalp drips in the moonlight.

"You're a monster," I whisper.

"And you're a fool," Kiersten says, rolling her shoulders back. "But I am not without mercy. I'll give you a choice. Embrace your magic . . . or face the woods."

The girls stand there, watching in anticipation.

I look to Gertie, but she's huddled in a tight ball on the ground, rocking back and forth like a broken seesaw.

"I can't . . . ," I whisper back. "I can't accept something I don't feel."

"So be it," Kiersten says with the wave of Gertie's scalp. "Good-bye."

"Now?" I ask, fighting for control of my breath. "I can't . . . it's dark . . . at least give me until morning."

"My mercy has run out."

"Wait," I say, trying to get her attention. "I can try. What do you want me to do? Take off my clothes, howl at the moon? Do you want me to put my hand in the fire, roll around in sumac?"

"Do you hear something?" she says mockingly, swatting the air in front of her. "There's an annoying gnat buzzing in my ear."

"Or I'll take the punishment. Do you want a finger . . .

an ear . . . my braid? I'll do whatever you want, but don't make me—"

"Get rid of her."

Without hesitation, the girls pick up the rocks from around the fire pit and start pelting them at me. One whizzes right past me, narrowly missing my temple, and I take off.

Stinging branches whip at my skin as I fight my way through dense foliage. I look up at the sky to get my bearings, but the moon and stars are hidden beneath the clouds as if they can't bear to lay witness. I'm running when something grabs me by my skirts. I start swinging my fists wildly but only make contact with a thicket. I'm trying to untangle myself when I hear it behind me. Or maybe it's right next to me. Is it a ghost, trying to take over my body? Or a wild animal starved for human flesh? Whatever it is, it's something I can feel over every inch of my skin. Something watching me.

Yanking my skirt free, I take off running in the opposite direction—at least I think it's the opposite direction. My heart is pounding, my limbs are burning with the strain, but my head is empty, some deeper part of me taking over.

I'm pummeling through the darkness, running blind, for what feels like hours, until I hit something solid.

Stunned from the impact, I stagger back; shocks of blunt pain ricochet through my limbs. At first I think I must've run into a giant tree, but when I reach out to touch it, it's too smooth, like it's been stripped clean.

"The fence," I whisper. Sinking down next to it, I'm happy to find something familiar. Something to anchor me to reality. As the heat of my escape quickly leaves me, the chill sinks in. I'm pulling my cloak tighter around me when I hear heavy breathing. I'm hoping it's my own, but when I place my hands over my mouth, it's still present, steady as the grandfather clock in our front hall.

"Is that you?" I whisper through my trembling fingers.

There's no reply, but I swear I can feel the heat from the poacher's body seeping through the cracks in the wood. It's the same feeling I had when I first encountered him on the trail.

"Why didn't you kill me?" I ask, pressing my palms to the fence. "Twice you've let me go."

I listen closely. There's a sound of a blade being released from a sheath.

"You won't hurt me," I whisper, resting my cheek against the splintery wood. "I know it."

As the cloud cover breaks, unveiling a full moon and a swath of bright stars, a blade comes shooting through the narrow gap in the fence, nicking my chin.

I jump to my feet. The sudden movement makes me dizzy, or maybe it's the warm blood coursing down my throat. As the glint of steel recedes, I peer inside the slit to find cold, dark eyes staring back at me. His breath is so loud in my ears now that it's all I can hear. I stagger back a few steps before the world tips on end, sending me crashing to the cold hard ground, a veil of darkness spreading over me like a thick lead blanket.

WINTER

Glittering bony branches hulk and sway above me. My breath hangs heavy in the air. Propping myself up to get a look at my surroundings, I flinch as the harsh wind hits my chin. I touch it—the sticky clotting of blood, the dirt caked beneath my nails, stinging the cut.

"Last night really happened," I whisper.

Peering through the gap in the fence where the blade came through, I can't believe I thought he wouldn't hurt me. I don't hear the breathing anymore, but I'm not going to get close enough to be certain. Father said that was one of my best traits: I didn't need to learn a lesson twice. Maybe the poacher assumed I was dead and moved on. The idea of him watching me while I lay there unconscious, bleeding, makes me sick to my stomach.

Staring into the dense forest, separating me from the camp, I know what I have to do. Ghosts or not, I won't last another day without water. Even thinking about it makes my tongue ache. The animals must be drinking from somewhere.

As I get to my feet, the dizziness sets back in. I have to lean over and brace my hands against my knees to get the world to stop spinning. I'm thinking I need to throw up, but I only dry-heave a few times. There's nothing in there. Not even spit.

Holding on to a sapling for balance, I take my first step back into the woods. The wind rustles through the high branches, making me shiver. Even the sound of the ground cover crunching beneath my boots feels sinister.

I used to love the woods. I'd spend every moment of my free time exploring the depths of hidden treasures, but this is different.

A bird lets out a shriek of warning. And I can't help wondering if the warning is for the other birds or for me.

"I am my father's daughter," I whisper, straightening my spine. I believe in medicine. In facts. In truths. I will not get caught up in superstition. Maybe the ghosts are something you have to believe in for them to hurt you. I need to think that way, because right now my nerves are dangling by a thread.

I have no idea where I am, how far I got from the camp last night, but as I look up to get my bearings, the sky is no help. It looks like it's been smeared with river clay—a drab, endless swath of pewter. Back home, I hardly thought about the sun, but out here, it's everything.

When it briefly pops out, I rush to a spot where it's beaming down, longing to feel it on my skin, but by the time I reach it, it's gone. It feels personal now, like Eve is toying with me.

As I crawl over a large cluster of limestone to try to catch another beam of light, I spot a patch of bright green algae clinging to the edge of a small pool of water. Just the sight of it makes my throat burn with thirst. How long has it been since I've had something to drink? Hours . . . days . . . I can't recall. But as I move toward it, I catch something. A swish of a tail. There's a creature hunched beside the pond. It raises its head—two beady black eyes glare back at me. I recognize the perky ears, the pointed nose, the copper coloring of its fur—but there's something wrong. Blinking hard, I see a fox, but it looks as if someone's painted a bright red smiley face over its mouth and whiskers. I've heard the rumors that the animals are mad in the woods, but when I look closer, I see the small rabbit splayed open at its feet. Blood oozes into the stagnant pool like a pot of ink tipped over in the rain.

My stomach lurches. My head feels so light, like it could float off my body at any moment. Pressing my face against the cool mossy stone, I try to get hold of myself. "You're okay. It will pass." I think about waiting for the fox to leave, drinking the bloody water, but as a breeze passes over me, I follow it up a steep incline, and remember my mother telling me that water is best when collected high on the spring. And that water had to come from somewhere.

Following the faint trickling sound, I use the holly bushes to guide me up the wooded hill, but every time I grab them, the points prick my fingers. My feet are unsteady. My vision blurs to the point that I have to stop every few yards to gain my composure, but when I finally reach the top, I'm met with the most welcome sight—water gushing through the limestone, forming a small deep pool. The water looks crystal clear, no sign of the algae . . . or blood . . . but I need to be careful. It's hard to know what's real anymore. Crawling toward the surface, I lean over, sinking my hands into the frigid water, scooping it into my mouth. Most of it dribbles down my chin, soaking my dress, but I don't care. It tastes clean—nothing like the water from the well.

As I go in for another drink, I see something twitch at the bottom of the pool. Clinging between two large rocks, there's a cluster of dark shells that look like rolled-up shoe leather. Mollusks of some kind.

I know I could catch my death going in after them, but I might very well die from hunger if I don't. Stripping off my clothes, I try to ease into the water at first, but every inch feels like I'm being skinned alive. Letting out three short pants, I plunge my entire body under the water. The shock seems to revive me a bit, making me move a little quicker. I pry two of them loose, but there's one that's really rooted in there. As I come up for air, I place the two shells on the edge and hop out to grab a jagged rock. The air feels so nice and warm that I don't want to go back under again, but I need as much food as I can get.

Diving back under the surface, I'm digging the rock into the crevice, trying to pry the third one free, when I think of a time my father took me to the big river. I was so keen on catching my first fish. First line in, I caught a beautiful rainbow trout. It fought so hard that it took all my strength to reel it in. Even when I got it to the shore, it flipped its body all over the place, thrashing its head from side to side, and when I went to hit it with a stick, my father unhooked it and threw it back in. "You have to respect something that wants to live that bad," he said. I remember being furious at him, but I understand it now.

This little one isn't ready to give in. And neither am I.

Pushing back to the surface, I pull myself out of the spring, grab my clothes, and immediately start working on the two shells I harvested, but I'm shivering so hard I can barely hold on to the rock. "Breathe, Tierney," I whisper.

Pulling up the hood of my cloak, I sink into a tight ball, blowing hot air into the gap until the feeling comes back in my fingers.

Trying it once again, with steady hands, I use the rock to gently pry open the shell. The cream-colored flesh, the pinks and blues and grays lining the inside of the shell—I don't know exactly what it is, but it's some kind of mussel or clam. I poke it and it flinches. At home, we'd slurp these down as quickly as possible so we wouldn't have to taste them, but I want to taste it. I want to taste anything other than bile. I only hope I can keep it down. Carefully separating the mussel from the shell, I take it in. I chew every bit of it, savoring it all the way to the very last drop of murky liquid. I wanted to save the other one for later, but I can't wait. Prying it open, I suck the mussel into my mouth, and immediately bite down on something hard. I'm thinking it's just a piece of shell that broke off, but as I spit it out into my hand, I realize it's a river clam pearl, just like the ones from my veiling day dress. Turning it over in my hand, I study every facet, every hint of iridescent color, every dent and rise. These are rare. And now I have two. I put it in my pocket, nestling it with the one June gave me. Maybe when I get home I can give these to Clara and Penny. And I realize that's the first time in months I've even thought about going home—about getting out of here alive.

A light brushing sound grabs my attention. It's too soft to be leaves. There's something about it that reminds me of home.

Climbing to the top of the ridge, above the spring, I find a wide plateau, covered in the shriveled remains of weeds, a tiny pop of color on the right side.

As I walk toward it, I'm trying not to get too carried away, but what if it's the flower from my dream?

Getting on my hands and knees, I see it's not the flower but the frayed end of a red ribbon. A surge of excitement rushes through me. If other grace year girls were here . . . if they survived the wood . . . then so can I.

I tug on the strand, but it seems to be stuck on something. As I adjust my body so I can pull it up with a little more force, I feel something crunch beneath my knee. It's an unnatural sound, like a broken piece of china. Pushing away the dead weeds and clumps of dirt, I find something solid. I'm trying to figure out what it is when my thumb jams through a hole in the rock.

Only it's not a hole . . . and this isn't a rock.

It's a human skull with molars still attached.

The red ribbon garroted around the neck bones.

My stomach tightens into a hard knot. Dropping the skull to the ground, I frantically try to cover it back up with dirt, but all I can think about is the girls who went into the woods and never came back.

Maybe the ghost stories are true.

Wanting to put as much distance as I can between my-self and whatever dark truth lies at the top of the ridge, I careen down the hill and immediately lose my footing, rolling the rest of the way down, bashing into a rotting tree stump. I'm lying on my back, staring up at the vast sky. There's a part of me that wonders if I'm already dead. If those are my bones. Maybe a hundred years have passed in the blink of an eye and I'm nothing but a shadow now. But as my vision slowly comes back into focus, so does the pain. Being dead shouldn't hurt this much. Using a tan-gle of exposed roots, I pull myself up. It takes a few min-utes for my brain to catch up with my body, but I don't have time to give in to whatever this is. The sun is begin-ning to wane.

The smell of oats burning in a cast-iron skillet draws me back toward the camp. I try to mark my path the best I can so I can find my way back to the spring, if need be. Settling in an evergreen near the perimeter, I watch them in the clearing, laughing, carrying on—as if they don't have a care in the world. They're happy I'm gone. I don't know if it's jealousy talking or my imagination gone askew, but there's something about them that reminds me of the trappers coming back from the outskirts, hopped up on hemlock silt, reeking of mischief. It's hard to believe that just a few days ago, I was one of them. It feels like a world away.

Gertrude walks across the clearing, the back of her head glistening in the dying light. I'm leaning forward to see if I can somehow get her attention, tell her I'm all right, when one of the branches snaps beneath me. It gets Gertie's attention, but unfortunately, it gets Kiersten's, as well.

I'm balancing my weight, trying not to make another sound, as the girls gravitate to the edge of the clearing.

"It's a ghost," Jenna whispers.

"Maybe it's Tierney," Helen says, nuzzling Dovey under her chin. "Looking for revenge."

"She wouldn't dare come back here, dead or alive," Kiersten says, narrowing her eyes. "There's a lot more I can cut off of Gertie if she decides to test me."

And I swear she's staring right at me, like she's whispering directly in my ear.

Jumping down, I back away from the tree . . . from Kiersten's eyes, and retreat into the woods.

Like a ghost, I walk through the night.

I don't know where I am . . . where I'm going, but I'm not lost, because there's no one looking for me. Nowhere to go. I thought being with the girls at the camp, watching them slowly slip into madness, was the loneliest I could ever feel.

I was wrong.

I spend my days memorizing the woods, cutting new paths, looking for food, and in the evenings, I batten down wherever I can, under a fallen log, a rain-whipped hollow in a rock, but I never stay in the same place twice. The abundance of animal tracks lets me know I'm not alone in here, and by the size of the prints, I can tell there are much more frightening things in here than ghosts.

The only upside is that being away from the camp seems to have given me some clarity. I still get dizzy from time to time, but I don't feel as unhinged, as if the earth might open up and swallow me whole. Maybe just being around each other is what's making the sickness spread. A poison of the mind.

Other than a lucked-upon scavenged root, or the occasional acorn a squirrel gave up on, I haven't eaten in weeks. My stomach doesn't growl anymore. It doesn't even hurt. When I take in a deep breath, I imagine the air filling me up, sustaining me. I don't know if it's good or bad, but it seems to be enough.

Occasionally, I get a whiff of chicory water or fatty meat roasting over an open flame, but I know the girls don't have anything like that in the camp. Even if they did, they're not in the right frame of mind to pull off a meal like that.

I follow the scent all the way to the fence. There's a part of me that wants to claw my way over the barrier to get to it, but maybe that's how they'll lure me out. Or maybe it's my mind playing tricks on me.

Father had a patient a few years ago who insisted he smelled dandelion greens in the dead of winter. That was right before something exploded inside his head and he bled out.

"No." I give my braid a hard tug. I need to stay focused—steer clear of the fence. I don't care that the girl from my dreams led me here.

I know enough from eavesdropping on the fur trappers returning from the wilds to understand that the real enemy out here isn't the wildlife or even the elements, it's your own mind. I always thought of myself as such a solitary creature—oh, how I longed to be alone—but I didn't real-ize until I got out here how much of that is false. Some-thing I told myself to feel strong . . . better than the rest. I spent most of my life watching people, judging them, sorting them into some category or another, because it kept the focus off myself. I wonder what I'd see if I came across Tierney James today. And now I'm talking about myself in the third person.

I try to stay busy, but it's harder than one might think. When I feel myself drifting to that shadowy realm behind my mind's eye, that place of doubt and blame, guilt and remorse, I pull myself back with little tasks. I weave a rope so I can pull myself up the incline easier. I remember Mi-chael and I doing that a few summers back so we could reach the bluff over Turtle Pond. I'll never forget that feeling, leaping off the ridge into nothing but air, hitting the cool water with a tremendous splash.

Thinking about him hurts. I'm not pining after him like some veil-hungry schoolgirl. It hurts to think about how wrong I was about his feelings for me. It makes me wonder if I've been wrong about other things, too. Important things.

Taking shelter from the wind behind a giant oak, I press my body against the bark. At first, it feels grounding, something to remind me that I'm still a human being, but my thoughts eventually turn into wondering if I'll be petrified here, if I'll become one with the tree. A hundred years from now people will pass by, and a girl will tug on her father's sleeve. "Do you see the girl in the tree?" she'll ask. And he'll pat her on her head. "You have a grand imagination." Maybe if she looks closely, she'll be able to see me blink. If she places her palm against the bark, she'll be able to feel my heart still beating.

On clear mornings, I climb past the spring, all the way to the ridge. Every day it gets a little harder, but it's worth it. Through a sea of barren branches, I get a glimpse of the entire island, encircled by a crust of ice, which slowly gives way to the deepest blue water I've ever seen.

If I didn't know what this place was, the horror of what goes on here, I'd say it's breathtaking.

But the bones are a constant reminder.

Whether it's the girl from my dreams or a nameless faceless girl from the county, she's always here to remind me of what could happen if I slip up. If I let my guard down.

However she met her end, I hope she had time to make her peace. Father once treated a trapper from the wilds with a hatchet lodged in his skull, his body convulsing with the slightest movement. My father gave him a choice. Pull it out and hemorrhage quickly or leave it in and die a slow death. The trapper chose the latter. I remember thinking it was the coward's choice, but now I'm not so sure. There's no such thing as a gentle death, so why give it a helping hand? He fought hard for his very last breath. Running my hand over the dirt, I want to believe she did the same. Maybe she crawled all the way from the camp, to the highest point on the island for refuge. Dying with a view like this wouldn't be the worst way to go.

But the darkest part of me can't help but wonder if her own kind did this to her. If that's what will happen to me.

Today, there's a large plume of smoke rising from the girls' camp. Clearly, they're using green wood. A number of other small wisps of smoke can be seen wafting up from the shore in every direction, which leads me to believe the poachers must have camps of their own. They appear to be stationed around the island in perfect intervals. It tells me they're organized. Methodical. I still haven't figured out how they get to us, how they break us down to poach us, but I'm doing my best to keep my wits about me.

I'd like to stay up on the ridge forever, but I tire easily now. Even standing up to the wind blowing against me feels like work. Sometimes I feel like it might pick me up and carry me off to another land. But that's magical thinking. There's nothing magical about starving and freezing to death.

As I climb down the ridge to start another mind-numbing

day of foraging for roots, I see a large rodent pop up from the spring with the last river clam perched between his teeth.

"Muskrat," I hiss.

As he takes off down the hill, I go barreling after him. I'm chasing him through the forest, past a huge grove of pines, all the way to the barrier, where he stops. I'm thinking I have him trapped when he turns and burrows his way under the fence. I lunge for him, reaching my hand all the way through the hole, but it's too late.

Resting my cheek on the ground, I start to weep. I know it's pathetic, but it felt like as long as that river clam survived, so could I. But the truth is, I'm running out of time. Out of resources.

I'm staring at the hole in the bottom of the fence, trying to think about what the hell I'm going to do, when it strikes me: the fence—Hans.

On our way to the encampment, Hans told me that he was in charge of maintaining the barrier, that he wanted to be close by. If the fence is reported as being damaged, he'll have to come and fix it. I know it's against the law to fraternize with the guards, but Hans is my friend. He's always protected me in the county as much as he could. If he threw my pack over the fence when we first got here, maybe he'd be willing to bring me food—even a blanket, just so I could get back on my feet.

But no one's ever going to notice a muskrat-sized hole this far from the gate. Checking out the wood, I see the enormous cedar log is rotting out. When I pick at it, chunks come off easily in my hand. But I don't have the time or energy to pick away at it for days. Using the heel of my boot, I kick at the soft wood until there's a hole big enough to pass a kettle through—surely something even the dumbest poacher would notice and report.

And so I sit.

And I wait.

It seems far-fetched, at best. But I'm desperate.

A vicious wind races through the gap in the fence; I pull my cloak tighter around my shoulders. I can't believe I used to love this time of year—all bundled up in woolen cocoons, to the point where no one could discern one child from the next. Not the women. After their grace year, their faces needed to be free and clear to make sure they weren't hiding their magic. The wives scarcely went outdoors during those months. But come spring, when they emerged, it was like watching butterflies shake free of their chrysalis. Little things, like taking the long way to the market. Moving to a different side of the lane just to catch a beam of sunlight.

Occasionally, I'd see one of them slip off her shoe, placing an unstockinged toe into the freshly sprung grass. A hint of wild decadence, a secret place within her heart that could never truly be tamed.

Lying down on a nest of gathered leaves and bark, I stare through the hole in the fence, memorizing every divot, every crack, every splinter in the rotten wood, and I can't help wondering if that's what my insides look like now, or if there's nothing left inside of me but a hollow space.

Turning my focus to the vast sky above, I let my mind wander over the land. There are times when it feels unfathomable that life is continuing elsewhere. The poachers are living their lives, the grace year girls are living theirs, my parents, my sisters, Michael—for everyone else, time is moving forward, but all I have is this. It feels as if I'm slowly losing touch with reality, with time, with even being a human. Everything's boiled down to the bare necessity. Eat. Evacuate. Sweat. Shiver. Sleep. This is what it means to exist. All those years at home, I was biding my time, waiting for my real life to begin, but *that* was my real life, as good as it would ever get, and I didn't even know it.

It's so cold, I can see my breath hovering around me. If I close my eyes I can smell the colors green and yellow, feel the sunshine on my skin, but when I open them all I see is gray and brown, the scent of death filling my nostrils, maybe my own. A slow deterioration of body and spirit.

I thought I only closed my eyes for a moment, but it must've been longer. A few hours, or maybe it's been days, but dark is on its way.

With just enough light to gather some wood that might be dry enough to catch, I scoop up a handful of leaves, making a small nest. Using my flint, I hover over it—spark after spark after spark until it finally ignites.

Gathering the nest in my hands, I gently blow. It makes me think of Michael, when we were kids, blowing on dandelions, making wishes.

I always wished for a truthful life. I never asked him what he wished for—I wonder if he wished for me.

At the unveiling ceremony, he said, *You don't have to change for me.* But that's not entirely true. In that moment, I became his property. A slower death for me than anything I'd face out here. As much as he thinks he loves me—his allegiance to his family, his faith, his sex will always prevail. I saw a flash of that when we got in an argument on veiling day. He can tell himself he's only trying to protect me, but there will always be something in him that wants to contain me, hide me from the world.

The nursery rhyme that Ami was singing lilts through the trees. Without thinking, I sing along with her.

Eve with the golden hair, sits on high in her rocking chair,

The wind doth blow, the night unfurls, weeping for all the men she's cursed.

Girls beware, if you don't behave, you'll be sent to an early grave.

I'm not sure how long I sit there, staring into the flames, singing her song, but the fire's dwindled to embers now, and mine is the only voice in the forest. Maybe she was never singing at all. And then I remember that Ami is dead.

Curling up into a tight ball next to the fire, I carefully tuck in my cloak around me. Once I'm satisfied that every gap has been tended to, I settle in. The trick is to lie perfectly still. One wrong move and the cold air will invade my space like a brutal army. And once the chill sets in, it'll be nearly impossible to shake.

I'm lying there shivering, praying for sleep, when I hear something enter my campsite. At first I think it might be the ghost, the girl buried on the ridge, but the footsteps are too heavy, the deep huffing of air too loud, the scent too foul. This is something entirely corporal. Animal.

I think about running, but I'm too tired to move, too weak to fight anything off, and if I leave this fire, if I leave my meager cocoon, I might very well freeze to death anyway. Instead, I lie perfectly still, staring into the embers, willing whatever it is to pass me by, but it only comes closer, so close that I can feel it hovering over me. It nudges my spine. My mind is telling me to flee, but I force my body to stay limp. Play dead. That's my only defense right now, which honestly isn't that far from the truth.

The animal lets out a horrifying groan; a long strand of drool drips onto my cheek. I know that sound. I know that smell. *Bear.* I have to clench my jaw to stop myself from screaming. It's nudging me with its snout, pawing at my side. The sound of its claws ripping through the wool of my cloak makes me feel faint. I'm thinking this is it, how I'll meet my end, when I hear something drop on the forest floor a few feet away. The bear must've heard it, too, because it decides to stop mauling me long enough to investigate. I hear gnashing teeth, followed by another thud, this time a little further away. And then another thud, even further. With every step it takes away from me, I breathe a little easier, and when I hear it reach the ravine, on the other side of the pines, I know it somehow decided to move on. Wanting to wipe the rancid drool from my face, I reach out to grab a leaf, and my hand brushes against something warm and wet. Picking up one of the burning logs, I hold it close, squinting into the void to find the fatty remains of a mangled piece of fresh meat. Without even thinking, I shove it in my mouth. I'm gagging and chewing at the same time, disgusted and grateful for this tiny miracle. Looking up at the trees, I'm wondering where it could've possibly dropped from, and that's when I hear it. There's someone on the other side of the fence.

Crawling forward, I whisper through the hole in the wood, "Hans, is that you?"

But the only reply is his retreating footsteps.

At the first hint of cold gray dawn, I brace my hands on the frozen ground to get up, then notice small flecks strewn all around me.

At first I think it might be snow—the air has felt that way for days—but it's the wrong shape, the wrong color: cream with specks of light red. I poke it with my boot; it rolls over. A bean. I'm sure of it. When I lean forward to pick it up, more beans fall to the ground.

Where did these come from? I'm thinking Hans might've thrown these in along with the meat, but when I stand, I see another one fall from my cloak.

Slipping my fingers inside the clawed edges of wool, I feel a series of small hard bumps. Carefully opening the stitches of the hem, I peel back the soft gray, revealing an intricate maze of seeds that have been sewn into each layer of the lining. Hundreds of them.

Pumpkin, tomato, celery, and a few I don't even recognize.

"June," I whisper, the realization taking the breath from my body. She must've worked on this for months, but how did she know I would need these? Unless what's happening to me happened to her. Clamping my hand over my mouth, I try to stifle a sobbing gasp, but it can't be stopped. Tears are streaming down my cheeks, and all I can think about is how much I want to see her again. How much I want to see all of them—my mother and father. Clara and Penny, Ivy . . . even Michael. I want to thank them, say I'm sorry, but in order to do that, I need to survive this.

For weeks, I've felt like I've been moving under thick water, but not today, not in this moment. Despite the gloomy weather, the cold nipping at my flesh, the emptiness festering inside of me, I have a spring in my step. A newfound bit of hope, one that I've been carrying with me all this time.

Climbing the incline, I pass the spring, the bones of the girl, and fight my way to the highest ridge. I remember June said she sewed in different layers of lining for each new season, but I'm just going to plant them all. I may not even make it to the next season.

I know next to nothing about gardening, just the little bits I've picked up from June's stories, but I seem to remember a little nursery song she taught Clara and Penny. I even remember the hand motions that go with it. I feel silly for doing it, but it brings an unexpected smile to my face. *"Dig, drop, cover, pat . . . water, sun, grow, eat."* I raise my head to the sky, willing the sun to come out, to give me a sign, when something falls in my eye. My skin prickles up in a fresh wave of goosebumps. "Snow," I whisper, my heart sinking in my chest.

At home, I would be ecstatic for the first snow. Michael and I would spend the whole day planning our snow kingdom, stuffing handfuls down each other's backside, wandering home at dusk with numb fingers, eyelashes caked with glittering ice. I'd thaw by the hearth, sipping mulled cider, peeling off one layer at a time, with the sound of my mother taking out her frustration on her knitting needles, the crinkle of Father's paper, the serene voices of Clara and Penny taking turns reading a chapter from a book.

Blinking hard, I try to erase the memories from my brain, but I'm too weak to stop them anymore. I need this garden to work.

Wiping away my tears, I frantically dig my fingers into the soil, but the ground is nearly frozen solid. Any sane person would wait until spring, but I don't have that luxury.

Using sharp rocks and sticks, I burn through the daylight, I burn through every last bit of my energy, tilling that soil, until I can no longer feel my hands. And as the sun begins to set, the cold air settles deep into my marrow, threatening to freeze me in place. A part of me wants to curl up, close my eyes, but I know I'll never be able to get up again. I'll die on this ridge, and as weak and tired as I am, I'm not ready to give up yet.

With bloody, battered fingers, I place each seed into the soil and cover it with the freezing earth. I say a silent prayer for each one of them. I know it's against the law for women to pray in silence, but I'm the only God here.

With the last seed in place, I take a look around to see the snow has blanketed the forest around me, like it's hiding me from the world, tucking me in for a long forgotten nightmare.

"Why are you doing this to me?" I whisper.

The clouds let out a deep groan, as if in response; goosebumps erupt over my entire body.

Thunder snow.

"It's just a coincidence. That's all," I say as I gather my things, but before I can descend the incline, another burst of thunder shakes the very ground beneath me.

Eve will not be denied.

The storm bears down on the island like a heavy omen.

I know I should find shelter until it passes, I've heard about storms like these from the trappers, but if this garden doesn't make it, neither will I.

Flipping up the hood of my cloak, I brace myself as I push against the ice, wind, and snow. It's hard to see the next step in front of me, let alone where the rows are so I can step between them.

A crack of lightning pierces the air, striking the ground in front of me. All my hair is standing on end, but I'm okay, I'm thinking the garden is okay, when the earth lets out a terrifying groan and the ground begins to shift. I'm rushing around the ridge, digging my freezing hands into the dirt, manically trying to push the soil back together, but it's disintegrating beneath me. Scrabbling upward, I manage to hold on to some vines as half of the ridge breaks off, thundering to the bottom of the ravine.

As I look down at the seeds, floating away down the eroding bank, I start to weep. That was everything I had. My last chance. And all I can do is watch it wash away, slip right through my fingers. Pulling myself back onto the ledge, I look up to the sky and I scream, "What did I do to deserve this?"

A burst of thunder seems to answer back, louder than lions, and I can feel her power, her ire, and it makes me angry—somehow I feel betrayed by her, but there were no promises made, no secret pacts to be broken. No one told me that this would be fair, that this would be easy. I can't help feeling that maybe I'm not meant to be here. Maybe I'm not meant to survive this. I scream as long and hard as I can, raging against everything that brought me here, and when I collapse into the frozen mud, a scream echoes back to me, a scream that isn't my own.

At first I think it might be a trapped animal, the final cry of a dying elk, but when it happens again, I know it's human. A blood-curdling scream, and it's coming from the direction of the camp.

"Gertrude," I whisper.

Abandoning the ruined garden, I run through the woods. I know the way by heart now, every fallen log, every wicked branch.

As I get closer, the screaming grows, but there's also laughing and singing. I break into the clearing to find girls spinning in circles, covering themselves in mud and snow. One of the girls is standing on top of the privy, waving her hands around, as if she's orchestrating the entire thing.

"Have you seen my veil?" A girl stumbles toward me, soaked to the bone, ice clinging to her dark lashes. It's Molly. I want to tell her she doesn't have a veil, but she's already wandered off in a daze.

I can't tell if they've gotten worse or I've just gotten better, but this is pure insanity.

Kiersten grabs Tamara's hand, pulling her into the center of the clearing. They're dancing wildly, spinning faster and faster, laughing and shrieking into the inky darkness, when a flash of lightning needles through the sky, striking the earth before them. I can smell the electricity in the air, but it's more than that. I smell burning hair and searing flesh. Tamara is on the ground, her body convulsing in a shallow puddle.

Helen staggers forward to get a closer look and then covers her mouth. It's hard to tell if she's laughing or crying—maybe she doesn't even know which.

Another flash of lightning beats down, making everyone duck for cover, everyone except Kiersten, who's grabbing Tamara's twitching arms, dragging her toward the fence. "Open the gate," Kiersten yells.

"Wait . . . what are you doing?" I run into the clearing, but Kiersten shoves me out of the way.

"I'm doing her a mercy," Kiersten says.

Tamara's eyes lock in on mine. She still can't speak, but I see the terror.

"You can't." I get back on my feet. "She's still breathing."

"Do you want her sisters to be sent to the outskirts?" Kiersten asks. "She deserves an honorable death."

As the girls rush forward to open the gate, I plead with them to stop, but it's as if they don't even see me . . . hear me.

Searching the clearing, I'm looking for anyone who'll listen when I see Gertrude hiding behind the punishment tree, tears streaming down her face. That's how I know she's still in there: no matter what's happening, no matter how far we fall, somewhere inside, she knows this is wrong.

As they lift Tamara's body to throw her out of the encampment, an enormous flash of lightning erupts over the camp, illuminating her face stretched into a soundless scream of horror.

The light dissipates; the dense thud of Tamara's body hits the ground. The eerie creak of the gate is followed by the clunk of the closing latch, like the final nail in a coffin.

Crowding against the fence, the girls press their faces against the gaps in the splintery wood, vying for a glimpse.

Sick caw noises echo from the shore.

As heavy footsteps descend on the other side of the gate, I back away.

I don't need to see it to know what's happening. I can hear it. I can feel it—blades ripping into flesh, Tamara's soundless scream winding up, building steam until that's all I can hear.

A few of the girls have to turn away, Jessica clenching her eyes shut, Martha crouching on the ground, everything in her stomach coming up at once, but they will never be able to escape what they've witnessed. What they've done. The rest stand there, unable to tear their eyes away from the carnage—this feels like judgment to them, God's will, but it's really just the will of Kiersten.

"You killed her," I say. "Tamara was one of your closest friends, and you murdered her."

Kiersten turns on me, a savage look in her eyes.

"Is . . . is that Tierney?" Helen staggers toward me, Dovey peeking out of the pocket of her cloak.

"She's back?" Katie asks, poking at my arm. "How?"

Jenna gets right in my face. Her pupils are so large they look like flat black marbles. "Is she a ghost?"

Kiersten picks up the axe resting against the fence. "There's only one way to find out."

As she stalks toward me, I'm backing up to the perimeter.

With every step, I feel the weight in my limbs, my blistered feet sloshing around in my boots, my heart throbbing in my throat.

The girls are buzzing all around me, like black flies on a fresh carcass.

"Everyone knows ghosts don't bleed . . . so all we have to do is—" Kiersten loses her balance and stumbles forward, slamming into me with such force that it makes me stagger back a few steps.

The girls look on with wide eyes. Kiersten's jaw goes slack; there's a low, nervous chuckle seeping from her throat.

And soon, they're all laughing.

Following their gaze, I look down to find the axe embedded between my shoulder and my chest. It looks fake—like the sawed-off iron spikes we glue onto Father Edmonds's hands and feet for the crucifixion ceremony at Passover.

Gripping the handle with both hands, I give it a hard tug, which only makes them laugh harder. I keep pulling until the axe finally gives, and with it comes the blood. Too much blood.

They're laughing so hard now that tears are streaming down their faces.

They think this is some kind of game.

But I'm still standing. And there's no one holding me back anymore.

Clutching the axe in my right hand, I take off running, barreling through the woods. I was sure they wouldn't follow. I was wrong. My only advantage is I know the terrain—but what the girls lack in know-how, they seem to make up for in determination.

"Over here," someone screams behind me.

Even tripping, running into tree branches, into each other, they seem to get right back up again, as if the pain doesn't affect them. Maybe it's magic or maybe it's whatever's infecting them, but my best bet is to hide, wait them out.

Leaping over a fallen cedar, I scoot back into the dark recess to catch my breath. Two girls vault over behind me; one of them lands wrong, and the sound of her ankle snapping makes me cringe, but somehow she manages to get right back up again, limping after the others.

I try to move my arm so I can get a good look at the damage, but it only makes the blood flow faster. I have to slow it down if I'm going to have any chance of making it through the night. Propping the axe between my knees, I reach under my skirts and rip a strip of cloth from the bottom of my chemise. The ripping sound is louder than I thought it would be. Quickly, I tie the cloth around my shoulder, but the ache is already starting to sharpen. I've seen enough of my father's patients to know that the shock is what's keeping me upright at the moment. Soon, it will wear off, and with that will come the pain. More than I can probably bear. If I can reach the spring, I can clean the cut out, assess the damage, but I have to get there first. I'm starting to gather my nerve to get up when I hear footsteps in the snow. One of the girls must've heard the ripping sound and doubled back. I'm holding my breath, keeping as still as possible. All I have to do is stay quiet, stay hidden until she moves on, but there seems to be something in here with me. A soft squeaking noise, tiny claws scratching against my boots. I glance down to see the tip of a skinny tail emerging from under my skirt.

Forest rat.

Now it's climbing up the outside of my skirt. I think the rat is heading for the torn hem of my cloak, searching for a stray seed, but it crawls right past the opening, toward the wound on my shoulder. A cold sweat breaks out on my brow. Rats carry disease, and we don't have proper medicine out here. I wait as long as I can, until I can't stand another second, before I use my good hand to fling the rat from my shoulder. It flies through the air, scrabbling for position, managing to grasp the head of the axe that's balanced between my legs. Before my mind can even process what's happening, the axe is careening toward the earth, impaling the rat—directly at the feet of a grace year girl.

Leaning over to peek into my hiding space, Meg Fisher whispers, "There you are."

I kick her hard in the face, she falls back, there's blood gushing from her nose, but all she does is laugh.

Grabbing the axe, I push past her, running to the only place I can think of, the one place no one, not even Meg, will be crazy enough to follow. Using the axe, I hack away at the rotting wood and dive headfirst into the gap in the bottom of the fence. I'm shimmying my way through when I feel cold fingers coil around my ankle.

"Where do you think you're going?" Meg says, jerking me back. Jagged bits of wood dig into my shoulder. The pain is so intense that it makes me lose my breath, but I can't let them take me.

Digging my nails into the frozen earth, I kick and scratch my way to the other side, but as soon as I get to my feet, I hear a caw echo from the south. Stumbling forward, I take cover behind a wind-ravaged pine.

"You can't hide from me," Meg calls out between grunting and laughing, straining to get through.

Whether it's the water or the food or the very air making her behave this way, this isn't the same girl I knew back home—the one who passed the giving basket at church, who collected Queen Anne's lace from the meadow in the early-morning hours so she could place it under the punishment tree after her mother faced the gallows. I want to tell her to stop, think about what she's doing, but she's not in her right mind.

There's another caw, closer this time.

I peek my head around the tree to find Meg's black eyes glinting in the moonlight. A huge grin takes over her face, as if the corners of her mouth are being pulled tight by invisible string.

"Got her," she screams back toward the fence. "She's right ove—"

A low hum hurtles through the night air and then abruptly stops.

Meg sinks to her knees, her eyes going wide; blood trickles from her open mouth.

I'm trying to comprehend what's happening when I catch a glint of shiny steel protruding from her neck. A throwing blade, just like the one that nearly hit Helen on the trail.

I'm about to crawl forward to help her when I see a black shadow emerge from the south.

Poacher.

I try to keep track of him, but he's moving so fast through the dark that my eyes can hardly keep up.

As he descends upon Meg's crumpled frame, I hear her trying to speak, but I can't make out any words beyond the gurgling of her blood-filled throat. Grabbing her by the hair, he yanks her head back, exposing the pale skin of her neck to the moonlight; that shrill caw escapes from beneath his shroud. It's echoed back.

The ground sways beneath me. Gripping the axe to my chest, I sink down against the tree, pressing my spine into the knotty bark, desperately trying to stay in the present, but I can feel the blood leaving my body. I can feel myself slowing down.

Soon, this place will be teeming with poachers. I won't be able to get back through the fence, not before I bleed out.

I'm teetering on the edge of consciousness. Maybe it's

the loss of blood, the sound of the poachers ripping into her flesh, the utter hopelessness I feel, but I begin to drift . . .

There's snow melting on my lips. For a moment, I'm back in the county, in the meadow, catching snowflakes on my tongue. I'm twelve years old. I know this because I still have a white ribbon. Michael and I are lying side by side making snow angels. When I roll over to get up, he gives me the queerest look—the space between his eyes crinkling up—the same way he looked when he held the rock over a dying deer in the woods last summer. "You're bleeding," he whispers.

I check my nose, my knees—there's nothing there, but he's right. There's blood on the snow, right where I was lying. At first, I think it must be a suffering animal that's burrowed its way beneath the snow, but the damp sticky feeling between my legs tells me otherwise.

I want to stuff it back in, pretend it didn't happen, but he knows. Soon everyone will know. I don't see it as a beautiful pain, something that will bring me closer to my purpose, closer to God, I see it as a sentence. Without another word, Michael gathers our things and walks me home. When we reach my door, he opens his mouth to say something, but nothing comes out. What is there to say?

I'm the suffering animal beneath the snow.

From across the great lake, the wind finds me, whispering in my ear. "Time is running out."

Looking up, I find the girl standing on the shore. I haven't seen her in so long, it brings a smile to my face.

I know I have a choice: stay here and die in my memories, or embrace one last adventure. I've followed her for so long now, what's once more?

The clouds seem to clear, unveiling a moon so bright, so full, that I'm afraid it might burst.

And suddenly, I know what she's been trying to tell me. Time is running out . . . on *me*.

Maybe surrendering my flesh is the only way I can still be of use.

Because isn't that the biggest sin of all for a woman?

Not to be of use.

Tightening my grip on the axe, I crawl forward. I don't look back. Instead, I focus on the smell of algae and wet clay, and when the wind unfurls around me again, I know I'm headed toward open water. Toward home.

When I reach the rocky shore, I use the axe to help me to my feet.

Looking out over the horizon, I see two moons.

One is real, the other a reflection.

It's just like the girl. Maybe that's all she ever was, a reflection of who I wanted to be.

Walking onto the ice, I wonder how far it goes . . . how long it will last. A few more feet . . . ten . . . twenty?

As the wind washes over me once again, I close my eyes and hold my arms out.

In this moment, I'd do anything for the magic to be true. I'd forsake everything just to be able to fly far away from here.

But nothing happens.

I feel nothing.

I don't even feel cold anymore.

The distinct sound of footfall on the rocky shore creeps up on me. But it's more than the sound, it's something I can feel deep inside of me. Like standing on a razor's edge.

Peering over my shoulder, I can't make out his features, but I know it's him—the way he moves, like heavy fog rolling in over the water.

With the dark gauzy fabric billowing around him, he looks like the angel of death. Nameless. Faceless. But isn't that exactly what death is?

As he steps onto the ice, I turn to face him.

A deep crack needles beneath us, making us both freeze in place.

I always thought if it came to this, I'd be able to face my death with dignity and grace, the same way I've seen countless women face the gallows in the square. But there's nothing dignified or graceful about dying like this, being skinned alive.

Lowering my chin, I square my feet, grip the axe with both hands, and stare him down.

Maybe it's Eve slipping under my skin, maybe it's the moonlight, or my feminine magic making me cruel and wily, but all I want to do in this moment is take him down with me.

Warmth is trailing down my arm, over my hands, making the handle slick with blood. But all I need is one good swing.

As if sensing my intentions, he holds his hands out in front of him, the way you'd try to calm a skittish horse before ensnaring it with a bridle.

I lift the axe. The moonlight glints off the blade, setting something off inside of me—a memory rising to the surface, something I thought I'd buried long ago: my mother standing over my bed, her eyes soft and moist, her metal thimble twitching in the lamplight. "Dream, little one. Dream of a better life. A truthful life."

And I wonder if she can see me now, if she can feel me, from across the great lake, over treacherous trails of thorn and thistle, if she somehow knew how all of this would end.

With tears streaming down my face, I whisper, "Forgive me."

Tightening my grip, I heave the axe into the ice.

At first, there's nothing, only the shock of impact reverberating up my arms, settling in my wound, making it throb with every beat of my heart, but then I hear it, a dull pop followed by a long continuous crack, as if my bones are being split in two.

He lunges for me, but it's too late. As the ice breaks beneath my feet, I plunge into the frigid water, a straight needle shooting toward the depths, but my skirts billow up around me, slowing my descent. Or maybe I'm not drifting down but up. Maybe it's the wind filling my skirts, making me soar high above the earth. My lungs are burning to take a deep breath. Whether I'll fill my chest with stardust or water, I cannot say, but I feel my body slowing down. My heart thrums in my ears, my throat, the tips of my fingers, like a funeral dirge.

Slow.

Slower.

Stop.

With the moon lighting the way, I drift under a sheet of glass. I'm watching the world pass me by. I don't feel sad, I don't feel lost, I feel a sense of peace knowing that

I left this world on my own terms. This is one thing they couldn't take from me.

I'm trailing my fingers against the surface when I hear a crash of thunder, a shattering of glass. Something tugs at my braid and I'm jerked toward the heavens. Jagged knots are being dragged against my back. There's something beating on my chest—a soft warmth on my lips. A burning sensation flares in my lungs; I'm heaving up liquid. When I take in a deep gasp, it burns—the air feels alien going into my lungs, a betrayal of some kind.

I'm walking, but I have no feet. I'm drifting through the woods on a cloud of smoke. There's a caw in the distance. A blood-drenched hand covers my mouth. My eyes focus on the one thing I can't make sense of—two black orbs staring back at me, the eyes of my executioner. My enemy.

Straining my neck, I bite down as hard as I can.

And then the world goes black.

I am nothing. I am no one.

Only skin and bones.

The sound of a serrated blade tearing through cloth seeps into my senses. There's blazing heat along my back, my spine. Long, even breath pulsing against the nape of my neck. A heavy weight on top of me, all around me. I try to stay disconnected from my body, unaware, the way I used to drift away during a punishment in the square, but as life returns to my limbs, so does the pain. A deep throbbing sensation on my left shoulder.

When the heat against my back leaves me, I see a man walk across the room, stark naked, pure muscle roiling beneath flesh. I want to scream, I want to wail, but I can't find the air. Every bit of my energy is being taken up with violent shivering. My teeth are clattering so hard I'm afraid they might break. A blur of charcoal fabric swells in the corner of the room and the poacher is back. Black eyes boring into me from the void.

Hovering over me, he pours rancid liquid down my throat. I try to spit it out, but he holds his hand over my mouth, forcing me to swallow.

A flash of gleaming steel, followed by the sharpest pain I've ever felt.

The blade digs into my flesh. It feels like he's tearing my arm off, but it happens again and again and again, more times than I have skin on my arm. I know they believe the more pain, the more potent the flesh, but it's a lie. I want to tell him the magic isn't real, that all he's doing is killing someone in cold blood, but something tells me it wouldn't even matter.

As the heavy liquid spreads through my chest, I know what this means. I know what this is. Death isn't just coming for me . . . it's here.

The wind howls around me, and with it comes the smell of witch hazel and rotting flesh.

Frantically, my eyes dart around the room. There are long strips of sinewy meat hanging from hooks. Tanned hides drying on a crudely made rack, and knives . . . so many knives, splayed across a rough butcher block table. My eyes quickly settle on a fawn-colored leather satchel, a series of small glass bottles lined up in front of it.

His kill kit.

The bottles are for me.

Panic courses through my muscles. My heart is beating so hard I'm afraid it will burst.

I try to get up, but I can't move my arms. I can't move my legs. The only thing I can move is my head, and even that feels so heavy, so bloated, that I can hardly keep it steady.

I look down to see what's become of me, but my body is hidden beneath heavy pelts. I wonder if the skin is gone from my entire body now, if beneath the covers I'm only a tangled labyrinth of veins and severed nerves being held together by congealed blood.

I try to scream, but there's something in my mouth preventing me from doing so. It tastes of cedar and blood. It makes me think of the horses from the county, with their braided manes, a bit inserted against the back of their jaw in order to control their movement. And I realize that's what I am now. Under someone else's control.

Noticing my agitation, the poacher emerges from the shadows, covered in charcoal-gray shrouds. He's been watching me this whole time. Probably enjoying it. He forces more of the noxious fluid down my throat. I'm choking on it, but he doesn't care. I can see it in his eyes. I'm nothing more than a pelt to him. An animal.

As the heavy liquid spreads through my body, I'm trying to decide if I should fight or give in, if I even have a choice, when I sense a glow moving from the hearth to my left side. It doesn't flicker like a candle; it's strong and steady as a northern star. As the light bends toward me, with it comes the pain. Agonizing pain. A soundless scream boils inside of me. The smell of burning flesh fills my nostrils. I remember hearing that some of the cruelest poachers like to brand their kill, play with their prey before death.

On the edge of passing out, I hear a sound—boots trudging through heavy snow, the clank of wind chimes, only the sound is too dull for metal or glass. It sounds like heavy blocks of petrified wood clattering together.

The poacher must hear it, too, because he lowers the iron from my flesh. A flash of fear in his eyes.

"Ryker, you there?" An unfamiliar voice penetrates the small space. It sounds like it's coming from far away.

I let out a moan for help, anything but this, and the poacher shoves his filthy hand over my mouth and nose. I'm struggling against the fleshy part of his palm, for even the smallest bit of air, but he's too strong. Meeting his cold dark eyes, I know that in a few short seconds he could snuff me out without the slightest hesitation, and maybe that would be for the best, but then I think of my mother and father, my sisters, even Michael. I promised that I would do everything in my power to make it home. Not in those glass bottles . . . but *alive*. And as long as there's breath in my body, I will fight.

But there are many ways to fight.

Blinking up at the poacher, I feel tears slip from the far corners of my eyes, pooling in my ears. I'm silently pleading with him to let go. He must understand, because just as I'm on the verge of death, he eases his hand away. I'm taking in wild gasping breaths when he whispers, "One more sound, and it will be your last. Do you understand?"

I nod my head. At least I think I'm nodding,

"C'mon, lazy," the stranger's voice calls. "You're missing out."

"Can't. Sick," the poacher replies, never once taking his eyes off me.

"Then I'll come up."

"No." The poacher bolts to his feet, showing me his knife belt, one last look of warning before slipping through the heavy door covering.

"Why are you wearing your shroud inside?" the other one asks. "Are you hurt? Did they try to pull you over the barrier?" There's urgency in his voice, but it sounds thin and distant, like he's talking through a narrow tube. "Have you been cursed?"

"Only a fever," the poacher replies. "I should be fine by the new moon."

I wonder how far away that is . . . days, weeks, if that's how long he plans on dragging this out before he finally kills me.

I'm struggling to get up, even lift my head enough so I can get a better sense of where I am . . . but it's no use. I must be tied down.

"Did you hear the news?" the other one says. "We got two a fortnight ago. One right by the gate. The other one made it clear over here to the southeast barrier. Your territory."

"Huh," the poacher says. "I guess I must've slept right through it."

He's lying, but it tells me something. They must not know about the rotting cedar, the gap under the fence. And by the way he's talking, it can't be far from here. If I can just make it out of here, maybe I can slip back through.

"First one lasted a couple of days, had burns on its back and chest, but Daniel was able to render most of the flesh."

"Tamara," I whisper, my eyes veering toward the glass bottles on the table.

"The second one drowned in its own blood before Niklaus even got off its fingertips. At least it wasn't burned." He laughs. "Dumb, lucky bastard."

My chin begins to quiver. She wasn't an *it*. She had a name. Meg.

"They said there was a third. Blood trail led right to the shore, to a big hole in the ice. I tried fishing it out, but only found this old rag."

"Is that wool?" the poacher asks, a strange tension in his voice. "I'll trade you for it."

"Why?" the other one asks. "It's all ripped up . . . filthy. Probably full of disease."

"I can boil it . . . make a nice satchel out of it."

"Got any hemlock silt?" the other one asks.

"Not yet, but I bet there'll be some down in the cove come spring. Got a nice elk hide, though."

"Why would you trade a fine pelt for *this*? What's going on?"

"Look, I don't like to rub it in." The poacher's tone changes. Light. Sunny. "But there's plenty more pelts around here . . . *if* you're skilled with a blade."

"Hey, I'm getting better," the other one says with a robust crack of laughter. "Just get me within ten feet of prey and I'll take it down. You'll see."

They're joking about killing . . . killing *us*.

"We got a deal?" the poacher says. "Take whichever one you want."

"Your loss."

I hear something heavy being pulled off a rod. The same sound as in the market when the reindeer hides come in from the north. And then I hear the poacher catch something.

As they say their good-byes, I'm straining my neck, determined to get a peek at my outside surroundings, but when he slips back through, all I can see . . . all I can focus on is the frozen gray clump in his hands.

My cloak.

Just the sight of him touching it fills me with rage. June

made that with her own two hands. For *me*. It's *mine*. He has no right to it. But clearly, he wants a trophy.

As he hangs it on a meat hook on the far end of the room, hot acid fills my throat, but instead of turning my head, letting it dribble out the corner of my mouth, like some pathetic victim, I swallow it. I swallow all of it.

I have no idea what he has planned for my body, but I have a plan of my own.

Most of the time, I can't see him, but I feel him watching me. I vaguely remember the sight of his naked backside, but I have no idea what his face looks like, what kind of deformity he's hiding under his shroud. In my head, he's a monster.

The only time I'm sure he's not watching is when he tends to the hearth, which he does with an almost religious fervor. It tells me he's disciplined. Careful. Vigilant. But I know how to make myself invisible, to play the broken bird. I'm a grace year girl, after all. I've been training for this my whole life.

So I stop fighting.

I stop spitting and screaming.

And after a few days, the bit comes out of my mouth.

When he raises the cup to my mouth, instead of trying to bite down on him like a wild animal, I part my lips, storing as much of the liquid as I can in my cheeks, and the moment he turns to set the pewter cup on the bench, I tilt my face, slowly releasing the liquid onto the peat mattress. The fetid smell of the insipid honeycomb used to mask the bitter taste of the poppy makes me gag, but nothing comes up anymore. Maybe that's part of his plan, what he's trying to do—dry me out like a piece of jerky.

As soon as I stop ingesting the liquid, the world begins to sharpen. Unfortunately, so does the pain. I hide it the best I can, biting down on the inside of my cheek when I feel it gnawing away at me, but the fever raging through my body will not be denied. I know he's just trying to keep me quiet so he can take his time, salvage every piece of me. I'm not sure if the blade or the infection will kill me first, but time is running out.

When he leaves twice a day for water and firewood, I practice moving my toes, flexing my calves and thigh muscles, but my movement is limited because of the ropes. Despite the restraint pinning down my right arm, it seems to be working just fine. The left arm is another matter. It doesn't seem to be tied down, but the slightest movement of my pinkie sends an unbearable bolt of pain ricocheting through my entire arm, settling deep inside my chest.

But I have to remind myself, pain is good.

No matter what he's done to me, it means that I still have an arm. That I'm still alive.

I count the steps that it takes for him to walk to the doorway. I imagine doing it myself, over and over and over again. Sometimes, I wake from a fitful sleep to think I've already done it, that I'm free, but the blur of gauzy char-coal fabric in my peripheral brings everything back to me . . . why I'm here.

When he leans over me, I try not to look him directly in the eyes. I don't want to give myself away, but it's more than that. I'm afraid of what I'll see reflected back. What's become of me. When I feel my strength waning, I stare at the crudely carved female figures perched on the man-tel. No doubt a display to remind him of how many girls he's killed. But I will not be joining them.

It takes eight more cups of forced liquid, and nine trips outside of the shelter for supplies, before he's careless enough to leave his blade belt on the bench next to me.

I try not to stare at it longingly, but this is it. This is everything.

As soon as he turns his attention to tend to the hearth, I lift my arm from beneath the pelts. The pain is so in-tense that I have to clench my teeth together so I don't scream out against my will. My arm is trembling, a cold sweat beads up on my forehead, but as soon as I grasp the hilt of the blade, something else in me takes over. A de-termination I haven't felt in months. I *will* get out of this. I *will* survive. As I ease the blade from the sheath, fresh blood seeps from my shoulder, dripping onto the wood floors, but I can't stop now. I can't let go.

Slipping the blade under the pelts, I start working on the restraint holding down my right arm. I'm prepared for a long arduous fight, but the blade slices right through, as if I'm cutting into a fresh block of lard. It startles me, but it's good. That means it's sharp.

Switching the blade to my right hand, I twist my body and quickly sever the restraints on my ankles.

As soon as I'm free, all I want to do is fling off the pelts and bolt for the door, but I have to be smart about this. I'm not foolish enough to think I can outrun him—not in my condition. Tightening my grip on the blade, I close my eyes and do one of the hardest things I've ever done in my life . . . I wait.

I try to listen for his steps, but he's so quiet—just like the first time I encountered him on the trail.

I concentrate on his breath, slow and steady as the metronome in Mrs. Wilkins's parlor. Everyone thought she was blind after she came back from her grace year, but I remember sneaking a candy from a silver dish once, her beady eyes darting toward me like an arrow.

What if this is the same? What if he left the belt there as a test . . . a trap? I'm praying that he doesn't notice the empty sheath . . . my blood on the wide planked floors . . . my body drenched in sweat.

The smell of pine, lake water, and smoke fills my nostrils, and I know he's close. All he has to do is lean over me, like he's done a hundred times before.

As he presses his wrist against my forehead, I hold my breath. I'm only going to get one shot at this, and if I miss . . . I can't even think about that.

Gripping the hilt as tight as I can, I kick off the heavy covers and lash out at him with the blade. A strange sound escapes his lips as he staggers back, clutching his lower abdomen. I'm not sure how much damage I did, but there's blood.

When I leap onto the cold floor, my bony legs begin to buckle, but I can't give in to this. If I don't get out of here now, I never will. Propelling myself toward the doorway, I push through the thick buffalo hide; the sun hits me like a bolt of lightning, blinding me, grinding me to a halt. The cold air bites into my flesh. I can't see the poacher behind me, but I can hear him, dragging his body across the floor. "Stop . . . don't take another step."

I don't know where I'm going, what's in store for me out there, but anything is better than this. As soon as tiny dots of muted color begin to prickle the backs of my eyes, I take my first step toward freedom . . . into nothing but air.

I'm plunging toward the depths when something catches me by the wrist. I try to scream, but the pain is so eviscerating that it robs me of my breath.

When the world slowly comes back into focus, I find myself dangling at least forty feet above the ground. The earth below is blanketed in thick snow, the northerly wind penetrating straight to my bones.

"Grab on to me with your other hand," a gravelly voice calls out. I look up to see the billowing charcoal silhouette of the poacher leaning over a narrow platform. Looking around, I'm shocked to discover that I've been in some kind of tree house this whole time . . . a *blind* . . . like they use back home for elk hunting. Only this isn't for elk. It's for hunting grace year girls. Hunting *me*.

"Just let me go," I say, tears stinging my eyes. "Do it, and all of this can be over."

"Is that what you want?" he asks.

"It's better than being skinned alive."

"Is that what you think I'm doing?"

Blinking up at him, I concentrate on his face. I'm expecting the same cold, inhuman gaze, but what I find confuses me. I don't know if it's the pain or the cold or the sickness making me see things that aren't there, but in this light, he almost looks . . . kind.

Reaching up with my other hand, I grasp his wrist and let him pull me up. I could be making the biggest mistake of my life, but even now, after everything that's happened, I'm still not ready to give up. Surrender.

I groan as my body scrapes against the side of the rough-hewn wood platform. My *naked* body. Searching the room for my clothes, all I find is strips of linen spread out by the small hearth.

"What did you do to my clothes . . . to *me*?" I ask, doing my best to cover up with my hands.

"Don't flatter yourself," he says as he grabs a strip of cloth, tying it around his bloody torso.

"But I'm naked . . . *you* were naked. I saw you—"

"You were freezing to death. It was the quickest way to warm you up," he says as he yanks a hide off the bed and tosses it at me. "You're welcome."

I wrap the pelt around me, ashamed by how good it

feels. "But I saw you with a knife . . . you skinned me . . . branded me." I peek inside the pelt. Just the sight of the fresh blood oozing from the bandage on my shoulder makes me sway a little on my feet.

"I didn't *brand* you," he snaps. "I had to cauterize the wound, which you've probably ripped open again." He moves toward me, and I back up against the wall, knocking over a pile of antlers.

"Don't touch me," I whisper, my fingertips grazing a pointy edge. I'm ready to protect myself if need be, but he softens his tone.

"May I?" he asks, taking a tentative step toward me, nodding toward my left arm.

I don't like that I can't see his face. It's disconcerting, but maybe that's the whole point. The same way the veils dehumanize us, the shrouds do the same for them. One symbolizes pure innocence, the other pure death.

Letting the pelt slip from my shoulder, he reaches out to unwrap the bandage.

His fingers feel like slivers of ice against my skin.

I take in a hissing breath. "What's that smell?" I ask.

I follow his gaze to the gaping flesh on my shoulder.

I've seen enough stab wounds in my father's care to know this one is bad, the kind that even the strongest men have succumbed to. A wave of dizziness swells inside of me, making me waver.

"Tierney, you should lie down, you're in no condition—"

"How do you know my name?" I stare up at him, but my vision is starting to blur. "Who are you?"

He doesn't reply, but there's a sound—like something heavy and wet, slowly sizzling in a pan.

A flash of movement catches my eye. I squint into my mangled flesh.

The room begins to lurch, but my feet are firmly planted on the ground.

"Maggots," I whisper. "The smell is coming from me. It's the smell of death."

I dream. Strangely enough, not of the girl, not of home, but of here—this place, this poacher. A cool rag on my forehead. Biting into soft wood when he cuts away decrepit flesh. The woozy droplets of blood being wrung from a bandage into a worn copper bowl. The steady sound of a thick needle. In and out. Out and in.

Sometimes I think I see hazy light spilling through the cracks in the wood; other times, it's so dark that it feels as if I'm floating through space, unmoored from the gravity holding me to this earth.

I try to keep track of time, but my mind is lost in shadow. In memories.

I imagine it's like being in the womb. The thrum of a heartbeat in the distance. The rushing sound of blood swirling all around me. I wasn't allowed in the room for Clara's birth because I hadn't bled yet, but I was there for Penny's. They say by your fifth, the baby just slides right out, but that's not what I witnessed. I saw violence. Pain. The shifting of bones. I tried to turn away, but my mother grabbed me, pulling me close. "*This* is the real magic," she whispered. At the time, I thought she was delirious, mad from exhaustion, but I wonder if she knew the truth. If she was trying to tell me something.

I feel myself teetering on a razor's edge, as if one grain of sand in the wrong direction could tip the scale, taking me down to the depths of nevermore, and yet I'm still here. I'm still breathing.

Sometimes I talk just to hear the sound of my voice. To know that I still have a tongue. A throat. I ask questions—*Who are you? Why haven't you killed me*—but they're never answered. Instead, the poacher sings. Songs of old. Songs I've only heard on the breeze, a passing whistle escaping the trappers' lips as they head back north. Or maybe he isn't singing at all. Maybe he's talking. Softly, the words bending in and out of my consciousness.

"Drink," he says, holding the cup to my lips.

I'm trying to focus in on him, but it's like smoke drifting through my fingers.

"How long have I been asleep?"

"Ten sunrises, nine moonfalls," he says, adjusting the rolled-up fabric beneath my head. "It's for the best, considering what I had to do to you."

I try to move my arms and my legs, just to know that I still have them, but it brings a fresh wave of pain.

I remember the last time I was awake. The last time we spoke. He said my name.

"How do you know my name?"

"You need to drink." He tilts the cup. It's hard to swallow the sweet thick liquid. It's hard to swallow at all. Like my body forgot how.

But I can feel the poppy spreading through my chest, my limbs, making my eyelids feel as if they've been threaded with heavy cinder.

"How do you know my name?" I ask again.

I'm expecting nothing, but instead, a soft voice emanates from beneath his shroud. "That was a mistake."

I study him, the wide space between his eyes that gets knotted up . . . I always thought it was anger, hatred, but maybe I was wrong . . . maybe it's concern.

"Please," I whisper. "We both know I'm probably not going to make it."

His eyes veer to my wound. "I never said that."

"You didn't need to."

There's a long unbearable pause. The heaviness that accompanies a deep, dark truth.

With only the sound of the wind howling through the trees, the slow crackle of the fire, he says, "I knew who you were as soon as I saw your eyes . . . you have the same eyes."

"The girl from my dreams," I say with a tight inhalation of breath, the memory of her coming back to me all at once. "You've seen her, too . . . who is she?"

"What girl?" He places his inner wrist against my forehead. I want to flinch away from his touch, but his cold skin feels like a much-needed balm to my burning flesh. "Your father," he says, staring down at me. "You have his eyes."

"My father?" I try to sit up, but the pain is too intense. I knew my father had been sneaking off to the outskirts for years, but I never imagined this. "Are we . . . ?" I try to finish the sentence, but it feels like there's a boulder in my throat. "Are we . . . *relations*?"

"Brother and sister? No." The poacher unwraps my bandage; his nostrils flare. Either the idea repulses him just as much as it repulses me, or it's in response to the wound. Maybe both. "Your father's not like that. He's a good man."

"Then why?" I ask, fighting to stave off the lull of the poppy. "Why does he go there?"

His eyes narrow on me. "You really don't know?"

I shake my head, but my skull feels like it's full of heavy water.

"He treats the women of the outskirts, the children . . . he saved Anders," he says as he gently crushes herbs in a small stone vessel.

"Anders?"

He lets out a sigh, as if he's mad at himself for saying too much. "You probably don't remember, but he paid me a visit a few weeks ago. "

"How could I forget." I wince as he smears a dark green poultice over my wound. "You nearly smothered me to death."

His eyes turn cold. "That would've been a pleasure compared to what he would've done to you had he discovered you here."

Staring past him, at the empty glass bottles lined up on the table, I think about Tamara and Meg. The horrible things they did to them. A shiver runs through me.

"We need to get this dirty ribbon away from—"

"No." I reach up, tucking the braid behind me. "The ribbon stays. The braid stays."

He lets out an irritated sigh. "Suit yourself."

"Who's Anders?" I ask, trying to soften my tone.

I can tell he's reluctant to talk, but I just keep asking until he gives.

"We grew up together," he says as he wraps a fresh strip of linen around my shoulder. "Last hunting season, the prey tried to take him over the barrier, bit him, cursed his entire family. Everyone died, but your father was able to save him."

"My father saved a *poacher*?" I ask. "But he would be exiled if anyone found out about that, and my mother, my sisters, we would be—"

"Of course that's your highest concern," he says, tying off the bandage tighter than need be.

"I didn't mean . . . it's just . . . *why*? Why would he risk it?"

"You still don't get it," he replies.

A caw echoes through the woods, making us both flinch.

"I don't underst—"

"I made a deal," he says, pushing away from the bedside, strapping on his knives. "In exchange for Anders's life, I promised that I would spare you if given the chance."

"But you stabbed me through the fence."

"I *barely* nicked you. You were getting too close . . . too comfortable."

"That night on the trail . . . the day I went over the barrier to help Gertrude," I say, getting short of breath.

"Honestly, if I'd known how much trouble you'd be, I would've thought twice," he says as he tosses a cold wet rag in my direction. "But now he and I are even." He blows out the candle and pulls back the door covering.

"Wait. Where are you going?"

"To do my job. What I should've been doing all along."

As I sit alone, shivering in the dark, I can't help thinking about the hurtful things I said to my father before I left the county, the pain in his eyes when he entered the church with the veil. "Vaer sa snill, tilgi meg," he whispered as he pressed the flower of my suitor into my hand.

I always thought he taught me things because he was selfishly practicing for a son, but maybe it was for this, so I could survive my grace year. Maybe he did all of this . . . for *me*.

Tears sting the back of my eyes. I want to get up and run, anything but sit here with my feelings, but as I get out of bed, my legs wobble as if they're made from straw and putty. I stagger forward, grabbing the edge of the table to try to catch myself; it begins to tilt; the tiny glass bottles roll toward me, the knives begin to slide. I right it just in time before everything goes crashing to the floor. As I'm leaning over the table, trying to catch my breath, I spot a small notebook, wedged behind the worn leather satchel. I open it to find sketches of muscles and veins, skeletal structures, similar to the field notebooks my father keeps on his patients. But when I turn to the last entry, I see a diagram of a girl—every mole, every scar, every blemish marked in great detail, from the brand of my father's sigil on the bottom of my right foot all the way to

the smallpox mark on my inner left thigh from a vaccination my father gave me last summer. This is a map of my
skin, the small dashes indicating where he'll cut. There's
even a detailed log planning out each piece of me that will
go in each corresponding bottle. One hundred in all. A
deep chill runs through my entire body.

The poacher kept his word to my father. But like he
said, they're even now.

Looking at the knives, the metal funnel, the pliers, the
hammer—it turns my stomach.

It's entirely possible he's simply preparing, just in case
the infection takes me, but there's an undeniable part of
him that wishes me dead. I run my finger along the dot-
ted lines of the sketch, and I can't stop thinking about the
fundamental rule of poaching, why they skin us alive instead of killing us first. The more pain, the more potent
the flesh. I look down at the fresh blood seeping through
the bandage. Maybe he hasn't been helping my wound at
all. Maybe he's been making it worse so I can suffer as
long as possible.

I think about grabbing my cloak, taking my chances
in the woods, but I'm in no condition.

If I'm going to survive this, I need for him to see me
not as an it, not as prey, but as a human being.

But I'm not so naïve as to think I don't need a backup
plan.

With trembling hands, I put back the bottles and the
notebook and grab the smallest knife from the table.
Dragging myself back to bed, I pull the thick pelts over
me and slip the knife beneath the mattress, practicing

pulling it out again and again, until I can no longer feel my arm. I want to stay up, wait for him, make sure he doesn't get the jump on me, but my eyes are too heavy to hold.

"Vaer sa snill, tilgi meg," I whisper on the breeze, hoping it will carry my message straight to my father's heart, but that's magical thinking, something I don't dare dabble in anymore.

Instead, I vow to make it home, so I can tell him myself.

I wake to the sound of breaking bones.

Letting out a gasping breath, I start to reach for the knife, then realize the poacher's clear across the room, sitting on a stool in front of the table, cutting away at something. I'm thinking the worst, wondering who it might be, when I catch a glimpse of a rabbit foot dangling over the edge of the table. Lurching to the side of the bed, I grab the pot, retching up everything in my stomach.

He doesn't even flinch.

Wiping the bile from my mouth, I lean back on my makeshift pillow. "Is that where you go at night? To hunt?"

He grunts out a reply. Could be yes. Could be no. He's clearly not in a mood to chat, but I can't let that stop me.

"Is it just rabbit, or do you hunt other things?" I know the answer, but I want to hear him say it.

He peers back at me, his eyes dark and narrow. "Whatever's careless enough to get in my path."

"Prey," I whisper, an icy current running through me. "That's what you call us, right?"

"Better than poachers," he says as he returns to his work, snapping the neck.

"Do you have a name?" I ask, trying to sit up, but the pain is still too much.

"Other than poacher?" he replies dryly. "Yes. I have a name."

I'm waiting for him to tell me, but it never comes.

"I'm not going to beg you."

"Good," he says as he continues to work on the rabbit.

The sound of his steady breath, the constant drip of the icicles on the eaves, it's driving me crazy—alone in the woods kind of crazy—only I'm not alone.

"Forget it," I say with a heavy sigh as I turn my head toward the door.

"It's Ryker," he says softly over his shoulder.

"Ryker," I repeat. "I knew that. I heard the other poacher call you that. It's an old Viking name." I perk up, trying to make a connection. "Det ere n fin kanin," I say, but he doesn't seem to understand.

My shoulder is throbbing now. A sheen of cold sweat covers my body.

"I think I could use some more medicine," I say as pleasantly as possible.

"No," he replies, without even looking at me.

"Why?" I blurt. "I'm in pain. Do you *want* me to be in pain . . . is that it?"

He turns to me, peeling back the rabbit fur in one long continuous stroke, as casually as if he's slipping off a silk stocking.

"You don't scare me," I whisper.

"Is that right?" he says as he drops the rabbit and abruptly gets up, blood staining his hands.

As he sits next to me, I ease my hand down to the edge of the mattress, slipping my fingers beneath for the comfort of the blade, but there's nothing there.

"Looking for this?" he asks, pulling the small blade from the sheath strapped to his ankle. "The next time you get out of bed to rifle through my things, you should make sure you're not leaving a trail of blood on the floor."

I reach out to hit him, but he catches my hand. "Save your energy. When you get well enough to return to the herd, you're going to need it."

I'm struggling to pull my hand free.

"You don't need the poppy anymore," he says as he releases me. "At this point, it will do more harm than good. It's up to the Gods now. You're either going to live or you're going to die."

"Why are you doing this?" I ask, tears streaming down my face. "I saw the notebook. You fulfilled your promise to my father, many times over. Why haven't you killed me yet or just let me die?"

A deep ridge settles between his eyes. "I keep asking myself the same question," he says, finally meeting my gaze. "But when I saw you . . . on the ice . . . you looked so . . ."

"Helpless," I whisper, disgusted and angry by the idea of that being what saved me.

"No," he says, his eyes glinting in the firelight. "Defiant. When you struck the ice with that axe . . . it was one of the bravest things I've ever seen."

Stark white light bleeds through the fluttering edge of the buffalo hide covering the door.

"I see you survived another night," he says as he stands over me, his clothes smelling of fresh snow and wood smoke. I can't tell if he's pleased or disappointed. Maybe he's not even sure.

I lurch to my side to throw up. He nudges a bucket closer with his boot, but there's no need. It's just a small bit of drool and bile. My insides are rejecting even the smallest thing now. "What's happening to me?"

"It's the infection," he says, sitting on the bench to inspect my wound. His fingers feel like they're made of ice.

I glance over at the angry red flesh. "I don't want to die here," I say with a sharp inhalation of breath.

"Then don't," he says, squeezing my arm tight, drawing the pus from the sutures.

My head lolls forward. I feel like I might pass out at any moment.

"How did this happen?" he asks, his voice harsh in my ears, insistent.

For a moment, I can't remember, maybe I don't want to remember, but slowly it comes back to me, nothing more than a flash of images—Gertie's scalp glinting in the moonlight. The woods. The seeds. The storm. Tamara's twitching body being shoved out of the gate.

"Kiersten," I whisper, my shoulder aching at the memory. "It was an axe."

Dabbing at the edges of my cut with witch hazel, he asks, "What did you do to her?"

"I didn't *do* anything," I say, my chin beginning to quiver. I try to pull up the pelts to hide my emotion, but I don't have the strength. "I only wanted to make things better . . . ," I whisper. "I wanted it to be . . . *different*."

"Why?" he asks, rewrapping my shoulder in a fresh bandage. I don't think he's that interested, he's probably just trying to keep me talking, keep me conscious, but I want to talk. I want to tell someone my story, just in case . . .

"The dreams," I reply. "The women of the county aren't allowed to dream, but I've dreamt of a girl ever since I can remember."

He looks at me curiously. "Is that the girl you were asking me about?"

I don't remember telling him about her; it makes me wonder what else I've told him in my addled state, but what does it matter anymore.

"I know it sounds crazy, but she was real to me. She showed me things . . . she made me believe that things could be different . . . not just for the grace year girls but for the laborers . . . the women of the outskirts, too."

He stops and stares at me. "Is that your magic?" he asks.

"No." I shake my head.

"Then what do you think it means?"

"I don't think it means anything anymore. It's just a fantasy. What I wanted my life to be." Reaching for the comfort of my braid, I pull it over my shoulder, tracing the red ribbon with my fingertips. "In the county, only our husbands are allowed to see us with our hair down, but when we arrived at the encampment, the girls took out their braids as a symbol that they've embraced their magic. I refused. That's the real reason they turned on me."

"Why would you refuse to embrace your magic?" he asks, unable to conceal his shock.

My eyes well up to the point that I can't see clearly, but I refuse to blink. "Because it isn't real." Saying it out loud feels dangerous but necessary.

Pressing his wrist against my forehead, he says, "We really need to get your fever down."

I jerk my head away from him. "I'm serious. I don't know if it's something in the air, the water, our food, but something is making them change . . . making them see and feel things that aren't real. It happened to me, too, but when they banished me from the camp, I got better. Clearer."

"You were starving to death when I found you, bleeding out—"

"Have you ever seen them fly?" I raise my voice. "Have you ever seen them disappear before your very eyes? Have you ever *seen* them do anything . . . but die?" The tears finally release, searing down my face.

"Drink this," he says, pouring a cup of steaming broth from a kettle.

My eyes widen. "I thought I couldn't have any more—"

"It's yarrow. It won't ease the pain, but it might help with the fever."

Sipping the broth, I try to forget about the pain nagging at my shoulder and think of anything else, but my thoughts keep coming back to my family. A different kind of pain. My little sisters. I bet they're worried sick about me, worried about what will happen to them if my body goes unaccounted for.

"If I die . . . promise you'll skin me," I say, swallowing the bitter liquid. "Give me an honorable death, so my sisters won't be punished."

"Of course," he says without the slightest hesitation.

"Of course?" I try to raise my head. "Can't you even say, *Hey, don't talk like that. I'm sure you're going to make it?*"

"I'm used to speaking my mind." He sets the cup on the table. "I say what I mean."

"What a luxury that must be." I laugh as I settle further back in the pelts, but it's not at all funny. "I don't think I've ever been able to do that."

"Why not?"

I try to focus on him, but I can feel the fever taking over. "In the county, there's nothing more dangerous than a woman who speaks her mind. That's what happened to Eve, you know, why we were cast out from heaven. We're dangerous creatures. Full of devil charms. If given the opportunity, we will use our magic to lure men to sin, to evil, to destruction." My eyes are getting heavy, too heavy to roll in a dramatic fashion. "That's why they send us here."

"To rid yourself of your magic," he says.

"No," I whisper as I drift off to sleep. "To break us."

A shrill caw in the distance jars me awake.

Ryker reaches for his knife belt and then stops, sinking back into the shadows.

"Aren't you going?" I ask.

"It's too far away. The call is coming all the way from the northwest."

That may be true, but I want to believe it's more than the distance, that maybe he's starting to see us in a different light.

As he tends to the fire, my eyes veer toward the glass bottles lined up on the table, set there like a constant reminder.

"How can you do it?" I ask, a dry hollow sound to my voice. "Kill innocent girls?"

"Innocent?" He looks back at me, staring pointedly at my shoulder. "No one is innocent in this. You of all people should know that."

"It was an accident."

"Accident or not, you have no idea what they're capable of. The curse. I've seen it with my own eyes." As he stokes the fire, his shoulders begin to relax. "Besides, nothing in this world is cut and dried. From death there is life . . . that's what my mother always says," he adds quietly.

"You have family?" I ask. I don't know why it never occurred to me that poachers would have feelings . . . a life before all of this.

He starts to speak but then clenches his jaw tight.

"Look, I don't want to be here just as much as you don't want me here. I'm only trying to pass the time."

He remains silent.

I let out a huff of air. "Fine."

"I have a mother. Six sisters," he says, staring up at the figurines on the hearth.

I count them. There are seven in all. I thought they represented the girls he'd killed, but now I'm thinking they might be his family.

"Six sisters?" I ask, trying to adjust my body so I can see better, but I'm still too weak. "I didn't think women of the outskirts had that many children."

"They don't." He sets the kettle over the flames. "They're not blood." He glances back at me but doesn't meet my eyes. "My mother . . . she takes in the young ones. The ones no one wants."

I'm trying to figure out what he means when the thought hits me right in the throat, making me choke on my own words. "Girls from the county? The girls who get banished?"

He stares into the flames, his eyes a million miles away. "Some of them are so traumatized they don't speak for months. At first, I hated them, I didn't understand, but I don't think about them that way anymore."

"As prey?" I ask, my voice trembling with anger . . . fear. "And *still* you poach us?"

"We're not poaching anything," he snaps. "We've been sanctioned to cull the herd, paid handsomely to deliver your flesh back to the county. Your fathers, brothers, husbands, mothers, sisters . . . *they* are the ones who consume you. Not *us*."

A sick feeling rushes through my entire body, making my eyes water. "I had no idea it was the county who did this."

"If I leave, if I don't take my place as a poacher, my family won't get my pay . . . they'll starve. And thanks to the county, I have a lot of mouths to feed."

"Who pays you?" I ask, trying to get control of my breath . . . my reeling thoughts.

"The same people who send you here," he says, pouring a steaming cup of broth. "On the final day of our hunting season, we line up outside the gate. Those who return empty-handed get just enough so our families can survive. Those who have prey present their kill. The bottles are counted, the brand verified. If it's healthy, properly rendered, they get a sack full of gold, enough to take their families west . . . leave this place for good."

"But there's nothing out there . . . nothing but death."

"Or maybe that's what they want us to believe," he says, barely above a whisper, as he lifts my head, helping me drink.

Another caw rings out over the woods, closer this time, making my skin prickle.

"How do they do it?" I ask, staring toward the doorway. "How do they lure the girls out of the encampment? Is it skill . . . brute force . . . the power of persuasion?"

Ryker sets down the broth. "We don't have to *do* anything." His gaze settles on my wound. "They do it to themselves. To each other."

His words feel like an axe, cutting me all over again.

"Have you ever killed a grace year girl?" I whisper, afraid of the answer, afraid not to ask.

"Almost," he says, pulling the pelts up, gently tucking me in. "But I'm glad I didn't."

"You're burning up," he says, pressing a cool rag to my forehead.

Prying my eyes open, I'm struggling to focus on him, to focus on anything. A dull clanking noise pulls my attention.

"What's that sound?" I whisper.

"The wind."

"The other sound. I've heard it before."

"The chimes?" he asks.

I let out a deep shiver. "I don't remember wind chimes sounding like that."

"They're made from bones."

"Why?" I ask, trying to keep my eyes open.

"Anders . . . he likes to make things with bones."

I think I heard him correctly, but I can't be sure of anything anymore.

I reach for the cloth draped over his mouth. "I need to see your face," I say through my chattering teeth.

He stops me, tucking my arm back under the pelts. "It's better this way."

"You don't have to worry about me . . . how I'll react," I say. "I've seen all kinds of deformities. My father has a book—"

"It's not that." He lowers his eyes. "It's forbidden."

"Why?" I try to wet my lips, but they only seem to crack open with the effort.

"Without our shrouds," he replies, glancing up at me through his dark lashes, "we'd have no protection from your magic."

"I told you, I have no magic." Once again, I reach for the gauzy fabric.

"You're wrong," he says, folding my outstretched fingers back into my sweaty palm. "You have more than you know."

There's something about his words, the way he says them, that makes me flustered; an unfamiliar heat rises to my cheeks. I want to argue, tell him the magic isn't real, but I don't have the energy.

"Please," I whisper. "I don't want to die without seeing the face of the person who tried to save me."

He stares at me intently. He's so quiet, I wonder if he even heard me.

With only the sound of the snow shifting from the eaves, the heavy hiss and crackle of the fire, he begins to unwrap the charcoal shroud. With each new sliver of exposed skin, my heart picks up speed. The sharp angle of his nose, his chin. Thin lips pressed together, dark hair curled up haphazardly around his shoulders. Is he handsome? Maybe not by the standards of the county, but I can't stop staring at him.

I wake to Ryker singing softly, his bare back to me, muscles rising beneath his skin as he stokes the fire. It's a song I recognize from the county. A real heartbreaker. His sisters must've taught it to him.

My hair is wet, my whole body is damp, but my lips and tongue are so dry they feel like the bark of a sycamore tree. I try to say something, eke out even the tiniest word, but nothing comes out. I'm so hot that it feels like I'm slowly roasting on a pyre. Using all my strength, I fling the pelts off of me.

Ryker startles when they hit the floor with a dull thud, but he doesn't reach for his shrouds.

Kneeling beside me, his brow knotted up in worry, he presses his inner wrist to my forehead. I swear I can feel his heart beating against my skull, or maybe it's my own, but as he looks down at me, his face softens, the faintest smile easing into the corners of his mouth.

"Your fever broke."

"Water," I manage to get out.

Scooping up the water from a bucket, he holds it to my lips. "Take it slow."

The first sip is so good, so cool against my throat, that I can't help grabbing his hands, gulping it down. Half of it runs down my chest, but I don't care. I'm alive. I pull the chemise away from my skin. *My chemise.* The crude stitches, the uneven hems. He's sewn it back together for me.

"Thank you," I whisper.

"Don't thank me yet," he says as he leans over me to unwrap the bandage from my shoulder. "You haven't seen my handiwork."

"Is this also your work?" I ask, skimming my thumb over the muted thick pink scar on the lower side of his abdomen.

He takes in a tight inhalation of breath, his skin prickling beneath my touch.

"Did I do this?" I ask, remembering lashing out at him with the blade when I tried to escape.

"I guess we both have something to remember each other by."

Looking over at my arm, what's left of the muscle on my shoulder, the jagged scars, the puckered skin, all I can feel is grateful. He saved my life more times than I can count, but I need to remember that he's still a poacher and I'm still a grace year girl.

"Is it daylight?" I ask, looking off toward the pelt covering the doorway.

"Would you like to see?"

"Even if I could move, isn't it too dangerous?" I ask.

Reaching up to the ceiling, he pushes open a hatch. I hear slushy snow slide to the forest floor.

The sunlight blinds me for a moment, but I don't care. The rush of cold air blowing in off the water seems to revive me a bit. I smell melting snow, lake water, river clay, and fresh-cut cedar.

When I can see clearly again, he's rolling up birch bark, placing it on the roof. "What's that for?"

"It's finally starting to thaw. This will keep the water from settling."

I'm still trying to get used to seeing him without the shroud, but I like it.

"Hungry?" he asks.

I think about it for a good minute. "Famished."

Ryker tosses a sack of walnuts onto the bed; they spill out, startling me.

"You need to start building muscle," he says, placing a steel cracker in my left hand.

"I can't."

"If you had enough strength to go for that knife hidden beneath the mattress, you have enough strength for this."

"That was self-preservation."

"So is this. Do you want to starve again? Eating whatever chunks of meat I decide to toss over the barrier?"

"That was you?" I ask.

"Who else?"

I thought it was Hans, but I keep it to myself.

"You need to start pitching in," Ryker says. "Take care of yourself."

Propping myself up, I reach out to grab a walnut. I'm trying to work the cracker, squeezing as hard as I can, but I'm not even making a dent.

"Like this," he says, cracking one wide open without the slightest effort, tipping the meat inside his mouth, grinning widely.

My stomach growls.

"I get what you're trying to do, you know." I glare up at him. "When I was five, I went to the orchards with my father. He could reach right up and pluck an apple from the limbs. I asked him to hold me up so I could get one, and he refused. He said, 'You're smart enough to get one on your own.' It made me furious, but he was right. Eventually, I grabbed a long stick and beat it out of the tree." I laugh at the memory. "I have to admit, it was the best apple I've ever had."

He smiles, but I see something behind his eyes. A tinge of sadness . . . regret.

"Do you know who your father is?" I ask.

"I was born in June." He looks at me like I should know what that means.

"April, for me."

"Figures," he says. "Stubborn. Obstinate. Try this one." He rolls another walnut my way. "I was born nine months from when the poachers returned for a new hunting season."

"Oh," I say, feeling heat rise in my cheeks. "So he's a poacher?"

"*Was* a poacher."

"I'm sorry . . . did he pass?"

"If you mean pass right over the mountain, then yes."

He cracks another one. "He got a kill, but he didn't take us with him. He offered to take my mom and me, but not the girls. He could never look at them as anything but the enemy."

"Like Anders?" I ask, thinking about the way he talks about the grace year girls.

He lets out a deep sigh. "Anders is complicated. His mother was once a grace year girl. She got rid of her magic, nearly died from it, has a scar clear across her face, but her husband-to-be didn't like the way she looked anymore, so they banished her."

"I know this story from my mother," I whisper. "She was a Wendell girl."

He shrugs. "She hated the county. Everything it stood for. She raised her boys the same."

"She had more than one boy?" I ask, sitting up a little taller.

"A rarity. I know." He nestles the empty shells together. "She loved them. Doted on them. Especially William, Anders's little brother. He was always so . . . *happy*. Anders wanted to get a kill so his little brother wouldn't have to. And now they're gone . . ." His voice trails off.

"The curse?" I ask.

Ryker nods. "My mother believes it happened for a reason, but she believes a lot of things. I guess if the curse never happened, if your father hadn't saved him, we wouldn't be here right now." He looks up at me. His eyes are the color of burned sugar. I never noticed that before.

I swallow hard. "Your mother sounds lovely. What's she like?"

"Kind, beautiful, full of life." As he says this, I watch his entire body relax. Normally he holds his frame like a tight wire, ready for anything, but I see an ease come over him. "But there are spells. She works hard, provides as much as she can, but she's getting older now. Before I came of age, it was my responsibility to take my sisters from the hut when she had a visitor . . . to help her when she needed to recover."

"Recover?"

His shoulders collapse. "Sometimes it's crying spells. A dark cloud hanging over her. Other times it's more serious and I have to send for the healer."

"Serious how?" I'm still trying to crack the shell, but I don't have the muscle strength.

"The wives are spared this," he says as he picks another walnut. "While you are vessels for sons, the women of the outskirts are vessels for their desire. Their rage." His eyes narrow. "There are certain men that will only be accepted inside a hut when the food is running low."

I think about the Tommy Pearsons and Geezer Fallows of the world, and a shiver runs through my blood.

"Or worse, the guards," he adds.

"The guards? But they've gone under the knife. They don't have any . . ." I finally manage to crack the walnut open.

He raises a brow; he almost seems amused by my sputtering. "It doesn't castrate their *minds*. If anything, it makes them worse."

"How?" I ask as I tip back the shell, finally getting something to eat.

"Because no matter what they do, they can never be truly . . . *satisfied.*"

I think about Hans, weeping in the healing house, ice nestled between his legs . . . the look of utter despair when he escorted the girls home from his first grace year, the girl he loved not being one of them. The tic he had of rubbing his heart, like he could somehow mend it. His trembling hand when he unsnagged my ribbon from the post. Maybe that's true for some, but not Hans.

"That's like saying all poachers are animals," I say.

"Maybe we are." He glances up at me, trying to gauge my reaction.

He wants to know what I think of him.

But I'm afraid of what will slip out if I open my mouth.

"Here," he says as he reaches over, putting his hand over mine to help me crack the next one.

I could still be delirious from the fever breaking, or high on the fresh air, but when he pulls his hand away, my fingers seem to hang there in the ether, as if longing for his return.

SPRING

The winter that came in like a lion has gone out like a lamb. The snow has melted under a clear mellow sun. The birds are singing, chlorophyll fills the air, and the full moon is upon us. Every night I see it growing through the hatch in the roof, which seems to mirror my own feelings for Ryker. Sometimes, when I look at him, it feels like my rib cage is being pried apart, expanding for extra air—it hurts, but it's a feeling I'm not sure I want to let go of.

To pass the time, keep our minds occupied, our curious hands busy, Ryker and I toss a dagger back and forth. At first, I could hardly bend my fingers enough to grasp the hilt, but I've gotten rather good at it. Quick. I've also taken to helping him rig up traps, fine finger work that takes a steady hand, using an entirely different set of muscles. Ironically, Ryker told me that I would make for a decent poacher.

When he's out hunting, I practice standing, walking, building my strength back in my legs, but it's also an excuse to explore the space around me. He's tidy, every nook seems to serve a purpose, but there are small personal touches here and there. A piece of driftwood in the shape of a swallow, a series of polished stones he's collected from the shore. The small figurines that he whittles away at when he's missing home. At the end of the hunting season he takes the figurines back to his family and then starts all over again to mark how much they've grown over the year.

At night, we talk for hours about everything and nothing. He teaches me about herbs; I teach him about the language of flowers. He knows a little from Anders. That's the one thing Anders's mother hung on to from the county.

There are days when it's enough to stand beneath the open hatch in the roof, feeling the spring air sink deep into my bones, and there are others where I long to be outside, when the soles of my feet begin to itch with the desire to explore, to be on my own. To answer to no one but myself. But that was never really the case. We all answer to someone.

We agreed that as soon as I was better, I'd return to the encampment.

I'm better now, and yet here I stand.

The second I hear his footsteps on the bottom rung of the ladder, I slip back into bed and feign weakness. I tell myself it's survival—here I have a warm bed, food in my belly, protection, but I know it's more than that. It's about him.

I don't know what his favorite color is, his favorite hymn, if he prefers blueberries over boysenberries, but I know the way he clenches his jaw when he's thinking, the rise and fall of his chest right before he drifts to sleep, the sound of his footsteps on the forest floor, the smell of his skin—salt, musk, lake water, and pine.

We come from completely different worlds, but I feel closer to him than I've ever felt to anyone.

We don't speak of the future or the past, so it's easy to pretend. When he leaves to hunt, I tell myself he's simply heading off to work—maybe a neighboring island. Or sometimes I make believe we're in exile, hiding from evil forces—which isn't entirely off base, but even that feels too close. Dangerous.

During twilight, that shadowy place between sleep and dreams—that's when it hurts the most. When reality worms its way between us.

In my weaker moments, I let myself fantasize that we could find a way. Maybe we could meet in the northern forest every year on the day of the unveiling ceremony, but it would never be enough.

The fact of the matter is, if I don't return to the county at the end of my grace year, my sisters will be punished in my stead, and if he goes missing, his family won't re-ceive his pay. They'll starve.

Ryker and I may be many things, but we could never willingly hurt the ones we love.

This will have to end before it even begins.

Tonight, when he returns, he takes off his shroud, his boots, unstraps his knives, pulls his shirt off, hanging it by the hearth, and then pauses. He's probably making sure I'm asleep before unbuttoning his trousers. I close my eyes, keeping my breath as even as possible. As soon as I hear them drop to the floor, I can't help but look. I remember feeling so afraid when I saw him like this on the first night he brought me here. I saw violence in the scars covering his body, I saw brute force in the way his muscles moved beneath his skin, but now I see something else. There is strength, but also restraint. There are scars, but also healing.

He kneels beside me, pressing the inside of his wrist against my forehead. Force of habit, or maybe it's just an excuse to touch me. Either way, I don't mind.

I pretend to stir awake.

Grabbing a pelt off the bed, he covers himself. "I hope I didn't scare you," he says, a beautiful flush covering his neck and cheeks.

"You don't," I whisper.

His eyes meet mine. And what should be an innocuous gesture feels entirely electric.

"Ryker, you there?" A voice pierces the air between us.

He presses his finger to my lips to keep me quiet, but I don't think I'd be able to utter a sound even if I wanted to.

It's not until we hear a foot hitting the bottom rung of the ladder that Ryker reacts. Bolting to his feet, he says, "Anders, sorry, I was sleeping." He gives me a look of apology before ducking behind the door covering.

"You're just wearing a rabbit skin now?" Anders asks, a lightness in his voice.

"Guess so." Ryker lets out a nervous laugh.

"Ned got one by the eastern fence," Anders says.

I sit up straight, tight as an arrow. That must've been the caw we heard last night.

"Hardly any meat on it, brains all scrambled, but Ned's set for life. You're missing out. That's the sixteenth one you've slept through."

"*Sixteen,*" I whisper.

"They're going down a lot earlier this season. Martin says the magic is really strong this year."

"Is that right?" Ryker replies, but I can sense the uneasiness in his voice, which means Anders can probably sense it, too.

I hear him take another step up the ladder. "How'd that wool work out for you?"

"Wool?"

My eyes shoot to my cloak, hanging by the hearth.

"You traded me an elk hide for it?"

"Oh, yeah, made a great herb satchel."

"Let's see." The poacher takes another step up the ladder.

A surge of panic rushes through me. If he gets all the way up here, I need to be ready to run . . . to fight.

"I haven't started yet," Ryker explains, "but I will as soon as the weather turns cooler."

Getting up as quietly as possible, I tiptoe across the room to fetch my cloak and boots. The floorboard lets out a deep groan.

There's an awkward pause. I'm waiting for Anders to come charging up the ladder to see what's going on when he says, "You know it was a year ago today that I was cursed . . . when you brought me home."

"That's right," Ryker replies, a soft haze slipping into his voice.

"I thought I was a dead man."

"But you made it. You survived."

"They owe me," Anders says, his voice darkening. "They killed my whole family. All I need is one clean shot. We'd have a lot better chance if you were out here with me. All we need is one kill, and we can take your family and get out of this place for good. Just like we planned."

"Take a look at that sky," Ryker says, clearly trying to change the subject. Or maybe he's trying to buy me some time.

Slipping into my boots, I grab a knife off the table.

"Yeah. Weather's changing fast," Anders replies. "Birds are flying low. Better batten down the hatches, close off the flue. Spring is about to go out with a bang."

I let out a shaky breath when I hear Anders step off the ladder, his feet hitting the ground, hard. "Hey," he calls up. "You know you can tell me anything. Whatever's going on with you, I'm here. Whatever you need."

As they say their good-byes, I sit on the edge of the bed, boots on, cloak around my shoulders, my body covered in a sheen of cold sweat.

"I'm sorry," Ryker whispers as he comes back inside. It's the first time he's ever said he's sorry to me.

"I wonder who it was last night," I murmur. "Could've been Nanette or Molly or Helen . . ."

He takes off my boots.

"Or maybe it was Ravenna, Katie, or Jessica."

He removes my cloak.

"Becca, Lucy, Martha . . . *Gertie* . . . ," I whisper, my chin beginning to tremble. "They don't deserve this. They don't owe him their lives."

Prying the knife out of my hand, he sits beside me.

"I know this is hard, but you don't know what the prey is capable of . . . I mean, the girls." He corrects himself. "When I found Anders last year, he was near death. It started with a rash near the bite mark, and by the time I got him back to the outskirts, it covered his entire body. He was burning up, vomiting blood, white bumps bursting to the touch. And within a week his entire family was dead."

"White bumps?" I ask, wiping away my tears with the back of my hand. "The size of early spring peas?"

"You've seen it?"

"Does Anders have scars?" I ask, trying to control my breath.

"Yes," he replies warily.

"Like the one on my thigh?"

He thinks about it for a minute and nods; his cheeks flush.

"It's from the vaccination my father gave to me."

"I have one, too," he says, pointing out a small spot on the back of his shoulder.

"Did my father give you a shot?" I ask, running my thumb over his scar.

"Yes," he replies. "After we made the agreement."

The memory comes flooding back to me. The ear in that glass bottle at the apothecary—covered in pustules. My father wasn't buying that vial for himself or even for my mother—he was buying it for *this*.

"It's not a curse," I whisper, tears running down my cheeks. "It's smallpox. A virus. I don't know why I never put it together before, but my father had been working on a cure for years. You need to tell the others," I say, shooting to my feet. "If you go to them and tell them the truth . . . they'll stop."

Ryker shakes his head. "They'd never believe me, and even if they did . . . think about it . . ." A look of horror passes over his face. "If they think the curse isn't real, what's to stop them from crossing the fence and hunting them down? They'd all be dead by sunrise."

I sink back down to the bed. I don't know how long we stay like this, sitting side by side, but the inch between us might as well be a mile.

"Ryker," I whisper into the dark.

The fire has nearly gone out, the last of the embers barely clinging to life. For a brief moment, I wonder if he's already left to go hunting for the night, but when I look toward the doorway, I glimpse the top of his head. He's sitting on the floor next to me, leaning back against the mattress. I can tell by his breathing that he's fast asleep.

I know it's wrong, but I find myself reaching out to touch his hair. Skimming my fingers over the twisted ends sends a surge of warmth rushing through me. I've touched Michael's hair a million times back in the county and never felt anything remotely like this. I know I should stop, but instead, I find myself threading my fingers in deeper.

Ryker sits up with a jolt.

Clenching my hand into a tight fist, I try to get control of my breath.

"Another nightmare?" I ask.

"Try to go back to sleep," he whispers, staring into the dark.

"What do you dream of?"

"It doesn't matter," he replies. "They're just dreams."

I know he's probably right, but it hurts to hear him say that, especially after I confided in him about the girl from my dreams, everything it meant to me.

As if he can sense my feelings, he forces his shoulders to relax and leans back against the bed, eyes fixed on the doorway. "I'm in the woods," he says softly. "I see water. It's close, but I can't seem to reach it."

"What are you doing there?" I ask, taking in his musky scent.

"I'm searching for something . . . *waiting* for something . . . but I don't know what it is. I walk through the forest, but my footsteps don't make a sound, they don't leave a trail. A buck comes charging through the trees. I take out my best blade, but the animal runs right through me." I watch his Adam's apple depress in the firelight. "And when I wake, I have this horrible feeling, this ache in my gut, like I'll never leave those woods. I'll never reach the shore. I'll be alone . . . forever."

I want to reach out to touch him again. I want to tell him that I'm here, that he's not alone, but what good would it do? No matter the circumstances that threw us together, he will always be a poacher. I will always be prey. Nothing will ever change that. As soon as I cross back over the fence, all of this will be nothing but a dream.

A great and terrible dream.

I wake to find that Ryker's set up a fishing line across a corner of the tiny cabin, draping pelts over it to hide a small metal tub, filled with steaming hot water.

"I thought you might want a bath," he says.

Pulling the chemise away from my damp skin, I tuck in my chin and take a whiff. He thought right.

As he tends to the hearth, I duck behind the pelts. There's a small jar of tea tree oil and a teakwood comb waiting for me.

I peek through the pelts. It seems silly. He's seen me naked a hundred times; he has a map to my skin, for God's sake, but everything's different now.

Slipping out of the chemise, I step into the tub. A low grumble of thunder rattles the tin beneath me.

"Anders was right about the storm," I say.

Pulling the ribbon from my hair, I let out the longest sigh of my life. I feel bad for swatting his hand away when he tried to take it out when I first arrived. I'm not sure if it was tradition or the idea of magic that set me off, but it makes me realize how ingrained the county runs in me.

Sinking into the water, it's so hot, I'm afraid I'll scald my skin, but it feels too good to stop. I can't imagine how many kettles he had to boil to fill this.

I'm rubbing the tea tree oil into my hair when I feel something brush against my leg. I'm about to jump out of the tub when I see it's a flower petal. I take in a quick breath. Wild roses. In the county, bathing with flowers is a sin, a perversion, punishable by whip.

"Is everything okay?" he asks. He's so attuned to me now. He probably hears the change in my breath.

"There are rose petals in the bath," I say, trying to sound as calm as possible.

"It's called a perfume bath. I'm told it's good for your skin. I thought it might help with your scars, but I can take them out if you don—"

"No. Of course. That's very kind," I say, rolling my eyes at how stupid I sound—like I'm accepting the arm of a gentleman to escort me over a puddle that I could damn well get over myself.

Sinking back into the water, I try to avoid touching the petals, but I have to admit, it's nice.

Another roar of thunder trembles beneath me, making me tense up. I remember the last time a huge storm came through. That didn't end so well. Smoothing the rose water over the scar tissue on my shoulder, I try to think of something else. Anything else.

"Do you have a nickname?" I ask.

"What's that?"

"Like, Ry or Ryker Striker or—"

"No." He lets out a tiny laugh. I don't think I've ever heard him laugh before. "Do you?"

I shrug. The pain in my shoulder seems to have dulled to the point that I hardly wince when I move it anymore. "Some of them call me Tierney the Terrible."

"Are you terrible?"

"Probably." I smile as I sink further into the water.

"Who gave you a veil?" he asks.

The question catches me by surprise. "A very foolish boy." I study him through the gap in the pelts, noticing the way he's clenching his jaw. "Why?"

"Just curious."

"You didn't think anyone would be crazy enough to give me a veil?" I say, twisting the water out of my hair.

"I didn't say that," he replies, staring intently into the waning fire.

"His name's Michael," I say as I comb through my hair. "Michael Welk. His father owns the apothecary. He'll be taking over as head of the council."

"You say this like it's a bad thing." He peers back at me. "What's wrong with him?"

"Nothing's *wrong* with him," I say as I start to weave the ribbon into my braid. "He's been my best friend since we were kids. That's why I thought he understood. He knew I didn't want to be a wife. He knew about the dreams. When he lifted my veil, I wanted to punch him in the face. And then he had the nerve to tell me that he's always loved me . . . that I didn't have to change for him."

"Maybe he's telling the truth. Maybe he wants to help you." He pokes at the logs. "It sounds like he could've turned you in at any point for having the dreams, but he chose to protect you. He sounds like a decent man."

I tie off the braid and glare at him through the gap. "Whose side are you on?"

"My own." He meets my gaze. "Always my own." He goes back to the hearth, but I can tell his mind is elsewhere. "Maybe you have an opportunity to change things. Maybe you can help the women of the outskirts, too. Like the usurper."

"You know about the usurper?" I jump out of the bath, pulling on my chemise. "Have you seen her?" I join him by the smoldering remains of the fire.

"No." He takes me in, his gaze lingering. "But I hear they meet with her on the border, in a hidden clearing. They stand together in a circle holding hands, talking late into the night."

"Who told you that?"

He reaches out to catch a drop of water dripping from the end of my braid. "Rachelle . . . ," he says, glancing up at me through his dark lashes. "A girl I know."

"Oh," I reply, which comes off snippier than I intended. "Is that . . . do you have a . . . a someone back home?" I ask, tripping over my own words.

He looks at me curiously. "We're hunters. We live a nomadic lifestyle. We're not allowed to form attachments . . . to spread our bastard seed."

I can't stop myself from looking down at his trousers. "So, you're like the guards, then?"

"No." He shifts his weight at the thought. "I'm all . . . intact."

"So you've never . . ."

"Of course I have," he says with a grin, the corners of his eyes crinkling up. "Who else do you think the women practice on?"

"I thought you weren't allowed to breed."

"There are plenty of other ways to be with a woman. Besides, they know their bodies. They know when they're fertile."

A searing heat takes over my face. I'm not sure why it bothers me. The girls in the county do the same in the meadow when trying to snare a husband. But this feels different. For some reason, I can't stop picturing the girl in Gertie's lithograph. Is that what he's used to? What it's like for them?

"We get to go home for a few days every year, between hunting seasons, but I'll be going home to see my mother, my sisters. So the answer is no." He looks at me intently, and my breath seems to catch in my throat. "There's no one special waiting for me back home."

I pretend to be interested in the stitching of my chemise, anything to divert my attention from the lawlessness I feel racing through my blood, but even the stitching reminds me of his hands, the fact that he sewed this back together for me to make me feel more at ease. I keep reminding myself that the only reason he didn't kill me is because of the deal he made with my father, but the why doesn't seem to matter anymore. Maybe it's the close quarters, the fact that he saved me more times than I can count, or maybe it's forbidden fruit that's making me feel this way, but I don't think about getting out of here anymore. I don't think about going home. I think about what it would feel like . . . the touch of his lips . . . his skin against mine.

A huge gust of air blows through the chimney, sending a whoosh of blazing embers shooting toward us. Ryker scoops me up in his arms, flinging me onto the bed.

As he snuffs out the sparks on my skin, I don't scream out in pain. I don't make a sound. The only thing I feel right now is the weight of his body leaning against mine.

"Easy now," he says as he lifts a stray damp strand of hair from my collarbone, gently blowing on my skin. I think he's trying to cool me down, but it only seems to fan something deeper inside of me. It's a different kind of heat. One that I don't know how to quell. One that I'm not even sure I want to.

Dipping a cloth in a jar of aloe water, he runs it over the tiny burn marks on my neck, across my collarbone. I'm staring up at him, getting lost in the bones of his face, when he stops short of the lace edging of my chemise; a drop of water trails down my chest. There's a weighted pause.

I want to ignore it, pretend this isn't happening, but in this moment, I wish he hadn't mended my slip. I wish there was nothing between us.

He stares down at me with the same intensity as when we first met, but what I once took as anger, I now know to be fear.

"Are you afraid of me?" I whisper. "My magic?"

"I'm not afraid of you," he says, watching my lips. "I'm afraid of the way you make me feel."

As we stare into each other's eyes, the world around us disappears. I forget all about the girls at the encampment, the poachers hunting them down. I forget about my dreams, the world I'll have to return to come fall.

I want to be lost.

I understand why the girls in the encampment cling to their magic. It's the same reason I cling to this. We're all yearning for escape. A respite from the life that's been chosen for us.

Right now, there's only this. And there are worse ways to pass the time.

I'm not sure if I'm lifting my head or if he's leaning forward, but we're so close now that I can feel his breath pulsing against my skin.

As he brushes his lips against mine, I feel a rush of heat move through my body, and when our tongues touch, something else inside of me takes over.

Threading my hands in his hair, wrapping myself around him, I'm pulling him closer . . . when he's ripped from my limbs.

A boy with madness in his eyes stands at the end of the bed, holding Ryker back. His shroud has slipped from his face, revealing a spray of tiny scars covering his cheeks. *Anders.*

"I knew something was wrong," he pants. "Did it bite you?"

"It's not what you think." Ryker gives me a pleading look.

"Don't look at it. It must've used its magic on you. Get your shroud, hurry, before it does something worse."

Ryker lets out a long sigh. "I'm getting my shroud."

Anders releases him and pulls a blade from the sheath on his belt. As he stalks toward me, Ryker reaches for the charcoal gauze hanging next to the hearth. I wonder if he really believes it . . . that I've somehow bewitched him.

I'm scooting back on the bed, all the way against the wall, when Ryker steps behind Anders, ensnaring his wrist with the shroud, twisting his arm back, forcing him to drop the blade. Before Anders can even react, Ryker has his hands tied behind him, the blade at his throat. "Don't make me hurt you," Ryker says.

"What are you doing?" Anders struggles to get free. "I'm not going to *take* it from you. It's *your* kill."

Ryker kicks the stool away from the table full of knives to in front of the hearth. "I want to explain this to you."

"There's nothing to explain. It put a spell on you. Anyone can see that."

"There's no spell," Ryker says, forcing him to sit.

Unfortunately, Anders is directly in my line of sight now, which he takes full advantage of by staring a million daggers into me.

"Her name is Tierney."

Anders shakes his head violently. "It doesn't have a name. It's prey. Nothing more."

"This is the daughter of Dr. James. The man who saved your life."

"So?"

"So . . . we owe him."

Anders lets out a strangled laugh. "You're just going to keep it . . . like a pet?"

"I don't know what I'm going to do yet."

"Look." Anders softens his tone. "I get it, you're lonely. We're all lonely. But you're going to have to kill it eventually. Or you could let me do it." His eyes light up. "You can keep it until the end of the season, and when you're done—"

"I don't want to kill her," Ryker says. "I want to be with her."

The admission stuns me almost as much as Anders.

"Y-you can't be serious?" he sputters. "We're poachers. We took an oath."

"There are higher oaths." Ryker glances back at me, and all I want to do is shrink into the wall. "We always said we'd leave if given the chance."

"*This* is our chance," Anders says, nodding at me. "If you skin it, we can take your family west, just like we planned. You can pick any girl you want from the outskirts—"

"There are other ways to leave," Ryker says.

"Wait . . . you're not . . ." Anders's face goes ashen. "You're not thinking of deserting, are you? What about your family? Your pay? They'll starve—"

"Not if you claim them as your own." Ryker leans forward, looking at him intently.

"You're serious," Anders whispers, his eyes tearing up.

"What about the guards? Have you thought about that? I've seen one of them sneaking around. He'll be dragging in timber to fix the breach any day now. If they catch her here—"

"They won't."

"Unless I tell," Anders mutters.

Ryker springs on him, holding the knife so close to his jugular that I hear it scraping against his whiskers. "I will die before I let anyone hurt her. Do you understand?"

"What about me?" Anders looks up at him, and I can almost feel his heart breaking. "What about our plans?"

"You are my brother," Ryker says, cradling the back of Anders's head. "That will never change. Once we're settled, I'll send for you and my family."

"You think you can just drift off into the sunset?" Anders's nostrils flare.

"Why not? There's plenty of land for the taking. I'm a good hunter."

"Not good enough," Anders says, staring at me.

"She's with me now." Ryker moves into his line of sight, breaking the fixation. "The question is, are you?" He tightens his grip on the knife. "I need to know right now where you stand."

"With you," Anders whispers. "I've always been with you, brother. Till the end."

Ryker looks back at me as if he's waiting for my approval. I nod. I don't know what else to do.

Bending to untie Anders's hands, Ryker says, "I know this is a lot to ask, but this is all going to work out. You'll see." He gives his shoulders a squeeze, before letting him go.

As Anders walks toward the door, I'm bracing myself for anything, but Ryker seems to have quelled his anger.

Anders pauses by the door. "I dropped a jar of hemlock silt around here somewhere. That's why I came . . . I wanted to show you. The storm kicked up a whole mess of it."

"That'll fetch a great price," Ryker says excitedly.

"There's more down in the third cove," Anders says. "We could haul it in together. Fifty-fifty."

"Nah, you can keep it, but I'll help you bring it in."

"You'd do that?" Anders asks sheepishly.

"We're still in this together," Ryker says. "Now there's just one more of us."

Anders looks my way. He still can't meet my eyes, but it's a start.

"First light, I'll meet you at the cove," Anders says with a slight smile. And for a brief second I can see the sweet boy Ryker told me about.

Immediately, I start cleaning up the cabin. I don't know what else to do . . . with my mind . . . my body.

Ryker leans against the wall, watching me. "Whatever you're thinking—"

"Thinking? What could I possibly be thinking?" I pick up the shroud off the floor. "Oh, I don't know . . . that

maybe you just had someone tied up with this . . . someone who wanted to kill me, or you to kill me, or kill me
together. I mean . . . kill *it*."

A pained look crosses his face. "You have to understand," he says as he moves toward me. "He was taken
over the barrier by prey, they *bit* him, he believes his entire family was wiped out by the curse . . . but he'll come
around. Just give him a chance. He would never do anything to hurt me."

"It's not you I'm worried about." I push past him, grabbing the stool, putting it back by the table. "And what's
this about *being* with me?" I scoff. "Don't you think you
should've at least asked me first? Or are you just going to
claim me like the men in the county?"

"I just thought . . . okay . . . fine," he says, following
close behind. "We can get married, if that's better."

"No!" I yell as I storm off to another corner, but it's only
a few feet away. There's nowhere to go. I accidentally kick
something; it rolls under the bed.

"You don't have to marry me," he says, throwing his
hands up in the air. "I just thought with the hair . . . and
the ribbon . . . the way you were raised . . . that it would
be . . . *important*."

Getting down on my hands and knees, I reach under
the bed to grab whatever it was that I kicked. It's a jar.
Holding it up to the light, my mind stutters.

"I'm trying to talk to you . . . will you please hear m—"

"Wait. Is this the hemlock silt Anders was talking about?"

"You found it," Ryker says, reaching for it.

"Are you *sure* this is it?" I tug back on it, forcing him to
meet my eyes.

"Positive," he says, clearly taken aback by my intensity. "You can tell by the bright green color and the way the edges spread out like—"

"What would this do to a person?"

"I've never touched the stuff, but the old crones use it in the northern woods for scrying work. If you even put a drop on your tongue, you'll have visions. They say it connects you to the spirit world, above *and* below."

"What about prolonged use . . . like all day . . . every day?"

"You'd go insane."

I put my hands over my mouth to stifle a sobbing gasp, but it leaks through my fingers. "I'm not crazy, then." I let out a sputtering burst of pent-up air. "Don't you get it?" With trembling hands, I grab on to him. "That's what's happening to the grace year girls. I knew it was something . . . the water . . . the food . . . the air . . . but it's *this* . . . the algae . . . it's inside the well. They all drink from it. When I was in the camp, I did, too. I was having dizzy spells, feeling things on my skin that weren't there. But after I was banished to the woods and started drinking the water from high on the spring, I felt better. Clearer." Fresh tears flood my eyes. "It's not magic . . . it's poison."

I get up and start pacing the floor. "They need to know. *Everyone* needs to know."

He shakes his head. "It wouldn't make any difference."

"How can you say that? It would make all the difference in the world. They wouldn't be losing their minds . . . they wouldn't be acting like this. The grace year could come to an end."

"The curse. The magic. Even if they believed us, it wouldn't really *change* anything," he says. "As long as there's a price on your flesh, there will always be poachers. There will always be a grace year."

"There has to be something we can do," I say, my eyes welling up.

"We can leave," he says, wiping a tear from my cheek. "Last year, a trapper from the north brought us a message from a family we knew. They made it over the mountains, beyond the plains, to a settlement where men and women live side by side, as equals. Where they're free."

I'm trying to even imagine what that would be like. Everything in me wants to say yes, run away from the pain, but a horrible feeling spreads from the pit of my stomach all the way to my throat. "Our families—"

"Anders will take care of my family. They'll get his pay, and as soon as we're settled—"

"What about my family? If my body is unaccounted for, my sisters will be punished, sent to the outskirts."

"If Michael is half the man you say he is, he would never let that happen."

I bristle at the mention of his name. It feels wrong coming out of Ryker's mouth. "Let's leave him out of this."

"Even if they were sent to the outskirts, my mother would take them in."

"But would they be expected to . . ."

"Not until they've bled," he says, matter-of-fact.

"And after that?" I ask, the realization gutting me.

"As soon as we're settled, we'll send for them."

"And if we never *settle*?" I ask, but I mean *live*, and I'm tired of not saying what I mean, so I ask again. "What if we don't *survive*? What happens to them?"

"We will . . . but why is it okay for my sisters to work in the outskirts and not yours?" he asks.

"It's not . . . ," I say, completely flustered. "But when I think of my sisters having to receive a man from the county, a man like Tommy Pearson, or any other man who's patted their head at church, watched them sing in the choir, watched them grow up, it makes me sick to my stomach."

"When I found you on the ice that night, you were ready to take your own life rather than hand it over to a poacher. Your sisters would've been sent to the outskirts. Why are you hesitating now?"

"I wasn't in my right mind." I raise my voice. "You saw me . . . I was dying."

He pulls me close, pressing his forehead against mine, letting out a heavy sigh. "I'm sorry. That wasn't fair."

The nearness of him, the warmth, feels like a soothing balm.

"Do you trust me?" he asks.

"Yes," I reply without hesitation.

"Then trust that we can do this," he says. "We have time to figure all of this out, but in the meantime, know that I will find a way. For all of us."

"Why do you want this?" I ask, searching his face for answers.

He traces his fingers down my braid, all the way to the end of the red silk ribbon. "I want to see you with your hair down, with the sun on your face."

Just before dawn, Ryker descends the ladder to meet Anders, and I feel hopeful for the first time in I don't even know how long. Lying down on the bed, breathing in his heavy scent, I imagine what it would be like, being with him, as man and wife, away from the county, away from all of this. I always thought the best I could hope for was to work in the fields. I never imagined anything more than that. I can tell myself it's because I'm a realist, but the truth is, I'm a coward. You can't be hurt if you don't try. I don't know when it happened—when I stopped reaching for things. Maybe around my first bleed, that first heavy reminder of our place in this world. But I think I'm ready to start striving for something more.

When I hear Ryker's boots on the ladder, I spring from the bed. He must've forgotten something, but I'm glad. I'm going to surprise him, tell him yes—but a dark-shrouded figure emerges through the door covering. Before I can grab one of the knives, he has me up against the wall, crushing the hilt of his blade against my windpipe.

"Anders . . ." I try to get free, but he only presses harder.

"Don't talk. Listen. Tonight, when the moon is highest

in the sky, you will leave." I'm blindly groping the walls behind me, desperate to find something I can use as a weapon. "There will be a candle and a shroud waiting for you at the foot of the ladder." I'm struggling against him, trying to grasp his arm, but it's no use. "I will make sure your path is clear and marked to the breach in the fence. There, you will take off the shrouds, leaving them behind, and then slither back into your hole, where you belong."

"Ryker . . . ," I whisper, straining to speak. "He'll kill you first."

"You need to know that I'll be coming back here at first light with every poacher in this camp. If you're not gone, and Ryker chooses to protect you, I won't be able to stop them."

"He'll never forgive you for this."

"If you breathe a word to him . . . if you don't follow my exact instructions, I will kill you. And if you think you're safe behind that wall, you're wrong. Do you see my face?" he says, forcing me to look him in the eyes. "I'm the only person who's ever survived the curse, which means I'm immune. If you try to get a message to him . . . if you try to lure him to the fence . . . if you so much as breathe in his direction, I'll know. And I'd rather watch him die a thousand deaths than watch him betray his family . . . his oath."

"You mean, betray *you*," I manage to get out.

He gets so close to my face that I can smell the bitter herbs clinging to his breath. "I would love nothing more than to peel the skin from your face like an overripe peach." He takes in a deep breath through his nostrils, regaining his composure. "But I don't want to hurt him. And I don't think you want to, either. Play nice, play by my rules. Or I will come for you."

I don't know how long I sit there, running through every possible scenario, but by the time I find the will to move, the day has passed me by. The sky is smudged in pinks and purples—not unlike the colors my neck will be, come morning.

Hearing boots on the bottom tread of the ladder, I start rushing around, gathering my meager belongings, my cloak, my boots, my stockings. I don't know what I'm going to say to him, but I don't even know if it's Ryker. What if it's Anders coming back to finish the job . . . or the guards . . . Even if it's Hans, how could I begin to explain this?

Grabbing a knife, I crouch next to the table. My hands are trembling.

A shrouded figure steps inside. I'm ready to slice his tendons wide open.

"Tierney?" Ryker calls out.

I let out a shuddering breath; he turns to find me crumpled on the floor.

"Hey . . . hey . . . it's okay," he says. "I'm here. I'm not going to let anything happen to you. I told you that."

As he pries the knife out of my hand and pulls me to my feet, I hold on to him, tighter than I've ever held on to anyone.

"Everything's good now. I talked with Anders. He's on our side. You have nothing to fear from him. He wants to help."

I'm opening my mouth to try and tell him what happened when he says, "I have something for you. Anders actually helped me find it. He knows a place."

He takes a piece of linen from his pocket, holding it as gently as if he's carrying a butterfly. Peeling back the layers, he reveals a tattered deep blue pansy.

I feel a distant memory tugging at me. My veiling day. I was on my way to meet Michael when I stopped to look at the flowers . . . there was a woman working in the greenhouse who told me that one day someone would give me a flower—that it would be a little withered around the edges, but it would mean just the same. A wave of raw emotion rises inside of me. What she didn't tell me was that it would mean so much more.

Looking up at him, I have to blink back the tears. I doubt Ryker knows what it means—he probably just thought it was pretty, but it's hard not to see it as a sign.

"This is the flower of good-bye," I whisper. "A bittersweet parting."

"I thought it meant everlasting love," he says.

"That's a blue violet," I explain.

"I guess Anders isn't as good with flowers as he thinks he is."

"It's a tricky one," I reply. But I think Anders knew exactly what he was doing when he picked this.

"Can we just pretend it's a violet?" He smiles.

Desperate to hide my feelings, I nod, and quickly turn away, placing the bloom on the edge of the table.

As he takes off his shroud, I realize how good I've gotten at pretending.

Pretending not to notice the knives covering nearly every surface—knives that were specially designed to peel my flesh. Pretending that eating preserves out of the same kind of jar they use to store our body parts in to sell back to the county is perfectly normal. Pretending this isn't crazy . . . that we could actually get away with it . . . live happily ever after.

But there's one thing in all of this that's not pretend.

I'm in love with him.

I may not be able to spend my life with him, grow old with him, but I can choose to give him my heart. My body. My soul. That's the one thing they will never be able to control in me.

Untying the bow from my ribbon, I wait for him.

He swallows hard before stepping toward me.

Taking in slow, measured breaths, he twirls the strand around his finger.

Our eyes meet. The energy radiating between us is so intense it feels like we might burn down the world.

As he pulls the strand, releasing my braid, I know I should avert my gaze, turn my eyes to God, the way we're taught, but in this moment, all I want is for him to see me. To be seen.

As he lifts my slip over my head, it's like lifting my veil.

As I unbutton his trousers, I'm accepting his flower.

When he presses his skin against mine, the bloom he chose for me opens up, filling the space with a heady perfume of longing and pain. Entirely ephemeral. Absolutely forbidden. And completely out of our control.

Dropping the ribbon to the floor, the last confine the county holds over me, I lead him to the bed.

He's a poacher. I'm prey. Nothing will ever change that. But in this small treetop cabin, away from our home, and the men who named us, we are still human beings, longing for connection, to feel something more than despair in this bleak year.

With nothing but the moon and the stars as our witness, he lies beside me. Pressing our palms together, entwining our fingers, we breathe in time. This is exactly where we need to be. There's no second-guessing, no thinking. And when his lips meet mine, the world disappears.

Like magic.

Tonight, as I lie next to him, I memorize every inch of him with my fingertips. Every scar. Every chiseled ridge. I whisper secrets into his skin, everything I've longed to tell him, and when I run out of breath, I place the deep blue flower in the palm of his hand. He'll know what it means.

As bittersweet as it is, I can't help thinking that maybe it survived for exactly this occasion. Because words would fail me, my lips would betray me. But this flower will tell him everything he wants to hear, everything he needs to tell himself. He can read into every petal, every fall, every rivet in the stem, but the meaning will remain the same. Good-bye.

He'll probably be wondering if he did something, said something to make me leave, or maybe he'll just think I was spooked by Anders. No matter the cause, no matter the pain, he'll understand it was for the best—inevitable.

He saved my life. And now it's time for me to save his.

Gathering my things, I descend the ladder. I see Anders was true to his word, placing the candle and the shroud beneath the blind, but the candle has burned down to the quick, leaving nothing but a pool of soft wax. As I look up at the sky, a feeling of dread presses down on me. I thought it was just before dawn, but the sun has been up for hours, hidden beneath thick dark clouds. I stayed too long.

Wrapping the shroud around my body, my face, I smell fetid meat and bitter herbs. It smells of Anders.

Bumping into something hanging from the ladder, I grab on to it to stop the noise. I know that sound. It's the wind chime Anders made. I can't help wondering if these are the discarded bones of grace year girls. If that's what will happen to me.

Stepping away from the shore, back toward the barrier, feels wrong. Like something my body isn't supposed to do. He said he'd mark the trail. I'm searching for a pattern, anything that stands out, when I spot the orange-yellow leaves of the butterfly weed marking the trail. The meaning couldn't be more clear—leave and never return. Anders definitely knows his flowers.

As I follow the trail of petals, there's a part of me that wonders if this is all an elaborate hoax, a path leading me straight into Anders's blade, but when I clear the last of the trees and come face-to-face with the towering fence, I know he meant what he said—every word of it. But where's the gap in the fence? I'm wondering if I'm too late, if Hans has already mended it, when I see a giant pile of leaves heaped against the side of the barrier. Getting down on my hands and knees, I start digging through it, relieved and heartbroken all at once to see that it's still there. The gap is smaller than I remember.

But the world was smaller then.

I'm getting ready to crawl back through when I hear a strange brushing sound behind me. Like silk against rough fingers. I told myself I wouldn't look back, but my head turns on pure instinct. There's nothing there. Nothing I can see, but with spring in full bloom, everything feels hidden from me. Even the top of Ryker's blind has been swallowed up by the foliage. Nothing but a memory. Another dream I once had.

Crawling through the gap, I rip off the shrouds, but I can't get away from Anders's scent, his blade against my throat.

I brace myself against a pine, trying to catch my breath, trying to pull myself together, but just being back inside the encampment brings that claustrophobic feeling back.

As I stare at the path ahead, I'm thinking I could hide in the woods, wait out the rest of the year. I picked up enough survival skills watching Ryker these past few months, but that would be the coward's way out. I'd never be able to live with myself knowing that I could've helped them. That I could've stopped this.

Despite everything they've done to me, they deserve to know the truth.

The woods look different than the last time I was here, every shade of green imaginable tucked in all around me, but the rocks, the trees, the jagged paths seem to be burned into my memory. With each step forward, I'm trying not to remember the madness, the cruelty, the chaos, but as soon as I reach the perimeter, the edge of the clearing, my heart starts beating hard against my rib cage, my palms are sweaty, my limbs feel weak. I have no idea what they'll do to me, but it's too late to turn back now.

Tying the red silk ribbon around my wrist, I step into the camp.

I'm expecting a flurry of commotion, the excited panic that comes when the trappers return from the wild—return from the dead—but no one seems to give me a second glance. In fact, the first few girls that pass seem to look right through me. I wonder if they think I'm a ghost, an apparition come back to haunt them. And for a moment, I wonder if it's true. Maybe I died that night, maybe Ryker skinned me alive, and all of this is an elaborate hallucination of my own making.

Because even without the influence of the well water, I feel dizzy in their presence. Transparent. Paper thin. Like one stiff breeze could turn me into stardust.

"I know you." A girl staggers toward me. I think it's Hannah, but it's hard to tell beneath all the dirt and grime. "Tierney the Terrible."

I nod.

"Someone was looking for you." She reaches up to scratch her head but ends up pulling out a clump of hair instead. "I can't remember who," she says before wandering off.

Cautiously, I walk the camp. The pots and kettles are piled up next to the fire, rotting food curdling at the bottom, rice scattered in the dirt, empty jars and cans strewn about. Roaches are battling it out for the remains. I pass Dovey's cage, thinking she's certainly dead by now, but huddled in the bottom corner there's a scrawny bird. She's not cooing, but when I slip my finger through the slats to try to pet her, she lashes out with a vicious squawk.

"That's how she says good morning." A soft voice passes behind me. I turn to find Vivi shuffling toward the gate, where a handful of other girls are huddled together.

The limbs of the punishment tree hang heavy, bloated with new trinkets, the soil beneath, caked in fresh blood. There's a girl standing behind the tree—she's so thin that I almost miss her. She's stroking a long copper braid that obviously used to be attached to her skull. It makes me think of Gertie. *Where is she?*

As I open the door to the lodging house, the smell hits me like a runaway coach.

Urine, disease, rot, and filth. I wonder if it smelled like this when I lived here or if this is something new.

There are a few girls lying in their cots. They're so still that for a moment I wonder if they're dead, but I can detect the faint rise and fall of their chests. I stare down at them, but they don't meet my eyes. They seem to be lost in a world of their own making.

I find the spot where my cot used to be. I remember how scared I was the last time I was here, but I also re-member Gertrude, Helen, Nanette, and Martha—talking late into the night. We were so full of hope in the begin-ning. We really thought we could change things, but one by one, they fell under the influence of the water . . . of Kiersten.

Their cots are gone now. I tell myself that maybe they've just moved their beds to the other side of the room, but when I look over at the swollen pile of iron frames stacked up in the corner, I know it's a lie.

I'd love to play dumb, pretend I've been in a soundless slumber, but I heard the caws in the woods, as I lay beside a poacher every night, doing nothing to help them. Nothing to warn them. "I'm so sorry, Gertie," I whisper through my trembling lips.

"She's not here," a voice calls out from the far corner of the room, making my skin crawl. I don't see anyone there, but as I walk toward the sound, a hand reaches out from under one of the beds, grasping my ankle.

I scream.

"Shhh . . . ," she whispers, peeking out from beneath the rusty springs. "Don't or you'll wake the ghosts."

It's Helen. Or what's left of Helen. There's a half-moon puckered scar where her right eye used to be.

"What happened to you?"

"You can see me?" she asks, a huge grin spreading across her face.

I nod, trying not to stare.

"I got so invisible that I couldn't see myself anymore. They had to take out my eye, so I could come back . . . but Gertie . . . ," she says, staring off in the distance. "They took her to the larder."

"The larder?" I ask. "Why?"

She tucks her chin into her chest. "Gertie was too dirty." She snickers, but her laughter quickly dissolves into soft tears.

Backing away from her, I leave the lodging house and walk across the clearing to the larder. Each step feels harder than the last, like I'm trudging against a strong current. People halt and stare, Jessica, Ravenna, but no one stops me. No one is coming after me. Not yet.

The sticky heat has made the door swell. As I pry it open, a flood of flies comes pouring out, but all I find is

a cot piled high with ratty blankets. And now I understand what Helen meant—the smell is unbearable. Covering my nose and mouth with my overskirt, I take a good
look around. The shelves have been emptied; a bucket
sits on the ground next to the cot, full of bile and filth.
There's a dark green cloak peeking out from beneath the
scratchy wool blankets.

"Gertie," I whisper.

Nothing.

I try one more time. "Gertrude?"

"Tierney?" a soft voice replies.

My breath hitches in my throat. Digging through the
blankets, I find her. She's bone thin, with skin the color
of a late January sky.

"Where have you been?" she asks.

It's all I can do to hold myself together. "I'm here now,"
I say, reaching for her hand. I feel her pulse, but it's so
weak I'm afraid her heart will stop at any moment.

"Let's get you situated," I say, peeling off the blankets,
squeezing her limbs, trying to get some blood flowing.
"Did they stop feeding you?" I whisper.

"No." She blinks up at me. "I just can't keep anything
down."

"How long have you been like this?"

"Is it the new year?" she asks.

"It's June." I'm lifting her neck to prop it up on a rolled-
up blanket when my fingers slip into something soft and
gooey.

Taking the dusty lamp from the hook in the corner, I
turn it up so I can take a look. The sight turns my stomach. I want to throw up, but I can't let her know how bad

it is. "Does this hurt?" I ask, pressing on the red swollen flesh edging the wound on the back of her skull.

"No. But I seem to have lost my braid," she says, moving her hand down an imaginary line where it once lay.

And I realize that's when time must've stopped moving for her—the day her braid was severed from her body. The day I was banished to the woods.

"Where is she?" Kiersten's voice ratchets up my spine. I could try to hide, make her come in and get me, but Gertie's been through enough.

"I'll be right back," I whisper as I pull a blanket over her and slip through the larder door to find Kiersten heading straight toward me from the eastern barrier, a swarm of girls hovering around her.

She moves like a wounded predator, her steps are slow but calculated, a rusty hatchet at her side. It takes all of my nerve to hold my ground.

"I have something for you," she says as she swings the hatchet in front of her.

Instinctively, I flinch, but she only drops the blade at my feet.

"We need firewood."

I look up at her, really look at her—the dull-yellow matted hair, sunken cheeks, sallow skin, her once-clear blue eyes completely swallowed up by her pupils—and I realize it's not just Gertie . . . Kiersten doesn't remember. None of them do.

As I lean down to pick up the hatchet, she places her foot on it. "Hold it. You're not allowed to take out your braid unless you've embraced your magic."

Everyone in the camp seems to snap to attention, as if they can smell the venom in the air.

"I have," I reply, a fresh surge of panic bubbling up in my chest. "You helped me. Remember?"

Her eyes narrow on me.

"You dared me to go into the woods. I was lost for a long time . . . near death—"

"You survived the woods . . . the ghosts?" Hannah asks.

"Yes." I glance back at the trees, remembering the ghost stories they used to tell around the fire. "They spoke to me . . . saved me . . . led me home."

I'm hoping my face isn't doing what my insides are doing. I feel like a coward for lying, but it's better than losing a tongue.

Kiersten reluctantly takes her foot off the blade.

I grip the hatchet. The handle is still warm from her touch. The heat moves through me, something I haven't felt in a long time. There's a part of me that wants to return the kindness, an eye for an eye, but I have to remind myself that it's the water making them behave like this. They're sick.

"Are they with us now?" Jenna asks, her eyes darting around the clearing like a scared animal.

Searching the camp, I'm trying to come up with something that might appease them when I see Meghan standing by the gate, who might as well be a ghost with that complexion. "There's one over there," I say, pointing in her direction. "But she's harmless. She's just trying to find a way out . . . she just wants to go home."

As they stare at the gate, I know they're thinking the exact same thing.

Kiersten steps close to me, so close that I can feel her breath on my skin. "How did you survive in the woods without food or water?"

I'm grasping for answers, trying to figure out what to say, when I think of the truth. Maybe there's a way I can use this to get them to stop drinking from the well of their own accord. "The ghosts . . . they led me to a spring in the woods. I was very ill, but the water healed me."

There are whispers buzzing all around me, like an agitated hive.

I'm thinking she's going to call my bluff, strike me down, but instead, she nudges the cauldron toward me. "Prove it." Roaches come skittering out onto her bare feet, but she doesn't even notice. "Bring this back full of ghost water, or don't bother coming back at all."

"Sure." I swallow hard. "I just want to check on Gertie first," I say, moving toward the larder.

Kiersten steps in front of me. "I'll take care of Gertie until you get back."

I know Kiersten well enough to know it isn't a kindness. It's a threat.

Taking the hatchet and the kettle, I back away into the woods. I don't dare turn my back on them.

It's not until I've been safely swallowed up by the foliage that I sink to the forest floor and finally let it out. I'm not sure if I'm crying for them or for me, but I have to find a way to make this right. To fix this.

I may have broken my vows, shamed my family name, but I'm still a grace year girl.

I'm one of them.

And if I don't help them, who will?

Tucking the hatchet into my skirt, I find the faint remains of the trail I made all those months ago. As I'm hacking my way through vines and hanging moss, a needling thought creeps in. What if I can't find the spring? What if it's been swallowed up by the forest or dried out? If I don't deliver the water, they'll never believe a word I say. Quickening my pace, I pull myself up the steep incline, relieved to find the spring still there. Collapsing beside it, all I want to do is strip off my clothes, jump in, cool off, but I need to get back to Gertie. I don't like the way Kiersten said she'd take care of her until I returned.

As I'm washing out the kettle, I hear a soft scratching noise, the same thing I heard this morning before I crossed over the barrier. Following the sound, I climb the ridge and see something I'm not quite ready for. How could anyone be ready for something like this? The dead girl. Her stark white bones exposed to the surface. The last time I was here, only her skull was peeking up from the earth. I know that storm was vicious, washed away half of the ridge, taking my seeds down with it, but I didn't think it could do something like *this*.

As I walk toward her body, I see that she's curled into a tight ball, every delicate bone in perfect formation; even the tattered remains of her ribbon are still coiled around the vertebrae in her neck.

There's a part of me that wishes I really could communicate with the dead. What would she tell me? Who did this to her and why? Leaving her body here is almost a bigger sin than the murder itself. We all know what an unclaimed body means to us . . . to our families. Whoever did this must've hated her so much that they were willing to condemn her entire family. Even after everything I've witnessed here, it's hard to imagine a grace year girl being capable of such a crime.

A wave of nausea rushes over me. Crawling to the ledge, I'm gulping down air, trying to calm myself, when I see the most astonishing thing. A pea shoot.

It doesn't sound like much, but grabbing on to some vines, I lean over as far as I dare.

There's life. So much life.

Squash, tomatoes, leeks, carrots, parsnips, corn, peppers, cabbage, and chard—a show of abundance, so rich that it takes my breath away. "June's garden," I whisper, tears stinging my eyes. "I can't believe it."

Grasping some leafy tops—the only ones I can reach—I pull up some plump carrots, and a few beets, before settling back on the ridge. It's the best I can manage until I rig up some ropes, but this will make for a better meal than they've probably had in months.

I want to sing and dance, kiss the ground, but the realization quickly sets in that I have no one to tell. Or the person I want to tell is on the other side of the barrier. He might as well be on the other side of the world.

Looking back at the dead girl, I think of Ryker's words.

From death there is life. My eyes start to well up, but I can't afford to think about him right now. I can't afford to go soft.

After chopping wood and filling up the kettle with fresh water, I dig out a clump of clay and place it in my stocking for safekeeping.

Using my overskirt as a satchel, I tie up the firewood and affix it to my back. The vegetables go in my pockets; the wild herbs and bloodroot I collect go in my bosom. Getting the full kettle of water down the slope and dragging it back to the camp is difficult, especially with the heavy load balanced on my back, but this is the only thing that's going to save them, save us all.

When I stop to take a breath, I realize this is the point in the forest where I used to veer off to the gap in the eastern fence, but that's not what has me choked up. There's a thyme flower nestled beneath a patch of clover. It's a low flower, one that's so common most people hardly think of it anymore, but in the old language, it symbolized forgiveness. My first instinct is to think of all the people I've hurt, the people I'd like to give it to—Ryker, Michael, my father, my mother, my sisters—but they're not here, and their forgiveness is out of my hands. There's one person who desperately needs it, though, someone I'm completely in control of—myself. I did the best I could with what I'd been given. I stuck to my beliefs. I survived against all odds. I fell in love and gave my heart freely, knowing that it would be broken. I can't regret the choices I've made, and so I must accept them. As I tuck the thyme flower into the top of my chemise, I hear something behind me.

I'm probably just being paranoid. With good reason,

considering that the last time I was in the encampment they tried to cut out my tongue.

"Kiersten, is that you?" I whisper.

There's no answer, but I hear the same light scratching sound I heard on the other side of the barrier . . . the ridge. It could be anything—a small creature skittering through the leaves, a boar in the distance rubbing its tusk against a tree—but I swear I can feel it. Eyes on my skin. Like the woods are staring back at me.

When I emerge from the forest, the girls gather round. They seem in awe that I've made it back alive—*again*—but even more so that I returned bearing gifts.

Kiersten pushes forward to inspect the water.

"Drink it." Her eyes fix on me and I realize she thinks I might be trying to poison her. Glancing over at the well, it almost makes me laugh. *Almost.*

Taking the clam shell from my pocket, I dip up some water and slurp it down. "See? It's good."

She goes to put her dirty hands in, and I stop her.

"The ghosts gave me this. I'll share it with you, but if you try to take it from me, there will be consequences." I nod toward the woods. "They say you can have one sip each, for now. The rest is for supper."

I'm waiting for her to knock me out, at the very least scream at me, but all she does is hold out her hands, as delicately as if she's accepting a sip of wine from the jeweled goblet at church.

I dip the shell into the water and hand it to her. She sips it, savoring each drop, just like Mother does with the last of the dandelion wine.

As she takes in the final bit, the girls line up for their turn. Kiersten stands guard, supervising them. I wonder what she's thinking—if by drinking this she'll become more powerful . . . or if this means the ghosts won't harm her . . . whatever's going on in her hemlock-silt-addled brain, I'm grateful for it.

When the last one has had her taste, Kiersten motions for them to back off.

As they slowly dissipate, I let out a long, quiet breath.

I've found the one thing that still scares them: the ghosts of the fallen grace year girls.

I'm not sure how long I'll be able to keep it up—hopefully long enough to get them clear of the hemlock silt—but my first priority is Gertrude. Not only because she's my friend, but because they always put her last, they put her out here to die, and I'll be damned if I'm going to let that happen.

As I drag her cot out of the rancid shack into the late-afternoon sun, Gertrude blinks up at it in disbelief and then gives me a hazy smile. I wonder how long it's been since she's seen the sun. Carefully, using the clump I brought back in my stocking, I spread clay over her hair, her scalp, and wash it clean with a bucket of well water. I then grind the bloodroot stems into a thick paste, applying it directly to her wound.

Limb by limb, I scrub Gertie's emaciated body with basil and sage leaves. I'm trying to be gentle with her, not expose too much skin at one time so she doesn't get too cold, but she's shivering so hard that it rattles the rusty springs beneath her. I ask her if she's okay, and she just smiles up at me. "Look how pretty the sky is," she whispers.

Fighting back tears, I look up and nod. She's so incredibly grateful, but she shouldn't have to feel grateful for this—for being treated like a basic human being. None of us should.

Outside of the infection, she seems clearer than the rest. Maybe because she hasn't been able to keep anything down—including the well water.

I give her little sips of fresh water.

"It tastes so good," she says, latching on to the cup, trying to gulp down the liquid.

I have to pry the cup away from her. "You need to take it slow."

I remember Ryker saying the exact same thing to me. It's hard to imagine him caring for me like this. Bathing me, cleaning up maggots and puke. I even stabbed him in the stomach and he still took care of me. But I can't think about Ryker right now. I can't think about anything other than getting the camp clear of this poison.

Shredding the kindling into long wispy threads, I arrange the firewood in the pit and hit the flint over and over and over again until I finally catch a spark. I'm out of practice, but the wood shavings catch like a charm. With the fire crackling, I stash some of the fresh water in an empty honey jug in the larder and use the rest to make a stew. Adding carrots, beets, wild onion, and herbs, I set the kettle over the fire, and soon every girl in the encampment is gravitating toward me. Even Kiersten makes an appearance, pacing the length of the clearing like a caged animal. She hasn't asked for the hatchet back, so I keep it close, just in case they try to jump me, but all they do is sit there, licking their lips, staring into the flames.

I wonder how long it's been since they've eaten a meal. There's a part of me that wants to refuse them, tell them this is only for me and Gertie—it would serve them right—but seeing them like this, emaciated, dirty, living-breathing-hollowed-out skulls, I have to remind myself, it's not their fault. It's the water that made them do all those things. As soon as I get them clear, everything will be different.

One by one, I dish out the portions, and we sit around the fire, just like we did on that first night, but there are a lot fewer mouths to feed now.

A noise rustles on the perimeter. The other girls must hear it, too, because all eyes are focused on the woods now. It's the same sound I've been hearing all day, but I think it goes back further than that . . . it's something familiar . . . a memory tugging at me . . . but I can't seem to place it.

"What are they saying?" Jenna asks.

They all look at me, and I realize they think it's the ghosts. My first instinct is to tell them they don't want us to drink from the well, but that's too clumsy. Too obvious. I need to find a way for Kiersten to think it's her idea. If I come on too strong, too soon, she'll know I'm up to something. Best to start small. And since I'm a terrible liar, I'll start with something I know to be true.

"It's Tamara," I whisper, the memory of her death making

my throat feel thick. "She lived for two more days, had burns on her back and chest from the lightning strike, but her poacher was able to render most of her flesh."

They all look to Kiersten, but she pretends not to notice, staring directly into the flames.

There's another sound, closer this time.

"Who's that?" Jenna asks, peeking up through her fingers.

"It's Meg," I reply.

The girls get very still.

"She disappeared months ago," Dena whispers, the memory of her best friend coming back to her. "We thought the ghosts took her."

"No," I whisper. "She escaped, under the eastern barrier . . . took a knife in the neck. Drowned in her own blood before her poacher even got off her fingertips."

"Stop . . . stop." Helen's shoulders begin to shake. At first I think she's laughing, like she did on that night they threw Tamara's twitching body out of the gate, but when she glances up at me, I see wet streaks running down her dirty cheeks. She opens her mouth to speak, but nothing comes out. Maybe she can't voice it yet, maybe she doesn't know how, but I can see it on her face—the seed of regret.

Looking around the campfire, it's hard to imagine that in a few short months, we'll be going home to become docile wives, compliant servers, laborers. Maybe for some, the true believers, they'll think nothing of it—that everything was God's will, a necessary evil so they could come home as purified women. Most have had their first taste of freedom—they might even like what they've become— but what of the others, the ones who only wanted to survive. When the "magic" wears off, when the memories come pouring in, how will they make peace with what happened here? The horror we inflicted on one another.

But maybe the well water will make them think it's all a hazy dream. They won't be able to distinguish fact from fiction, dream from reality. Maybe that's the look the women always get after they return, the one I can never decipher. Maybe they don't even know what they're feeling.

Desperately trying to remember, but blessed to forget.

After cleaning out the larder, I move Gertrude back inside. They made it clear they would make room for us in the lodging house, but I don't trust the girls, not until they're clear of the hemlock silt.

Settling in beside her, I feed her a special broth I made with yarrow, ginger, and the remaining bloodroot. I've seen my father make it for his infected patients a hundred times before.

"This should help ease your stomach, your fever."

"It's good." She takes a few sips through her chattering teeth, and when she looks up at me, I notice the same chalky red residue clinging to the corners of her mouth that I saw on my mother the night before I left.

My mind stumbles over the memory. It wasn't the

blood of grace year girls, it was the broth. I remember the cold sweat on my mother's brow, her trembling fingers, her near-fainting spell at the church. She must've been ill, but why would they try to hide it from me?

Gertrude reaches back to scratch her head; I catch her hand. "No more scratching." Ripping off a strip of my underskirt, I wrap the linen around her hands, tying them off like mittens. "That's why you're sick. Your wound is badly infected."

"Wound," she whispers, the memory of what happened slipping over her like the darkest of veils. "How will Geezer Fallow like me now?" She tries to make a joke out of it, but it's no use.

We sit in silence for some time before Gertrude speaks again.

"Kiersten . . ." She swallows hard. "I need to tell you what happened."

"You don't have to tell me anything, you don't owe me any expla—"

"I want to," she insists. "I *need* to."

I squeeze her hand.

I had the same urge to speak when I was sick, the need to share my story . . . just in case.

"Kiersten found the lithograph in her father's study. She asked me to meet her at church, in the confessional booth, before lessons so she could show it to me." I wipe a cool rag over her forehead; she shivers. "It was the middle of July. Blistering outside, but the confessional was cool in comparison." She stares at the flame of the candle. "I remember the smell of frankincense, the dark red velvet cushion pressing against the back of my knees. The ooze of beeswax dripping onto the pedestal." A faint smile plays slowly across her lips. "Kiersten was squeezed in next to me so tight that I could feel her heart beating against my shoulder. When she pulled the parchment from her under-skirt, it took me a minute to even understand what I was seeing. I thought . . ." Her eyes are on the verge of tearing up. "I thought she was trying to tell me something. I thought she was giving me some kind of a sign." Her bot-tom lip begins to quiver. "I kissed her," she says. "Like we've done a dozen times before. But we got caught. I wasn't asking her to do those things in the lithograph. All I was trying to do was tell her that I loved her. It wasn't dirty. I'm not dirty . . ."

"I know that." I smooth my hand down her cheeks, wip-ing away her tears.

"When Kiersten threatened to tell you, I played along. I thought . . ."

"What?"

"I thought if you knew, you wouldn't want to be friends with me anymore."

"You thought wrong," I say.

She studies me, a deep rift settling into her brow.

As she reaches up to try to scratch the back of her head again, I stop her.

"You need to heal."

She stares at me intently, a haunted look coming over her. "Can we ever really heal from this?" she whispers.

I know what she means. I know what she's asking.

Pulling the thyme blossom from my chemise, I offer it to her. Tears fill her eyes. Pawing at it, she tries to accept it, but it's no use with the linen wrapped around her hands.

We both start laughing. And in this tiny gesture, this minuscule moment, I know we're okay . . . that Gertrude is going to be okay.

"What happened to us?" she asks, staring into my eyes. "One minute we were building things, changing things, and then . . ."

"It's not your fault. It's no one's fault . . . not even Kiersten's."

"How can you say that?" she asks.

I'm not sure how much of this she'll be able to take in, but I can trust Gertie. And it feels like if I don't tell her, then it's not real somehow. Leaning in close, I whisper, "It's the well water. The algae . . . it's hemlock silt. The same thing the crones use in the outskirts to speak with the dead."

She stares up at me, and I can see her starting to put the pieces together. "The dizziness, the hallucinations, the violent impulses, it's all from the well water? But if the magic isn't real . . . ," she says, reaching out to touch my hair. "The ghosts in the woods . . . Tamara, Meg, you made all that up?"

"The ghost part, yes, but that's the truth about what happened to them . . . how they died."

"How do you know that?"

I think of Meg's face—the look in her eyes when the dagger pierced the side of her neck. "Because I was there," I whisper.

I see a chill race over Gertie's flesh. "But if the ghosts aren't real . . . how did you make those sounds happen?"

I want to put her at ease, tell her I planned the entire thing, but I've never been able to lie to Gertie. "I didn't,"

I whisper, trying not to imagine what else could be out there. Trying not to think of Anders's threat.

"When you left . . . I thought . . ." Gertie's eyes are getting heavy. She's fighting it, just like Clara used to do at bedtime. "It's like . . . you're back from the dead."

"Maybe I am," I whisper, tucking the blankets in around her.

"Then tell me about heaven . . . what's it like?" she asks as her eyelids finally come to a close.

As the last bit of the flame sputters out, I whisper, "Heaven is a boy in a treehouse, with cold hands and a warm heart."

"He said he'd come back for you," she says.

It takes me a minute to recognize her, to realize I'm dreaming, but then I notice the shaved head, the small red mark beneath her eye.

"Where have you been?" I ask.

"I've been waiting," she replies, standing in front of the door.

"Waiting for what?"

"For you to remember . . . for you to open your eyes." She pushes the door ajar.

I snap awake to find myself hunched over Gertie's cot,

the slightest whiff of bay leaves and lime in the air. It re-minds me of the apothecary . . . of home. I used to love that smell, but now it seems too harsh . . . astringent.

But if it was just a dream, why is the door ajar? I'm cer-tain I pulled it shut last night. I was so tired I suppose I could've opened it myself and not even remembered. Just because I'm back in the camp doesn't mean I'm going to go crazy. Taking a deep breath, I try to concentrate on something pleasant, something real—dawn is slipping in, gray-pink on the verge of spilling into gold. I think this is my favorite time of day, maybe because it reminds me of Ryker. If I close my eyes I can hear him climb the ladder, remove his shrouds, and slip in next to me, the smell of night and musk clinging to his skin.

"See, I didn't scratch," Gertie says, startling me.

I look back to see her holding up her makeshift mit-tens. "Good." I smile up at her, thankful for the interrup-tion, but even more thankful to see the slightest bit of color return to her cheeks.

I catch her staring at my left shoulder, the deep inden-tation of missing flesh and muscle; I pull on my cloak.

"Sorry," she whispers. "I can't imagine the horror you must've faced out there."

I want to tell her about Ryker . . . about how he saved my life, that the only reason I left him was to save his . . . but not all secrets are equal. In the county, if Gertie's se-cret got out, she would be banished to the outskirts, but if my secret got out, it would mean the gallows.

"You need to teach me how to do a braid like that," she says, trying to lighten the mood. "I mean . . . when my hair grows back," she adds.

Lifting my hands to my hair, I find it's been done up in an elaborate box braid.

Yanking the ends free, I shake it loose, as if it's full of snakes. There's no way I could've done something like that in my sleep. I don't even know how to make a braid like that, but I know someone who does—Kiersten. She wore a similar braid on veiling day. I remember on our first night at the encampment, the girls talking about Olga Vetrone, the girl who disappeared in the woods. They said she was being haunted, that the ghosts would braid her hair at night, tie up her ribbon in strange configurations. Made her go crazy. *Nice try, Kiersten.*

After I get Gertie situated, I go outside to find Kiersten and the others gathered around the well. As soon as I start walking across the clearing to the privy, they stop talking. They turn to watch me. I can feel their eyes on me like a dozen weighted lures sinking into my flesh.

"Come here," Kiersten says, the tone of her voice making my insides shrivel.

I look behind me, praying she isn't talking to me, but there's no one else.

Reluctantly, I walk toward her. I'm trying not to panic, but I can't help wondering if she heard me whispering to Gertie last night, if she remembers that I was banished . . . that she stabbed me with an axe.

"Closer," she says, holding up the bucket of water. The patch of bright green algae clinging to the rope brings that vile taste back—the feeling that your tongue is being coated in dank velvet.

Jenna loses her balance, accidentally bumping into

Kiersten's arm, causing some water to spill. Kiersten's eyes flash.

Before I have a chance to even take in a breath, Kiersten slams the bucket into Jenna's face. The sound of cracking teeth makes me cringe. Blood's gushing from Jenna's mouth, but she doesn't scream . . . she doesn't even flinch. The other girls just stand around as if they're accustomed to these sudden bursts of violence. Or maybe I've forgotten what it's like to live among them.

"This is for Tierney," Kiersten says, offering me the bucket.

Jenna's blood is dripping from the edge, making my stomach turn, but if I refuse, Kiersten will never trust me. This is a test.

Taking it from her, I'm pretending to take a sip when Kiersten tilts the bucket, forcing the liquid into my mouth. I'm choking on hemlock silt, blood, and malice, and they're all laughing; their crazed pupils boring into me.

I barely make it into the woods before I hunch over, throwing up every last bit of liquid inside my stomach. I'm panting in my own filth, wondering if I've made a horrible mistake by coming back here. I should've used the shrouds to walk right out of this place and never come back—

"The shrouds," I gasp. *Anders.* Is that what the girl was trying to tell me? He said he'd come back for me if I didn't follow his exact orders—I was supposed to leave the shrouds on the other side of the fence.

Running to the breach in the eastern barrier, I come skidding to a stop when I see the shrouds are gone. I pace the area, trying to figure out what happened to them. Maybe I shoved them back through and forgot. I was upset. I just remember wanting to get them off me as soon as possible. Or maybe an animal carried them off—they smelled bad enough. Anders could've slipped through and grabbed them. He made it clear he wasn't afraid of crossing the barrier—the barrier—it's been mended. Sinking down next to it, running my hand over the thin cut of cedar that's been wedged inside, I feel a mood slip over me. I thought it would take at least a few days to fix, that they'd be replacing the entire log. Yes, it's shoddy work, but I'm trying to figure out why I care so much. Maybe I just wanted to see a friendly face, to thank Hans for getting my supplies back to me when we first arrived, but it's more than that.

The window to Ryker has been closed.

And it feels like the final word.

Turning my back on the fence, I make a promise never to come back. No good can come of it.

Instead, I focus on the task in front of me—bringing the girls back to the world . . . back to themselves. The easiest thing would be to lead them to the spring, but I don't think that even when they're high on hemlock silt I'd ever be able to convince them to follow me into the woods. The ghost stories are too ingrained, too real to them, and I certainly didn't help matters with my stories from last night.

I'm going to have to bring the spring to them.

Since the camp is at a lower elevation, I'm thinking I can make some kind of irrigation system, but without pipes or proper tools, I'm going to have to get creative.

When I brace my hand against a birch to avoid stepping on a cluster of deer scat, the bark lifts up under my sweaty palm. I remember Ryker telling me he used rolled-up bark on his roof to get the melting snow to drain.

Using the hatchet, I make a clean cut in the bark, lifting off a huge strip. If I roll up enough of these and link them together, maybe I can form a pipe. It's a tedious task, peeling every birch I can find, but there's something cathartic about it. I was laid up for so long, I forgot how good it feels to use your hands, your mind, for something constructive.

I nestle them together to form one long tube, then start to dig. I remember trying to till the soil for the garden in the dead of winter, how hard that was, but it's nearly summer now, and the soil gives way to me with only the slightest amount of pressure from the hatchet. After burying the tube all the way up the incline, I'm faced with the difficult task of diverting the brook. I have no idea if this will even work, but I've come this far. Digging out a trench, I watch the water flow into the tube. I'm running down the hill, elated to see it pouring from the bottom. Once I've filled the kettles, I realize I need to find a way to control the flow. I search the woods for a cork tree. I know I saw a couple of them around here. I figure if it's good enough to hold the ale in the casks at home, it will be good enough for this. I spot one on the northern wooded slope and pry off a chunk. Whittling it down to the right size, I jam it in, but the water pressure causes it to shoot right out. I need something to hold it in place. Rolling a boulder over, I hold the cork over the tube and use my knees to nudge the rock beneath. I'm waiting for the bark to blow, the earth to reject the water like a spouting whale, but it seems to hold. For now. And all I can worry about is now. I'm thankful for it, because if I start thinking too far ahead, it will lead me all the way back to the county, to a very dark place.

Covered in mud and bark and leaves, I drag myself back up the incline, into the creek, letting the cool water wash over me.

An apple blossom drifts down to the surface, reminding me of the rose bath Ryker made for me. Flicking it out of the pool, I plunge myself under the water, trying to force the memory out of my head. As I come up for air, I hear the faint scratching sound again. Happy for a distraction, I jump out of the pool, following the sound all the way to the top of the ridge, to the girl's remains—the tattered end of her ribbon rubbing against the bones of her neck. This can't be the same sound I heard in the camp, or clear on the other side of the fence. The distance is far too great. But that's not the only thing that has me on edge. There appears to be something wedged inside her rib cage. Something I didn't see before.

Sinking next to her, I peer inside to find a flower. A red chrysanthemum. The flower of rebirth. My skin explodes in goosebumps. How did this get here? I reach in to grab it, being careful not to touch her bones. It's a little tattered and bruised, but the stem is cut on the bias, with precision and care. I wonder if Kiersten did this to mess with me, but I've never seen a flower like this in the encampment before. I can't help thinking of the bloom Ryker gave me—the one Anders helped him find—and I wonder if this came from outside the barrier.

"Stop it, Tierney," I whisper to myself, pulverizing it between my fingers. "Don't get paranoid. It's just a flower."

But a flower is never just a flower.

I blink long and hard as if I can somehow make things right in my head, but when I open them, nothing has changed.

Maybe it's just traces of unpurged well water working their way through my system, or exhaustion, but there's a part of me that can't help wondering if by claiming the magic, telling them that I could communicate with the dead, I somehow raised her ghost.

SUMMER

The first few days with the girls are the worst—crying fits, bursts of anger, wanting to claw their own skin off. I remember feeling like that when I got banished to the woods, staggering around, trying to find my way back to some form of reality.

But in the passing months, we seem to settle into an uneasy routine.

On the first full moon, they all bleed at the same time—no punishments have been ordered, no new wild claims of magic have come forth, but I still feel out of sync. Out of time.

Though I haven't had a drop of the well water, sometimes it feels as if I had. Little things: the scratching noise that seems to follow me wherever I go; the bones on the ridge that seem to shift a little every day, her head tilting more toward the sun, her toes pointing down toward the earth, the slight angle of her hip—as if at any moment, she could rise. Maybe it's merely the power of suggestion making me feel this way. I've been telling ghost stories every night to satisfy the girls. Maybe I'm starting to believe my own lies, but nearly every morning, I wake to the smell of lime and bay leaves, my hair braided. I don't mention it to anyone, because I don't want to give Kiersten the satisfaction, but I can see it in her eyes, her growing frustration with me.

My biggest obstacle by far is keeping my thoughts from slipping under the fence, walking toward the shore, climbing the ladder to the best feeling I've ever known.

When I have the strength, I get up and move, find something to keep myself occupied—weaving rope, rebuilding the rain barrels, clearing the trail, leveling it off so it's wide enough for the wagon to carry the water without spilling a drop—but at night when everyone is sleeping, and my body has failed me, I have no choice but to sit here, my mind playing through every detail of my last night with Ryker on a constant torturous loop. Sometimes, I close my eyes and try to meet him in my dreams, but I don't dream anymore. Of anything. Even the girl feels like a distant memory, someone I used to know—just another thing that's left me.

Although the girls have access to plenty of fresh water now, they still drink from the well on occasion. Maybe it's self-preservation, knowing what their body needs.

I remember Father treating trappers from the north, feeding them thimblefuls of whisky on the hour. It wasn't enough to satisfy them, but just enough to keep them from going into the throes of withdrawal. And that's exactly what this is—a withdrawal. I can't imagine going cold turkey from the hemlock silt, marching for two days straight while you purge everything from your body. No wonder the girls are so out of it when they return—they're half dead, and the other half only wishes they were.

Doing it this way will take longer, but they won't feel like their bones are being turned inside out. Hopefully it will feel natural, like their magic is slowly leaving them, which isn't that far from the truth.

A few of the girls are well enough that they've shown an interest in helping me around the camp. At first, I found it unnerving, their dark beady eyes staring into me, but as they slowly come back to the world, I give them small tasks. One of them is minding Helen. She's been following me around like a shadow, nicking whatever I've left behind. If a spoon is missing, I'll find it under Helen's bed. If a button has gone astray, I'll find it in her pocket. It's hard to get upset with her. She hasn't recovered as well as the others. It makes me wonder if she ever will.

On a bright note, Dovey has resumed her usual cheery coo. Helen even offered to let me carry the bird around for a while, but it's best not to get too attached. I remind Helen that we'll have to leave her behind when the guards come for us, but she doesn't want to hear it. The women aren't allowed to own pets in the county. *We* are the pets.

Other than the disturbing night visits, Kiersten has steered clear of me, but the one thing I've learned about Kiersten is you can never let your guard down. I've been watching her, sometimes staying up all night to try to catch her sneaking off into the woods to move the bones, but she doesn't seem to leave the camp. She's been watching me, too. Sometimes, when we're gathered around the fire, I catch her tracking me like prey. I try to ignore it, pretend it doesn't spook me, but the fact of the matter is, the more I help them, the more they will remember.

And as the second full moon draws near, I find myself moving in shadows. I don't feel at ease anywhere anymore. Not even in my own body. My skin.

It's not just the sound of the ribbon, or the shifting of the bones on the ridge, it's a presence I feel hanging over me everywhere I turn. Even the girls, who I thought would be further along by now, still spend most of their time listening to the wind, getting lost in the clouds, speaking of their magic like it's a living, breathing thing. At first, I thought it was just to please Kiersten, a means of survival, but I'm afraid it goes much deeper than that. Maybe it's something they don't even want to give up.

Tonight, as the sun gives way to the moon, a million stars making me feel smaller than a speck of dust, I stand on the perimeter, listening to the incessant scratching noise. It's so dark I can hardly see a few feet in front of me, but I can't stop picturing her standing there, the ribbon snared around her neck, grating against the bones of her throat.

"Tierney." Gertrude nudges me. "They asked you a question."

I look back to find the entire camp staring at me.

"Well?" Jenna prods. "What are they saying?"

I haven't spoken of the girl on the ridge yet; maybe it felt too sacred, too real, like it would be a betrayal of some kind. But maybe this is the one secret I don't have to carry all by myself.

"I don't know her name," I reply. "But her bones lie on the highest ridge of the island." As I turn my back on the woods, the scratching noise seems to grow more insistent . . . furious, but I don't let it deter me. "Do you hear that? It's the sound of the frayed red ribbon coiled around the bones of her throat. She was strangled so violently that her ribbon ripped in two."

"Maybe she's trying to find the other half," Jenna says. "Just like the story of Tahvo."

"Is that the Viking one?" Lucy asks.

Jenna nods excitedly. "His entire crew turned on him, stabbed him one hundred times before he fell. Instead of burning his flesh, a proper burial for a warrior, they left his bones to rot on a distant shore." Jenna leans forward, the firelight dancing in her eyes. "But every full moon he rose from the dead to take his revenge. It took him eight years to hunt down every single one of them and their kin. Only then could he earn the pyre that would carry his soul to the heavens."

I'm trying not to let my imagination get away from me, but what if the dead girl's own grace year girls did this to her? Maybe she's looking for revenge. And if she's bound to the encampment forever . . . maybe we're the next best thing.

As Gertrude and I settle into the larder, sweat soaking through our clothes, she says, "If you won't keep the door open, you should at least take off your cloak."

"I'm fine," I say, pulling it tighter around me.

"If you're worried about Helen taking it from you—"

"I told you I'm fine," I say, shorter than I'd like, clutching the hatchet to my chest.

The sound of her skimming her fingers over the healed stubble on the back of her head grates on my nerves.

"You haven't been drinking from the well, have you?" she asks.

"No." I look at her sharply. "Of course not."

"Then what is it . . . what aren't you telling me?"

I take in a deep breath. "You know how I talked about the bones on the ridge?"

"That was a really good one tonight. And then when Jenna said the thing about the Viking . . . I almost believed it—"

"I think it might be real."

"What?" she asks, trying to hide the goosebumps on her arms.

"The sound I hear in the camp . . . it's the same sound I hear when I'm on the ridge . . . the ribbon scratching against her bones."

She looks at me for a moment and then bursts out laughing. "Very funny."

I laugh along with her and then turn on my side so she can't see the tears in my eyes.

"You're finally up," Gertie says, straightening the jars of preserves on the shelf behind her. "I've been begging you to keep the door open all summer, and now that it's finally cooled down you decide to open it?"

"I didn't," I say, sitting up, peeling the cloak away from my skin.

"I heard you do it." She rolls her eyes. "Oh, and nice touch, blowing out the candle, scratching at your ribbon like that. The girls are going to eat that up tonight."

"What are you talking ab—"

Reaching for the ribbon that was tied around my wrist, I freeze. It's not there. It's not in my hair. Panicking, I get on the floor to start looking for it.

"Missing something?" she asks.

"Helen," I say with a deep sigh as I get to my feet and head to the lodging house. She's got to stop doing this. Sneaking around, taking people's things. I don't want to get cross with her, but she needs to straighten up if she's going to make it back in the county.

As I pass the well, I glance down and catch my reflection, a bright red slit running across my throat. Doubling back, I stare into the water. Then my fingers fly to my neck, cringing when they graze against the silk.

Tugging at it, I'm trying to free myself, but it's knotted so tight I can't get it loose. I'm fumbling with the knot, but it only seems to make the ribbon coil tighter.

I'm leaning over, fighting for air, when I see Kiersten's reflection directly behind me.

"Careful, now," she says as she reaches her hands around my throat, deftly untying the knot. "Poacher's Kiss," she whispers in my ear.

"What?" I gasp, bracing myself against the side of the well.

"That's the name of the knot," she says, lacing the ribbon around my wrist, fashioning a gentle bow. "The harder you pull, the tighter it gets."

"How do you know that?" I ask, staring at her reflection in the water.

"The last time I saw someone stare into the water like that, I made them drown. You remember Laura, don't you?"

I swallow hard.

"As I recall, you didn't think my magic was the cause . . . you didn't think our magic was real at all."

"I was wrong," I whisper as I turn to face her. "That was before I went into the woods. You helped me understand."

She looks me dead in the eyes. I can't help the shiver racing over my flesh. I thought the large black pupils were scary, but now that her irises have returned, the cool blue hue is even more chilling.

Whether she's the one who did this or not, she's remembering.

As she walks away, I can't help wondering how long it

will take until Kiersten remembers that she wants me
dead.

As I set out for the spring, the ridge, I don't look at the
bones. I don't listen to the ribbon scraping against her
neck. I keep to what I know to be true. The land doesn't lie.

Lowering myself over the ridge, I notice the tomatoes,
squash, and peppers have given way to turnips, broccoli,
and beans. The sumac leaves near the shore have just
started to turn. Even the air feels crisper. The season is
on the verge of change. So am I.

I'll never forget Ivy returning from her grace year.
When she staggered back into the square, I didn't even
recognize her. Clumps of her hair were missing; her eyes
looked unreal, like the large buttons from Father's winter
coat. She collapsed in the square before her husband even
got her home. There was a time when they thought she
wouldn't make it.

They let me sit with her once, while my father spoke
with her husband about her care. I remember leaning in
close to look at her, trying to decide if it was really her. I
thought maybe she'd shed her skin out there, like the
changelings from the old fairy tales. I think that's what
always scared me the most about the grace year, that I
would somehow lose myself, come back an entirely different person.

We just get better at hiding things.

I used to wonder how the women could turn a blind
eye to things in the county, things that were happening

right in front of them, but some truths are so horrifying that you can't even admit them to yourself.

I understand that now.

On the way back to the camp, when I hear a twig snap behind me, I don't stop to listen, to wonder, I just keep pushing the cart down the path. I'm the one who gives this thing power, and I'm not willing to do that anymore. No more games. No more distractions.

Tonight, as we settle around the fire, and they ask me what the ghosts are saying, I reply, "I don't hear them anymore."

It's for the good of the camp. For the good of me.

There's a long pause. A silence so loud I can feel it echoing around the campfire, like a dying ember begging to be reignited.

I'm thinking this is it, the end of all this, when Jenna sits up tall, staring into the woods. "I hear them now. Ever since I started drinking the ghost water."

"Me, too," Ravenna chimes in.

"So do I," Hannah says, nodding her head so fast that it reminds me of a bird getting ready to feed its young.

And then one after another they begin telling ghost stories of their own. Far more terrifying than anything I could ever come up with.

Gertrude looks at me, confusion in her eyes.

But I get it.

The hemlock silt simply helped them see what they already believed.

I wake to footsteps in the clearing. It's probably Helen; she has a tendency to wander at night. I'm waiting for one of the girls to get up and fetch her, but they never do. They've grown tired of babysitting her. We all have. As I get up to open the door, I hear the scratching sound of the ribbon enter my bloodstream. I want to tell myself it's just Kiersten trying to scare me, but I feel a dark presence oozing from beneath the door.

The handle of the larder door compresses. I'm bracing myself, ready to come face-to-face with whatever's been haunting me, when a blood-curdling scream rings out from the direction of the lodging house. Gertie snaps awake. I'm yanking on the door trying to open it, but the wood must still be swollen. By the time I finally get it open, I only catch a glimpse of a figure moving past the perimeter, like a passing shadow.

The girls are huddled outside of the lodging house, screaming and crying.

Running across the clearing, I find Becca sheltered in the mass, her eyes wide, her body trembling.

"I was going to the privy . . . and I saw it . . . ," she snivels. "A ghost hovering near the larder door."

"Has anyone seen Dovey?" Helen asks.

Ravenna pushes her out of the way. "Was it Ami or Meg?"

"No. It wasn't like that . . ."

"Dovey, where are you?" Helen calls out.

Everyone shushes her.

"I didn't see arms or legs," Becca continues. "I only saw *eyes*. Dark gleaming eyes staring at me from the shadows. I don't know how to explain it, but whatever it was . . . it felt evil."

Poacher. My skin erupts in goosebumps. Could Anders be here in the camp?

I know I was late crossing over. I might have forgotten to put the shrouds on the other side of the fence, but I did what he asked. I left Ryker, the only real chance I had at happiness. Wasn't that enough?

While the others settle back in the lodging house to sleep, I sit on one of the logs around the fire. I don't face the flames, staring at what could've been. I stare out into the woods, at what will be.

For months, I've felt something building, moving in shadows all around me; as much as I've tried to reason it away, hold it at bay, it's come knocking at my door. No more hiding. No more denial.

"If you want me, come and get me," I whisper to the woods.

The only reply is the ribbon grating against my very last nerve.

Whether it's Anders or a ghost, I'm finally ready to face the truth.

All of it.

Long strands of hair tickle my arms.

At first, I think I'm dreaming of home, that it's Clara and Penny crawling under the covers to wake me, but the weight is too heavy, the breath too foul. I open my eyes to find Kiersten crouched over me, the hatchet to my throat, her eyes shining like sapphires in the early-morning light.

"Why did you come back here?" she hisses in my ear.

"T-to get rid of my magic," I stammer. "Just like you."

As the other girls begin to gather around, Kiersten pulls the blade back, but I can almost see the wheels turning in her head—she's grasping at memories, trying to make sense of things. She studies me in a way that makes me think she's one tick away from remembering everything.

Getting off of me, she walks back toward the lodging house and slams the door behind her.

As I sit there, dusting off my elbows, I'm looking around trying to figure out what went wrong. They're pretty much clean of the hemlock silt. I can see it in their eyes, and yet they're still behaving like wild animals.

Gertie rushes over. "Here, let me help y—" Her breath halts as she stares down at me.

"My cloak," I whisper, wrapping my arms around my threadbare chemise, trying to cover myself the best I can.

"You can borrow mine," she says, backing away from me, like she's just seen a ghost.

"If you're looking for Helen," Vivi says, creeping along the perimeter, "I saw her just before dawn. She was out searching for Dovey. If you ask me, it's about time that bird flew away. Her wing's been fixed for months now." She drags her hand along the branches of an evergreen, tearing off a sprig. "I don't know why you're always wearing that ratty thing anyways, even when it was hot as hades."

"None of your business," I snap. But as soon as she skitters away, I feel bad.

"Helen's probably out by the western fence," Gertie says as she hands me her cloak. I put it on. It's too small for me, but it'll do. "If you want, I can go ou—"

"I don't have time for this," I say as I head for the perimeter.

"Why? What's wrong?"

"Nothing's wrong," I try to assure her, but inside I'm screaming. "I just want to get the last of the summer berries on the far south end of the encampment. I'll camp in the woods tonight . . . be back first thing in the morning," I say as I cross into the forest, desperate to escape her sympathetic gaze. I'm afraid I've already said too much . . . that she knows too much, but I can't worry about that. I have bigger problems right now.

As I'm walking toward the brook, there are light quick steps behind me. My first instinct is to turn around, try to catch them in the act, but maybe that's exactly what they want me to do. Up to this point, all I've done is react, and they've played me like an expert at marbles, sending me crashing all over the place, but I need to be smart about this.

So instead, I take a deep breath and think about where I can lead them. Where I can get an advantage. There's a giant oak up ahead that I took refuge behind many times last winter.

Being as sly as possible, I reach down and grab a fist-sized rock. It makes me think of Laura, slipping rocks into the hems of her skirts on the way to the encampment. That was so long ago, and yet the image of her sinking to the bottom of the lake seems to be etched into the back of my eyelids. One good swing, for Laura. That's all I need.

As I near the oak, I have to force myself not to speed up, not to let my breath get away from me. Ducking around the girth of the tree, I press my spine against the bark, waiting . . . hoping they take the bait.

The footsteps are getting closer.

Closer.

I haul back the rock, ready to swing, when I hear a high-pitched scream.

"Gertrude?" I exhale.

She's standing there, eyes wider than a girl's at her first hanging.

"You almost killed me," she says, staring at the rock in my hand.

"What are you doing here?" I search the woods behind her. "You shouldn't sneak up on me like that."

"I . . . I just wanted to help. I'm feeling better now . . . or I was." She looks down at the trail of urine trickling over her boot.

I let out a deep sigh. "Let's get you cleaned up," I say as I lead her up the incline, to the brook.

"You did all this?" she says, looking at all the various ropes and contraptions I've set up.

"Here, put your underclothes in this," I say, showing her the netting I've rigged up in the spring for wash.

Wriggling out of her bloomers, she tucks them in the water. "You're using your veil for *this*?" She chuckles.

"Seemed fitting."

"I'm sorry I followed you," she says, "it's just—"

"It's for the best," I say, checking on the birch pipe. "You need to know how to take care of yourself . . . the others . . . just in case."

"In case of what?" She steps into my line of sight.

I try to play it off, but it's impossible for me to lie to Gertie. My eyes start to well up, just thinking about the things I have to say to her.

"I don't know exactly what happened to you out there," she says, "but I know certain things . . ."

I pull the cloak tighter around me.

"A boy in a treehouse with cold hands and a warm heart," she adds.

"You heard that?" I whisper.

She nods.

"Ryker . . . ," I say, running my hand over the deep scar on my shoulder.

A pained look crosses her face. "Did he . . ."

"No. He saved me . . . nursed me back to health." My chin begins to tremble at the thought. "He wanted to run away with me. Start a life together."

"Then why did you come back?" Her brow knots up.

"I have a duty—"

"Everything's different now," she says, taking my hands in hers. "You must know that."

"I can't do this right now," I say, climbing the ridge, trying to escape her words.

"You're running out of time," she says.

It stops me in my tracks. That's the same thing the girl said to me right before I met Ryker on the frozen lake.

"If it's because of your sisters," she says, following after me, "I can speak up for them."

"And risk being banished to the outskirts?"

"It couldn't be any worse than having to marry Geezer Fallow," she says. "Exceptions can be made . . . especially with Michael taking over as head of the council."

Michael. It's been so long since I thought of him that I can hardly conjure his face. It's like a portrait that's been left out in the rain.

Gertie gasps when she reaches the top of the ridge. "You were telling the truth," she says, gravitating to the stark bones.

I join her. "Yesterday, she was lying on her right side, with her legs curled up."

"And now she's flat on her back?" she asks, blinking rapidly. "Are you saying the ghost is real?"

"I hope so." I stare down at the ribbon fluttering in the breeze.

"How can you say that?"

"Because the alternative is even more frightening."

"Tierney. You're scaring me," she says, taking a step back. "What could be worse than a vengeful ghost?"

"A vengeful poacher," I whisper. "Anders." Even saying his name makes me feel sick to my stomach. "He found me with Ryker, told me that if I didn't cross back over he would kill us both."

"Does Ryker know ab—"

"No. No." I squeeze her hand tight. I can't bear to hear her say another word.

"But the curse . . ."

"There is no curse," I say, thinking of the vial at the apothecary. "It's smallpox. Anders survived a bout of it last year, and now he believes he's immune. He said he'd come back for me if I didn't follow his orders."

"But you followed his orders, right?" she asks, getting short of breath.

I wince in her direction.

"Oh God, Tierney." She starts to pace. "But that still doesn't explain *this*." She nods toward the girl.

"Anders," I say, swallowing hard. "He likes to play with bones."

"What do you mean, *likes* to play with bones?"

"He makes . . . wind chimes and things out of them."

"Tierney!" She raises her voice. "A poacher was *in* the camp . . . we have to tell the others . . . we have to warn them."

"No," I say in a panic. "Not yet. Not until I'm certain."

"You sound pretty convincing to me."

"Tonight, I'm going to stay here, hidden on the ridge," I say as I pick up the harness to show her. "I need to see it with my own eyes first."

"Fine," she says, putting her hands on her hips. "Then I'm staying with you."

"You can't." I drop the rope.

"Of course I can. I'm a part of this now."

"This isn't a game." I grab her by the shoulders. "You don't know what they're like . . . what they do to us." Her face goes ashen and I soften my grip. "Besides, I need you to take care of the others. If something happens to me . . ." I set my jaw. I'm struggling to finish my thought when Gertie rescues me.

"I'll do it. But I have conditions."

"Name it."

"When you're back, when you're sure, you need to tell them the truth."

I open my mouth to argue; she cuts me off. "Non-negotiable."

"Fine," I reluctantly agree.

"And when this is done," she says, her eyes welling up,

"you need to go back to him. You have no choice. You took care of me out here. Now let me take care of you."

I nod. Anything to get her to stop, to not say another word.

We spend the rest of the day on the ridge. I show her the garden, telling her about the seeds June sewed into the lining of my cloak, how the storm washed it all away, and the miracle I came back to.

As we share the last summer tomato, we sit on the edge of the spring, talking for hours, until our feet are wrinkled up like old prunes. For a brief moment, I forget about everything, all of the horror we've witnessed, but as soon as the sun begins to set, and I have to send her back to the camp, it all comes back to me. That's the problem with letting the light in—after it's been taken away from you, it feels even darker than it was before.

As the moon starts to rise, I get into the harness and lower myself over the ridge, just low enough that I'm covered, but high enough that if I stretch my neck, I can still see her bones. It's torture having to stay still for this long, but at least I have my back turned to the shore, to the tip of Ryker's shelter that I imagine I can see peeking up through the trees. Even that small thought seems to open up a fresh wound in me. I know Gertie's right, about everything, but I have to get through this first.

Gripping the rope, I concentrate on what's in front of me. June's garden clinging to the hillside. I decide to count everything. What can be more mind numbing than that? Twelve squash, sixty-one beans, eighteen scallions—I do it over and over again until numbers are meaningless, just lines and swirls held together by connective tissue. And when the moon is highest in the sky, and I can no longer feel my legs, I'm thinking about calling it, just going back to the camp, accepting that this was just my imagination getting the better of me, when I hear something splash in the spring. It could be the muskrat hoping for another mollusk, but it sounds bigger than that. Unafraid.

As heavy wet steps climb the ridge, I hear breath. In and out. Out and in. And when the footsteps reach the top of the ridge, that familiar sound swells in my ears: the scratching of the ribbon—slow, steady, deliberate, obsessive—followed by the clattering of bones.

Stretching up to peek over the ledge, I accidentally brush my knee against the hillside, causing a small clump of dirt to tumble to the depths.

I'm holding my breath, hoping I didn't give myself away, when the scratching sound stops. The bones go still.

Heavy steps walk straight toward me. I'm clinging to the ropes, praying I'm hidden enough in the darkness to avoid being seen. But the moon is so bright. Fertile. Relentless.

The tip of a boot edges over the ridge. I'm afraid to look up. Afraid not to.

As I slowly raise my eyes, a breeze rushes in from the west, causing the charcoal-gray fabric to billow over me, hiding me from sight, covering me in a darkness so deep that it feels like I'm in a freefall.

When I come to, there's an eerie red glow shining over the horizon. At home, we call this a devil's morn. They say if you're caught in this light, great misfortune will come your way. But what could be worse than this? I must've passed out, but if he'd seen me, I'd be dead right now. I guess I owe my life to the western wind. To Eve. Maybe we're even now.

As I pull myself up to the ridge and crawl out of the harness, I feel like a woman who's been lost at sea for years. My body aches, the indentations from the ropes feel like they'll never recover, my legs and arms tingle as if they've been asleep for days, but that's nothing compared to what's been done to her.

Dragging my body over to the dead girl's remains, I have to choke back the bile clinging to the back of my throat. There, for everyone to see, the girl's bones have been laid out in painstaking detail, spread-eagle with two black calla lilies placed in her eye sockets—the flower of ill will. Death. "Legs spread, arms flat, eyes to God," I whisper.

As I pluck the bad omens from her eyes, I notice the dark red stain smeared across the mandible, all the way around, where her lips would've been.

Spitting on the bottom of my chemise, I'm trying to rub it away, when I realize it's blood.

I wrench up whatever's left in my stomach.

There's only one person who's not afraid of the curse . . . who likes to play with bones . . .

who knows the language of flowers and where to procure them.

Anders said he'd come back for me. He kept his promise.

Now maybe it's time to break mine.

As I head back to camp, there are no eager faces around the campfire waiting to be fed, no Gertie tidying up the larder. No Dovey annoying me with her incessant coo. I'm wondering if everyone's still asleep, but when I peek in the lodging house, I find it's empty.

A horrifying thought creeps in. Ryker told me that if the poachers no longer feared the curse, every girl in the camp would be dead by sunrise.

Running into the clearing, I'm starting to panic when I hear hushed voices, weeping, coming from the back of the lodging house.

I should be relieved to see them unharmed, but the way they're huddled together in a tight circle, staring down at the ground, gives me pause.

"What is it?" I ask, unable to hide the nervous tremor in my voice. "What's happened?"

Before anyone has a chance to answer, Kiersten advances on me, fire in her eyes, veins bulging from her neck. "Give me your hands," she screams. "Let me see your hands!"

I'm looking around, desperately trying to figure out what's going on. Gertrude meets my gaze, but all she can do is shake her head, tears streaming down her face.

Kiersten grabs my hands, inspecting them from every angle. "She must've scrubbed it off."

"Scrubbed what off?" I ask, my breath shallow in my chest.

"Don't play innocent with me. Where did the blood come from?"

"I have no idea what you're talking about."

"*This.*" She yanks me over so I'm standing directly in front of the back wall of the lodging house.

There, written in dark red blood, is the word WHORE.

And below it, on the soft dirt, lies a bird, neck snapped, wings spread, a yellow nasturtium placed on its chest. The symbol of betrayal.

"Dovey," I whisper.

Looking around at their distraught faces, I realize they

think I did this. This is exactly what Anders wants. He wants them to turn on me. Cast me out.

"I . . . I didn't do this . . . ," I sputter.

"I suppose you want us to believe a ghost did this. How could you do this to Helen? The weakest among us—"

"Wait . . . where is Helen?" I ask.

"If this is about your stupid cloak, you can ju—"

"Where's Helen?" I shout.

"We thought she was with you," Becca says, looking up at me, eyes red with tears.

"Why would you think that?" I ask.

"Last night, we saw her skipping into the woods," Martha says.

"Was she wearing my cloak?" I whisper.

"We tried to get it from her," Nanette says, "but she said it gave her powers."

As I take off running toward the woods, Kiersten's yelling after me, "This isn't over, Tierney. You have to answer for what you've done."

My heart is hammering. My stomach is so tight you could pound it like a drum. I'm tearing down the path, calling out her name, when I see the tattered hem of my cloak peeking out from beneath a willow.

The dread I feel is overwhelming, but when I pull the edge of the wool and realize it's not attached to her body, I let out a huge burst of air. "Calm down," I whisper. She probably just got too warm and dropped it, but as I dust it off and put it back on, I notice something odd: a wide swath of clean fresh dirt leading under the tree. As if someone had been dragged—

Clawing through the veil of stringy limbs, I find her hidden underneath. "Helen." I gently shake her shoulder, but she's already gone cold. Sinking beside her, I see her red ribbon is coiled around her throat so tightly, it cut into her skin. Just like the girl on the ridge. I'm racking my brain, searching for answers, but I can't understand why he would just leave her body here? A kill like this is all he needs.

But it's not about that, is it? This is personal. This is about me.

He won't stop until he gets what he wants.

And I'm going to give it to him.

As they load Helen's body onto the wagon, Kiersten drags me by my hair to the punishment tree.

"Get the hatchet," she calls out.

I'm trying to think of anything I can say to get out of this, but I'm tired of lying—to them, to myself. Gertie's right. The truth has come to the surface, whether I'm ready for it or not.

"There's a poacher in the encampment," I yell.

Kiersten laughs as she drops me in front of the tree. "It's always someone else's fault, right, Tierney?"

"It's *my* fault. It's all my fault," I say. "*I'm* the reason Helen's dead." My eyes well up as I look back at Helen's body. "She was wearing my cloak. He thought it was me."

"Is that why you were so upset about it going missing?" Vivi asks.

"Don't listen to her lies. She's just trying to trick us," Kiersten says.

"It's all true." Gertie steps forward. "The ghost you saw in the clearing, the sound we kept hearing in the woods, it's a poacher. Tierney escaped from him, climbed back through a breach in the eastern fence, and now he's come to claim his prize . . . the kill that got away from him."

"The figure at the larder door," Hannah says with wide eyes. "I thought it was a ghost, but it was the shrouds they wear."

"You're not seriously listening to this, are you?" Kiersten grabs the hatchet from Jenna and raises it.

"If you kill me," I say, holding up my hands, "he'll take revenge on every single one of you. He wants *me*. I'm the only one who can stop this."

"I think she might be telling the truth." Jenna sidles next to her. "Why else would he have left Helen's body behind?"

Kiersten kicks the edge of my boot. "How?"

"I'll go into the woods. I'll wait for him."

"And we're supposed to trust you?" She huffs, tightening her grip.

"What do you have to lose?" I say. "Either way, you win. If I kill him or he kills me . . . all of this will end."

"Kiersten, please." Jenna pulls on her arm. "We're so close to going home. Let him have her."

Kiersten takes in a deep breath through her nostrils, and then lowers the blade.

I'm shocked she's agreeing to this so easily, but I'm not about to wait around for her to change her mind.

As I turn and walk toward the perimeter she says, "But first, you have to put Helen outside the gate."

My body freezes in place. "I can't," I whisper.

"You want her sisters to be punished? You want her body to be unaccounted for? She deserves an honorable death. And since it was your fault—"

"Don't make me do this," I say, my face contorting in agony, but I know she's right. This is my responsibility.

As I walk toward Helen's body, the girls step back, giving me a wide berth. Gertie gives me a supportive nod, but I can see she's on the verge of falling apart. We all are.

I push the wagon to the barrier, then open the gate; the high-pitched groan of the rusty hinges settles deep inside my gut. Putting my hands under her arms, I lift her off the wagon, but I'm so shaky that I end up dropping her in an ugly heap. Tears are streaming down my face. I can hardly catch my breath. This is not what she deserves.

Even though I can hear the call of the poachers, see their shadowy figures emerging from the tree line, I take my time. I've seen plenty of dead bodies in the healing house before, but never one that's been a friend.

And Helen was my friend.

Straightening out her limbs, her dress, I close her eyelid and place her hands together on her chest. Out of respect. Love.

I only hope someone will do the same for me.

Walking to the ridge feels like something out of a dream . . .
a nightmare.

I feel dead inside. But maybe that's exactly what I need
to get through this.

Setting up a guide rope, I gather as many fallen branches
as I can find and start to dig.

I dig through the morning, I dig through the afternoon,
and when the sun begins to set, still red on the horizon, I
stop. I wanted to dig so deep that I'd reach the devil himself, but this will have to do.

Honing the branches into needle-sharp points, twenty
in all, I bury the blunt ends into the bottom of the pit. It's
primitive, but so is Anders.

With bloodied, blistered hands, I climb the rope to the
surface. It feels good to breathe again. To feel the air on my
face. I head down to the spring and plunge my aching hands
into the cool water. I want to leave them there until I can't
feel them anymore, but I'm done trying to numb myself.
Untying the veil from the rocks, I stretch it over the pit until
it's taut and then tack down the sides with hawthorn spikes.
It would be a lot easier to use rocks, but I can't afford anything to impede his steps. I need a clean drop.

Sprinkling a thin layer of fresh dirt over the surface, I stand back to survey my work.

This is the best I can do.

This is all I have left in me.

As I sit on the ridge, staring past the woods, the barrier, beyond the shore, I acknowledge the three moons that have passed since I last saw Ryker. I want to tell myself it's easier now, that sometimes I can't remember his face, or the sound of his voice, but I cling to the memories like stolen jewels, only to be taken out on special occasions. But it's no use hiding them away anymore. He's with me all the time now.

As dark comes, I don't bother trying to conceal myself. I want him to see me. And who would dare try to hide from this moon?

Just before dawn, I hear footsteps coming up the incline, past the spring, toward the ridge. It takes everything I have not to look back, but I won't give him the satisfaction of seeing my fear.

When he reaches the top of the ridge, I know the moment he sees me, because the scratching sound grows more intense . . . fevered.

With each step closer, it feels like he's hacking away pieces of me, until I'm nothing but a pile of discarded flesh.

I'm convinced he's seen my trap, that he's making his way around it right now to slit my throat, when I hear the most beautiful sound in the world—the wet crunching sound of his body being impaled.

In the dim early light, I walk to the edge of the trap. I've spent the entire night fantasizing about what I'm going to say to him, but as I gaze down at the figure, flesh twisted around spikes, I see a face I never expected to see. It's so shocking that it takes me a minute to even place him . . . to form his name. "H-Hans," I finally manage to get out. "What are you doing here?"

"The barrier. I thought you needed my help," he whispers, coughing up a fresh stream of blood. "I told you I'd come for you."

"But you're not supposed to be here." I put my hands to my throat. I'm shaking so hard that I can barely speak.

"Please, can you help me?" he whispers.

"I'm so sorry . . . so sorry," I murmur as I climb down the rope, carefully navigating around the spikes so I don't cause him any more pain. "Where are you hurt?" I ask, kneeling as close to him as I can. He tries to move. That's when I see the damage—a spike going through his groin, his right side, his left arm, and shoulder, pinning him down like a specimen in Father's study. It's a miracle he hasn't bled out by now.

"This wasn't meant for you," I try to explain, but I'm

crying so hard, he probably can't understand me. "There's a poacher who's been terrorizing the camp . . ."

"My left arm." He cringes in pain. "Can you take out the spike so I can move my arm?"

I nod, quickly trying to pull myself together for his sake. The least I can do is try to make him more comfortable, hold his hand in the end.

I'm leaning across his body, trying to figure out how to pry up the spike without hurting him any more, when I see the glint of a blade buried in the earth, the hilt in the palm of his clenched fist. Maybe he was trying to cut through the spike, but how could he have reached for it with his arm pinned like that, unless he already had it in his hand when he fell? Taking in a deep breath, I smell it— bay leaves and lime, the same odor I always detected in the larder when I woke up with my hair done up in elaborate braids. That's the cologne Hans buys from the apothecary, but there's something beneath that. Fetid meat and bitter herbs. Anders's scent. I'm starting to recoil from him when I feel the scratchy fabric between my fingers. I know that sensation by heart. It's the feel of a shroud. I look down to find he's swathed in charcoal fabric. This is Anders's shroud. But the most damning thing by far is the sound—the incessant scratching of the ribbon. Following the noise, I see him rubbing his hand over his breast pocket, the way he's always done back in the county, but now I see the reason why—the frayed end of a faded red ribbon peeking out from his pocket, like it's begging to be seen.

The ribbon. The knife. The braids. The missing shrouds.

The scent of his cologne. He said he'd come back for me, just like the girl warned.

It was never Anders in the encampment. It was Hans, all along.

My skin explodes in goosebumps.

Glancing up toward the surface, toward the ridge, I know who the dead girl is.

"Olga Vetrone," I whisper as I sit up, rigid as a plank. "You killed her. Why?"

Reaching out with his right hand, he tries to grasp my throat, but I'm just out of his reach.

"She was a whore who deserved to die," he says, veins bulging in his neck. "I faced the knife for her." He's trying to catch his breath, but I can hear the fluid filling his lungs. "And when I came back to get her, she acted like she didn't know me. That what we had wasn't real." When he's finally exhausted himself, he leans his head back, returning to the ribbon. The obsessive rubbing. He's been doing it for so long now, I wonder if he even notices it anymore. "And when I came back for you . . ." A look of anguish passes over his face. "You're just like her. You betrayed me."

"How did I betray you?" I ask, my body trembling.

"You were supposed to be with *me*," he says. "The first time I saw you . . . I knew what you wanted."

Tears are streaming down my face—not out of sadness but out of pure rage. "I was seven years old . . . trying to be *kind*."

"You wanted me," he screams. "I know you did." He coughs up blood. "You're all a bunch of whores. And look at you now. You soiled your flesh with a poacher," he whispers, blood bubbling through his teeth like venom. "That's right. I heard you with him that night. And soon everyone will know exactly what you are."

There's nothing I can say, nothing I can do, but climb out of this pit.

I don't belong here.

But he does.

I don't mind the obscenities he screams at me, because the more he yells, the quicker he'll drown in his own blood.

I'm heading down the incline from the ridge when I see Gertie running up the path.

"What is it?" I ask, rushing down to meet her. "Did they hurt you?"

She's shaking her head rapidly, struggling to take in enough air. "I tried to stop them, but they wouldn't listen . . . they took a poacher . . . he was lingering by the breach in the eastern fence. Tall. Dark hair."

"Ryker," I whisper.

Taking off back toward the camp, I don't think about watching my step, I don't think about Gertie struggling to keep up, all I can think about is what they could do to him. What I've seen them do to their own kind is horrific enough, but given the chance with a poacher, they're capable of anything. *God, please let me get there in time.*

As I break through the trees behind the lodging house and make my way into the clearing, it's like coming upon a battlefield, long after the last cannon has been fired.

Girls are standing around in a daze, some are throwing up, a few are down on their knees praying.

Kiersten walks toward me, chin held high, a streak of blood across her face. "We took care of it for you," she says, glancing back toward the punishment tree.

Following her gaze, I see a man, stripped naked, lying still on the ground. Dead still.

As I walk toward him, there's a low thrum hammering in my ears. I don't want to remember him like this, but I need to see him one more time . . . to say I'm sorry . . . to say good-bye.

Kneeling next to him, I press my ear against his chest, hoping that by some miracle he's still clinging to life, but there's nothing. Only a cold bloody shell. But a shell belonging to a different man. Looking beyond the blood, the broken bones, I know in my heart this isn't Ryker.

As I get to my feet, I let out a burst of noise. I'm not sure if I'm laughing or crying, maybe something in between, but as I look around at their ravaged faces, I realize they're looking at me like *I'm* the lunatic here. "I don't know what to say . . ."

"Thank you would be a good start," Kiersten says.

"The intruder is dead in a pit in the woods," I say, enunciating each word. "You took this man against his will. His family will now starve because of you."

"Who cares?" Kiersten snaps. "He's a poacher. Our enemy. He deserved to die."

"It's *murder*."

"It's the grace year!" Kiersten screams back at me.

"Our magic made us do it," Jenna adds, quietly.

"There is no magic," I yell, dragging my fingers through my tangled hair. "It's the well water . . . the algae . . . it's hemlock silt. That's what's been making you see things, hear things, feel things that aren't real. And you've been nearly clear of it for months. You're better," I say as I look each one of them in the eyes. "But you don't *want* to be better, because then you'll have to face what you've done."

"Don't listen to her. She's poison," Kiersten says. "I told you that from the beginning."

"Think about it," Martha says, staring down at the well. "We only started feeling better when Tierney came back with fresh water."

"I knew this was wrong," Hannah says, looking at her trembling hands, caked in blood. "I told you this was wrong."

"Hemlock silt wouldn't give us powers," Kiersten says.

"No." I raise my chin. "You did that all on your own."

"I'm not listening to this heretic anymore." Kiersten starts to walk off, but no one seems to notice.

"I understand how it happens now . . . how we become this," I say as I walk around the clearing. "I thought it was just the water, but I was wrong. Even without the hemlock silt, there were times when I got so caught up in it that I nearly succumbed. I mean . . . who doesn't want to feel powerful? Who doesn't want to feel like they're in control for once in their lives? Because without it, what would we be?" Looking up at the bloated limbs of the punishment tree, I say, "We hurt each other because it's the only way we're permitted to show our anger. When our choices are taken from us, the fire builds within. Sometimes I feel like we might burn down the world to cindery bits, with our love, our rage, and everything in between."

A few of the girls are crying, but I have no idea if I've really gotten through to them.

And it's not my problem anymore. Gertie's right. I have other things to think about now.

Tying my red ribbon to the punishment tree, I walk away.

From all of it.

I have no idea if I'll make it back to Ryker's shelter. If he'll even have me. But I have to try.

Just as I clear the perimeter, I feel someone lace her pinkie through mine. I don't need to look to know who it is. *"Gertie,"* I whisper. Tears fill my eyes. My chin is trembling. "Please tell Michael I'm sorry. That he deserves so much better. But for everything we were, everything he wanted our lives to be, to spare my sisters. Please don't punish them for my sins."

"You have my word," she says without hesitation, tears running down her face. "You're doing the right thing."

We embrace, and I realize this is probably the last time I'll ever see her.

I squeeze her tight. "I wish I could take you with me."

"I'll be okay," she says, but her entire body is shaking. "Knowing that you're out there . . . knowing that you're free is enough for me."

I want to believe her, but I've seen what the county does to us. "Don't let them break you," I whisper.

She nods, burying her wet face in my neck. "At sundown I'll create a diversion by the gate. Run and don't look back," she says. "Be well. Be happy."

There's so much more I want to say to her . . . but I'm afraid if I start, I'll never be able to stop . . . I'll never be able to leave her behind.

Climbing back inside the pit, I take Hans's knife and cut the shrouds from his body. I'm trying to pull the severed ribbon free, but he's clenching it so hard in death that I end up having to break his fingers, one by one, in order to get it loose.

I'm happy to do it. I'd break every bone in his body if I had to. He doesn't deserve to be buried with her ribbon. It doesn't belong to him. Never did.

As I shovel heaps of mother earth over him, I don't say a prayer. I don't shed a tear. He's nothing but another ghost to me.

Unsnagging the shredded ribbon from Olga's vertebrae, I unite it with the other half and fold it in the bones of her hand.

One could look at it like she's hanging on to it—one could look at it like she's letting go.

I know what I see.

Tucking hawthorn branches, leaves, and herbs in the spaces between her bones, I work the flint until it catches. Hawthorn is seldom used in the county anymore, but in the old language, it signified ascension. A higher purpose. I have to believe that she'll find peace.

As I fan the flames, they grow higher and higher, until I'm sure God himself can see the smoke.

I tend to her remains as if they belonged to one of my sisters, releasing her to the wind . . . the water . . . the air . . . wherever she wants to roam.

It's a pyre fit for a warrior, which is exactly what she was.

With the sun melting into the horizon, the forest still tinged in bloodred glow, I wash the shrouds clean of every bit of hate, then hurry through the woods toward the eastern fence. This time, I'm not running from something, I'm running *to,* compelled forward by something much greater than fear.

Hope.

Wrapping myself in the torn shrouds, I peek my head out of the breach, making sure it's clear, and then start to pull myself through. It's harder this time. I have to contort my body differently, but as soon as I get my torso through, the rest comes easily. As I stand up and face the shore, the endless water stretched out before me, I can't help thinking of the last time I did this. I was bleeding out, freezing to death, dying, and now I'm full of life.

I dart between the trees, trying to remember the way back to Ryker's shelter, when I hear voices on the shore. Ducking behind a cluster of evergreens, I see men of all ages, getting into canoes, passing a bottle around.

"He was a good man," a hunter with a fresh scar running down his neck bellows.

"He was a prick," another man says as he climbs in, grabbing the bottle. "But no one deserves that kind of death. Not even Leonard."

"And so close to the end of the season," a boy says as he pushes them off.

"Poor bastard. Probably cursed his entire family," another one says as he climbs into the next canoe.

I can't figure out why they're leaving. The guards don't come back for us for another two days.

I'm getting ready to edge closer, see if I can spot Ryker among them, when I'm grabbed from behind, a hand over my mouth, jerking me away from the shore. My limbs are flailing, I'm trying to get away, but he's too strong for me. When we reach the cover of a blind, he lets out a ragged whisper in my ear, "Tierney, stop. It's me . . . Ryker."

My whole body goes limp in his arms. I don't know if it's the sheer emotion of hearing his voice or knowing that he's okay, but my chest is heaving . . . I'm trying to find the air. "I thought . . . I thought it was you in the camp . . . I thought you were dead."

Spinning around in his arms, I pull the shroud from his face, kissing him with a fierceness that not even I recognize. He runs his hands down my body, over my waist, and then stops—

"Tierney," he says with a heavy breath.

I open my mouth to say something, but words fail me. For a moment, I'd almost forgotten. Forgotten how much time has passed. That I owe him an explanation for all of this.

Leaning my forehead against his, I say, "The day I left, Anders came to your shelter. He said if I didn't leave by first light, he'd come back for me . . . that they would come for you, too. I wanted to save your life, the way you saved mine, and I realize coming back here now, like this, is the most selfish thing I'll ever do . . ." My voice is starting to tremble. "But being without you isn't an option anymore. If you don't feel the same, if you don't want to be with me, if this is too much, I'll understand, I'll turn around and—"

Sinking to his knees, he wraps his arms around me, pressing his face into my skirts. "We'll find a way."

Climbing the ladder to Ryker's shelter feels like a choice this time, one that I would make again and again. Even the air smells like home to me—pine and lake water, sun-drenched salty skin. My happiest and most painful hours have been spent here. It feels impossible to separate the two, and honestly, I don't think I'd want to.

We're more careful with each other now, but tonight,

every kiss, every caress, every loving gaze feels weighted with the past, present, and future. No more floating among the stars; tonight I feel grounded to the earth, as if we've taken root in the soil.

Under the eyes of God and Eve, we open up to each other and accept our fate. But we face it together.

In this dark wood, in this cursed place, we've found a bit of grace.

We stay up all night, talking, touching, basking in each other's company, and when every last feeling has been revealed, he speaks to me of the future. Something I never allowed before. But instead of tensing up, I stay soft, like raw clay in his hands.

"We'll leave just before dawn," he says, wrapping clean bandages over the open blisters on my hands. "We'll take one of the canoes. Most of the hunters left today to get more time at home."

"They don't stay until the end?"

"A few of the first-years will stick around, hoping for a miracle, but it's extremely rare to get prey this close to the end."

"What about supplies?"

"Knives, pelts, food," he says as he looks around the blind. "I've been preserving all summer for the next hunting season. We'll take as much as we can carry. Go east. We'll drift until we find an island of our own or a settlement where we can live as man and wife. Even if there's nothing else out there, I'm a good hunter. You're resourceful and sharp as a blade. If anyone can make it, it's us."

"And what about Anders?" I ask.

I feel his muscles tense at the mere mention of his name. "We were supposed to meet in two days to go back to the outskirts together. I'd like to tell him good-bye, but I'm afraid if I see him, I'll have to kill him." He lets out a deep sigh, leaning back on the bed. "He shouldn't be a problem, though. He's been preoccupied lately, spooked by a guard who's been lingering between our territories."

"A guard?" I ask, my breath hitching in my throat.

"Anders is convinced this guard knows about us, knows that I harbored a grace year girl. I thought he was just being paranoid, but now I think it was probably the guilt eating away at him."

Now it's my turn to tense up.

"Whatever we face out there, Anders or a guard, I can handle it. I will protect you."

Curling up in his arms, I let it go. Some secrets are best left buried.

Just before dawn, we pack up whatever we can carry. While Ryker tends to the weapons, the heavy jars of food, I use my overskirt to bundle up the pelts and blankets, then hoist them onto my back. I can tell he doesn't like me carrying anything, but he's smart enough to keep it to himself.

The sun is on the cusp of rising, the softest orange glow making the water look like it's on fire, which seems fitting— Ryker and I running straight into the flames.

As we walk toward the shore, I notice how much the leaves have changed; how much I've changed with them. Instead of thinking about all the ways I could die, I start planning for all the ways I want to live.

I think about waking up alongside him, our children tugging at our covers, tending to our garden, laughter all around us, and at night, sitting around a roaring fire, telling long-forgotten tales of the grace year. I'll miss my family. I'll miss seeing my sisters grow up. But we've been given a chance at another life, and we have to take it. Sometimes I wonder if I'm so accustomed to struggling that anything else feels foreign to me, like something I'm not supposed to feel, but here we are. We're really doing this. Together.

As we clear the last of the trees, we keep our heads down, bodies hunched low. Moving in the open like this is dangerous under any circumstances, but I can see the shore. I can feel the sun on my face.

Hearing a noise behind us, the rhythmic crunch of leaves, a clipped huffing sound, we both freeze midstep. Slowly, Ryker peers over his shoulder and holds out his hand, signaling for me to stay put. Still.

The rhythm is getting closer, so close that I can feel it pounding up from the earth. I'm about to dive for cover when I see the rise of Ryker's cheek. The start of a smile.

Glancing back, I see a deer running straight toward us. A young buck. I'm thinking we should move out of its path, but Ryker stands his ground, watching in awe as it thunders past.

And I know exactly what he's thinking—it's just like his dream, only the stag didn't run right through him.

Smiling back at me, he reaches out for my hand, but before I can grab on to his, I stagger forward to my knees, as if I've been shoved from behind. I look over my shoulder to see a dagger embedded in the pelts.

"Ryker?" I whisper.

He has the strangest expression on his face. His skin has turned to ash; his breath is coming out in short bursts. "Run for the gate. Head straight south, follow the barrier."

His words . . . his face . . . nothing makes sense . . . and then I see the hilt of a blade protruding from his stomach.

"I'm not leaving you," I say as I start to get up.

"Then stay down . . . close your eyes," he grunts. "But if something happens . . . I need you to run."

I nod. I think I nod. I know he told me to close my eyes, but I can't do it.

Grabbing the hilt of the blade, he pulls it out, blood dripping from eight inches of etched steel. That's when I hear the caw. It's more than a warning. More than a call to run. It's the sound of death.

"They're coming," he says, his eyes focused somewhere behind me. Holding the blade to his side, he widens his stance and takes a deep breath through his nostrils.

Two sets of heavy footsteps approach. "We only want the prey," one of them says. "Leave right now and we can forget all about this."

"We'll even cut you in," the other one says.

Ryker doesn't answer. Not with words.

Tightening his grip on the blade, he starts swinging.

There are boots stamping all around me; I hear a scream, the slicing of flesh, the grinding of bone. I'm praying that it's not Ryker when a body slams to the ground, one hazel eye locked on me, the other with a dagger pierced right through it.

"Stop," I hear someone call from the distance.

Beyond Ryker fighting the other poacher for control of the knife, there's a third poacher coming toward us. I have to do something. I can't just lie here and play dead, no matter what I promised.

Slipping out of the pack, I grab the knife embedded in the hides and get to my feet. I want to help, I'm trying to help, but they're moving so fast. The last thing I want to do is hurt Ryker even more, but if I don't do something, we may never make it to the shore. I'm on the verge of throwing myself into the fray when the poacher kicks Ryker's legs out from under him, holding a knife to his throat. Ryker's eyes land on the knife in my hand, and I know what he wants me to do—toss it to him, the way we used to pass the time last winter.

With trembling hands, I lob it toward him. I'm thinking I didn't use enough force when he manages to snatch it right out of the air, swinging his arm back, plunging the steel into his assailant's ribs, but not before the poacher drags the knife across Ryker's throat.

There's a moment of complete and utter silence.

The world stops turning.

The birds stop singing.

And in the next breath, everything seems to speed up, faster than I can even process.

"Run," Ryker manages to get out, before he crumples to the ground in a sea of his own blood.

I'm standing there, frozen, not knowing what to do, how to breathe, when the third poacher reaches us. He takes one look at Ryker, the two poachers lying on the ground, and lets out a horrifying growl. "It was only supposed to be you."

It's enough to snap me out of this . . . enough to run.

Taking off toward the south, I'm scrambling past the poachers' abandoned blinds, following the barrier the best I can, but tears are stinging my eyes, clouding my vision. I hear fast footsteps behind me, but I can't look, I can't bear to see Ryker's body. The place of his death. A knife slices through the air right next to my head, nicking my ear. I weave between the trees trying to lose him, but he stays right with me. Diving for me, he manages to grasp my cloak, ripping half of the wool from my body, but I kick him as hard as I can and keep going. I keep striving. For what, I have no idea, but Ryker told me to run and that's all I can focus on right now.

"Open the gate," I yell as I get closer.

I hear the girls arguing, but I don't have time for this. I'll never be able to scale it like I did before. Not now.

"Please," I scream as I bang against the wood. Tears are streaming down my face; my entire body is trembling. Pressing my back against the gate, I'm trying not to think of Ryker, the look in his eyes when he told me to run. The blood. The bodies. As I stare down the long path, I get the faintest glimpse of the vast lake in the distance, and I can't help wondering if this is punishment for believing I could somehow escape this . . . that I could be happy. After everything that's happened, surviving the woods, being stabbed with an axe, being hunted by a guard, having my heart broken into a million pieces, I can't believe this is how it ends. On the final day of my grace year, hunched outside the gate of the encampment, condemned to death by my own kind.

I close my eyes, finally ready to accept my fate. Then I'm pulled inside.

Covered in blood and filth, my torn cloak exposing my body for all to see, I sink to my knees before them.

They stand there in shock, staring down at me.

Gertie is reaching out to comfort me when Kiersten

screams, "Don't touch her . . . she's a whore." She's dragging a rain barrel to a huge pile of supplies in the middle
of the clearing. Everything I built to keep them going this
past year. "We need to burn everything . . . burn her with
it," Kiersten says as she hacks into one of my barrels, splitting it into pieces. "Get the torches," she yells.

"You can't be serious," Gertie says through her split lip.
I'm sure it was a fight to even get them to open the gate.

"She can't go back with us," Kiersten says, taking out
her rage on my cooking stand. "Not after everything that's
happened here. And if we don't burn everything, the next
year's grace year girls will never suffer, and if they don't
suffer, they won't be able to get rid of their magic."

"Haven't we all suffered enough?" Gertie says, her voice
trembling.

"Shut up," Kiersten says.

"No . . . she's right." Jenna steps forward. "My little sister is in the next year. Allie. She's never done anything
wrong . . . been good her whole life . . . followed all the
rules. Why should she have to suffer for something that's
not even real?"

"The magic is *real*," Kiersten screams. "Jenna . . . you
can fly, Dena . . . you can talk to animals, Ravenna . . .
you can control the sun and the moon."

But the girls just stand there in silence.

"Fine," Kiersten says as she stomps toward the gate.
"I'm putting an end to this right now."

"What are you doing?" Jenna asks.

"I can *prove* the magic is real." Kiersten yanks open the
gate. "Watch. No harm will come to me," she says as she
steps over the threshold.

I know most of the poachers have already left the island, but there's at least one more out there.

Counting her steps, Kiersten seems to gain confidence with each stride, and when she reaches ten, she turns to face us, spreading her arms out wide. "See. I told you. Nothing can touch me. My magic forbids it. Come, join me and you'll see."

A few of the girls are edging closer when a dark figure stumbles from the brush.

The girls freeze at the sight of him.

Kiersten glances at him over her shoulder and laughs. "Look, he's trembling. He can't come any closer."

The poacher stands there, eyes darting wildly around the scene, trying to decipher if this is some kind of a trap or madness. Tentatively, he takes a step toward her.

Kiersten's manic smile begins to waver, but she stands her ground. "That's as close as my magic will allow. Watch."

Slipping the knife from his sheath, he takes another step.

"Stop. I command you. Don't come any closer . . . or else," she says, her voice starting to betray her.

Lunging forward, the poacher grabs her from behind, holding a blade to her throat, so close that when she murmurs, "What's happening . . . ," the steel bites into her skin.

With blood trickling down her chest, her confusion swiftly turns to terror.

There's a part of me that should feel satisfied—Kiersten's finally getting what she deserves—but I only feel tired. Tired of hating each other. Tired of feeling small. Tired of being used. Tired of men deciding our fate, and for what?

Picking up a shattered piece of the rain barrel, I hold it in my hands, feeling the weight of the solid wood.

"Enough," I whisper.

The girls look at me, then look at each other, and without a word, they pick up whatever they can get their hands on—rocks, buckets, ribbons, nails.

As we step over the threshold, I feel something swell inside of me—it's more than anger, more than fear, more than anything they tried to pin on us, it's a sense of belonging . . . that we're a part of something bigger than ourselves. And isn't that what we've all been searching for?

We may be without powers, but we are not powerless.

As we march forward as one, the poacher digs the knife in further.

"Come any closer and I'll skin her right in front of you."

"Please . . . help me," Kiersten whispers, a fresh trail of blood seeping down her neck.

The girls are following my lead, waiting for a signal, but as the poacher's eyes scan the crowd, I recognize something. I'll never forget those eyes, the ones I saw when he climbed the ladder to Ryker's shelter to threaten me.

And suddenly, I don't see a poacher, I see a boy, who lost his entire family, whose eyes are still wet from witnessing the death of his best friend. We have that much in common.

It's not just the grace year girls that are victims of the county. It's the poachers, the guards, the wives, the laborers, the women of the outskirts . . . we're all a part of this. We're the same.

Lowering the wood plank, I say, "Go home, Anders. There's a family that needs you."

He looks at me, all of me, and his eyes seem to soften.

As he lowers the blade, they grab Kiersten, carrying her inside the encampment.

Anders and I watch each other until he backs away into the foliage, until all I can hear is his heavy breath . . . until all I can hear is my own.

Huddling on the floor of the lodging house, I realize we're right back where we started. But that's not entirely true.

"What do we do now?" Kiersten asks, wiping away her tears, and I realize she's looking to me. They all are.

There's a part of me that wants to tell them they're on their own, this isn't my fight anymore, but I promised myself that as long as I had breath in my body, I would strive for a better life. A truthful life. Looking around at the empty iron bed frames stacked up around us, I think about Betsy, Laura, Ami, Tamara, Meg, Patrice, Molly, Ellie, Helen, and so many others.

"We can start by leaving this place how we would've liked to have found it."

Whispers erupt among them.

"Despite everything that's happened here, I've seen glimpses of strength, mercy, and warmth from every single one of you," I say as I meet their eyes. "Imagine if we were able to let that shine, how bright the world could be. I want to live in that world. For however much time I have left. My father always told me that it's the small decisions you make when no one is watching that make you who you are. Who do we want to be?"

A hush falls over the room, but as I look around, I realize it's a good hush. A necessary hush.

"But what about you?" Gertie asks, her chin quivering. "You can't go back . . . not now . . . not after everything that's happened—"

"You're right. I can't go back to the county to be a wife, but I can tell the truth. I can look them in the eyes and tell them what the grace year really is." It takes everything I have not to lose it right then and there, but I have to stay strong. One crack in the veneer, one chink in my armor could dismantle me completely, sending me crashing to the floor. I'll let myself feel, I'll let myself grieve when they light the match for my pyre. But not until then.

No one says a word, but I can tell they're worried about being punished themselves—guilt by association. And I don't blame them.

"I'm not asking you to join in. No grand gestures," I assure them. "When we reach the gates of the county, I want you to step away from me, pretend you don't know me, but I will say my piece. I owe it to every fallen grace year girl. I owe it to myself."

———

We spend the last night doing what we should have done all along.

After washing out the privy, cleaning the larder, tidying the clearing, we get to work untangling the bed frames. The girls decide to set up the beds in one large continuous circle. There's something about it that gets to me. I think about Ryker telling me about the women in the outskirts who meet with the usurper in the woods, how they join hands and stand in a circle. It's easy for the men of the county to scoff at such things, the silly work of women, but they must not think it's all that silly or they wouldn't be working so hard to stop the usurper. I hope they haven't caught her—I hope she's still out there.

Someone tugs at my cloak and I flinch.

"I just want to mend it for you," Martha says.

Taking a deep breath, I let it go, laying it in her hands as if it's made of gold. And for me, it is. It saved my life more than once out here. "Thank you." I squeeze her hand. I'm grateful she thought of mending it. I want June to see that it survived. That I made full use of her gift.

As I walk around the camp, taking it all in, I see they managed to bind together enough timber to cover the well. They even scorched POISON into the wood for good measure.

The only thing left hanging over us, hanging over the entire encampment, is the punishment tree. Forty-seven years of hate and violence dangling from its limbs.

"Maybe we can strip the branches. Bury the offerings," Jessica says.

"We can do better than that," Gertie says as she pries the hatchet from the chopping block. Back home, vandalizing the punishment tree would be sacrilege, instant death, but who's going to tell, who's going to see? Kiersten was right about one thing—we are the only Gods here.

Taking turns, pouring all of our sadness and rage into each swing, we hack into the trunk. Braids, toes, fingers, and teeth rattle in the trembling branches, and when the tree finally drops, I feel the weight of it in every inch of my body. Even though I won't be here to see the ramifications of this, it's enough to witness its demise. I know I'm a far cry from the girl from my dreams, but I want to believe there's a part of her that lives in me . . . in every single one of us.

After burning the hacked-up tree and everything it stood for, we bury the ashes and decorate the stump with weeds—clover, wood sorrel, and buttercups. They're low flowers, seldom used anymore in the county, but they once symbolized fragility, peace, and solitude.

Just seeing the display makes me realize how much we've lost out here, but maybe we had to destroy everything in order for something to be born anew.

From death there is life.

Just before dawn, we cut a fresh trail to the ridge, setting up markers as we go, so the next year of girls will be able to find the spring . . . June's garden.

When we reach the top of the incline, Martha begins to hum. The women of the county aren't allowed to hum—the men think it's a way we can hide magic spells—but maybe that's exactly what we need right now, a spell to make this okay.

Taking off our clothes, we lay them on the rocks and beat out a year's worth of dirt and blood, lies and secrets. The girls try not to stare, but I can feel their eyes on my skin.

As we step into the cold water to bathe under the waning moon, we open up to each other, giving voice to every fallen girl's name, telling stories to remember them by. Maybe it's the moonlight or the gravity of going home, but it feels pure. Like we can finally be clean of this. It makes me wonder if Eve is looking down at us now with a benevolent gaze. Maybe this is all she ever wanted.

When the sun rises, mellow and hazy on the eastern shore, we sit on the edge of the ridge and braid each other's hair, tidy up our rags, shine our tattered boots.

It may seem futile, a lost cause, something the men will never notice, but we're not doing it for them. It's for us . . . for the women of the outskirts, the county, young and old, wives and laborers alike. When they see us marching home, they'll know change is in the air.

THE
RETURN

As the guards approach the gate, clubs in hand, their thick-soled boots heavy against the earth, we don't wait for them to come knocking. We open the gate wide, filing out in silence.

We keep our heads bowed to the ground, and not only so they'll think we've dispelled our magic. We do it out of reverence for everyone who's walked this path before. Everyone who will be forced to walk it in the future.

When I hear the gate close behind me, a tightness spreads throughout my chest. Leaving this place feels like I'm leaving Ryker, but then the wind finds me, rustling a strand of hair loose from my braid. Maybe he's standing right next to me, whispering my name.

"It won't be long," I whisper back.

"This one's talking to herself." A guard nods toward me.

"Better than last year. Remember the Barnes girl, the one with half her ear missing? She pissed herself before we even reached the shore."

They snicker as they push past, but I don't mind. Let them think I'm crazy.

Out of the corner of my eye, I catch a flash of red. As I walk toward it, my heart picks up speed. The flower. I'd almost forgotten about it. Pretending to trip, I crawl over to it, skimming my fingers over the perfectly formed petals, but now there are two. Maybe this is how it spreads. One at a time. Slow, but sure.

It's easy to think of your life as being meaningless out here, a tiny forgotten imprint that can easily be washed away by the next passing storm, but instead of making me feel small, it gives everything more purpose, more meaning. I'm no more or less important than a small seedling trying to burst through the soil. We all play a part on this earth. And however small, I intend to play mine.

"On your feet." Two of the guards pick me up by my elbows. I want to fight them off, but I force myself to go limp.

As they put us in boats and we cross the water, it's impossible not to notice how much we've dwindled in size, not just from hunger, and supplies, but in sheer numbers. I count for the first time—eighteen of us have fallen. Out of those, four had veils, which means four men will be choosing new wives among the survivors. Even after everything that's happened, I wonder how many of the remaining girls are still hoping for a veil. It was enough to get them to leave the camp untorched, but truly believing, giving up everything they were raised on, will take time. Something I'm quickly running out of.

The open water, the breeze, the unobstructed sun glaring down on us—it feels like freedom, but we know it's a lie. This is how they break us. They take everything away, our very dignity, and anything we get in return feels like a gift.

In front of the guards, we're silent; we don't meet their gaze. I keep my cloak wrapped tight around me, our secrets even closer, but at night, with the steady purr of their drunken slumber, the girls whisper in the dark, about the black ribbons they'll receive, what's expected in the marital bed, which labor houses they'll be assigned to, finally giving way to what the council will do to me after I tell them the truth . . . how I'll be punished . . . how I'll die.

The gallows would be a kindness. Most likely they'll burn me alive, but at least my sisters won't be punished in my absence. There will be a stain on my family name, but in time, it will fade. My mother will smile a little harder, my sisters will toe the line, play their part, and hopefully, by the time their grace year comes around, my treachery will be nothing but a distant memory.

On the second day of our march, as we approach the outskirts, the pit in my stomach begins to grow. I wonder if I'll recognize Ryker's family. I wonder if they've already gotten word of his death.

When I get my first whiff of wood smoke, musk, and flowering herbs, I trail behind the others. I'm suddenly painfully aware of my secret. Searching the sea of women, I stop when I see Ryker staring back at me—not Ryker, but a woman with his eyes, his lips, surrounded by six girls. It brings a fresh wave of pain to the surface, but also relief. In some way, he will live on.

There are so many things I want to say—how much I loved him. How he wanted a better life for them, how he died with his eyes wide open, under a northern star. But before I can gather the nerve to speak, his mother says, "It's you . . . you look just like her."

I have no idea what she's talking about, but as I open my mouth to ask, a guard comes up behind me, grabbing my arm, pulling me away.

As I look back, she pulls her hair away from her shoulder, revealing a tiny red bloom pinned to her tunic.

"Wait . . . ," I whisper, but as I try to go back, the guard yanks me to his side.

"It's too late to run. You belong to the county now. You belong to Mr. Welk."

When we reach the gate, the guards hold the line. The church bell tolls for each one of us. We hear a gasp from the people of the county on the other side of the fence: it's the bloodiest season in grace year history. Out of the thirty-three girls, only fifteen of us are coming home alive.

The clinking of coin cuts through the atmosphere, drawing my attention to the guard station, where men are lined up, the same as when we left for the encampment last year. It's not until I spot a few heavy leather satchels among them that I realize they're not here to watch the broken birds, they're here for payment. For a brief second, I catch myself searching for Ryker's face, but he's gone now. And he's never coming back.

The gates open, jarring me back to the present. As the new grace year girls funnel out in a prim line, it takes me by surprise. They look so young, so pretty, like dolls being dressed up for a dance—not being sent for slaughter. I think about the way the returning girls looked at us when we passed them last year, as if they despised us, and I wonder what these new girls see in us. I hope they know the leap of faith we've committed, that we tried to make things better for them.

Though my chin is quivering, I try to smile. "Take care of each other," I whisper on the breeze.

And as the last girls disappear, I turn to face the open gate.

My eyes fill with tears, my body feels welded in place, but somehow I move. Maybe it's the momentum of the crowd; maybe it's something more primal than that.

My moment of truth.

The heaviness is palpable. I feel it in every part of my body, but I feel it from the other girls as well. They know what this means for me . . . that this is the end of the line.

As we move into the square, people are craning their necks trying to see which girls made it. There are sighs of relief, disappointed gasps.

The men who offered a veil take their places, standing in front of the girl of their choosing, a black silk ribbon in hand. I see the tips of Michael's fine boots in front of me, but I can't bear to meet his eyes.

Four new girls are chosen to replace the fallen brides,

but there are whispers. Peering down the line, I see Mr. Welk standing before Gertie.

He places his hand on her shoulder; I see her recoil. "We're sorry to inform you that Mr. Fallow passed this winter. Please accept our condolences."

Gertie puts her hands over her mouth, taking in a gasping breath.

"Look how broken up she is," I hear someone comment from the crowd.

"I heard they're sending her to the fields."

She looks over at me, a flash of wild excitement in her eyes, but her secret reverie dies as she takes in Michael standing in front of me.

And I know the longer I put this off, the harder it's going to be . . . for all of us.

Unbuttoning the clasp of my cloak, I let it slip from my shoulders. As the tattered wool hits the ground, I raise my chin to face the crowd. The first person I see is Michael. He's standing before me, a gardenia in his lapel. The flower he chose for me—the flower of purity. He smiles at me, the way I always remembered him, standing in the meadow, his shirtsleeves rolled up, the sun glinting through his hair, but as the autumn breeze seeps through my threadbare chemise, making the fabric cling to my swollen belly, I see the blood drain from his face, hurt and shock welling up in his eyes.

I blink long and slow, hoping to erase the image from my mind, but when I open them again, I immediately spot my family standing in the front row. My father's gritting his teeth; Ivy and June are covering Clara and Penny's eyes.

My mother stands like a statue, stone cold indifference, as if I'm already dead to her.

But it's nothing compared to the chill I feel from the county.

There are hisses and whispers, demands for punishment.

Someone throws a flower at me, hitting me square in the cheek—an orange lily, the flower of anger, hatred. Disgust. Picking it up off the ground, I trace my finger along the razor-curved edges, but I can't allow myself to disappear right now. As much as it hurts, I have to stay present, I have to stay in my body, in this moment.

Back in the encampment, I was so full of purpose, but now that I'm here, standing before them, I can't help but feel regret. Not for what I did—being with Ryker was the closest I've ever felt to God—but I feel bad for doing this to my family, to Michael. They don't deserve this humiliation. None of us do.

The unpleasant din sweeping through the crowd quickly escalates to shouts and accusations. "Whore. Heretic. Burn her."

My knees start to give way, but I lock them in place. I have to be brave—for Ryker, for the grace year girls . . . because I know the truth.

Michael's father steps forward, wearing a mask of concern, but I see what lies beneath. The glint in his eyes. He's thrilled to be rid of me.

"Never in my years has a crime been so apparent," he adds, motioning toward my protruding belly.

A screeching wail breaks out in the crowd; women

come rushing toward me, hissing, spitting, grabbing at me. As the guards pull them away, I see my mother's face among them. Of course, she's one of them. The hurt I feel is overwhelming, but the shame is unbearable, a death all its own. As they're dragging her away, she lifts her skirts, baring her naked ankle, a jagged scar running down the side. I'm wondering why she did that, what it means, when a shoe comes hurtling my way. I duck just in time. The crowd is screaming for blood. My whole body is trembling. But I have to calm myself. I have to be able to speak clearly. Speak the truth. I won't let them scare me into silence.

I don't remember clenching my fist, but when I uncurl my fingers, I find the most startling thing. A tiny red flower. Five petals perfectly formed. The flower from my dreams. But how did it get here?

My breath grows shallow in my chest. I'm searching the crowd, looking for an answer, when my eyes settle on my mother. Her glassy eyes are locked on mine; her bottom lip has the slightest quiver. Pushing aside the scarf draped around her neck, she reveals a tiny red flower, pinned over her heart. The realization hits me so hard that I have to brace my hands against my knees so I don't pass out.

It's her.

The scar on her ankle—it's from the trap the guards set the night before veiling day. That's why she had blood running down her leg, why she was drinking bloodroot, to stave off infection. And the reason she was always first to join in on a punishment was so she could offer a kind word, a flower, a bit of comfort. Ryker's mother said *you look like her*—it had nothing to do with the girl from my dream; it was because my mother is the one that's been meeting with the women of the outskirts all this time.

She is the usurper the county has been whispering about, hunting.

I want to run to her, thank her . . . for letting me dream, for risking her life to try to help the women of the county, but I can't. All I can do is stand here and swallow it, like we have to swallow everything else. I'm trying to hold back my emotions, but I can feel my face contorting. That strange heat moving to my cheeks. I always thought it was magic moving through me, but now I know it to be *rage*.

Mr. Welk puts his hand on Michael's slumped shoulders. "As you know, today is the day I relinquish my role as head of the council to you, but given the grave nature of the offense, I will take on this burden for you."

I'm waiting for him to say it, aching for him to deliver my sentence, because once that happens, I'll be able to speak my truth. It's the law that every woman must stand with open eyes, open ears, for the duration of a punishment. And even if they try to cut me off, it takes a long time for a body to burn.

Mr. Welk proudly addresses the crowd. "As my final act of service, a gift to my son, I hereby sentence Tierney James to—"

"The child is mine," Michael says, his eyes still trained on the ground in front of him.

A collective gasp rises from the crowd. From me.

"There, now." Mr. Welk holds his hands out in front of him. "We all know Michael hasn't left the county in the past year. He's in shock, that's all, he's confused. Just give him a moment." He turns to his son. "I know you're up-set, but—"

Michael pulls away from him. "Tierney came to me in a dream." He speaks directly to the crowd. "Night after night we lay together in the meadow. That's how strong our bond is. *That* was Tierney's magic."

"That's not possible," someone calls out. "She's a whore, anyone can see that."

Mr. Welk motions for the guards to seize me, but Michael squares his body in front of me. "If you need to punish someone, punish me," Michael says. "I'm to blame. I commanded her to come to me in her dreams, I made her lie with me, because I was selfish and couldn't wait an entire year to be with her."

I study his face—I can't tell if he's delusional enough to truly believe this or if he's lying to protect me.

"I know of Tierney's dreams." Gertie steps beside me. "They're as real as she's standing before you."

"It's witchery," a voice booms from the crowd. "Those two are in on it together. Depraved."

I'm telling Gertie to stand down, don't get in trouble for me, when Kiersten follows suit. One by one, the girls fall in around me. It nearly brings me to my knees. Never in my life have I seen a group of women stand together in this way. And as I look around the square, I can tell it doesn't go unnoticed. The men are too caught up in their rhetoric, screaming red-faced into the void, but the women stand in soft silence, as if they've been waiting for this their whole lives. And like smoke signals on a distant mountain, I see a flash of red spread throughout the crowd.

A tiny red flower under the apron bib of the woman from the flower stand; she gave me a purple iris before I left, the symbol of hope. There's a red flower beneath the ruffle of Aunt Linny's dress; I remember her telling me to stay in the woods where I belong, even dropping a sprig of holly, just like the bushes leading to the ridge. There's a red flower pinned underneath June's collar; June sewed every single seed into my cloak . . . in secret. And my mother, telling me that water was best when it came from high on the spring.

They risked everything to try to help me and I didn't even know it. All I can hear is my mother's words. "Your eyes are wide open, but you see nothing," I whisper.

Tears burn my eyes, but I don't dare blink; I don't want to miss a single moment.

"This has gone too far," Mr. Welk says, signaling to the guards.

"Are you calling them liars?" Michael asks. "*All* of them?"

Mr. Welk grabs his elbow. "I understand what you're trying to do, it's noble, but you don't know what you're dealing with. This could get out of hand."

Michael jerks his arm free. "Or maybe you're calling *me* a liar?" he exclaims, loud enough so everyone in the county can hear. "Because if you don't accept this, what you're really saying is that the magic isn't real."

"Don't be ludicrous," Mr. Welk says with a forced chuckle. "Of course the magic is real." He swallows hard. "I think the real issue here is *safety*." He appeals to the crowd. "How do we know she won't come for us in our dreams . . . murder us in our sleep?"

"Tierney's magic is gone. I can feel it when I look at her," Michael says as he stands before me, and yet he still can't meet my eyes. "Come . . . see for yourself."

The men press forward, scrutinizing every inch of me. I want to claw their eyes out, but I force myself to stand still.

"Enough of this nonsense." Mr. Welk signals to one of the guards. "Get the torches."

Michael stares his father down. "I'm warning you. If you burn Tierney, you burn me with her."

The color leaches from Mr. Welk's face. And in that brief moment, I see how much he loves his son, how he'd rather endure anything than give him up. Even me.

"Tell you what . . ." He signals to the guards to hold off. "*I'll* examine her," he says through his teeth, as if it's causing him physical pain to be near me. As he stares me dead in the eyes, I can feel the hatred pouring out of him, but there's something more than that. *Fear.* He's losing control, and we both know it. And like he said to me when he was whipping my backside in the apothecary that night, lack of respect is a slippery slope.

"My son speaks the truth." His shoulders slump as he turns to face the crowd. "The magic has left her."

The men let out a disappointed groan.

"But this is *proof* that the girls' magic is getting stronger," Mr. Welk says with a newfound lilt. "This proves that we need the grace year more than ever."

It takes everything I have to keep my mouth shut, to listen to him stoke fear in the community, creating an even bigger lie, but when I look around at the women, I see the slightest shift. Hope spreading like a balm over an angry rash. It's not the rebellion of my dreams, it's not a show of strength like the girl possessed, but maybe it's the start of something . . . something bigger than ourselves.

"Please, don't do this, son," Mr. Welk pleads. "She's not worth it. She's making a fool out of you."

Michael holds up the black ribbon, telling me to turn around.

I know this is my last chance to speak up, to be heard, but in that moment, I feel the child move inside of me. Ryker's child. If I don't stand down, if I don't accept this kindness, Ryker's line will die with me.

I turn, tears streaming down my face.

Knotting the black silk around my braid, he rips out the red strand with more force than necessary, but I don't mind. In this moment, I need to feel anything but this— anything to distract me from the pain of being silenced once and for all. But this isn't about me anymore.

A guard rushes forward with a rolled sheet of parchment, handing it to Mr. Welk.

He breaks the seal and studies the register; there's a dark glint in his eye. "I believe this falls upon you, Michael. Your first official duty as head of the council."

As he hands it over, I can tell this is something bad. A way to get back at him for choosing me.

Michael grits his jaw, taking in a deep breath through his nostrils, before calling out, "It's come to my attention that Laura Clayton's body is unaccounted for."

Laura. The haunted look on her face before she keeled over the side of the canoe.

As the county turns their attention to the Clayton family, Mrs. Clayton stands there seemingly unaffected, but then I see her fingers blanch around her youngest daughter's shoulder.

"Don't," I whisper to Michael. "Please don't do this."

"I've used up all of my goodwill on you," he replies through his teeth. "Priscilla Clayton . . ." Michael raises his chin. "Step forward."

Mr. Clayton pries the girl away from her mother's grasp and gives her a nudge in our direction.

As the girl walks to the center of the square, nearly tripping on her errant shoelace, she pulls her plait over her shoulder, nervously fidgeting with the white ribbon. I recognize her from Clara's year. She's only seven years old.

"Are you ready to accept your sister's punishment?" Michael asks.

Tears spring to her eyes, but she doesn't make a sound.

"On behalf of God and the chosen men," Michael says, the slightest waver in his voice, "I hereby banish you to the outskirts for the rest of your days."

The sound of the massive gate creaking open makes me flinch.

As she takes her first wobbly step toward the outskirts, Michael stops her.

I let out a shaky breath thinking he's had a change of heart, that he won't go through with this, but all he does is reach down, pulling the white ribbon from her hair, letting it fall to the ground.

I look up at him in disgust. How could he do this? But he's one of them now.

Kneeling down to tie her boot lace, I whisper, "Laura wanted me to tell you that she's sorry." I double-knot it. "Find Ryker's mother. She'll watch over you." I look up, expecting a soft smile, a teary thank-you, but I'm met with a cold flash of anger. And why shouldn't she feel angry? We all should.

As the labor houses are assigned, the black ribbons administered, I follow the white strand of abandoned silk as it twists in the breeze, drags in the dirt, all the way beyond the gate, across the great lake, back to the woods where I left part of my heart, and I wonder if Ryker's still out there, if he can see me. What he must think of me.

As the ceremony ends and the crowd disperses, I watch the guards carry unmarked crates from the gate to the apothecary. I'm looking around wondering if anyone else can see what I see, but the women give away nothing, their eyes a million miles away. In wonderment. In horror.

The things we do to girls. Whether we put them on pedestals only to tear them down, or use them for parts and holes, we're all complicit in this. But everything touches everything else, and I have to believe that some good will come out of all this destruction.

The men will never end the grace year.

But maybe we can.

In strained silence, Michael escorts me to our new home, a tidy row house filled with gardenias. I'm almost choking on the heavy perfume, on his good intentions.

As soon as the door closes, I say, "Michael, you need to know . . . I wasn't taken . . . against my will."

The look on his face is so gutting I almost wish they'd just burned me alive. "Don't . . . ," he says, taking the gardenia from his lapel, crushing it in his fist.

"I didn't ask for any of this. I didn't ask you to lie for me."

A maid clears her throat as she comes in from the parlor.

"Take her," Michael says, handing me off like an unruly child, before stepping outside.

"Where would you like her, sir?" she asks.

He turns, and his anger, the pure rage burning behind his eyes, sends a chill through me. It's the first time I've felt afraid of him.

"She can wait for me in our bedroom," he says as he slams the door behind him.

Walking up the plush carpeted stairs, I skim my fingers over the wallpaper, rich swirls of dark burgundy. "Padded shackles, but shackles just the same," I whisper.

"What'd you say, ma'am?" the maid asks.

Ma'am. How did this happen to me? How did I get here?

At the top of the stairs, there are four closed doors. The gas lamps flicker beneath etched glass. There's a painting on the wall. A child. A little girl lying in the grass. I wonder what she sees? Maybe it reminds him of me, the way we used to lie in the meadow. But I can't help wondering if she's dead. If they left her there to die.

"Mr. Welk would like you to wait in here, ma'am."

Mr. Welk. That's his name now. It's not Michael anymore.

She opens the second door on the right. I step inside. I notice she never turns her back on me. I wonder if that's a holdover from her grace year . . . if she thinks of me as her enemy.

Normally, we come back twitching and seething, wailing from our dying violence. But maybe I'm even more unnerving this way.

Backing out of the room, she closes the door and locks it behind her.

I pace the room, counting my steps. There's a carved mahogany four-poster bed. A small rolltop desk with paper, ink, and quill. There's a Bible next to the bed. Thick black leather, silky pages with gold edging. The inscription on the first page makes me want to set it on fire. *To my son. My most prized possession.* And I remember how much Michael hated that. Feeling pressured to follow in his father's footsteps. Feeling trapped by all of this.

But that was Michael. Mr. Welk seems more than comfortable with all this now.

I'm crouching to look under the bed when something slips under my skin, like an old memory, or maybe it's déjà vu—something my heart has already leapt into before my mind has had a chance to catch up. It's the sound of an axe biting into hard wood. Peeking through the lace curtain, I see a man below, chopping timber. Viciously, he swings the blade, over and over and over. His body is a tight wire, the strain showing in his neck. There's no finesse, no sense of preservation behind his cutting. He's doing this to let out his rage . . . or to gather it.

And when he stops and looks up at my window, I realize it's Michael. Mr. Welk.

I duck back, hoping he didn't see me, but when I peek out again, he's gone . . . and so is the axe.

Hearing the front door slam open, heavy boots inside the foyer, I'm darting around the room looking for anything I can defend myself with, but what would be the point? Here, I am his property. He can do what he likes to me. No questions asked. And besides, everyone would know I had this coming.

Unlocking the door, he shoves it open. He's standing there, covered in sweat, the axe by his side.

"Sit," he says, pointing to the bed.

I do as I'm told. I have no idea what he expects of me, what more I can endure, but I try to think back on my instructions. Legs spread, arms limp, eyes to God.

Setting his axe down on the bedside table, he stands before me, the smell of rage spoiling on his skin. I grit my jaw, expecting the worst, but he does something so unexpected that I lose my words, I lose my breath.

Kneeling before me, he unlaces my filthy boots.

As he pries them off of my battered feet, he says, "I didn't lie. I dreamt that I was with you every single night."

With tears streaming down my face, he places the key on the bedside table, picks up the axe, and leaves the room.

A few moments later, there's a light knock on the door. I bolt up expecting him to come back to me, so we can talk, work this out, but it's only the maid.

I'm surprised by how disappointed I feel.

Drawing a bath, she helps me out of my clothes. She looks away when she sees my swollen belly, and I wonder what she must think of me. What they all must think of me.

I recognize her from the year before Ivy's grace year. Her name is Bridget. She seems nervous, fidgety, but she doesn't ask any questions. Instead, she talks nonstop about the goings-on of the county. Not much of it sinks in, but I'm happy for the noise, a sense of normalcy.

Using a fine boar-bristle brush, she scrubs my body clean with a soap made from honey that she buys at the market. She washes my hair with lavender and comfrey. The hot water feels so good that I don't want to get out, but the lure of broth and tea awaiting me in the other room is a powerful motivator. Helping me into a stiff white cotton nightgown, she sits me down at the dressing table, encouraging me to eat while she brushes out my hair. She doesn't have the gentlest touch, so most of the broth spills out of the spoon before it reaches my mouth. Eventually, I just pick up the bowl and drink it. It's warm and salty and rich. She tells me that if I keep it down, I can move on to solids tomorrow, which is lucky for me, because it's pot roast night. As she braids the black silk ribbon into my hair, she goes on and on about the menu, the wash schedule, the music at church, and when she finally tucks me into bed, I pretend to fall fast asleep, just to get her to leave.

Finally, alone, I lie there in utter silence, but it's not silent at all.

There's the low woozy hiss of the gas lamps in the hall, the steady tick of the grandfather clock at the bottom of the stairs. Staring up at the pale blue ceiling, the crisp white trim, I wonder how I got here. How this came to pass. Three days ago, I lost Ryker and was certain I'd be marching to my own death, and now, I'm here, in this strange clean box, married to a man that's both home and a stranger to me. Hearing his footstep on the stairs, I grab the key to lock the door, but hesitate to turn the latch. Instead, I stand there, waiting, listening, watching his shadow beneath the door. He pauses, and I wonder if he has his hand on the knob, if he's one heartbeat away from coming in here, but he passes by, walking to the end of the hall, where he opens another door and closes it behind him.

For weeks, this goes on.

I know I could ease his suffering with a single word, but instead I hold my breath.

What could we possibly say to each other that would make this okay?

But with each passing day, I begin to unthaw.

I find myself singing a tune in the bath. I even laugh out loud remembering a time when Michael and I fell from an oak, scaring the pants off of Gill and Stacy in the meadow one night. Slowly, I return to the world. To some form of myself.

Sometimes I try to visualize Ryker, conjure his smell, his touch, but all I see is here. All I feel is now. It's only when I look in the mirror at my swollen belly that I realize I'll get to see Ryker every day. Not in my dreams, but in my arms. Michael has given me this gift. And despite everything, I'm grateful.

Soon, I begin to dress in the fine gowns laid out for me. I braid my hair, securing it with the black strand of silk. I sit at the window watching life go by through the sun-filled curtains. And when the clock strikes midnight, I venture downstairs to sit in front of the roaring fire in the parlor. I'm not afraid to stare into the flames anymore. What I wouldn't give for a bit of magic right now. Real or imagined.

Night after night, I can feel Michael standing in the doorway behind me, watching, waiting for a kind word, a simple gesture, but I can't seem to bring myself to do it.

Sometimes, I find myself wondering what would've happened if he'd told me how he felt sooner. Would we have kissed under a starlit sky, before the grace year ever fell upon us?

But we can't go back. He's the head of the council now. In charge of the apothecary, the very place that deals in the body parts of dead grace year girls. No matter what we once were to each other, I need to remember that the Michael I knew is gone. This is Mr. Welk.

When a month has passed, a respectable amount of time for a returning grace year girl to recover from the brink of madness, I'm encouraged to go out. Encouraged is a mild way of saying they force me out the door and lock it behind me. It's what's expected of me. But more importantly, I need to show them that I belong here. Establish my new position. There's no more hiding my belly, even if I wanted to.

It's odd moving through the narrow lanes now. I find the men avert their eyes. It's disconcerting at first, but then I realize how freeing it is. The women, on the other hand, meet my gaze head-on, eyes wide open. It's the slightest shift, and something the men would never detect, but I feel it.

The women aren't allowed to congregate outside of sanctioned holidays, but I crave their company. Before my grace year, I avoided the market like the plague, but now

I find myself making excuses to go there. Every exchange, every look has a deeper meaning. Removing a glove to reveal a missing fingertip. Tilting the chin to display a mangled earlobe. We all carry our wounds, some more visible than others. It's a language all its own, one that I have yet to master. But I'm learning.

With the exception of the greenhouse, I visit the honey stand the most. People must think I have the most outrageous sweet tooth or that I take more baths than a Grecian goddess, but it's mainly to see Gertie. Only the usual pleasantries are exchanged, but it's amazing how many subtleties you can put into a simple "good morning." I smooth my hands over my skirts to show her how much I've grown, and in exchange, she smiles toward a girl working alongside her; the girl smiles back—flushed cheeks, bright eyes, a hint of a smile curling her lips—and I wonder if Gertie's found happiness. Bliss. Something better than the lithograph.

I've only seen Kiersten a few times, always escorted by her maids, pretty as ever, but when she looks at me and smiles, it's like she's looking right through me. Lost in a dream. Maybe it's better that way. For all of us.

There's always a bit of gossip you can gather from the market—not from the women, they know better, but from the men. Maybe their tongues are loose from whisky, or maybe they want us to hear about another man's misfortune, but as I pass the chestnut stand, I learn there was a small fire at the apothecary. I can't believe Michael didn't mention it to me, but why would he? This is men's business. I don't like the way they're speaking about him, as if he's bitten off more than he can chew, but when I think about the apothecary, what they sell from secret shelves, I can't deny there's a small part of me that wishes it had burned to the ground.

Every afternoon, I walk to the west, past my old house, hoping for a glimpse of my mother, and today I'm finally rewarded.

I desperately want her to meet my eyes, just once, but her gaze seems to skim right over me.

I'm about to move along when I notice the dark pink petunia she's twirling between her fingers. This flower can signify resentment, but in the old language it was an urgent message. *Your presence is needed.*

I know it's dangerous to linger like this, but I'm convinced the message is for me.

As she walks due west, on the lane that cuts through the forest, I follow.

I shadowed my father a million times before, watching him sneak off to the outskirts, but it never occurred to me to follow my mother—that she would have a life of her own.

As she cuts off to the north, I quicken my pace. I want to make sure I keep a safe distance, but if I lose her trail, I'm afraid I'll never be able to find her.

Reaching the tree where she veered off, I search for her, to no avail. I can almost hear her voice in my head. *Your eyes are wide open, but you see nothing.*

Breathing in the woods, I hear something, nothing more than a whisper, probably just the wind moving through the dying leaves, but it's enough to lull me forward. Letting my senses guide me, I walk beyond a grove of evergreens, through a veil of leafy vines, to a small barren clearing.

In the center there are traces of a fire, the smell of moss, cypress, and black ash lingering in the air.

To the north, I hear voices—women's voices, boisterous, untethered—and I realize I must be near the border of the outskirts. It could be a campsite used by the trappers, but around the fire there are traces of Queen Anne's lace and valerian root. I remember hearing about the gatherings from Ryker. This is clearly a place for women's work.

"We meet here on full moons," my mother says. "You'll receive a flower as an invitation, but not until the baby is born."

I turn my head, searching for her, but she's hidden among the trees. As I take a closer look around, it dawns on me. This is the place from my dreams. The trees are shorter, the light is different, and the forest floor isn't blanketed with the mysterious red blooms, but this is definitely it.

"I've dreamt of this place," I say.

"That's because you were here once, when you were small," she says.

"Was I?" I ask, trying to seek her out.

"You must've followed me here, because you got lost," she says; her voice seems to swirl all around me. "Mrs. Fallow found you. Brought you home. We were so worried you would talk about what you'd seen here, but you were always good at keeping secrets."

I'm scraping my memory for a hint of what I'd seen. Flames, dancing, women joining hands. "For the longest time, I thought the dreams were real," I say, searching for her behind the cascading vines. "I thought it was my magic creeping in, but it was me all along, talking to myself, showing me what my unconscious mind couldn't bear to name," I say.

It's only when she steps out from behind a balsam that I see her.

"Mother," I whisper. I start running toward her, but she holds up her hand to stop me.

She's right. I can't get carried away. I've forgotten what it's like here. How dangerous this is.

Stepping next to a fir, we speak to each other from different sides of the forest path. Each of us concealed in shadow.

"Are my sisters involved?" I ask.

"June, yes, she's a great help to me, but Ivy isn't cut out for such things."

"How do I know who's safe? Who's one of us?"

"You won't," she replies. "Start with those closest to you. Little confidences to test the waters, but nothing that carries a punishment more than a whipping. You don't want to draw attention to yourself."

"I should've known it was you, behind everything," I say, my eyes misting over.

"I didn't do it alone. Your father is a good man. But all good men need a helping hand sometimes. Like Michael, with the fire at the apothecary."

"What about it?"

She smiles. "Curious how only one cabinet was affected by the flames."

I stare at the charred remnants of the campfire, trying

to grasp her meaning, and when I look back to tell her I had nothing to do with that, my mother is gone. I turn just in time to catch the tail end of her black silk ribbon disappearing down the lane.

I want to run, call out Michael's name in the square, but my mother's right, I can't draw attention to myself. Using every ounce of restraint that I have in me, I shorten my gait, slow my pace, until it looks as if I'm out for nothing more than a bit of fresh air.

I stop at the apothecary first, but he's already locked up for the night, the CLOSED sign dangling from a thin silver chain.

As I peek into the windows, the memory of catching my father buying one of the vials from Mr. Welk quickly rises to the surface, but now there's only a charred shadow where the cabinet used to be.

"It's true," I whisper. Michael did this for me and he didn't even tell me about it. Then again, I never gave him a chance.

For the past few months, all I've done is push him away, and for what? He saved my life, accepted another man's child as his own, asking for nothing in return. I think I did it because I feel guilty for being so horrible to him when he lifted my veil. I feel guilty for betraying him by falling in love with someone else, and I feel guilty for not trusting him to be exactly what I've always known him to be—a good man.

Choking back my emotions, I make my way home, with slow, measured steps, but as soon as the front door closes behind me, I tear off my wool cape and run through the house, smacking right into Bridget at the top of the stairs. "Where is he?" I ask. "Where's Mr. We— where's Michael?"

"Council meeting," she says, in a fluster. "He won't be home till late. Is something wrong with the b—"

"No . . . no . . . nothing like that," I say, smoothing down my skirts. "It's nothing."

She looks me over. "Why don't you sit and rest," she says, ushering me into the bedroom. "And I'll bring up supper in a few."

As I sit on the edge of the bed, she bends down, silently digging cockleburs from the hems of my skirts. Just like the ones I used to find on June.

I glance up at her, trying to figure out if she suspects anything, if I've somehow given myself away, but as she leaves, I notice the tiniest change. She doesn't back out of the room anymore.

When Bridget comes up with dinner, I pick at it, pretend nothing's happened, but everything's different now. I'm different. It's not just the news of the fire in the apothecary that has me feeling this way, although the gesture means more to me than he could ever imagine; this is about growing up, accepting responsibility, accepting kindness, accepting love.

As I step into the bath, Bridget fills the silence, babbling on and on about the flowers at church. I find myself leaning over the side of the tub to pluck a soft pink rose petal from the small arrangement on the tray. My mother told me to test the water with people who are closest to me. Who's closer to me than Bridget? She was once a grace year girl, just like me. With deliberate intent, I drop the petal into the bath, watching it swirl around my ankles lasciviously.

Bridget stops talking. Her breath halts in her chest. I look up at her, waiting for her to snatch it out of the water, run and tell the head of the house of my transgression, but instead, I see the faintest rise in the corner of her mouth. And I know this is a new beginning. For all of us.

Tonight, as the clock strikes twelve, I descend the stairs, my silk robes swishing against the thick rugs, and curl up on the settee and wait. Michael hardly makes a sound when he comes in, but I know he's there; I can smell his amber cologne. Matching my breath to his own, I will him to enter, but when he turns to leave, I whisper, "Please. Join me."

He clears his throat before stepping into the room as if he's making sure that I was speaking to him.

He sits beside me, being careful not to get so close as to make me skittish. We stay like this for a long time, staring at the flames, and I remember Ryker telling me that Michael sounded like a decent man. I think he said that, or maybe that's what I need to tell myself to make peace with this. Taking in a deep breath I say, "I owe you an explan—"

"You owe me nothing," he whispers. "I love you. I have

always loved you. I will always love you. I only hope that in time you will grow to love me, too."

My eyes begin to well up. "The fire at the apothecary . . . I know it was you. I know you did that for me."

He lets out a burst of pent-up air. "For someone who's right about so many things, when you're wrong, you're spectacularly wrong."

I look up at him, trying to understand.

"I did it for *me*," he says, his brow knotting up. "All those years we spent together as kids, running around the county, trying to figure out clues about the grace year, it meant something to me. The girl from your dreams . . . she meant something to me, too. I always believed, in you, in her, in change, you just didn't believe in *me*."

Tears are searing down my cheeks now.

Tentatively, he places his hand next to mine on the settee, the heat of his flesh drawing me in. I stretch out my fingers to take his hand in mine. At first, I flinch at the full weight of his palm, the weight of this moment, but it feels good. It feels real. Not a betrayal of Ryker, but that my heart is big enough to love two people at the same time, in two different ways.

And this is how it starts, how we grow our friendship into something more.

More than I ever expected.

Through the winter, Michael and I ease into our expected roles, until it doesn't feel like a role anymore. We eat together, stroll through the market, attend church, go to social functions, arm in arm. On occasion, I'm allowed to help him in the apothecary, which has given me purpose, something to do, but also given me insight into the women of the county. It's a delicate negotiation, trying to suss out who is amenable to change and who would sooner cut my tongue out if given the chance. But all of this will take time. Something I've finally come to accept that I have plenty of.

In the meantime, we enjoy each other's company. I no longer flinch when he touches me; instead, I lean into him, for comfort and warmth. At night, we speak of everything under the sun, but never the grace year. That is the one vow I will never break. It doesn't belong to him.

As the full moon of my ninth month draws near, I feel it in my body, the duality of wanting to hang on but needing to let go.

I used to dread the full moon. I saw it as a dark, wild place where madness dwells. But I think the full moon shows us who we really are . . . what we're meant to be.

Tonight, when I open my eyes, the girl is lying beside me. I haven't dreamt of her in so long, it startles me. She looks different . . . worried.

"Everything's going to be okay," I tell her, but when I reach out to touch her face, my hand goes right through her.

A jolt of pain shoots through me, making me crunch up in a tight ball. It starts in my lower abdomen, radiating throughout my limbs. It's so intense, so sudden, that I let out a sharp scream.

"What is it?" Michael bolts up in bed. "Another nightmare? I'm here. You're safe. You're home."

I try to stand, but the next wave of pain hits me like a runaway colt. "Whoa," I manage to exhale.

"What can I do?" he asks.

I lean forward, trying to ease the pressure, when I notice tiny specks floating outside the window.

"Snow," I whisper as I peer through the gap in the heavy damask curtains.

"Do you want me to open the window for you?" he asks, easing his warm hand over my lower back.

I nod.

As he opens it, the blast of freezing air brings me right back to the encampment—facing Ryker on the frozen lake. A fresh wave of pain comes over me, but it's not physical this time. I try to get up so I can see the snow more clearly, but when I rise from the bed, Michael stammers, "Tierney . . . you're bleeding."

Without taking my eyes off the falling snow, I say, "I know."

As he bolts out of the room, yelling at the maids to

fetch the midwife, I can't help wondering if this is a sign. A late snow sent by Eve. But what is she trying to tell me?

Another surge of pain comes, making my knees buckle.

Michael bursts into the room, dragging the midwife with him. She still looks half asleep, but once she sees the state I'm in, she snaps to.

"Dear child," she says, pressing her hand to my forehead. I'm sticky with sweat and burning up with fever, but I try to smile. Another wave of pain hits, and I let out a deep groan.

As she helps me to the bed to examine me, I watch my stomach roiling in the lamplight. Tiny elbows and knees, struggling to get out.

"I need towels, hot water, ice, and iodine," she barks at Michael. *"Now."*

"What's wrong?" I pant. "Is there something wrong with the baby?"

As he rushes out of the room, hollering at the staff, I'm asking a million questions, but she just ignores me, removing the tools from her satchel. It reminds me of Ryker, the tools from his kill kit.

There's a commotion downstairs. The midwife props up my body with the pillows. Even this small amount of jostling is excruciating. I have to bite down on a rag to stop myself from screaming out.

People are racing up the stairs; my mother and two older sisters barge into the room. Clara and Penny aren't allowed, not until they've bled.

As they hover around me, I hear my father outside the room, trying to calm Michael down. "It's going to be okay. Tierney is as strong as they come. She can do this."

My mother presses a cool cloth to my head.

"I'm scared," I whisper.

She pauses, her face ravaged with worry. "Frykt ikke for min kjærlighet er evig."

"Fear not, for my love is everlasting," I whisper back. It brings fresh tears to my eyes. It reminds me of a time when I was small, curled up next to my mother in her room after Penny's birth, the smell of blood and freesia hanging all around us. She was burning up with fever, and I knew by the look on my father's face that it might be the last time I'd see her. As I clung to her soft warm flesh, burrowing my face in the musky linens, she told me to be strong. She pressed my hand over her heart. "There's a place inside us where they can't reach us, they can't see. What burns in you burns in all of us."

I ran to the woods that night, hiding in the tall grass. Hiding from all my fears.

The fear of growing older, the shame of not bearing sons. The wounds the women held so close that they had to clamp their mouths shut for fear of it slipping out. I saw the hurt and the anger seeping from their pores, making them lash out at the women around them. Jealous of their daughters. Jealous of the wind that could move over the cliffs without a care in the world. I thought if they cut us open they'd find an endless maze of locks and bolts, dams and bricked-over dead ends. A heart with walls so tall that it slowly suffocates, choking on its own secrets. But here, in this room, my mother and my sisters gathered around me, I understand there's so much more to us . . . a world hidden in the tiny gestures that I could never see before. They were there all along.

As my mother pulls away to help the midwife, June and Ivy step in to comfort me. "We're here," June says, taking my hand.

"It's okay to scream," Ivy says, taking my other hand. "I screamed my head off with little Agnes. It's the one time we're allowed, might as well make the most of it."

"Ivy," June hisses, but she can't stop the small smile taking over the corner of her mouth. "We can scream together . . . if you'd like," June adds.

I nod, a hazy smile coming over me as I squeeze their hands.

As the midwife presses down on my belly, she shakes her head.

"What is it?" my mother asks.

"The baby's in a bad position. I'm going to have to reach in and turn it."

My sisters hold on to me even tighter. We've all heard the stories. Childbirth is dangerous business under the most normal of circumstances, but rarely do babies make it out of a breech.

"Brace yourself," the midwife says as she grips my belly with one hand and reaches inside me with the other.

The pain is cutting at first, but it quickly shifts to something dull and deep. A guttural moan escapes my lips as I bear down.

"Don't push," she says.

But I can't help it. The pressure is unbearable. I'm exhausted. Panting. Sweat seeping from every pore, my hair soaking wet, the bedsheets stained with blood. I don't know how much longer I can hang on. And then I look outside at the gently falling snow and I think of Ryker. He would never let me give up. He would never let me be weak. Or I would never want to seem weak in front of him. I close my eyes and imagine he's here with me, and maybe I'm delirious, on the edge of bleeding out, but I swear I can feel his presence.

I hear the men outside my room, glasses clinking, the faint hint of whisky seeping from beneath the door. "May you be blessed with a son," Father Edmonds bellows.

"We should pray," Ivy says, fear in her eyes.

As my mother and sisters gather round, they join hands. "Dear Lord, use me as your holy vessel to deliver thy son—"

"No. Not that." I shake my head, my breath shallow in my chest. "If you feel the need to pray, then pray for a girl."

"That's blasphemy," Ivy whispers, looking back at the door to make sure the men didn't hear.

"For Tierney," my mother says.

The women look at each other, an unspoken understanding falling over the room.

They rejoin hands. "Dear Lord, use me as your holy vessel to deliver thy . . . *daughter*—"

As they pray, I bear down.

"Feet," the midwife calls out. "Legs. Arms. Head." But her tone grows more somber in the end. "The child is clear."

"Can I see?" I cry.

The midwife looks to my mother. She gives her a stern nod.

As the midwife lays the child on top of me, the tears come. "It's a girl," I say with a soft laugh.

But she just lies there completely still.

"Please breathe . . . please," I whisper.

As I wipe the blood from her perfect little face, I note that she has my eyes, my lips, Ryker's dark hair, the slight dimple in her chin, but there's a spot that won't come clean. A small strawberry mark below her right eye.

And in the second of her first weighted breath, I realize it's her—the girl that I've been searching for.

Letting out a sobbing gasp, I hold her close, kissing her softly.

The magic is real. Maybe not in the way they believe, but if you're willing to open your eyes, open your heart, it's all around us, inside us, waiting to be recognized. I'm a part of her, as is Ryker, and Michael, and all the girls who stood with me in that square to make this come to pass.

She belongs to all of us.

"I've dreamed of you my whole life," I say as I kiss her. "You are wanted. You are loved."

As if she understands, she wraps her tiny fingers around mine.

"What's her name?" my mother asks, her chin trembling.

I don't even have to think about it; it's as if I've always known. "Her name is Grace," I whisper. "Grace Ryker Welk. And she's the one who's going to change everything."

My mother leans over to kiss her granddaughter, slipping a small red flower with five petals into my hand.

I look up at her and whisper, "My eyes are wide open, and I see everything now."

With tears streaming down her face, my mother smooths

her hand down my braid, releasing me from the black ribbon. And everything it means.

As I close my eyes and let out my next endless breath, I find myself walking in the woods, weightless, free.

I've been here before. Or maybe I never left.

A shadowy figure emerges on the trail ahead, dark shrouds billowing around him like smoke. With every step forward, he comes into clearer focus.

Ryker.

I can't tell if he recognizes me or not, but he's walking straight toward me.

Holding my ground, I wait to see if he'll take me in his arms or simply pass right through me.

ACKNOWLEDGMENTS

Three years ago, 10:00 A.M., Penn Station:

I'm staring up at the board, willing my train to arrive, when I notice a girl in front of me. Probably thirteen or fourteen, long and lean, bouncing on the tips of her toes, thoroughly annoying her parents, grandparents, and younger siblings. She has the nervous energy of a girl on the verge of womanhood. Of change.

A man in a business suit walks by, instinctively looking her way, stem to stern, as they say. I know that look. She's fair game now. Prey.

And then I notice a middle-aged woman pass, drawn to that same energy, but I imagine for entirely different reasons. As she surveys the girl, a look of sadness, possibly disdain, clouds her eyes. Maybe it's a reminder of everything she's lost . . . everything she thinks she'll never get back, but this girl is now competition.

As the family's train is announced, they rush to the gate and say their goodbyes. They're clearly sending the girl back to boarding school. She waves the entire escalator ride down, and I can't help but notice the look of relief on her parents' faces. For another year, she'll be tucked away from the world. Safe.

"The things we do to young girls," I whisper under my breath.

In a daze, I walk to my train, and when I sit down in my seat, I start to weep. I cry for that girl. I cry for my daughter, my mother, my sister, my grandmothers.

I open my computer and by the time I get to D.C. the book is completely plotted. The beginning and ending has been written, and I know I don't have a choice. I have to write this book.

It felt like magic.

I whispered the idea to a few friends, I worked in isolation, in silence. I experienced the despair of the election, the demise of my marriage, the joy of a new one, and through it all, I had *The Grace Year*.

But no one does this alone. My editor, Sara Goodman, took a big chance on me. She recognized what I was trying to accomplish and guided me through each draft with tough love and passion. She pushed me in all the best ways possible. I couldn't be more grateful and proud of the work we've done together. That goes for everyone at Wednesday Books/St. Martin's Press—from the stunning cover to the thoughtful planning of how to get this book into people's hands, I hit the publisher jackpot. Many thanks to Jennifer Enderlin, Kerri Resnick, DJ DeSmyter, Jessica Preeg, Brant Janeway, Anne Marie Tallberg, Natalie Tsay, Dana Aprigliano, Jennie Conway, and Elizabeth Catalano.

My powerhouse of an agent, Joannna Volpe, was by my

side the entire way, always available to talk through story, brainstorm, and strategize. She gave me a lot of encouragement when I felt like I was failing. She's also the first person I would call in a zombie apocalypse. Thank you for taking me on. Thank you for changing my life.

On that note, I have a slew of people to thank at New Leaf Literary: Mia Roman for her blind faith in me, Veronica Grijalva, Abbie Donoghue, Jordan Hill, Meredith Barnes, Kelsey Lewis, Devin Ross, and special mention to Jaida Temperly, who restored my faith in the business. I am forever thankful that you came into my life.

To Pouya Shahbazian, Elizabeth Banks, Alison Small, Max Handelman, Karl Austin, Marissa Linden, and everyone at Brownstone Productions and Universal for believing in Tierney and her story.

So much gratitude to Kelly Link, Jasmine Warga, Sabaa Tahir, Libba Bray, Melissa Albert, Sara Grochowski, Sami Thomason, and Allison Senecal for offering their early support. It was far more than a seed of kindness; it meant the world to me.

My writing confidants—Libba Bray, Erin Morgenstern, and Jasmine Warga.

These are the people I lean on the most. Whether it's long-distance writing sprints or endless hours talking about story and books and life, you were a vital part of this journey. You have all of my love and respect.

To Kara Thomas, Alexis Bass, and Virginia Boecker. Thank you for making me laugh every single day.

Many thanks to Nova Ren Suma, Lorin Oberweger, Holly Black, Maggie Hall, Jodi Kendal, Veronica Rossi, Gina Carey, Bess Cozby, and Rebecca Behrens.

Art inspires art, so I must tip my hat to Laura Marling and Karilise Alexander.

To my parents, John and Joyce; my sister, Cristie; Ed, Regan, and Evan, thank you for always supporting me.

For my partner, Larry. You've shown me unconditional love. You believed in me when I had a hard time believing in myself. You are such a warm ray of light in my life. For Kim, Haley, and Matt, thank you for welcoming me into the family with open arms. I love you all.

To my daughter, Madeline, and my son, Rahm, nothing in this world has given me greater pride than being your mother. You inspire me to be a better person, to keep fighting, to keep reaching. You make this world a better place, simply by being in it.

And for the girl at the train station. I see you. Not as prey or competition. I see hope.